I0781256

Endless Horizon

Endless Horizon

JT McKinley

Deeds Publishing | Athens

Published by Deeds Publishing in Athens, GA
www.deedspublishing.com

Printed in The United States of America

Cover and interior design by Deeds Publishing

ISBN 978-1-961505-36-0

Books are available in quantity for promotional or premium use. For information, email info@deedspublishing.com.

First Edition, 2024

10 9 8 7 6 5 4 3 2 1

Writing a book has been a life-long dream. As a result, my heart is full of gratitude for a great many people as I type this dedication page. But until my eyes were opened to the power of surrender by my wife, the folks at Blue Ridge Mountain Recovery Center, and the people I met there in the North Georgia mountains and in meetings elsewhere since, that dream would never have come to fruition. I dedicate this work to all who have helped with my addiction to alcohol and all who continue to walk alongside me on this journey to recovery. I know in my soul that Heather A. and Grayson C. are reading this somewhere, somehow, and smiling.

If you or someone you love is struggling with addiction, know that both help, and a better life is out here. It all starts with surrendering—to something bigger and infinitely better. It starts with turning the page.

Contents

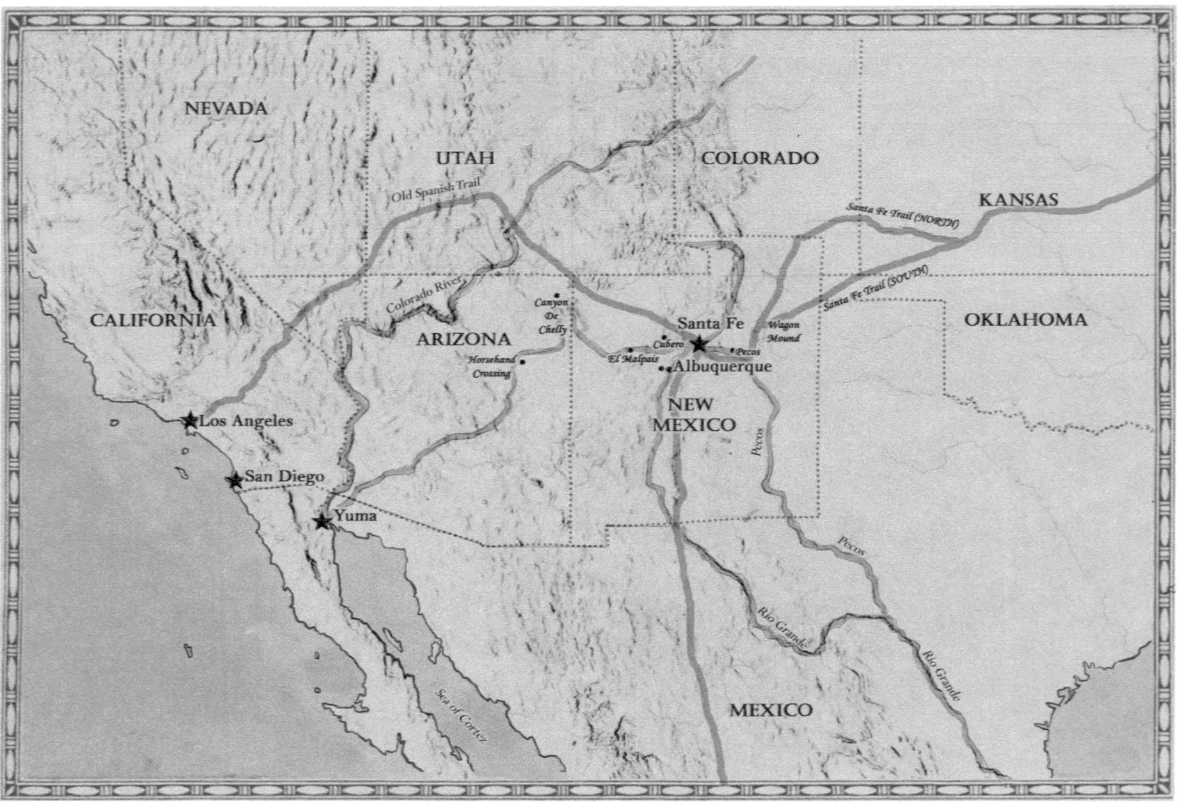

NEVADA
UTAH
COLORADO
KANSAS
CALIFORNIA
ARIZONA
OKLAHOMA
NEW MEXICO
MEXICO
Old Spanish Trail
Santa Fe Trail (NORTH)
Santa Fe Trail (SOUTH)
Colorado River
Canyon De Chelly
Santa Fe
Wagon Mound
Cubero
Pecos
El Malpais
Albuquerque
Horsehand Crossing
Los Angeles
San Diego
Yuma
Pecos
Pecos
Rio Grande
Rio Grande
Sea of Cortez

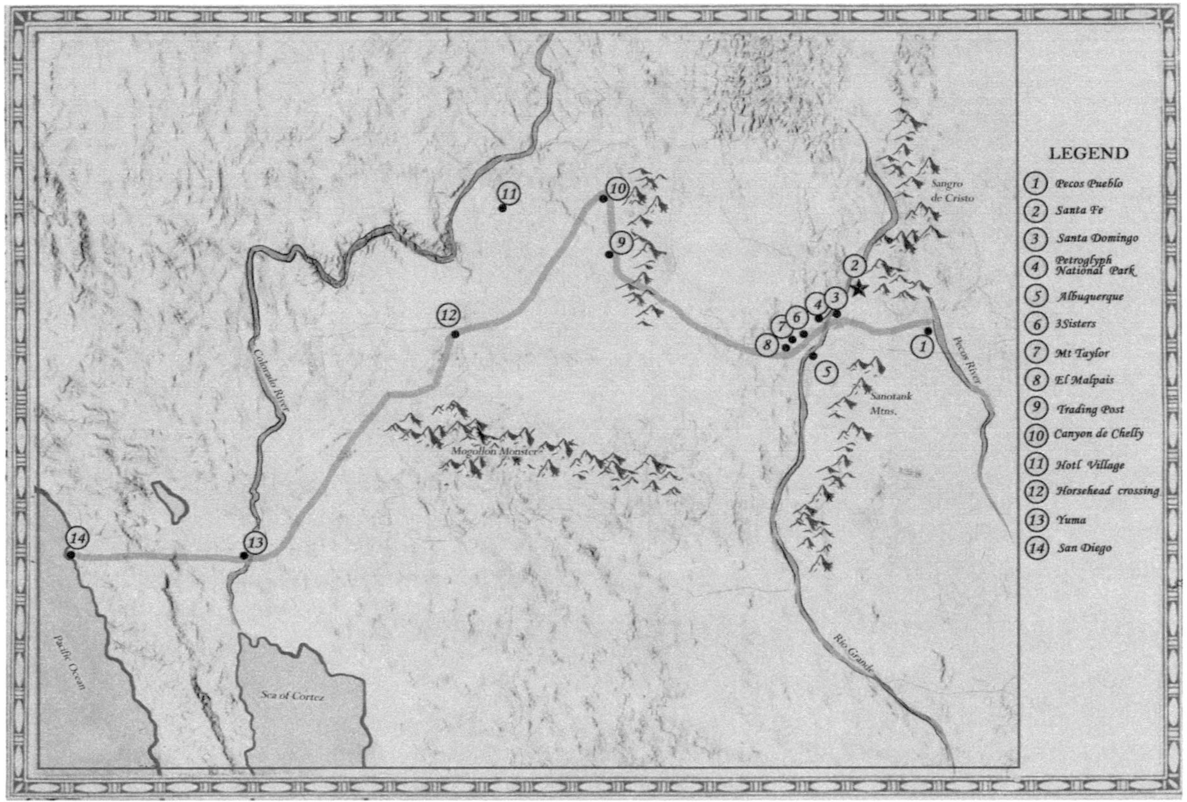

LEGEND
1 Pecos Pueblo
2 Santa Fe
3 Santa Domingo
4 Petroglyph National Park
5 Albuquerque
6 3Sisters
7 Mt Taylor
8 El Malpais
9 Trading Post
10 Canyon de Chelly
11 Hotl Village
12 Horsehead crossing
13 Yuma
14 San Diego
Sangro de Cristo
Pecos River
Sanotank Mtns.
Rio Grande
Colorado River
Mogollon Monster
Pacific Ocean
Sea of Cortez

Cast of Characters

Governor Manuel Armijo: Governor of New Mexico prior to arrival of the Army of the West

Auguste: Right hand man to Jules, soldier in the Swiss Guard

Bisahalani 'Bisa': Navajo kidnapped by Utes as a boy, travels with Larrañaga

Colonel Alexander Donovan: Commander of the Dragoons, Army of the West

Eduardo 'Lalo' Larrañaga Garcia: nephew and 'right hand man' of Larrañaga

Queen Isabella II: Queen of Spain who sent Larrañaga on his mission

Jules: Officer in the Swiss Guard, Pope Pious IX's emissary in the New World

General Steven Watts Kearny: Commander of the United States Army of the West

Cristóval Maria Larrañaga: Uncle of 'Lalo,' doctor by trade, archeologist

James McClendon: Son of Jonathan and Santa Fe Trail pioneer

Jonathan McClendon: Father of Jonathan, history professor by trade, Santa Fe Trail pioneer

Chief Narbona: Navajo chief and elder

Juan Felipe Ortiz: Father of Manuel Ortiz, Spanish settler in Taos

Father Manuel Ortiz: Son of Juan Felipe Ortiz, Catholic priest in Santa Fe

Pope Pious IX: Head of the Catholic Church, last Pope to rule over Papal States (Italy)

Francisco Eduardo Pizarro: Ancestor of Larrañaga and Lalo, Governor of New Castille (Peru)

President James Polk: Commander in Chief of the U.S. Army

Robert 'Bob' Quinn: Husband of Fiona, father of Maire, Pony Express branch boss

Fiona Quinn: Wife of Bob, mother of Maire, owner/operator of 'The Quinn'

Maire Quinn: Daughter of Bob and Fiona Quinn.

Corporal Sampson: Runner/aide for General Kearny

Smythe: Recorder assigned by President Polk to document all activities of the Army of the West

Lieutenant Colonel Peter Thompson: Second in command of the Dragoons, Army of the West

Bishop Zumbria: Head of the Catholic Church of Northern Mexico

*"Truth is stranger than fiction, but it is because
Fiction is obliged to stick to possibilities; Truth isn't."*

—Mark Twain

1. June 1846 — Santa Fe Trail

The Conestoga wagon, packed nearly to the brim with food stores, water barrels, and trunks, wasn't made for flight, but that didn't keep it from launching into the air as it left the well-worn, dusty ruts of the most desolate and unforgiving stretch of the Santa Fe Trail: the Cimarron Desert. James, a lanky seventeen-year-old boy who had been half-asleep in the back of the hot wagon bed, jolted awake as the wooden wheels left the ground. What happened next came like a kaleidoscope: flashes of white canopy, blue sky, the greying wood of the airborne trunks and barrels, all overlaid with the sounds of shattering wheels and terrified screams and the pungent smell of smoke. For James, the almost too calm, even boring crossing changed instantly.

Once out of the rut, the wide-eyed, braying mules half pulled, and half dragged the now one-wheeled wagon across the uneven ground. With surging adrenaline, James gathered his bearings and grasped the wooden tailgate for balance. Kneeling as if before an altar he looked out, his lizard brain immediately registering the danger of the bare-chested, face-painted Indians who drew and released flaming arrows with each step their horses took, both performed with graceful and deadly precision. After only a moment's hesitation, James leapt from the back of the doomed, fire-engulfed wagon.

* * * * *

Ravens traced circles and voiced their grating caws over the still-form young man. James' wavy, unkempt auburn hair rustled in the dry prairie breeze along with the short, lifeless grass that even the pack mules wouldn't bother eating. The sun, far past its zenith, bathed the western horizon in a red-orange glow, its usually crisp edges obscured by layers of reflective dust held aloft as if by some invisible hand. Dried blood crusted between and around his closed eyes from a gash across his forehead, a call of its own for the ancient, winged scavengers whose numbers grew as darkness hastened. The strongest of the birds, or perhaps the most anxious to demonstrate its prowess, dove.

James' eyes flickered at the weight landing on his shoulder. Sharp claws broke through his torn shirt vest. And when the black beak pierced his sunburned cheek, the combination of pain and surprise evoked its own primitive reaction. James swatted the scavenger and leapt to his feet, the bird fluttering away with a damaged wing, only to fall to his knees and then back to the dirt this time face down, unconscious once again. The dust of the 167-mile-long lifeless stretch of desert settled around him, embraced him. Darkness fell soon after his eyelids and the aviary harbingers of death retreated to wherever they go.

* * * * *

James found himself sitting on the end of the wooden pier that extended out over the marshy lowlands bordering his family's farm just outside of Charleston, South Carolina. His bare feet dangled just above the brackish water. Behind him he could hear the sounds of his mother and father singing John Howard Payne's popular ballad, 'Home! Sweet Home!'

Embraced by the familiar summer heat and humidity, he felt completely at peace as he heard the slightly off-key duet sing the final verse,

An exile from home splendor dazzles in vain
Oh give me my lowly thatched cottage again
The birds singing gaily that came at my call
And gave me the peace of mind dearer than all
Home, home, sweet, sweet home
There's no place like home, there's no place like home!

* * * * *

James awoke, the voices of his parents replaced by a new sound and a sky as murky as the marsh back home. The nearly full moon from the previous night had not yet announced its presence but beckoned just below the horizon. The coyotes, however, had. Still a ways off, as far as he could tell. James gathered his hands under his chest and pushed himself up and off of the rugged ground. His head spun with hazy memories of the previous day. The burning wagon. The Indians. The jump. He longed to be back in the dream. He longed for home.

As his eyes adjusted to the growing darkness, an almost incapacitating sense of solitude overtook him. And with it, fear. *Where is my father? The others?* James stumbled around, looking for…anything. And then he not only heard but felt, deep in his core, the howling again—closer this time.

His mind, more attuned to the immediate four-legged danger than his aching heart, called for action—something he'd never shied away from. Searching for something to protect himself, James tripped over the ruins of a wagon. Squinting through unfocused, blood- and dust-encrusted eyes, James realized it was only part of a wagon, the bed part. Then he remembered. The four-wagon caravan he had been a part of, had been traveling in with his father and eleven others, had been heading for 'Wagon Bed Spring.' *Was that this morning? Yesterday?* They'd traveled for days without finding water and if they didn't replenish their nearly-gone stores soon, the silver-haired guide whose face looked like a dried-out grape but whose voice conveyed both wisdom and confidence had said, "We'll all be in a heap of trouble—or dust." James replayed the conversation in his mind.

"Wagon Bed Spring. That there is what will get us across the rest of this godforsaken desert. It's just a wagon bed, courtesy of the famous Jedidiah Smith, God rest his soul. Anyways, he cut a hole in the middle and sank it into the ground a bit, so it only fills up with water, not muck. And it's easier to spot."

And then James remembered his father later telling him that Jedidiah Smith, the famed American trapper, mountain main, and explorer had vanished from around here during a crossing in 1831. His body had never been found.

A close and prolonged coyote shrill broke James out of his memory. Tapping into a strength as primordial as the underground river beneath the spring, he bent down next to the partially submerged wooden wagon bed and pried it up. One side. Then another. Silently he thanked his father for making him do all those chores back on the farm—like building the pier. The sucking sound of the rising bed invigorated him. *Water.* Standing it on end, the young man flipped the bed over and began lowering it to the flat and dry ground next to the spring. A split second before the structure hit, James wedged himself under it, grateful that he fit in the hastily crafted hideout. Water dripped down onto his face and out of reflex and with gratitude he lapped as much as he could from the bloated wood.

The snarling and pawing at the box commenced mere moments later, just as the light of the moon filled the hole. *Even in the darkness, there is light,* James remembered his pastor saying. He prayed—fast and furiously he prayed. For himself. For his father.

Angry and determined to sink their sharp teeth into their cornered prey, the barks of the ravenous beasts echoed like a summer thunderstorm. James trembled as he did when he heard those storms as a young child. He hollered back, trying in vain to match their screams of frustration, hoping the ruckus would scare them away. After what seemed like an eternity, the canine cacophony decreased both in tempo and volume. James' did as well. These frustrated scavengers, like the ones before, abandoned their hunt.

As they pulled away from the upturned bed, James heard them dipping their tongues into the exposed spring, filling their bellies with something other than what they had wanted, but something, nonetheless. Life would go on, for all of them. Their soft and rapid footsteps retreated into the night.

For the first time since the Indian attack, James' heart wasn't trying to leap out of his chest and his head, while sensitive to the touch, was clear. That clarity, however, did not sit well with him as the life he and his father had left in Charleston flashed in front of his eyes. James' mother Annie, the daughter of the dean of the College of Charleston, had been the rock in the McClendon family and possessed the rare quality of treating everyone she met with unconditional positive regard. Words, not violence, were her go-to and she employed them expertly.

His father, the grandson of a signer of the Declaration of Independence, had been first a student and then a respected professor at the College of Charleston. James' parents shared a passion for life and family and poured themselves into James and their community. And then his mother and unborn sister died in childbirth.

James' parents had lived and loved together in the thriving port town since before James' birth. The future seemed as bright and full of possibility as the ocean their small farmhouse overlooked. James had considered, until the devastating event earlier this year, joining the ranks of the military. His spirit was full of a desire to experience and explore and serve as did his grandfather. *A boat captain, perhaps,* he'd thought and imagined as he'd studied the waves and currents near his home. But the day his mother died changed everything. For all of them.

Tears fell from James' eyes further depleting, he chided himself, what little moisture was left in his body. Only this time he did so not for himself but for his old life, "*home sweet home.*" Oh, how he longed to hear his parents' voices again. His swollen eyes focused on the pinpricks of light in the night sky through the hole in the wagon bed. *They'd seen it all,* he thought. Then he slept.

For the third time something awakened the young man. With dawn's early light replacing that of the stars and moon through the hole in the bed, James discerned heavy footfalls and human voices. He strained to listen over the grumbling of his empty stomach, the throbbing pain in his head and face. Horses stopped not far from the overturned bed and James could hear them, even picture them dipping their heads into the spring and drinking. James licked his own cracked and painful lips. The sound of feet hitting the ground nearby made James flinch, the heel of his boot striking the wood loudly.

He heard a voice say something in what he thought was Spanish and as this registered in his mind the bed flipped over, bathing James in the bright morning light which highlighted the outlines of two dark haired, bearded men draped in what looked like long blankets with circles cut out for their heads. Atop those heads were round hats. The fact that these strangers were not Indians pacified, to some degree, James' frightened mind. Trying to stand quickly after spending hours wedged underneath the wooden structure, James slipped and fell at the feet of one of the men.

Embarrassed, he took his time getting up and noticed the man's maroon boots that nearly reached the wearer's knees. As James' eyes adjusted to the light, he noticed a third, younger person, similarly dressed, but a fair amount shorter, high cheekbones and no facial hair. He stood behind the two bearded men with a rifle across his shoulders.

"Buenos días," the older of the two bearded men said to James, his gravelly voice as foreign as it was non-threatening. Turning to his partner, the one with the maroon boots, he pointed at the overturned wagon bed and said, "and you thought we'd find a *brujo*—a witch? You have always been the superstitious one mi sobrino." Both laughed. Mr. Boots shook his head and turned back to his horse.

When he once again faced James, he held a tin cup. James, propped up on an elbow but still on the hard ground watched intently, each passing moment increasing, he hoped, the likelihood that these men would not harm him. Everything about these two bespoke confidence and grace, characteristics his parents had admired and encouraged. More importantly, they seemed to want to help. Mr. Boots bent over and dipped the cup in the spring and held it out to the older man, shook his head and muttered, "siempre el Buen Samaritano."

If time had stopped when the young man first heard the approaching riders, it started again with the offering of the cup. James propped himself up on shaky knees, then got to his feet, angry at the tears once again welling up in his eyes. He recalled the "cup of life" sermon and his First Communion—the symbolism not lost on the young man. The strangers stepped back, giving James some space, and wordlessly hoisted the displaced wagon bed back over the top of the spring. For James, the chaos and terror of the last couple of days seemed to slip away like the coyotes had the previous night.

Coming back to James with a dripping cloth, the one Mr. Boots had called the "Good Samaritan" carefully began to wipe the young man's wound and face, removing, he thought, the two most commonly found elements in these parts, *la mugre y la sangre*. Dirt and blood.

"My father …," James started, his eyes tracing the line of the horizon pausing only briefly at the scattered, smoldering hulks of what had been his wagon train. "Have you seen him?"

The pleading look on the young man's face went unanswered. The strangers had seen it countless times; people who had lost so much holding onto a hope for restoration of what had once been. But now was not.

"We should get going," Mr. Boots said to no one in particular, his English also heavily accented. "While the spring gives life," he paused and surveyed the wreckage, "la Muerte is never far."

"Si. Trouble rarely gives warning," said the man who'd been called the good Samaritan.

James' eyes settled on the other fellow, the one without facial hair who he quickly surmised was an Indian. Knowing not what else to do, James awkwardly waved as the Indian slid his rifle into the scabbard on the side of his saddle and hopped up. The other two—Mexicans, James guessed—checked their gear and tightened the latigos on their horses. As James took another drink he watched them, quickly discerning two things.

First, they were experienced travelers. The rigging on each man's horse held packs and water containers of many shapes and sizes. Second, sitting atop their mounts, they were clearly not planning to stay. James panicked and thought, *what about my father?* Trying to hide his fear and give himself time to think, James brushed the dust off his pants and shirt vest and took stock of his condition and possessions. Outside of his throbbing head and the gash on his cheek, he seemed okay. Hungry, but okay. He'd been in fights before; the kind teenage boys often have as they seek to lay claim their place in the world. But this time he knew was different.

The war cry of the Indians still rang in his ears. He'd lost his father. But he hadn't lost his scalp, nor had he lost the 1840 Buffalo Horn Handle Bowie knife his father had bought him in St. Louis that still hung on his belt. He was far from familiar ground, and it seemed that every living thing in this godforsaken country, present company excluded, was after his hide. For James, the Santa Fe Trail that had held such promise of and for a new life instead had taken nearly everything he had left in the world away. Looking one last time at the water in the spring, he saw his own reflection and wondered, *what am I going to do?*

The Good Samaritan put the toe of his boot in the stirrup and threw his leg over his horse's back in a well-practiced move, scanned the horizon, and then focused his kind eyes on James. "We too are crossers, heading to Santa Fe. And you are welcome to join us." With that, Mr. Boots leaned down from his mount and extended an arm. "Vamos. Let's go."

James held on to Mr. Boots like his life depended on it, because it did. Grateful to be a part of something after seemingly all had been lost, James' mood lightened, knowing he was not alone. He took strength from their presence, even if they were strangers. Moving side to side with the swaying of the horse, he listened to the sounds of the wind and scanned the now-simmering landscape. *How could such a desolate place have such a well-worn trail?* He wondered.

As the sun reached higher into the sky, James closed his eyes as if doing so would silence the memories. The fears. The unknown. Exhaustion overcame him: twice he nearly fell off the horse and on both occasions the men laughed and said something he couldn't understand. James didn't mind. In fact, he laughed too.

"What's your name, mijo?" the Good Samaritan asked, pulling his horse alongside his partner's. Clearly at ease with the proximity, James noticed the horses adjusted their gait and walked in step as if connected in some silent way. The look of vigilance and determination that had been fixed on the man's face softened once again to one of compassion.

"James. James McClendon."

"And where are you from James?" the Good Samaritan asked.

"South Carolina, sir. My father was a professor of history at the College of Charleston. We had a small farm. My mother…" his voice trailed off, sadness overcoming him. The man's eyes did not leave James'. And to the man's surprise, neither did James look away. Both felt the connection.

"Mi nombre es Cristóval Maria Larrañaga. You are riding with my nephew Lalo. And the talkative young man with all of our supplies back there is Bisa," the Good Samaritan said with a sarcastic flair. "Your father sounds like an intelligent and resourceful man."

James caught the way Larrañaga used the present tense with regards to his father. It almost made him smile—something else Larrañaga did not miss. "Yes sir. He…is." The horses continued to follow the wagon ruts, and the wind continued to blow in their faces and the sun did what it always had done. After a few moments of reflective silence, James continued, "Where are we, sir?"

Larrañaga straightened his back before speaking, taking on an almost regal manner. "This is what many call the *Journada del Muerte*—The Journey of Death—for reasons that I should think are obvious. This is the most direct route from St. Louis to Santa Fe. Wagons can move easily here, across the flat plains and dry, shallow riverbeds. But it is also the most dangerous. Little water, poor grass…," his voice drifted off, the silence filled with the footfalls of their horses, "and of course, los Indios. There is talk in your government of closing this route because of raids like the one that brought you to us."

He shook his head. "This desolate place is why Spain did not come east in force hundreds of years ago. It is why so few norteamericanos are now moving west *this* way, opting instead for the easier but longer northern route. The Cimarron Desert is a barrier more formidable than any ocean, especially now that more of los Indios have made their way here. The good news is that we are more than halfway through it." He paused, scanning the endless horizon. "We are all just trying to survive, each in our own way."

James felt Lalo chuckle at the last, but he listened intently to Larrañaga's confident voice. James' old wagon driver had had a similar voice, save for the Spanish accent. The young man had enjoyed listening to and learning about the history of this place and the people here from the driver and he sensed he'd feel the same about Larrañaga. "So what's our next landmark?" James asked, knowing that crossers used unique landmarks and geological features to measure their progress and keep them heading in the right direction.

Using his bearded chin as a pointer, Larrañaga indicated in the direction they were heading. "Up there you can just make out the summit of Perillo Hills, a place called Point of Rocks, the highest point around. There's shelter from the wind up there and more importantly, a spring. It should not be too much longer now. We will attend to the horses, have some food, and get some rest," he said and took a hard look at James. "And I need to take another look at your ..."

"I'm fine," James interrupted.

"I will take another look at your wound, James. Infection is not something you want out here. Where was I? Ah yes. Tomorrow we will ride to Autograph Rock where people for generations have made their marks on those sandstone cliffs. Maybe you'll see something you recognize. After that, Wagon Mound. That's where the northern branch of the Santa Fe Trail links up with this one. We'll try to find your people ..."

"My people?" James again interrupted.

Larrañaga silently chided the South Carolinian with the stern look of a schoolteacher. "Norteamericanos," he said. "And we shall find the supplies and information we need there."

James' red face broadcast his embarrassment. But the manner in which the Good Samaritan—Larrañaga—had said all this reassured the anxious young man. It was then that he noticed Larrañaga's unique saddle, distinguishable by its much bigger horn. James had never seen anything like it. He asked, "Are you from Mexico?"

Larrañaga took off his hat and ran his fingers through his more salt than pepper shoulder length hair before responding. "I am a Spaniard, born to a noble family with a long history of service to God and country. I have always had a passion for helping people, so I became a doctor. After completing my education, I accepted a position, a mission, offered by my Queen and encouraged by my family. That mission involved coming to Mexico…"

As he reminisced, the wrinkles on his face seemed to vanish. He radiated pride and sat up a bit straighter in his saddle. "A very important mission. *Terrae veritas invenietur.*" He took a deep breath as if to begin a long story. "In the bones of the earth shall the truth be found."

Again he paused, "Lalo and I sailed from Spain to Veracruz and then traveled on horseback to Mexico City, and similarly north on the Silver Road to Santa Fe. Along the way I witnessed tremendous suffering and sickness—largely the result of illnesses we Spanish brought here. The smallpox…what it did…*'no imaginable.'* It killed one out of every three of los Indios."

Tears now welled in his eyes. "For ten years now I have helped bring the vaccine to the people of this land. In fact, that's why we're here on the trail. We had to pick up more vaccines in St. Louis. Ah, lo siento. Pardon my digression. I stopped counting after I'd given my two thousandth shot. Some call us the 'saviors of a generation.' But I am no closer to completing my *real* mission."

He paused, choosing his words carefully. It seemed to James that the older man's wrinkles had returned. "I am looking for something. Something very important." Even before the final syllable left his mouth Larrañaga spurred his mount forward and away he galloped.

Lalo, for the first time since their initial meeting, spoke. "My Tío, my uncle, is a saint. He has a pura *cora-*

zón– a pure heart. I never stopped counting. He's saved 2,834 people at great personal risk. Spent a fortune of his own money." Turning his head to look at James, he corrected himself. "2,835 people. But it is neither fame nor fortune he seeks."

James waited for more but more did not follow. The crossers rode on in silence towards the Point of Rocks as the afternoon progressed.

At the boulder strewn hilltop, the small band reunited. Larrañaga, Lalo told James, had ridden ahead to verify his earlier proclamations regarding safety and to see if any 'personas malas'—bad people—were visible from the west or the north. With that accomplished and Lalo, James, and Bisa's arrival, they all wearily slid their legs over their saddles and planted their feet on the rocky ground. Larrañaga wasted no time and issued commands first in Spanish, then English.

"James, you and I will corral the horses there, up against those big boulders. Lalo (who had told James his real name was Eduardo, shortened to Lalo) *tiene que vigilar* –keep a watch out. Bisa, preparar la cena por favor. Everyone has a role to play," Larrañaga said almost lyrically.

Larrañaga and James corralled, fed, and watered the horses and afterwards, the Spaniard cleaned and applied some ointment to James' head wound. And then it was time for the men to eat. James' stomach grumbled loudly, and everyone laughed at the noise. Dinner was a simple, "cold" meal of bread, corn, and jerked meat. Wood was as scarce as water out here, and Larrañaga told James he had no desire to light a beacon that might attract the wrong kind of attention.

After they'd finished, James gratefully accepting a second and third helping, Larrañaga said, "Tomorrow we will start early. As we ride, mijo," Larrañaga continued, "I will tell you about the people we will find at our destination, the people of the pueblos. And perhaps we'll get Bisahalani to live up to his name and tell you about his people. Now it is time for rest." He sat down, laid back against his saddle, and pulled a blanket over his head.

"Great Speaker. That what Bisahalani—or Bisa—means," Lalo whispered before tossing a blanket to James and pulling one over his own face. As James reclined, he realized that in this place, with these men, he was not alone. They were all travelers from faraway places doing their best to survive.

* * * * *

Lalo's boot on James' chest brought the South Carolinian out of a dream-laden sleep. He'd been watching, detached from himself, as his father fought an Indian over James' prone, still body. In his dream, James stood next to his mother who was also watching, holding her infant daughter. He saw the wagons of the caravan, now without their animals and any useful cargo, riddled with burning arrows, the fires rapidly engulfing the wooden frames. He saw his father plunge a knife deep into the torso of the bare-chested Indian and James called out to him, tried to run to him but with each step his father seemed further away. Lalo's boot and soft voice pulled James away from the horrible scene. "It's time."

The travelers ate stale bread and cold beans in silence. Only as the cold, syrupy coffee crossed their lips was the silence broken. Larrañaga told them that the next leg in their journey would be the most dangerous. They'd have to stay alert at all times, he said, looking each in their eyes. That about shut down all other conversation, so after finishing their cups they packed and readied the horses and cleared the site of all evidence of their presence. Jumping up into his saddle, Larrañaga exclaimed, "Vamanos compadres. Let's go!"

Guided by the light of a partially obscured moon sitting low on the horizon, the four continued their journey south and west. The darkness and danger called for continued silence, so that is how they rode. As the sun's rising slowly pulled back the curtains of night and the slow, careful walking of the horses sped up, gunshots in the distance shattered the silence. Larrañaga, Lalo, and Bisa reined in their horses, willing their eyes to pick up the source of the commotion.

After a few long moments, the scene came to light. A raid in progress. Far ahead James counted twelve armed Indians riding through a loose circle of wagons, shooting into and then pillaging their contents. Only two from the wagon train, using one of the wagons for cover, returned fire. They were not faring well. Panic and poorly aimed shots would be their downfall. It was not long in coming.

In moments, all firing ceased, but that did not stop Larrañaga from urging his horse into a full out run, the other two horses following closely behind. James held on to Lalo tightly while latches on hip pistols and straps keeping short-barreled Winchester lever-action rifles in their scabbards were removed or loosened.

Larrañaga fired two shots in the air, hoping, praying that there was someone left to save. In the dim, pre-dawn light, James could see a dust trail rising behind the startled raiding party as they quickly fled the scene. Larrañaga got to the site of all the action well before Lalo, James, and Bisa. James watched as Larrañaga jumped from his horse and began to check for survivors while Bisa fired a couple of rounds at the fleeing Indians. All their horses were lathered in sweat in the growing heat of the morning.

While James dismounted and went to grab the reins of Larrañaga's riderless horse, the Spainard knelt next to each of the dead and offered a silent prayer. Rising from the last he looked in the direction the Indians rode off in and then hollered at the group. "There's nothing more we can do here. Los Indios might come back once they see there are just four of us."

As he walked towards James, Larrañaga picked up one of the recently deceased men's hats and banged it against his pantleg before handing it to James. "You need a hat. And I am sure Lalo would appreciate it if you rounded up those two loose horses there and took one as your own."

* * * * *

Desperate for water and weary from the sun and being

on constant alert, the sight of the bluffs marked with the names of fellow passers-by could not have inspired more gratitude. Upon arrival they dismounted, corralled their horses, and Bisa grabbed his rifle and scaled the hundred-foot cliff to keep watch. Larrañaga and James walked stiffly up to the wall where the elder found his name, traced his fingers over the rough, etched surface.

James looked for any sign of his father's name, but to no avail. Meanwhile, Lalo anxiously searched around the base of the cliff for the spring. After a few minutes he hollered and all, but Bisa came running. The trio filled their hats with water, dousing their heads, drinking, and scrubbing as if maybe by doing the latter they could wash away the horrors they'd witnessed earlier.

The events of the day weighed heavily on their hearts. Again they ate cold rations, set up a rotation for the watch, and unwrapped their bedrolls. As the sun dipped below the horizon, Larrañaga pulled James aside and together they walked along the wall of the cliff. James could almost picture people writing their names or drawing pictures on the rock's face. He picked up a rock and turned to Larrañaga as if for approval. The Spaniard smiled and nodded.

James found some open space and began to etch his own name. When he finished, Larrañaga smiled again and pointed at a drawing just a few feet away from James' name. It was a drawing—concentric circles, one inside another, emanating from a single point in the center.

"The circle of life," Larrañaga said in a voice barely audible over the steady wind. "Todo esta connectado—everything is connected." As the Spaniard said this, he gestured to all the other names on the cliff wall. The two stood silently for a few moments, deep in their own thoughts.

James reached out and traced a finger backwards on the circle and quietly asked, "Does this mean that what happened to me in the past determines my future?"

"An excellent question James—one that dips its toes in science, philosophy, and religion." Larrañaga was quiet for a moment and continued, "Since your father is a professor, then you likely know the name of Charles Darwin. Darwin wrote, 'It is not the strongest of species that survives, nor the most intelligent, but the one most responsive to change.' I believe what happens to us and those we love in life provides…opportunities…to learn and grow. When I think of my past, I know that those experiences have helped me define what it is I value and as a result have influenced my ability to respond in good ways. But no, my past does not define me or determine my future. God has already done that." Larrañaga placed his arm around James' shoulders and whispered, "solo Dios."

* * * * *

No dreams visited James that night and thankfully so. Once again, the small band climbed atop their horses and were back on the trail before the sun crested the eastern horizon. For the past three days, the landscape consisted largely of the sparse grassy plain and dry, meandering creek beds, a view as featureless as a blank sheet of paper, James thought.

As their long shadows diminished in size and the sun approached its apex in the cloudless sky, James began to discern several changes. First, he noticed the gradual but incessant incline of the well-worn trail. Soon after, he caught the faint outlines of mountains on the western horizon. Mountains covered, James noticed as they grew in clarity, in the green of what must be large trees. His mind jumped back to the farm in Charleston where Live Oaks draped in thick Spanish Moss outlined three sides of their property—the ocean had the fourth.

As if reading James' mind, Larrañaga said with a flare of the dramatic, "those are the Sangre de Cristo Mountains, covered in Ponderosa Pines. The smaller trees you see just ahead are Pinyons. And at the base of those mountains," he pointed his gloved finger, "is Wagon Mound."

With the change in scenery crystalizing before their eyes, the heaviness of the trail began to dissipate. "I believe we are now in New Mexico," Larrañaga said with a hint of a laugh. "New Mexico existed as a named entity even before Mexico declared its independence from Spain in 1821. It is known as the land of the pueblos—well-established villages, some with several thousands of Puebloans who hunt, farm, and trade and have done so for thousands of years. These pueblos are something to behold. Many have four and five story buildings built around grand courtyards or as we say, plazas.

"People travel from all over for Puebloan pottery and their tightly woven blankets. But what sets them apart from others in this difficult land is their very close tie with the past—the place, si, but even more so the people and their beliefs. The Puebloan People honor their ancestors, passing along their stories and beliefs with words and pictures—like the ones we saw on the rocks. The Navajo call the ancestors of the Puebloans the Anasazi which means...." Tio said and glanced at Bisa, beckoning him to continue.

"Old ones." Bisa finally broke his silence, his deep voice not altogether a match for his youthful appearance, James thought. Bisa did not expand past that, so Larrañaga continued.

"Some, interpret the Navajo word "Anasazi" to mean 'ancient enemy.' James, one thing I have learned is that names can be troublesome, sometimes paint false pictures, convey untruths. Names have power...," Larrañaga's voice drifted off momentarily, stepping his horse around a spike-ridden cane cholla. They all noted the juniper and pinyon thickets up ahead and adjusted their course to miss them.

"But enough about names. With the help of the Navajo, the Spanish and Mexican governments have been able to learn much about the Anasazi," Larrañaga said excitedly. "One of the things we've learned is that the Anasazi's creation story is different than what we read in the Christian Bible. They believe that people as we now know and see them journeyed as spirits through a series of underworlds before emerging from a hole in the ground, from within mother earth. When people die, they believe, their spirit rejoins those of all the others and helps those who are still living lead a good life. The cycle of life." With this, Larrañaga looked at James and traced the concentric circle pattern in the air.

"Now," he continued, carefully guiding his horse down into a rocky arroyo, a dry creek bed, "the Anasazi did not worship in an ornate, mountain top church but, recognizing their arrival from underground, constructed pit houses called *kivas* for their spiritual activities and religious ceremonies. The entrance to these is through a portal in the roof and down a ladder. These kivas are round, expertly crafted to blend into their surroundings, and have a hard dirt floor. The timbers that support the mud and clay roof are gigantic and often have been hauled tens of miles, or in some cases, hundreds of miles to get to where they are needed. How—we have no idea. No man or horse could carry them. Ah, again I digress. And here is the most interesting thing. Most kivas have another hole, called a sipapu, that leads further underground."

As they approached the hustle and bustle around Wagon Mound, Larrañaga knew he needed to quickly make one last point. "As I mentioned, the Puebloans convey their history, their culture, through storytelling. And it is worth noting that when an elder Puebloan tells a story, it is his responsibility to tell it accurately and it is the responsibility of the hearer to listen intently, memorize what is said, and be able to pass it along. James, that means no *interrupting*," and everyone laughed. "Both the teller and the hearer are connected, via the story. This connection cannot be broken—that is where their strength comes from, their ability to not only survive but ensure their wisdom and beliefs pass from one generation to the next."

He wanted to say much more but his audience's attention had shifted to the sight of dozens of wagons lined up just a few miles ahead.

* * * * *

Wagon Mound, a make-shift town that looked like it could blow over in a stiff wind situated at the base of a butte—an isolated hill with steep sides and a flat top—shaped roughly like a Conestoga wagon, was known for two things. First, it served as the first (for the east bound travelers) or last (for the westbound) natural landmark of the Santa Fe Trail. Second, just south of the geological feature was the convergence point of the mountain (northern) branch of the trail and Cimarron desert (southern) branch. This meant that travelers of all types and from all directions funneled past this waystation.

* * * * *

Larrañaga called his foursome to a halt and, scanning the area, found who he was looking for: Manuel Armijo, three-term governor of New Mexico. The pear-shaped, elegantly dressed man stood just to the side of the brand-new Barouche carriage. The garish, four wheeled, open top carriage was known to be the favorite of the rich and powerful and looked as out of place here in eastern New

Mexico as an Anasazi would in Charleson. Armijo wore tight-fitting brown pants, a matching buttoned waistcoat, and white high collared linen shirt that also set him apart from all the others at Wagon Mound. *Interesting*, Larrañaga thought, *he is not wearing his military uniform.*

Lalo saw him as well, knew that his Tío needed to speak with the man, and turned to James and Bisa and said, beckoning, "Vamanos. Let's go water the horses at the Oja de Santa Clara, the spring in that canyon." While they trotted off, Larrañaga galloped towards the governor.

"It has been some time," the governor said, "since our paths crossed. I have some news."

2. July 25, 1846 — Border of New Mexico

The first ever invasion of a foreign country by the United States military began without incident or fanfare, *just the way I hoped*, the nearly fifty-three-year-old Brigadier General Steven Watts Kearny thought as he watched the first of his troops cross what he believed to be the border of New Mexico.

The Santa Fe Trail, a name that elicited both dread and excitement, an entity that took as much as it gave, appeared the same on one side of the border as it did on the other. And the Army of the West, under Kearny's command, had followed the northern or "mountain" branch towards the trail's namesake — Santa Fe. Armed with thirty years of experience from the Arkansas to Yellowstone rivers and tasked with a mission unlike any other in his nation's short history, the commanding general exuded vigilance and confidence atop his mount. "Stay sharp," he commanded. "And welcome to New Mexico." Bugles sounded. Cheers echoed up and down the line. The last American outpost they'd passed was Branson,

Colorado. The trail here snaked thought the Chico Hills, bordered on the east by a long, flat, down slope that led to the brown, dust-enshrouded Great Plains. To the west was the tree-lined north-south ridgeline of the Sangre de Cristo Mountains. And just beyond stood Santa Fe. The highly anticipated first confrontation with Mexican troops could happen at any moment.

* * * * *

On May 13, 1846, Congress authorized a force of two thousand troops and five hundred more support personnel for the Army of the West following President Polk's petition to declare war on Mexico. General Kearny, respected by friends and foes alike for bravery, intelligence, and the ability to overcome incredible odds, both natural and man-made, was appointed the commanding officer. His first and perhaps most daunting task was to cobble together a unit he knew could accomplish the mission. He recruited heavily from the St. Louis area: men skilled in trades, horsemanship, and frontier life. What these new recruits lacked in military experience, they endeavored to make up for with patriotic pride. "Death before dishonor" and "The love of country is the love of God" were commonly heard phrases as the men signed their service contracts.

To add some much-needed experience and to serve as the pointy end of the sword that he knew he'd need, General Kearny added the five-hundred-man Mormon Battalion and three hundred Dragoons from the First

Dragoon Regiment—a unit that Kearny himself had recruited, trained, and led for years.

These mounted infantrymen were, at least on the American frontier, the most feared, the most capable fighting force around. They were cavalrymen of the finest sort, made famous by their ability to travel vast distances in record time, track anything that moved, and strike with precision and brutality anywhere, anytime. They fought and thought like the natives they most often pursued.

Kearny hand-picked his protégé, Colonel Alexander Donovan for the role of commander of the Dragoons when he'd been named to lead the Army of the West. Donovan, an excellent horseman who wore his emotions on his sleeve, grew up in a protestant-Irish family and as such possessed unfaltering sense of—and need to be—a self-made man. These, combined with Donovan's imposing 6'6" height, made him the perfect choice.

Amidst a carnival-like atmosphere, the caravan of wagons and mounted and dismounted soldiers marched out of the gates of Fort Leavenworth to the sound of bugles in late June. Even "Old Fuss and Feathers" Winfield Scott, the Commanding General of the United States Army, attended the event. General Kearny knew, as he rendered his final salute to Scott and the political VIPs and flag-waving civilians gathered in the streets, that the first half of the journey would be more of a training exercise than a formal military campaign for his cobbled-together unit. *A good thing,* he wrote in his journal. While most of the new recruits displayed trepidation from the very start, fearful that the enemy might be lurking just outside the fort, those with experience knew no raiding force existed that would attempt to take on this Army. Not here. Not now. Maybe not ever.

The well-worn northern branch of the Santa Fe Trail beckoned them across the plains and up the steep slope to the base of the Rocky Mountains. The hot and dry northwesterly wind blew incessantly in their faces; those in the back of the procession grudgingly suffering the dust storm kicked up by those before them. Between that and blisters from new boots caused many a grumble in the ranks.

Blisters, snakebites, and dehydration kept the medical unit busy right from the start. Unfortunately, while hurrying off to the latest series of dropouts, the elderly Colonel John Kelly, senior medical officer, fell from his horse but that is not what killed him. A heart attack did. This would not delay Kearny, however, who placed a junior officer in command of the unit.

Over the course of the next few days, the junior officer's personal conduct combined with his hesitant reactions to the most mundane of situations forced General Kearny to make an executive decision and relieve the officer of his command.

As this drama unfolded, a wagon train heading east approached the mile-long caravan of the Army of the West. On it was a handful of survivors from a recent Indian raid, one in particular possessed a quick wit and a presence that bespoke a quiet confidence—qualities General Kearny looked for in his officer corps. This man was not a doctor, but even after just a few minutes, Kearny deduced he was both well-educated had a capacity to lead. An added plus was his deep knowledge of history.

After hearing the man's heart-wrenching story, General Kearny swore him in as the new commander of the medical support unit and ordered the supply officer to issue the newly minted Captain Jonathan McClendon a horse, uniform, and sidearm. Trotting down the line to take his place amongst the Santa Fe-bound troops, McClendon wiped away a tear. Hope flowed in his veins for the first time since losing James.

The rest of the journey across the plains and up the gradual slope to the base of the Rockies passed uneventfully. Kearny pushed the men to their limits and a bit beyond, constantly evaluating his officers and making changes or giving direction and encouragement as needed. Kearny took pride in knowing which levers to pull and when to pull them to get the job done. He knew not only how to lead men, but was also an expert logistician, fully aware that a fighting force — a conquering force — could not be successful without the appropriate supplies and support, particularly on the nearly 900-mile-long Santa Fe Trail that started at 444 feet of elevation on the banks of the Mississippi and rose to over 7,200 at its namesake city.

* * * * *

In the hot days immediately following the crossing of the border of New Mexico, the Sangre de Cristo peaks towered forebodingly over the Army of the West; the tallest more than 5,000 feet higher than the rock-studded desert plain and the dust-enshrouded caravan. Hushed voices and silent prayers called for the late summer monsoon season with its brief yet torrential downpours. As the weary men and horses struggled to put one worn out boot or shoe in front of the other, Ponderosa pines and Douglas firs effortlessly climbed the 13,000-foot peaks.

After a mid-day break in a shady grove overwatched by Aspen trees, General Kearny and his leadership entourage decided to ride at the head of the Army. Cresting a small hill, the commanding officer discerned their next—and final—planned stopping point before Santa Fe: Wagon Mound. The latest report from his Dragoon scouts offered that all Mexican troops in New Mexico had either dispersed or hunkered down in and around Santa Fe, but he was not one who liked surprises. General Kearny ordered Colonel Donovan and his Dragoons to break off from the main element to clear and secure Wagon Mound for the Army of the West.

Moments after motioning Colonel Donovan and the Dragoons ahead, General Kearny turned to his entourage and beckoned Corporal Sampson, one of his most dependable runners. The runners had a critical role: deliver messages to his subordinate commanders with speed and accuracy and return just as fast with their recipients' responses. Typically young, educated, and out of necessity good horsemen, these men also could fill in 'gaps' in the leadership structure as officers invariably went down in battle.

Alongside the runners, and for the first time in the

history of the United States Army, two gray-haired, well-educated men committed Kearny's actions and words to paper in real time or as close to it as the situation permitted. They were recorders, assigned by and rumored to be close associates of President Polk to capture all of the Army's activities in detail. While the runners were soldiers first and foremost, the recorders were not. As such, they did not wear uniforms or carry weapons. In fact, they looked more like professors than the former professor now commanding the medical unit.

Sampson trotted up alongside the general. "Yes sir?"

"Inform the commanders to meet me in the shade of those trees up ahead. And when you see Captain McClendon, tell him I need to speak with him privately after the meeting."

Sampson repeated the order, received a nod of confirmation, turned, and galloped away. One of the recorders—Smythe, he was called, just Smythe—nodded to his partner, a man by the name of Tellefson before pulling out his journal.

As the Army of the West continued its march towards Wagon Mound, the command staff, which included Kearny, the commanders of the Dragoons, the First and Second infantry regiments of Fort Leavenworth, the artillery and medical detachment, and the Mormon Battalion, as well as the Army's executive, intelligence, planning, and supply officers, and of course the runners, recorders, flag bearers, and aides as each of those roles desired, broke off from the main element and gathered on the east side of the trail at the designated grove of trees as if to keep some distance from the prying eyes that Kearny suspected were tracking their progress in the nearby mountains.

When all but Donovan had arrived, Kearny reiterated the plan. The Army of the West was to link up with the Dragoons, occupy the high ground around Wagon Mound with a heavy southwest orientation, form up and establish security for the wagon train, clean their weapons, rest and water the horses. And to always maintain a high level of security. Only then were the men to eat and rest themselves.

The general asked for questions but neither expected nor received any. He dismissed them all except for Captain McClendon. Smythe, however, remained. McClendon caught the frustrated, yet resigned glance Kearny flashed the recorder's way. The General clearly was not used to having to deal with civilians in his ranks, McClendon thought. Kearny dismounted and by doing so invited the others to do the same.

"Jon, I'm sorry I haven't been able to get to this sooner, but as you know we've been a bit busy," Kearny said as he looked over the heads of his immediate audience at his beloved units as they passed. Then he paused, looked down at the long, brown Side oats grass of the high prairie. He returned his gaze to the captain, crossed his arms, and started anew. "You know our primary mission—to capture and control all the land between here and the Pacific, starting with Santa Fe. But we have a secondary mission I've not yet told you about. It's one I think I can entrust to you now."

"Of course, whatever it is, I will do my best to help, Sir." McClendon said, mindful of military etiquette.

Kearny continued. "Every country worth its salt is focused on finding ancient structures and artifacts that possess significant political, cultural, or even religious significance. What used to be a personal, albeit morbid, hobby, is now of national interest. The Spanish, French, British, and yes, even the United States of America are sponsoring major quests for items, I reckon, to put in a museum. And there are some who believe that some of these artifacts may have…some unique attributes…which only further increases the national interest."

Kearny shifted his eyes from McClendon to the ridgeline to the west before continuing. "President Polk wants to show that the U.S. is indeed worth its salt and that's what this expedition is all about: taking the land and everything in it. So, he has ordered the Army of the West—us—to keep a sharp eye out for anything that might be…useful…in this regard. Are you following me?"

Unsure where this was going, McClendon responded, "Yes, sir."

Kearny bent over and scooped up a handful of dirt and rock before continuing. "As you likely know, where we are standing right now is thought to be the edge of some of the oldest land in the world. The dryness of the environment means anything found here could be even more ancient and therefore more…*significant* than anything else in a museum today."

Kearny opened his hand, dumped out the contents,

and clapped his hands together before pointing to the southwest. "Soon we'll be in Santa Fe. The political and military capital of New Mexico. It is also a religious mecca of sorts, if my sources are correct. You probably know that the cathedral in Santa Fe was built even before the pilgrims landed in Massachusetts.

"Well, sources tell me the Catholic Archbishop from Mexico City and his emissaries from across Mexico are frequently there, and they've had their clergy out all across this land, not only to bring civilization to the natives, but also to retrieve and/or destroy artifacts of political, cultural, or spiritual significance as the Spanish have throughout their colonies."

He paused and laughed to himself. "By the look on your face I can tell you are wondering why I am telling you all of this. Well, from our discussions over the past month I can tell you know your history. And, unlike all of my officers, you have not dedicated your life to the business of soldiering and harbor no political ambitions. Soldiering is, well, messy. Destructive by nature. Full of egos—just like politics. Given that the kinds of artifacts the President hopes we will find will be fragile, even sensitive in nature, I need to be able to rely on someone who appreciates these things and will act, well, not like a soldier. I am making you my chief—and this is a relatively new term I understand—*archaeologist*.

"When we get to Wagon Mound, I want you to link up with Colonel Donovan. I've asked him to assign ten of his trusted Dragoons to your command. And in the meantime, I want you to place someone you know can do the job to take over your role as commander of the medical detachment."

With that, Kearny ceased talking and looked at Smythe, who was scribbling in his journal. Turning back to McClendon, Kearny concluded the conversation by grabbing ahold of his saddle and hoisting himself up. "Now let's get back to the troops."

"That was interesting," McClendon said as the most powerful man west of the Mississippi galloped off. A few moments passed while Smythe finished what he was writing. Then he closed his book and approached McClendon until they stood almost toe to toe. It was only then that McClendon noticed the older man's piercing, steel-blue eyes. McClendon felt the hairs on the back of his neck rise to attention and he remembered how he felt the first time he stood before a new class, as if he was being assessed, even judged, in every way.

Unlike the oftentimes boisterous students, Smythe said nothing. Desperate to break the awkward silence, McClendon simultaneously stepped back and tipped his hat to the grey-haired civilian before jumping up into his own saddle and riding away.

* * * * *

To the casual observer, the presence and disposition of the Army of the West on and around the Conestoga-shaped butte made the scene look like an ant hill: coordinated movement of things both large and small, uniform colors, and even a "queen" in the form of the General and his command staff. Unlike an anthill, the Army of the West could not be stepped over or ignored. Indians of various tribes, as well as Mexican army scouts, often working in tandem surreptitiously counted troops and horses, assessed strengths and weaknesses.

At the same time, the presence of the Army of the West did not stop the flow of people either at the beginning or end of their crossing of the Santa Fe Trail. Wagon trains, single riders, and all those making their living off of travelers got the unmistakably clear message from the United States' troops: *we are here.*

* * * * *

As the sun set behind the Sangre de Cristos and their immense shadow fell over the encamped Army of the West, Captain McClendon made his way from the medical unit to the headquarters tent. He'd selected and transitioned his command to his second in charge—a necessarily easy and quick process in the military. As McClendon climbed the hill to the large white tent, Corporal Sampson ran down to meet him, saluted, and handed him a small leather pouch.

"Compliments of General Kearny, sir."

Opening the pouch, McClendon found two silver eagle pins and a brief note from the General. *Congratulations on the promotion. This should help you get the job done. And as the old Irish proverb states, Believe nothing that you hear and only half of what you see. Stephen Watts Kearny, Brigadier General, Commanding.*

Too stunned to move, now *Colonel* McClendon took in the scene of the army in motion around him. He looked up at the mountains that bore witness to this event — and so many others throughout history. His mind and heart raced. A month ago, he had lost his son. All his worldly possessions. Since the turn of the year, he'd lost his wife and daughter, his job, his home. *Why? And now this?*

Both overwhelmed and exhilarated, he fell to his knees. As a religious man, he knew in his soul that God had a plan. For him and for all things. But at that moment, kneeling there in the uniform of an officer in the United States Army, Jonathan McClendon felt as out of place as a pig in a church. Alone.

And then from somewhere deep inside, he heard his father's soldierly voice say, "Pull yourself together, son." McClendon had admired his father's courage, his passion for serving, and took those words to heart. He stood and reread the message from General Kearny. "Get the job done," he said to himself.

He'd been entrusted with a vague yet exciting task, and a vaunted title to boot. Looking around, it dawned on McClendon that for the first time in his life he was in a foreign country that he knew little about. And a people he knew nothing about. That would have to change.

* * * * *

Later that evening, Colonel Donovan of the Dragoons spotted McClendon after dinner at the officer's mess and walked over, a smile on his ruddy face. Half a foot taller and a full foot broader than the South Carolinian, the commander of the Dragoons wrapped an arm the size of a normal man's leg around the former professor's shoulders. While the two colonels had spoken a few times during the course of their crossing, both would later recall that this was the first "significant" interaction the two had.

"I heard the news, Jonathan," Donovan said a few decibels too loudly, the smell of whisky on his breath. "From captain to colonel in one month. Now that does not happen every day, especially without firing a shot! Well done, sir. And ten of my finest. Well, I've hand-picked and briefed them and set you up with a tent near theirs right over there," Donovan pointed, leaning just a bit too much on the smaller man. "You know, its customary for the newly promoted to buy a round of drinks. I'll hold you to that once you get settled in and meet the boys."

The next morning, Colonel Donovan gave General Kearny and his staff a detailed status report about how he and his Dragoons expertly completed scouting all viable routes from Wagon Mound to Santa Fe. From the sound of things, there was only one that would work for the Army of the West. Donovan wisely said that the Mexican army assuredly knew the same. That route was, of course, the Santa Fe Trail that took them south from Wagon Mound, past the abandoned Pecos Pueblo, west up and over Glorietta Pass, and then down into Santa Fe.

At the conclusion of his part of the briefing, Donovan confirmed that Colonel McClendon's "team" had been briefed and were standing by for orders, as was he and the Dragoons. Something in his voice worried McClendon. And it felt like Donovan was going to keep McClendon under his wing, whether he liked it or not.

* * * * *

Days passed without news or orders. July turned to August; the hot days followed by what could almost be called cool nights with occasional brief thunderstorms providing a welcome respite. The Army of the West—and all others around, it seemed—were in constant motion. Training. Trading. Eating. Telling stories. Getting drunk. A few drank just a bit, but most drank to excess. McClendon did not and neither did General Kearny, who struck McClendon as a puppeteer waiting until his audience was ready to begin pulling the strings.

Who is your real audience? McClendon wondered more than once. One evening, while sitting at a table with Kearny, the commanding officer offered a personal observation. "Did you know that 'alcohol' in Arabic is 'al-kuhl'? Al-kuhl means 'body eating spirit'." He shook his head while watching many of the officers under his command consume whatever local concoction Donovan had rounded up for the officers. Kearny continued, "I have long been advising the Indians to stay away from booze. I hope they heed that advice better than soldiers do."

It was listening to stories and insights like that which interested Colonel McClendon the most. Walking around Wagon Mound became routine for the former professor.

He'd stop and introduce himself to anyone who looked like they had a story to tell, and that was just about everyone. Especially if they'd been drinking.

One Sunday morning as the sun came up over the flat, open terrain to the east where he hoped James somehow had survived the raid, McClendon mounted his horse and walked it though the hasty campsites of travelers outside the security perimeter of the Army of the West. Working his way up into the foothills of the Sangre de Cristos, he came across a few dozen people of all kinds sitting or kneeling on a small rocky slope that formed somewhat of a natural amphitheater. A dark-skinned, rather portly priest in a brown robe tied loosely around his waist by a single rope preached, alternating between Spanish, English, and Latin.

After a few minutes the priest blessed the cup and the bread and served communion to those who wanted it. *It's been a long time, Jonathan,* the officer thought, as he dismounted and joined the cue for the holy offering.

After the service concluded, McClendon remained and assisted the priest pack his things in his small, two-wheeled carriage. "Bless you, my son," the priest responded. Together they made short order of the task and, with the heat rising along with their level of familiarity with each other, the two found some shade and sat down to rest. And talk.

"Father, tell me of the people here. They seem to be such a...diverse group," McClendon started.

After a few moments of contemplation, the priest responded, "While from atop your horse you might see

Spanish, Mestizo, Indian, Black, or White, underneath the surface we are all alike. Most are doing all they can to survive in this difficult world. And to love God to the best of their ability.

"In your profession, you know that nothing can be accomplished alone. We know that here as well and do our best to not let our own pride get in the way of being connected. If you look closely enough, you'll see the mystery of God working through each and every one of us. Look over there—you see that man wearing a white shirt and knee-length brown pants? He is the son of a holy man from one of the pueblos near here. He runs a trading post that provides all the essentials travelers need. Food. Clothing. Even grease for the wagon wheels.

"When people do not have enough money or goods to trade, he finds a way to get them what they need. And that man, over there in the carriage. He travels here every week from Albuquerque with mail, providing those here with a connection to family and friends deep in Mexico. And that man, riding away on the beautiful white and brown horse. He is called the "savior of a generation." He's a Spanish doctor who immunizes los Indios against the terrible smallpox. We all have a role to play, my son. What is yours?"

* * * * *

The evening of August 7th began with a refreshing downpour. But water wasn't the only thing in the air. The soft rumble throughout the Army of the West was that something important was about to happen. And sure enough, Donovan's briefing that night turned the rumble into an earthquake. He informed the command element that the vaunted mayor of Santa Fe, who also served as the senior most military officer, had delegated his authority to his second in command and was seen fleeing Santa Fe in the company of a small number of Mexican troops.

According to Donovan, the mayor had left in order to "convince Mexico City to send more troops." The soldiers who remained had abandoned their posts along Glorietta Pass and had not set up any kind of defensive positions around the city.

"Thank you, Colonel Donovan. This army would be blind without you, sir. Gentlemen, this is the news we've been waiting for," General Kearny said with confidence and excitement, tugging at his dark blue coat emblazoned with the single gold star.

He took a drink of coffee and continued, "Gentlemen, the main element will begin our 100 mile march to Santa Fe at first light. Colonel Donovan, you and the Dragoons will depart at 4 am. You will secure Glorietta Pass by the morning of the 10th, to provide overwatch both east towards Santa Fe and west for our approach.

"We will execute the plan we've discussed, using the Santa Fe Trail to maximize our speed of advance. And with God by our side, we will be raising the flag of the United States of America over the Palace of the Governors on the 13th."

Loud, confident HOOOAAAAHHHs echoed

throughout the room. The officers in the room stood, snapped to attention, and saluted the man who would soon be known as the latest conqueror of New Mexico.

45

3. August 9, 1846 — Pecos Pueblo, New Mexico

They'd worked through the night digging through the rubble of what had once been a grand Spanish Catholic church. Only three of the four walls remained standing as the entire west-facing side where the 18-foot-tall double doors, as well as the roof and everything inside, had been burned down or destroyed by the Pecos Puebloans in a revolt against the Spanish who had occupied nearly every facet of their lives for well over a hundred years.

Shards of metal from the imported bell that had once proudly if not ominously filled the entire valley with its ringing lay scattered on the hard packed dirt floor. At 7,000 feet above sea level, the cool night air smelled of smoke from fires both old and new. Lanterns provided just enough light in the predawn darkness to continue the search for a small door or hole along the baseboards amidst the charred beams and piles of adobe bricks. That, they had been told, was where they'd find what they'd been looking for.

The informant, a Navajo man, had approached Governor Armijo with a promise of an "ancient relic" in exchange, of course, for money. Armijo, knowing that the Americans had their sights set on Santa Fe just a day's ride west from Pecos Pueblo along the Santa Fe Trail, had to act fast. He needed help from someone he trusted and only one name came to mind: Cristoval Maria Larrañaga. Together Armijo and Larrañaga met with the Navajo. The meeting point, Pecos Pueblo. The mission, find the relic before the Americans arrived.

* * * * *

Some 30 million years prior, amidst tremendous tectonic pressure along spider-webbed fault lines, what had once been a great ocean floor rose, creating the Sangre de Cristo Mountain range. Blanca Peak, the range's highest point, reaches 14,326 feet, more than double the elevation of Mount Mitchell, the highest peak east of the Mississippi.

Pecos, located at the southeastern corner of the Sangre de Cristos sits in a high valley with an abundant, spring and river-fed water supply, making it an almost idyllic location for civilization. Glorietta Mesa marks the southern boundary, lower than the range's peaks to the north and west, but still hundreds of vertical feet above the rolling valley it watches over. The geologically younger, and slightly lower still Tecalote Range forms the eastern boundary of the high valley.

The area's namesake river, the Pecos, runs west to east through the valley before turning south and heading towards the Gulf of Mexico. And the far younger Santa Fe

Trail that was first documented in American journals and newspapers in 1821 by William Becknell, approaches its terminus from the east side of Pecos, winding westward through and up the valley where Pecos sits, and exits via Glorietta Pass. From there, Santa Fe and its surrounding villages are within sight.

History whispers that the Anasazi first occupied the Pecos area around 11,500 BC. For thousands of years, they lived as hunters and gatherers, following and depending initially on the great mammoths and mastodons and later, on bison and pronghorn. Around 5500 BC, the Anasazi began cultivating corn, initiating a transition to an agriculture-based society. This more sedentary lifestyle required more established protection from the elements—in other words, better housing.

By the turn of the 16th century, Pecos Pueblo was one of the largest of over one hundred known pueblos in and around New Mexico. Hosting a quadrangle formed by multi-story buildings with over 600 rooms and at least 2,000 people, the Pecos location and civilization attracted travelers and trade, as evidenced by the far-reaching variety of people and artifacts found there by the Spanish conquistadors.

The Puebloans even designated a field just outside and below their village for travelers and traders to pitch their tents, making the area somewhat of a modern flea market. This influx of new faces and beliefs was welcomed, but not without concern. The people of Pecos Pueblo developed and maintained a 500 man strong warrior force. Newcomers were welcomed but forewarned.

The Anasazi, it is said, believed in balance and harmony and passed that along from one generation to the next. They hunted and farmed and produced what they needed to sustain their lives, their community. Relationship—with others and with the natural world—meant everything.

At birth, children were immediately accepted as belonging to a family, clan, and community. Everyone contributed to the good of the community, whether that be through hunting or construction, farming or food preparation, pot-making or spiritual leadership. The journey of the people was often depicted as a series of concentric circles, emanating from a central, common point. Only in this connected way, they believed, could people not only survive but live in balance and harmony.

Balance and harmony were not a part of Holy Roman Emperor and King of Spain Charles V's plan that led to the crossing of the Atlantic in force in the early 16th century. His plan, like those of so many other world leaders, was conquest. Hernan Cortez set the standard for this when he led the expedition to take control of the Aztec empire—Mexico—in 1521.

Within a decade of Cortez's success, the Spanish managed to disassemble the vast Inca Empire that stretched for thousands of miles along the "new" continent's Pacific coast. To accomplish these amazing feats was one thing. To hold the territory was another. To do this, the conquistadors brought with them Governors from the politically connected class in Spain and Catholic priests from the Roman Catholic Church to win both the hearts and the minds of the native populations for God and Spain.

Names have meaning and *Catholic*, derived from the Greek adjective *katholikos* means 'universal.' Armed with the mission of spreading what they believed to be the universal religion, Spanish soldiers, priests, and settlers laid their lives on the line as far north in the 'New World' as a place they called San Francisco (37th parallel north) and as far south as the Maule River (35th parallel south).

To accomplish their mission, they brought metal tools and weapons that the natives had never seen anything like and could not defend against, even with their vastly superior numbers. The Spanish brought livestock such as horses, goats, and sheep that were much more suited to thrive in water-scarce environments than what had previously existed there. And they brought disease. Measles, influenza, and pneumonia raged through any population that encountered the Spanish. Perhaps the most impactful Spanish addition to the new world was smallpox. This highly infectious disease caused the deaths of more than half of the indigenous population of "New Spain" by the end of the Sixteenth Century.

At the end of the 16th century—1598 to be exact—the Spanish reached Santa Fe and Pecos Pueblo. There, soldiers, priests, and settlers continued their colonization, their mission of converting the indigenous people to Catholicism, and their quest for treasure of legendary proportions.

A significant element of their strategy was to not only discourage but ultimately destroy all non-Catholic traditions—to quite literally turn the lives of the locals around. One example of this involved the Catholic Church in the Pecos Pueblo which officially opened its doors in 1618. All Puebloan structures there were oriented east, towards the sunrise and the valley below where traders and travelers would stay.

The Spanish Church, however, was built facing west, towards the multi-story dwellings of the Puebloans. Perhaps this was to show los Indios just where the power and control now emanated from. But this is just conjecture. The mission and movement to eliminate all ancient traditions was as real as the steel breastplates they wore. In 1619, a Catholic priest living in Pecos wrote in his journal, "Today we destroyed the last of the kivas and all the statues we could find." And before the Spanish had arrived, there were at least a dozen kivas in the Pecos Pueblo.

The Spanish weren't the only people out to get the Puebloans: The Apache Indians also took a toll on them, both before and after the Spanish arrived. The oldest Apache artifacts found in the Pecos area date back to 1000 AD, well after the pueblo became a thriving, almost metropolitan village. Taking horses, sheep, goats, and even people for slaves or trade during their hit-and-run raids, the Apache people preyed on the Puebloans often and without remorse. Those who claim to know say Apache raids is why the Puebloans developed their own warrior force.

By 1680, the Pecos Puebloans had had enough of the Spanish and the Apaches. Over the course of a week, they revolted, burning down the massive Catholic Church and killing or forcing out all of the Spanish. Pecos Pueblo returned to their ancient traditions and rebuilt their kivas. For twelve years they held the Spanish and Apache off. But the Spanish regained control in 1692, returning Pecos Pueblo to the Spanish way of life.

In 1821, Mexico successfully gained its independence from Spain. New Mexico, as it had been called even while governed by Spain, became a part of Mexico. But without the protection of the Spanish soldiers or a standing Mexican army, the Pecos Puebloans were forced to flee their village in fear of their lives. Home, for them, was about relationships, not a physical location. By 1838, Pecos Pueblo was a ghost town, the departed souls of the past its only inhabitants.

* * * * *

The six exhausted men finished their search of the church ruins just after the sun climbed above the hills to the east and reflected its light off the rocky, treeless face of the Glorietta Mesa. They hadn't found the promised opening or door in the floor or baseboards. The lack of success, paired with the sleepless night, made for bad moods all around, especially for Governor Armijo who teetered on the precipice of losing not only his position but also his livelihood.

He turned to his aide, Tomás, who had been clearing rubble and debris by his side all night and said, "I think we are done here. Pinche Navajo!" Turning to Larrañaga,

Lalo, James, and Bisa he continued, "Gentlemen, I don't know what to say. Lo siento—I'm sorry."

Larrañaga, much more familiar with overcoming failure than Governor Armijo, was not ready to give up. "Mi amigo, this is *un pueblo grande*. Perhaps we are looking in the wrong place. Bisa, James, could you tend to the fire? Perhaps some coffee will spur some ideas." Tomás hurried after the two young men, anxious to be away from his employer.

Armijo, Larrañaga, and Lalo sat down with their backs against the remains of the eastern wall of the church and looked out in silence over the buffalo grass field below. Larrañaga pictured the diverse travelers, traders, and peoples who had camped there over the course of millennia. *If I wanted to hide something here, with so many people coming and going, where would I do it?* Larrañaga pondered.

* * * * *

Back in late June when they met at Wagon Mound, Armijo had told Larrañaga that the Americans were coming. And soon. He had told Larrañaga that he was working behind the scenes, getting valuable information from a personal friend within the U.S. government who had conveyed not only the size and composition of the newly created Army of the West that was tasked with taking the capital city and, further west, the coastal town of El Pueblo de Nuestra Señora la Reina de Los Ángeles del Río de la Porcuincula—the Port of Los Angeles, but also their secondary mission: to seize any and all artifacts of cultural, religious, or political significance.

What Armijo hadn't told Larrañaga was that he'd made a deal with his politically connected friend in the Polk Administration. In exchange for a U.S-sponsored retirement from government service, the Governor of New Mexico would surrender Santa Fe without a shot being fired and hand over all valuable artifacts. With the smell of freshly cut pinon heating up their breakfast, Armijo felt like his plan was going up in smoke.

* * * * *

Lalo sat quietly next to his uncle, deep in his own thoughts. The prospect of finding ancient artifacts had made his uncle's offer over ten years ago impossible to turn down. He'd pledged his allegiance then, promising never to abandon him or the mission. But after years of searching, more near-death experiences than he could count, and the knowledge that each day that passed was one less he'd be able to spend with his wife and now fifteen-year-old son, that commitment waned as Spain had when they'd sailed away from her all those year ago.

His wife and son lived in Chihuahua City, hundreds of miles to the south, with his wife's parents who'd come over from Spain. Lalo had last seen them two years ago and during quiet moments like these, his heart ached. Just before stumbling across James under the wagon box, he'd tried to convince his uncle that they should think about giving up on their mission, or at least setting it aside for a spell so they could live a normal life in the beautiful town of Santa Fe or Taos. Larrañaga shook off the idea like a horse's tail dispatches flies.

Lalo then had proposed to bring his wife and son to Santa Fe, but both Larrañaga and New Mexico's Bishop Zumbria, who served as something of a mentor to Larrañaga, had strongly advised leaving them in Chihuahua City. A much safer place for a woman and child, they echoed.

Sitting there in the rubble, Lalo said a quiet prayer for his family, their safety, and his swift return to them. Especially after what happened to James' father in the Cimarron Desert. *So much sorrow and death here*, he thought.

* * * * *

Larrañaga wasn't thinking about running away or deals with governments. He'd spent his entire adult life piecing bits of information together—from legends, journals, and people—and here, today, he felt closer than they'd ever been to finding what he sought. This burst of confidence stemmed from a discussion he'd had with Father Manuel Ortiz the previous Sunday in Wagon Mound. Father Ortiz, the only ordained priest for hundreds of miles, traveled all across the high desert plain of New Mexico and into the surrounding mountains to bring the word of God to the Spanish and Mexican settlers, as well as any interested Indians—and there were many. As such, he kept his finger on the pulse of all that happened in New Mexico, good and bad.

Father Ortiz told Larrañaga about a conversation he and an old Puebloan had after a mass two weeks prior. The message Father Ortiz had offered the congregants centered on the "greatest commandments" as written in Matthew 22:36-40. According to Father Ortiz, the old man said the ancient ones tell of a story very similar to that which the Catholic priest offered. The story of a great man, both physically and spiritually, who came to teach them to live with love, for him and for each other.

This great man, the Puebloan had told him, visited the people during periods of great turmoil when the people needed him the most. He used his miraculous abilities to further his teachings and improve the lives of those who lived according to his will.

When Father Ortiz asked how the story of this great man ended, the old Puebloan said that, like Jesus, this great man was killed by those who did not accept his teachings, by those who took great pleasure in asserting their own power over others. *But something of this great man survived.* Something that still yields his miraculous, life-changing powers. And that something is *here*, in New Mexico. When Father Ortiz asked the man where, the Puebloan said "Pecos Pueblo."

This was not the first time Larrañaga had heard of this great mythical entity.

* * * * *

James stepped out from behind the church. "Coffee's ready, gentlemen." Armijo stood and stretched his aching back. Larrañaga stood as well but kept his eyes on the trail.

"Looks like we shall soon have company," the elder Spaniard said. "No hats. Dark hair pulled back underneath headbands. White shirts."

Bisa stepped out. He followed Larrañaga's eyes and said, "Navajo."

"Grab the rifles, mi sobrino, just in case," Larrañaga called over his shoulder to Lalo. "You and James provide us with some overwatch from here."

Larrañaga, Bisa, and Armijo walked down the hill from the church towards the trail. As the riders approached and saw the trio, they slowed. Larrañaga and Bisa both made a motion with their hands, first pointing at their heart and then extending their arm out from their chests.

Back at the church, Lalo whispered to James, "That means 'Yá'át'ééh,' Navajo for 'all is good.'"

Both riders returned the signal, seemed to relax a bit, and walked their lathered yet beautiful "painted" horses right up to the three men. After a few minutes, the riders continued west and Larrañaga, Bisa, and Armijo walked back up the hill to where the others stood.

"They say about 200 mounted soldiers are heading this way. Wearing the Yankee blue," Larrañaga said. "Several hours out." Bisa nodded. "Let's have our coffee and figure out a plan." Together the men fast stepped through the church to where the horses were tied and the coffee and food sat. While they ate, Larrañaga showed James the important hand signal they'd just used, telling him that from a distance this is how the Navajo know someone is friendly. *He has a lot to learn*, the Spaniard thought. *But he picks things up quickly. Bueno.*

Seeing a look of confusion on James' face, Larrañaga offered, "The Mexicans and the Spanish before them have employed the Navajo in a variety of ways. Artifact hunting and grave digging is one such way, but that is not something they like, si amigo?" This last he said to Bisa. "The Governor also uses the Navajo as his eyes and ears in the mountains and countryside around Santa Fe."

Barely making it through his breakfast, a visibly anxious Armijo stood and began to gather his things. His aide had already watered their horses and readied their saddles. After checking and double-checking their kits, Armijo pulled his friend aside. Leaning in close so the others could not hear, he said, "The time has come, my friend. I need to keep up appearances now. I am going to make my way to El Paso del Norte and plead for more troops to fend off the blue coats. If you find anything, get word to me there. We cannot let the Americans take anything this is rightfully ours."

Armijo and Larrañaga shook hands, and the former mounted his horse. Armijo yelled, "vaya con Dios!" and departed in the direction the Navajo riders had gone.

Lalo walked up behind Larrañaga as the Governor and his aide dropped from sight. "It looks like we're on our own once again, Tío. What's the plan?"

* * * * *

As the late afternoon sun neared the rim of the mountains to the west, Lalo, who had taken the watch while the others caught up on some sleep, made his way up a hill a few hundred meters north of the ruins of the church. He carried with him the field glass case he kept in his saddlebag. Focusing on the northeast, he immediately picked up two columns of blue-clad soldiers moving up the hill valley towards Pecos. They moved fast, their speed indicating that they did not expect any resistance. Lalo hustled down to the shaded riverbed where the horses were corralled, and the others were sleeping. He shook Larrañaga's shoulder, quickly gave him the update, and ran back up the hill. Looking through the field glasses at the men closest to him, he scanned their kit. Carbines. Pistols. And Sabers. The last identified them as the Dragoons out of Fort Smith. "No bueno," he muttered.

Larrañaga and James joined Lalo in the shade of the pine tree atop the hill while Bisa remained with the horses, preparing them for a quick departure should the need arise. The three on the hill took a knee to lower their profile. "I stopped counting at 200," Lalo said, winking at James.

"That's nearly their full contingent of Dragoons," Larrañaga said quietly.

"Hold on. There's more!" James proclaimed, startling the other two and pointing to the furthest visible rise in the trail. The dust cloud from the first, larger group still hung in the air as the second, half a mile back, rode right through it. Taking the field glasses from Lalo, Larrañaga scanned the first group again and then the second. He knew a few of the faces. The broad-shouldered, beast of a man next to the flag of the first unit was Colonel Donovan. He and Larrañaga had some history. The leader of the second unit, the one without the flag, Larrañaga did not recognize. In fact, judging by his riding skills and lack of saber, Larrañaga deduced the leader of the second unit was not a Dragoon at all. *Interesting…*

Larrañaga, Lalo, and James watched as the first unit of the Dragoons circled up and dismounted on the southwest side of the hill between the ruins of the church and Glorietta Creek, just below the mesa. Donovan's well-trained and experienced unit quickly established a perimeter, took the horses down to the creek, and removed the gear they'd need for setting up a temporary camp. "Looks like they're staying," Lalo said.

Larrañaga's mind played out several scenarios. His group was not in immediate danger, he figured, even if the Dragoons found them. They were just civilians, after all. Travelers like so many others here. A doctor and his assistants. But something started nagging at him as the second, smaller group with the non-Dragoon leader closed in. And when they turned off the trail, they headed not towards the lead group, but towards the northern side of the pueblo and the ruins of the Puebloan structures. And Larrañaga.

Shifting gears from thought to action, Larrañaga motioned to the others to remain crouched down but to follow him off the hill, back down to the horses. A small voice inside Larrañaga's head told him to leave, quickly. But a deeper voice, this one soothing and confident, told him to stay. To wait. To watch. "Tranquilo," he said to Lalo and the others, hoping that his voice communicated the same confidence. "Let's stay and see what God brings our way." Lalo crossed himself. James and Bisa looked questioningly at each other.

The last rays of light in the evening sky highlighted Larrañaga's outline as he once again climbed the hill towards the Pueblo. *He can still move like un puma*, Lalo thought. Larrañaga reached the top and peered down into the pueblo below. He counted eleven men in the closer, second group. Unlike the first group, this one was setting up two rows of three tents facing each other on the field he'd overlooked earlier in the day, the one where travelers long since gone had camped.

The larger contingent of Dragoons was mostly hidden on the south side of the abandoned pueblo. Apart from the security element, the rest of that group seemed to be resting and not setting up tents. But there was Donovan, walking amidst the rubble of the church. The man who up near Pagosa Springs, Colorado, had nearly taken his life two winters ago.

* * * * *

On a cold, clear winter day, smoke from cooking fires combined with the steam from the Pagosa[1] Hot Springs gave the narrow, pine-lined valley an ethereal hue. For hundreds of years, the Utes had wintered next to the

---

1. *Pagosa* is a Ute word for healing, or boiling water.

Pagosa River as elk, bighorn sheep, and beavers provided ample food and the hills surrounding the river valley made them feel safe, protected.

West and south of the hot springs was the high point of Chimney Rock, an ancient tower of sandstone with a clear line of sight to several over high points adjacent to other pueblos as far away as Chaco Canyon. The Anasazi had once lived there and those that climb up out of the valley to the base of the 325' tall tower of rock that gives the place its name are rewarded with not only a breathtaking view but also the remains of a 36 room village and one of the largest kivas in the region. It was from here that the ancients aligned their lives with the sun and stars, communicated with the spirits of the past and the people of the present, always in balance and harmony.

A thirty-man platoon of Dragoons under the command of newly promoted Captain Donovan had been ordered to the area after a series of Apache attacks on American and French trappers. Beavers were a highly lucrative commodity, and the trappers typically lived and hunted in small numbers, far away from the protection of military outposts or established towns. The Apache knew this. Donovan and his men approached Pagosa Springs from the northeast, coming down the valley between Saddle Mountain and Flat Top Mountain. At the same time, unaware of the attacks and the plan to address them, Larrañaga and Lalo made their way up the valley from the southwest.

When the Dragoons saw Indians going through their morning routines near the springs, the soldiers assumed they were the ones to blame for the recent deaths of the trappers. Heavy hoofbeats on the hard ground echoed off the valley walls. The Utes didn't put up much of a fight and by the time Larrañaga and Lalo arrived at the scene, ready to help whoever was in trouble, the deed was nearly done. The Ute's domed, willow-covered dwellings were ablaze, and Ute bodies were scattered throughout the village, some dying and some already dead, their blood casting horrific shadows on the otherwise pristine snow.

Three Utes, an elder, a woman who was likely his wife, and a child were sitting in the middle of the village surrounded by a dozen Dragoons. And Donovan.

Larrañaga and Lalo, dressed like frontiersmen but with full medical kits strapped to the two mules they had in tow as a part of their vaccination mission, were neither attacked nor welcomed by the Dragoons as they approached the scene. They were, however, escorted under guard to the captain who was interrogating the Utes. Unfortunately for all, Donovan's knowledge of Shoshonean — the language of the Ute — was sorely lacking.

As the stoic elder and sobbing woman attempted to communicate with Donovan, the reality that they were not speaking the Athabaskan language of the Apache set in. Larrañaga, taking this all in, explained to the broad shouldered, saber-toting soldier that these were not Apaches. He pleaded with Donovan to leave them in peace. Donovan, his adrenaline pumping, did not seem to — or maybe didn't want to — believe. Larrañaga swallowed hard and stepped between Donovan and the Utes.

"These are not Apache, sir," the Spaniard commanded. "Please, harm them no further and let us tend to the wounded," he said, gesturing back to his pack mules. The wailing of the woman filled his ears. The groaning of the peaceful village filled his heart.

Donovan's internal conflict was plastered on his red face, evident in his non-stop shifting from his right side to his left. "We have our orders." He paused as if considering. Turning his attention from the Spaniard back to the kneeling Indians, it was clear to all he'd made his decision. "We will finish the job." And with that Donovan turned to his second in command and nodded.

Larrañaga didn't hesitate—it just wasn't his nature. The Spaniard took two steps towards Donovan who anticipated Larrañaga's move and spun. Before Larrañaga could get a third step in a rifle butt struck him in the side of the head and the world went dark.

He came back to consciousness sometime later to the sound of Lalo's voice. Save for the two of them, the village was devoid of life. The elder Ute, the woman, and the child lay still ten steps away. The fires had gone out. The Dragoons were gone.

* * * * *

Larrañaga snapped back to the present and rubbed the scar on his left temple. Belly-crawling off the hilltop he made his way back to the campsite. "I imagine the first group will move out before dawn. They haven't set up any tents. They will go to Glorietta Pass to secure it for the infantry and wagon trails. But the second group…," he paused, thinking. "The second group has set up tents and seems to be planning to stay awhile. Let's break out some food and get some rest. Tomorrow is sure to be an eventful day."

4. August 10, 1846 — Pecos Pueblo, New Mexico

Lalo listened as the morning birds began to stretch their vocal chords. As the first hint of dawn crossed the horizon. He'd had the final watch of the night, and as the scene unfolded in and around the pueblo below, he silently confirmed his uncle's prediction before slowly making his way down to the others who had just begun to emerge from beneath their blankets. "You were right, Tío," he said, which earned him a smirk. "Donovan's group is gone. They are heading towards Glorietta Pass. The second group has eaten their breakfast and is walking up towards the pueblo.

Larrañaga rubbed his chin, deep in thought. He looked from Lalo to Bisa to James, at the same time appreciating and slightly concerned for their presence. "Here's what we're going to do."

* * * * *

Trotting their horses two abreast on the Santa Fe Trail

towards Pecos Pueblo in the late morning sun, the foursome looked no different than any other travelers. They had circled around to the north and east, out of sight of the second group of Dragoons whose attention seemed to be squarely on the deserted Indian village. The hulking remains of the church seemed to watch them though, a sense of foreboding permeating not only the landscape but their very beings.

As they neared the pueblo, Larrañaga gave a signal to Bisa and James behind him. The younger twosome broke off, found the shade of a nearby pine tree, and watched Larrañaga and Lalo ride up to the base of the hill just below the ruins of the church. After pausing for a few moments in anticipation of a reaction from the smaller group of Dragoons but drawing none, they rode up the hill first to the church and then into the abandoned pueblo where the Dragoons were picking through some rubble. Almost immediately, one of them spotted the pair, hollered to the others, and drew their sidearms.

"Hey, you!" the twang of a Kentuckian bounced off the mud-brick walls. Those down in the kivas scampered up, grabbed their rifles, and assumed a defensive posture. Several other Dragoons ran out of what had been a multi-story structure, weapons in hand. Both Larrañaga and Lalo, still atop their horses, raised their hands as they had planned to do.

"That's 10. Where's the other?" Lalo whispered. He and Larrañaga slowly dismounted their horses and led them, on foot, hands still raised, along the hilltop towards the Dragoons. "There he is," he said, pointing to a pile of rocks below the hilltop.

Moments later, the Dragoons, having been joined by their commander, encircled Larrañaga and Lalo who introduced themselves, making a point not to give off any kind of threatening demeanor. In reality, they weren't. Larrañaga's plan bore fruit. At the command of the officer in charge, the Dragoons lowered their weapons. The officer, a tall, thin, blond-haired man with a clean-shaven face walked towards the Spaniards with his hand extended.

"A pleasure to meet you, gentlemen. Please, put your hands down. My name is Jonathan McClendon, ah, Colonel McClendon of the Army of the West." He paused, looked curiously at Larrañaga as they shook hands, and continued. "Sir, you look familiar. Have we met before?"

The name. The accent. Larrañaga was too stunned to speak. It was Lalo who broke the silence.

"Colonel McClendon, we are on our way to Santa Fe after a difficult crossing. My uncle is a doctor, and I am his assistant. Might we trouble you for some food and drink?

"Of course," McClendon responded and gestured back towards the tents to one of his men to go get some canteens and something to eat. Turning back towards the ruins of the pueblo he said, "This is an incredible place. Do you know what happened here?"

Having regained his composure, Larrañaga turned to his nephew and said, "Go get the others, mi sobrino. Take the horses to the creek and then rejoin me up here." Lalo tried hard to stifle his smile, silently thanking God that the task forced him to turn away.

For half an hour, Larrañaga regaled the Dragoons with what he knew of the history of the Pecos Puebloans and the Anasazi before them. Larrañaga's Spanish accent, newfound energy despite having been up all night, and flair for the dramatic captured the attention of the *norteamericanos*. He concluded the story with the bait he had thought of earlier. "Legend has it that something very important is hidden here," he said. "Something that can do as much for our lives today as it did for the ancients."

The Dragoons looked at each other and then, as one, at McClendon whose face looked like a child's on Christmas morning. Clearing his throat to buy a moment of time. "That's interesting. Very interesting." He finally said, drawing out each syllable in his Low Country drawl. "Lieutenant, let's get the men back to work." He said to a short, energetic young man.

The lieutenant gave the order, and the soldiers begrudgingly stood and brushed themselves off. As they walked back to where they had been prior to the Spaniards' arrival, McClendon took a step closer to Larrañaga and said, "Tell me more about this legend."

And at that moment, Lalo, Bisa, and James emerged from the tree-shrouded creek and caught the eye of Larrañaga. Of McClendon.

Like a flash of late-summer lightning, Jonathan McClendon forgot about ancient artifacts, military etiquette, and national interests when he saw his son walking up the hill. He dropped the gloves he was holding and yelled,

"James!" James, whose mind hadn't yet registered what his eyes were seeing, stopped cold in his tracks, processing, but only for a moment. He ran to and embraced his father.

Larrañaga stepped back from the two McClendons and stroked his bearded chin, giving their joy- and tear-filled reunion some time and space and thanking God for putting him in the right place at the right time to help enable this.

Larrañaga then called the lieutenant and together with Bisa and Lalo they set off on a walk around the circumference of the hilltop. He called out the different parts of the village, describing what they must have looked like prior to the revolt, the destruction, the abandonment. The lieutenant listened closely. And all the while Larrañaga was thinking…both about the clues that Armijo and Father Ortiz had provided and about how to best leverage this new situation to his advantage. An idea began to form just as they arrived back at the site of the reunion.

Father and son sat on the raised edge of one of the many circular pithouses of the village, regaling each other with animated tales of their crossings. Streaks of tears glistened on their otherwise dirty, smiling faces. As the four men approached, they stood. All had tears in their eyes now, realizing that this reunion was nothing short of a miracle.

The Colonel adjusted his uniform and wiped a handkerchief across his face. "Senor Larrañaga, I do not know what to say. You—and your men—saved my son's life. You've brought us back together. For that, gentlemen, I am eternally grateful and woefully in your debt. Please, let's head down to the tents and allow me to feed you a meal. I for one would like to hear more about your mission, 'Savior of a Generation.'"

Turning to the lieutenant, McClendon said, "Please round up the troops and have them meet us there."

As the sun dipped towards the ridge to the west, the eleven Dragoons and four members of Larrañaga's party finished eating, trading stories, and strategizing for a comprehensive search of the village. Larrañaga skillfully guided the creation of the search strategy, suggesting they break off into teams of two or three to find and search each kiva. Larrañaga volunteered his trio for the largest, most central kiva, thinking that was the most likely location for anything of value. With full stomachs and a clear plan, all agreed to do their best to complete the searches before dark. Fortunately, more than one thought, the longer summer days afforded them several more hours of light.

Broken, burned timbers and mud bricks more than halfway filled the exposed, sunken kivas. Some were larger than others and, judging by their locations around the pueblo, some were more important than others, but all were about ten feet deep which made the task of hoisting debris out of the once sacred spaces an arduous task. But the men worked in hopeful silence. Every now and again someone would holler that they'd found something. In each instance, after a few moments of palpable anticipation, a negative report would follow.

The steady evening wind picked up in strength and with it swirling dust and dark, cumulous clouds signaled to all that a storm would shortly follow. *Being in a pit during a deluge is no bueno,* Larrañaga thought, watching the light fade from the sky. *And the Army of the West will be here tomorrow so we must keep at it!* No sooner did he complete that thought than the metallic smell of rain filled his dusty nostrils. Larrañaga's kiva was just about empty and neither he nor Lalo and Bisa had found anything of interest in the pit they'd been working. He cast a glance out in the direction of the other pits. *God, if it is your will, please help us,* he prayed silently and then began humming Veni Creator Spiritus, a Georgian chant that, throughout his life, seemed to bring him closer to God than his own thoughts.

As the first rain drops fell, Larrañaga decided to check on the others. He hopped up out of his own kiva and walked quickly down the line of pits to assess progress and to advise, once again, what to look for. He reminded them the Puebloans were known to have either a hiding space or tunnel in every structure they built and especially the kivas—both for hiding and for escape. In his own experience, Larrañaga had relayed, the vast majority of hidden compartments were built into the north side of kivas. In all likelihood, whatever they were looking for would be inside one of these.

Shouts of excitement broke the silence, popping out of the sunken spaces like kernels of corn. He heard Bisa's voice, then that of the lieutenant he'd spoken with earlier, and within the space of a few minutes what had been a quiet pueblo resonated with voices announcing they'd found a secret compartment.

Larrañaga ran back along the line of kivas, each separated by thirty or forty paces, shouting, "Now see what you find in there!"

Arriving out of breath at the one he, Lalo, and Bisa had been working on, Larrañaga barely broke stride and jumped down into the pit, twisting his ankle severely. But instead of pain in his ankle he felt a pulsing of energy in his soul. Lalo pointed to a small square hole cut into the floor and stood on one side of it, grinning from ear to ear and pointing at an object just barely visible amidst the dirt and darkness.

Just then the skies opened up, the cool rain drenching his back and legs and turning the floor of the kiva to mud. Thunder echoed off the surrounding heights. Lalo carefully reached into the hole and wrapped his hands around a glazed polychrome jar—a pot with a wide bottom that narrowed slightly at the top—of the kind he remembered seeing in Father Ortiz's Puebloan collection in Santa Fe.

Slowly he pulled the pot out and set it on the muddy floor. A colored band with paintings of water creatures spanned its circumference. Capable of holding several gallons of water, this pot held something else. Something wrapped loosely in the hide of a deer. Larrañaga reached in and pulled the something out, holding it as he would a newborn and began to unwrap it. A polished, dark stone face emerged. The figure's arms crossed over its heart.

"What is it?" a soldier asked from atop the kiva.

"It's a religious artifact—a stone effigy. The Puebloans used these in many of their ceremonies. It looks like it's been broken—probably by the priests—and expertly repaired. Bisa, take this," Larrañaga said, handing the carved stone to his friend. Then the Spaniard carefully climbed out of the pit. He looked down and noted the look of disdain on the Navajo's face as Bisa held the artifact away from his body.

Larrañaga scanned the skies, the mountains to the north and west, the flat top mesa to the south, and Santa Fe Trail to east. *Is someone or something out there?* He thought. "We have to hurry." Larrañaga started to run but after one step the pain in his ankle hit him like a galloping horse. Limping as fast as he could, he caught sight of James and his father atop the far kiva waving their arms wildly. With the help of Lalo and Bisa on either side, the threesome made their way there.

Bisa, anxious to rid himself of the stone effigy handed it to the waiting Colonel McClendon. While Lalo explained what it was, James helped Larrañaga down into the pit. Together they knelt in the mud on the floor of the kiva next to what looked like an entrance to a tunnel on the north side of the kiva. Surrounded above by dark skies and a growing number of Dragoons who were fixated on the artifact in their commander's hands, Larrañaga looked at James and said excitedly, "Think you can fit in there, mi hijo?"

The soaked young man answered by lowering his hands and then his head and shoulders into the tight, dark, slick space. Larrañaga watched James squirm headfirst through the hole in the ground; the water and mud acting like grease on a wagon wheel and within moments only James' ankles and feet remained visible to the crowd. Larraña-ga called for a rope, and someone tossed one down. The Spaniard quickly tied it around James' boot. Moments later the young man had completely disappeared inside what was clearly a tunnel and yelled back, his voice barely audible now, "Looks like this goes out a ways."

The Spaniard tossed the end of the rope up to one of the soldiers and told him to hold onto it and pull James out if need be. He then climbed up to the rim of the pit, wincing through the pain in his ankle and looked out, past the kiva, in the direction James seemed to be heading. *The backside of the hill. A downslope. Loose gravel and pottery chards…*, Larrañaga's mind processed what he saw and then it hit: "Puebloan trash! Of course!" Judging by the direction and angle James had taken, the Spainard guessed where the tunnel exit might be and limped his way there. Lalo followed. Larrañaga pointed and Lalo started kicking away the first few inches of mud, rocks, and long-abandoned rubbish.

They could hear James' muffled voice hollering from inside and added their hands to the clearing effort. With pounding hearts, they dug. Almost a foot into the side of the hill they ran into a large, flat slab of sandstone that prevented them from getting any deeper. "*La Puerta — the door!*" The Spaniards frantically searched to find its edges and, on finding them, worked their fingers underneath the wagon-wheel-sized, one-inch-thick slab. Using the slope to their advantage, the men got on the uphill side and squatted, placing their hands under the edges and readied themselves to flip the slab over and down the hill.

"Uno, dos,…," Larrañaga said and on three the men lifted and pushed the stone over, revealing the dark, open space of the tunnel.

"I see something…something glowing!" James' now louder voice filled Larrañaga's ears—and heart—with renewed excitement.

Crawling in, Larrañaga could just make out James' hands. And he was holding something. Something long and skinny, like a rifle, that emitted some kind of faint blue light. Amidst cheers of encouragement in both Spanish and English, James snaked his way towards Larrañaga and the dusky light at the end of the tunnel. As he emerged, covered in mud, in his hands was a long, narrow bundle wrapped in what appeared to be some kind of animal hide. "Hiding in the trash pile…" Larrañaga thought more than said.

The Spaniard pulled back into a kneeling position, careful not to further injure his ankle and took the bundle from James' mud-covered hands as he wiggled out of the tunnel. Lalo, anxious to help, grabbed the young man's torso from above and hoisted James to his feet. James' white teeth revealing a smile a country mile wide, a stark contrast to the rest of his mud-covered face and body.

Moments later they all were back on the top of the hill next to the kiva. Soaked but excited. Laughter mixed with the drone of the rain which now seemed to be diminishing. The stone effigy passed from soldier to soldier, each almost caressing the statue. But the hide-wrapped bundle which no longer glowed had the attention of James and the Spaniards and, as a result, Colonel McClendon.

The commanding officer pointed to a partially collapsed structure that appeared to provide some shelter from the rain. "Let's go in there, find some dry space." Entering and still carrying the faintly glowing bundle, Larrañaga realized he no longer felt pain in his ankle. *That's strange*, he thought. With the heavy clouds retreating from the high valley out over the low ground to the northeast, the sun now rested just above Glorietta Pass to the southwest as if it wanted to provide just a few more minutes of daylight.

Colonel McClendon turned to Larrañaga with outstretched arms and said, "May I?" Reluctantly, Larrañaga handed over the dripping bundle.

The Colonel's now ungloved hands gingerly laid it down on a flat rock that likely had served as a table. He started at one end and carefully removed the mud-covered hide, piece by piece. *It looks like a bone*, he thought, and said as much to the small group. He continued to remove the wrappings and as the full length became visible it was clear that this was no ordinary bone. "It looks like a femur. Doctor do you agree?" McClendon said, his slow, South Carolinian drawl somehow accentuating the uniqueness of their discovery.

The shaft is over three feet long. Dios mío! Larrañaga thought as he stepped forward and examined the ends of the bone and then used his hands to measure it. The length of his hand from the tip of his middle finger to the start of his wrist was ten inches — a fact he'd relied on often to measure newborn babies. When Larrañaga finished measuring, he did it again more to convince himself than out of fear of having made an error. When he was sure, he looked up at the group. "Sí. This is a *human* femur of … tremendous proportions," Larrañaga said and wiped his face with the back of his trembling hand. He pointed out and provided the medical names for the proximal, shaft, and distal parts of the femur.

Pausing, he then added critical context, "The length of a typical human femur is between sixteen and eighteen inches and accounts for approximately one quarter of a person's height. This femur …" he paused and started again. "The length of this femur is fifty-six inches." And with that his arms widened to encompass the entirety of the bone. "The person who this came from was between eighteen and twenty feet tall." James, now standing beside Larrañaga, reached out and touched the bone which had ceased glowing.

Silence filled the room and now, it was Larrañaga's turn to weep. Overcome with a flood of emotion at finding what he'd been after for the better part of his adult life, the Spaniard sank to his knees in humility and gratitude and sobbed like Lalo had never seen before. Finding this after years of searching, after leaving his home and traveling so many miles, witnessing so much human suffering, and enduring hardships that would kill—did kill—other men, filled his spirit, made him feel … *whole*.

The sun dipped down beneath the western ridgeline and the light in the small space began to fade as the realization of what they'd found sank in for the rest of the small group. Breaking the silence, Colonel McClendon said with a laugh, "Gentlemen, we really are soaked to the bone." They all chuckled. Colonel McClendon helped Larrañaga to his feet and together they rewrapped the bone. And then he handed it back to Larrañaga with a wink and motioned for the others to follow him back outside.

The soldiers, still enamored by the stone effigy, turned their attention back to their commander with inquiring looks on their faces. "It's a bone—looks like this kiva might have been a burial ground." McClendon paused and then continued, downplaying the significance of the femur. . "It's been quite a day." "You all should be proud. Lieutenant, take that stone … what was it? Effigy? Take it down to the camp and find a secure place for it. The rest of you get back and get cleaned up and dried off as best we can. Then it's time to celebrate."

The lieutenant, empowered by McClendon's trust took over, shooing the men downhill towards the camp. Wet and tired, the adrenaline of the find wearing off, the soldiers did not grumble at this order. They knew that tomorrow the Army of the West would arrive. And now they'd have something to show their beloved General.

Later, with the flames of a small fire illuminating their faces, the two McClendons, the Spanish gentlemen, and Bisa reclined against their saddlebags. The lieutenant had constructed a pile of rocks and set the stone effigy on top so that the whole thing looked a bit like a temple in the middle of all the tents. A small fire and those soldiers who were not pulling security surrounded it. The now cleaned and dried hide-wrapped bone rested between the elder McClendon and Larrañaga.

The sky clear, the men fed and dry, the fragrant pinon cackling in the fire the only sound, save for the occasional soldier banter or coyote yelp. After getting up to throw another couple of logs on the fire, Larrañaga returned to his gear. McClendon turned his head to Larrañaga and said, "I noticed your ankle doesn't seem to be troubling you any longer." Larrañaga nodded but appeared to be a thousand miles away, deep in thought.

Then the Spaniard reached back into the saddlebag and pulled out a worn leather brown book with yellowing pages. He flipped through it for a moment, searching for something. The flickering light of the fire revealing all eyes were fixed on the Spaniard. Finding what he was after, he cleared his throat and started.

This is an exerpt from Father Hernando de Luque's diary dated:

July 23, 1526 In the Incan city of Cuzco

This Incan Empire is full of mysteries and traditions so foreign to ours but by no means less established or meaningful. I met with a spiritual man, a native leader here in this Andean highland city, and asked him to tell me about his beliefs. What I have scribbled below is, to the best of my note-taking ability, what he said to me.

*Here in Cuzco (which means 'the earth's navel') and throughout the land, all people pray to Inti, the first ancestor and sun god. But the most important god of all is named **Viracocha**. Viracocha brought* *meaning and purpose to our lives and gave us our greatest moments and achievements as a people whenever he walked among us—And he has! Many times. His name—Viracocha—means "foam of the sea," and when he came he always did so from the sea and all but once left by the sea. Sometimes he brought helpers who, like him—and like you—were light-skinned. They were very tall—taller than three men. They wore beards, and long, flowing cloaks and san-dals. I can see on your face you do not believe. That is fine. But what I say is true, as the elders have passed from generation to generation. Let me tell you more.*

With Viracocha, we created paved roads that run from north to south, east to west, all across our vast land. Who else could do this? With Viracocha, we have built bridges across great rivers and tunnels through solid rock. Again I ask, what man or men could do this? With Viracocha we built the citadel of Sacsayhauman with huge boulders that normal men could never move, let alone carry over the moun-tains from the quarry. The entrance to this citadel is a doorway three men tall and two men laying down wide and the boulder that crosses the top of the entrance weighs more than your three boats put together.

But that is not all Viracocha has done for us. He taught us about the stars in the sky. In Tiahuanoco, Viracocha not only constructed our Gateway to the Sun monolith, again using material too large and too dense for any man or tool to manipulate, but he taught us how to align them with the stars as they would have been hundreds of generations ago. Check it, if you can.

Most importantly, Viracocha taught us how to live, with great love and kindness. To bear no ill will towards each other. To have a giving and grateful heart. Viracocha not only said these things but did these things. He lived by example, always helping, always providing, always looking after his people. That reminds me, Viracocha was also a healer. Everywhere he went, he sought out the sick and the blind. Everyone he touched was instantly healed.

You are probably wondering, where Viracocha is now? Viracocha would always leave the people when he could no longer tolerate their disobedience, when even his punishments would not stop the bad ones from pursuing their own interests. The last time was different. As Viracocha prepared to once again leave by sea, the bad ones lured him into a deep pit and stoned him to death, burying him under the stones. It is said that after Viracocha died, those who loved him came and took his bones to spread his love and powers throughout the world.

Spoken through an Incan-Spanish translator over the course of two interviews.

Signed. R.O. Molina

Larrañaga took a drink of his now cold coffee. Looking at each of the faces in his audience, he saw wide eyes and a few open mouths. The only one who didn't seem completely captured by the reading was Bisa, who had nodded off, propped up against his saddle. "To answer your question, Colonel McClendon, yes, my ankle is feeling much better, thank you. But perhaps I should be thanking Viracocha."

5. August 11, 1846 Pecos — Pueblo

The dawn's light came quickly for the small, emotionally exhausted group who'd experienced two miracles in the span of 24 hours: the reunion and the discovery of a lifetime. The air was so still that smoke from the ashes of the fire rose straight up in a pencil-thin line and the dirt was as dry as if the previous evening's downpour had been a figment of their imagination. Colonel McClendon, like the rest, had chosen to fall asleep next to the glowing embers under the ageless stars. But with the rising sun, they too slowly rose, stretching their sore backs and legs. The detachment of Dragoons had been up for a while, all tents and gear stowed, breakfast finished. Bisa, always an early riser, approached from across the field with an armful of wood. He squatted next to what was left of the fire and stoked it back to life.

"Larrañaga, let's you and me go grab a coffee and take a walk," Colonel McClendon said after stifling a yawn. Grabbing the coats they had been using as blankets and pillows, both men walked stiffly towards where the soldiers had kept a pot ready for them. They could smell the hot brew well outside of fifty feet. "This … bone," the

Colonel said in a low voice, drawing out the last word. "What do you propose we do with it?" Without waiting for a response, he continued. "General Kearny would surely love to have it. So would President Polk."

"Jonathan," Larrañaga decided to use the officer's first name, after all they'd been through together. "I have been learning about and searching for this for most of my life. My Queen sent me here to find it so she can add it to her collection of treasures. The Catholic Church…ay Dios mío. The Pope and his more conservative followers who supported the elimination of the Incans and Aztec want it found and destroyed. And my family has an interest—dating back to one of my ancestors."

"And what do you think the Anasazi and Puebloans would want? They have kept this hidden for…God knows how long," McClendon asked. This surprised Larrañaga.

"Protect it." Bisa said from behind, surprising both men. In his hands was a five-foot section of a tree which he'd split in half along its length and hollowed out. McClendon and Larrañaga looked first at the log, realizing it was a place to hide the bone, then at each other and finally at Bisa.

"Well done, Bisa." McClendon said. "Let's put this to immediate use. I don't want anything to happen to it." With a nod, Bisa turned and walked away.

"Un momento," Larrañaga shouted, stopping Bisa in his tracks. "Make another that looks exactly the same—and remember, salvation often lies in the smallest of details." Bisa smiled and took off at a run.

McClendon nodded to Larrañaga, adding admiration

to the list of sentiments he held for the Spanish doctor whose selfless character distinguished him from most other men he'd known. Looking up the hill to where they'd found the bone, Jonathan said, "Why do you think people like artifacts and ruins so much?"

"These things remind us that we are not alone. That we are a part of something bigger, connected in some way to a presence that's always been around and always will be." Larrañaga said. "But that is a frightening thought for some — especially those in power. As the world gets smaller and people with different beliefs are thrust together, those who have power fear losing it, especially to something or someone they don't understand."

He paused. Thought. Continued. "The 'truths' they've told us, the ones they hold dear, are at risk when things like this are found because it is not for 'something bigger' that they live. It is for themselves. As St. John tells us, 'You shall know the truth and the truth shall set you free.' Queens, Popes, Presidents, and even ordinary people like you and me — there are many who don't have either the desire or ability to believe in something bigger than themselves. But those are just the ramblings of a tired old man," Larrañaga concluded humbly. The men continued walking.

"One thing I'm sure of," Larrañaga said, stepping close to McClendon. "Those who have been hiding this would not want those in power to have it."

Again, McClendon nodded in agreement. "So, let's figure out what we're going to tell General Kearny."

* * * * *

A short time later, one of the men on McClendon's security detail shouted, "Three riders are approaching fast, sir. One mile out." He pointed southwest—the direction of Glorietta Pass. McClendon and Larrañaga, now sitting in the grass field below the hill with Lalo, James, and Bisa, finished tightening identical leather straps around each of the two "logs." They all stood and reflexively picked up their rifles. Colonel McClendon looked at James.

"Take the empty log and hide it in your bedroll. Now!" he ordered. McClendon picked up the second one, the one with the bone, and put it under a few regular logs by the firepit. Together, McClendon, Larrañaga, and Lalo ran up the hill.

By the time he stopped next to his sentry, Colonel McClendon could easily distinguish the three riders. "Colonel Donovan," he hollered down. Larrañaga and Lalo exchanged uneasy glances and slowly began walking towards their horses who stood, packed and ready, along with all the other corralled horses. McClendon ran down the hill to the two Spaniards. "Hey," the out of breath officer said, so that only they could hear. "It's too late. He'll see you riding off and that will look bad—for all of us."

Lalo stopped first and Larrañaga followed. The elder Spaniard picked up a stone and threw it in frustration. "Tranquilo, Tío," Lalo said.

"Tranquilo? ¿Cómo puedo mantener la calma cuando viene un hombre que intentó matarme? Larrañaga said with a fire in his eyes.

"Gentlemen," McClendon said, trying to bring the emotions down a few notches. "We have a plan that I think will work. Let's stick to it," he said. "Now, go stand by the effigy and let me do my part."

Larrañaga had no sooner sat down on a rock next to the effigy than Donovan and his Dragoon escorts galloped over the hill to where McClendon now stood. Being of equal rank, McClendon did not offer a salute, and this seemed to irritate the mounted commander. Dismounting, the two escorts took hold of Donovan's horse's reins and led them over to the creek and corral. McClendon extended a hand and said, "Good day, Donovan. How are things at the Pass?"

Still irritated by the lack of a formal greeting, Donovan ignored the pleasantries. "We came down to escort General Kearny there upon his arrival. My scouts tell me he should be here within the next hour or two." He paused, his keen eyes raking over the new piles of debris outside of the kivas, and continued, "Looks like my men have been busy. Find anything?"

Clearing his throat, keenly aware that these next few minutes would make or break the plan he and Larrañaga had hatched, McClendon responded, "We have. Something remarkable." McClendon pointed at the rockpile where Larrañaga, Lalo, James, Bisa, and several of the Dragoons stood around the stone effigy.

Donovan shifted his gaze from McClendon to the rockpile and then back to McClendon. "Perhaps we should go take a look together."

The polished stone effigy brilliantly reflected the mid-day sun. As Donovan and McClendon approached, the rest of the Dragoons stood a bit taller, their animated conversations ceasing altogether. Larrañaga and Lalo pulled their hats down just a bit further over their faces. Donovan's eyes instantly registered the presence of the non-uniformed personnel and locked in on James. "And who might these folks be?" he demanded.

McClendon walked to James and placed an arm around him. "This is my son, James. I still cannot believe he's here." The astonishment in his voice made the officer sound almost giddy. "These three gentlemen found him on the prairie and helped him get…here." McClendon gestured towards the Spaniards and Bisa.

This time it was Donovan who stepped forward, towards the Spaniards, apparently missing the fact that McClendon's presumed dead boy was still very much alive. Standing directly in front of Larrañaga, who had gotten to his feet just moments before, the two men stood inches apart, fires burning behind their eyes. "I remember you, *doctor*. How is your head?"

With fists balled and jaw clenched, Larrañaga said through gritted teeth, "And I remember you." Catching himself, Larrañaga paused, stepped back, and tried his best to relax his jaw. *Breathe. The plan is what is most important*, he reminded himself.

As if the wave of anger had passed completely, a smile broke out on Donovan's face and the big man clapped Larrañaga on the back. "Never mind the past. Clearly you have more than made up for that by rescuing the young McClendon. I am sure he is very grateful." The Dragoons whooped with support and bravado. "Now show me what you've found!"

Colonel McClendon couldn't help but respect the way his peer could work a crowd. The men shifted, formed a circle around the effigy and their leader. All of this set the stage for the next step in the plan. McClendon motioned for Bisa to come forward, "Colonel, Bisa is our resident Indian expert. He was the one who found this…treasure."

Donovan cast a wary eye towards both McClendon and Bisa. "So what am I looking at other than a shiny rock that looks like a child's toy?"

Bisa, as rehearsed, began. "Sir, this is an Anasazi stone effigy. It is Mesa Verde style, made of stone native to the distant peaks there." Bisa picked up the effigy and handing it to the officer, continued, "Every ceremony of the ancients started with a placing of hands on this. It united them. It is said that the power of all who have ever placed hands on this can be transferred to whoever possesses it. The Anasazi believed that all who have come before remain as spirits, waiting to be summoned for the good of the people." A stunned silence followed. Bisa's smoothness of delivery and the impact of the message on its hearers raised goosebumps—even for Colonel Mc-Clendon who almost clapped.

Larrañaga didn't think Donovan was convinced. The Colonel had nodded along during Bisa's speech, but the intangibility of the power of the artifact seemed too am-biguous for the big man of action. "Can you show me what it can do? What theses spirits can do? Now?"

Bisa looked to Larrañaga for support, but McClendon stepped forward. "Colonel, my understanding is that this power can only be tapped into for a righteous cause. Perhaps we could keep it at the front of our troops to protect them as they take Santa Fe." McClendon's shakily plucked arrow struck home. Donovan's eyes widened as he pictured the scene, knowing what this victory would do for his career. He wanted nothing more than to have his own Army one day.

"Well done, gentlemen," Donovan turned and said to his men, forgetting that it was Bisa who found the artifact. As the words came out of his mouth, the sound of footfalls of hundreds of horses echoed throughout the valley. The Army of the West.

The Mormon Battalion with its "Bear" emblazoned flag led the way. The hundreds of mounted blue coats created a sight even the bravest of adversaries would think twice about confronting. And right behind them, flanked by the Stars and Stripes and the command element, was General Kearny. The men on the field below the pueblo whooped at his impending arrival.

Donovan called for and remounted his horse. The Dragoons who had accompanied him down from Glorietta Pass followed suit and together they rode out to guide the general in. McClendon, Larrañaga, Lalo, Bisa, and James exchanged worried glances but nodded, relieved that so far the plan was still working. "Stay focused," Colonel McClendon whispered to his son, once again grateful for his presence and once again remembering his debt to Larrañaga.

The sharp bugle call for "make camp" resonated throughout the pine-filled valley and McClendon's Dragoons, in unison, sprang to action. The lieutenant barked out orders for placement of a security detachment around the hilltop, so they picked up their packs and hustled off, leaving only the McClendons, Spaniards, and Bisa in the open field below the pueblo.

The first riders of the Mormon Battalion arrived minutes later, circling around the open field like a choreographed dance. When all had arrived and the circle was complete, save for a path for Kearny and his entourage, the men adjusted their hats and uniforms and sat up straight in their saddles. The command element trotted into the center and stopped just short of Colonel McClendon.

Coming to the position of attention and rendering a crisp salute, McClendon said, "Welcome to Pecos Pueblo, General Kearny." Larrañaga and Lalo even stood up a bit taller. Hundreds of pairs of eyes bore down the odd mixture of men standing in the middle of the now not-so-open field. In fact, Larrañaga was beginning to feel claustrophobic. Behind Kearny, Donovan sat on his shifting horse, his eyes boring into the elder Spaniard.

Kearny, still mounted, returned the salute and turned his attention to the ruins of the Spanish church which stood atop the hill just a hundred meters away. "It seems someone beat us to the punch here," he joked, threw his leg over the horse, and dismounted.

"Yes, sir. The Puebloans cared for the Spanish about as much as we do," the lieutenant said before looking around at his present company and blushing with regret for speaking out of turn. Kearny seemed to sense this and shifted his eyes to those standing behind McClendon.

"And who do we have here, Colonel?"

Pulling James in front of him McClendon said, "Sir, I am proud to introduce you to my son, James. He was rescued by this man and his small band of…helpers." Turning to those behind him, McClendon continued, "May I present Doctor Cristóval Maria Larrañaga and his traveling companions Eduardo and Bisa. Gentlemen," McClendon said, turning back to the front, "This is General Steven Watts Kearny, the commander of the Army of the West."

Pleasantries exchanged and horses drawn away by attendants, General Kearny turned his attention back to the command element and issued orders. "Gentlemen, it has been a long trip. We are nearly there." He pointed west, towards Glorietta Pass and Santa Fe beyond, the troops hollered in excitement, and then he continued. "Tonight we will remain here. Rest the horses, tend to and refit the men. The wagon trains, God willing, shall arrive tomorrow and then they will do the same. We'll use this…pueblo…as our staging point for the taking of Santa Fe."

He paused, then continued. "At first light tomorrow, Colonel Donovan, his Dragoons, and I will advance to Glorietta Pass for a look at our objective. Once we have a good lay of the land and the disposition of any potential threat, we will ride into Santa Fe and claim this entire territory as belonging to the United States of America!"

This last was a change of the previously defined operation order. The faces of the men conveyed their surprise, and for just the briefest of moments delayed the boisterous reaction General Kearny had hoped his stirring speech would receive. The commanders and support officers, having their orders, dispersed after the smattering of shouts and applause died down.

Everyone knew their jobs. Tents would be raised, equipment cleaned, and fires started. Once again, the bowl-shaped valley would be alive with civilization.

It was then that McClendon heard pleading from one section of the larger circle—the sounds of a man in serious pain. General Kearny noted McClendon's diverted attention and reported, "We ran into some Apache on the trail a couple of hours ago. They got off a few shots at our lead horsemen and then took off once they realized the size of our element." McClendon and Larrañaga looked at each other, the same thought running through their minds. *The healing bone.* Colonel McClendon excused himself and ran towards the sounds of the wounded man. Larrañaga and James followed.

The wounded man had an arrow through his upper right leg. It had entered from the side and the bloody, chiseled tip just barely protruded through the inside of his light blue trousers. Colonel McClendon stepped to the side allowing Larrañaga to more closely examine the man.

"The arrow angles slightly down from entry to exit, which is a good thing because it decreases the chances of slicing your femoral artery," the doctor said in a calming, confident manner to the wounded soldier. Larrañaga reached into his coat pocket and extracted a knife, an ornately inscribed navaja or folding knife and cut the blood-soaked pants away to do a closer inspection. Meanwhile, McClendon told James to hold the man's right foot up in the air. Larrañaga nodded.

"It looks like you've lost a lot of blood and elevating the foot will help decrease the flow," Larrañaga told the wounded soldier. "We have to get the arrow out and then clean the wound. Soldier, we're going to get you fixed up pronto. Cómo te llamas—What's your name?"

Through gritted teeth and amidst tear-streaked cheeks the soldier shook with pain. "Frank. Frank Edwards—from St. Louis," he said.

"Bueno Frank from St. Louis, here's what we're going to do," Larrañaga said. "I'm going to put your belt in your mouth, and I want you to bite down on it. This will hurt and I don't need you locking your jaw down on your tongue." Larrañaga had already taken the belt from the man's trousers and put it lengthwise into the soldier's mouth who bit down with eyes full of fear.

Looking up at the crowd around him he said, "We need some clean bandages and water." Larrañaga then turned to James who was now right next to him and whispered. "Go get the bone. He's not going to make it."

The elder McClendon nodded in support. "Go. Fast!"

James ran. As fast as he could, he ran. A life depended on it. Questions raced through his mind as tried not to trip over the prairie dog holes in the grassy, uneven field. Bisa and Lalo watched this from a distance and knew what was happening. They ran to where McClendon had stashed the log and met James there. Lalo unwrapped the bedroll and retrieved the hollowed-out log. Bisa did his best to shield all of this from view of the soldiers. It helped that everyone's attention was on the wounded man and the men tending him. Almost everyone.

James untied the leather strap holding the two halves of the hollowed-out log together and pulled out the wrapped bone. The three looked at each other, knowing this was a point of no return, a break from their plan, but did they have a choice? Could they let a man die to keep this hidden? The muffled scream behind them answered their unspoken questions. With a nod, Lalo handed it to James who turned and ran back.

By the time James returned, the arrow was out and his father held two once white now deep crimson shirts against either side of the man's leg. James relieved his father and handed over the bundle he'd retrieved. Looking up at the crowd now gathered around, Larrañaga's eyes connected with Donovan's who was watching with an intense curiosity. Returning his focus to the passed-out soldier as he knelt and held the bone, he put his other hand on the man's leg between where James pressed his bloody hands against the wound.

The soldier who had fainted as Larrañaga pulled out the arrow opened his eyes wide. His face was white as snow. His chest completely still. In that instant, all who surrounded him thought he'd lost the battle. Some even turned away. But then the wounded man's chest started rising and falling again. Someone yelled, "Hey—look!"

Larrañaga sat back on the dry grass behind him and looked on in shock and awe, just like all the rest.

"What did you do?" a voice from the crowd demanded. Slowly, carefully, the wounded man sat up. His eyes fixed on the leg that was still red with blood, but the gaping, ugly entrance and exit wounds had closed up, leaving no evidence of ever having been there.

"Doc, what did you do?" the wounded man echoed. Unsure how to answer, Larrañaga got to his feet, buying him a few much-needed moments to figure out what to do, just how much to say. *Think!* As they did, the crowd closed in on the man, hoisted him to his feet, and began slapping him on his back. McClendon and Larrañaga used the distraction to step back, move away.

As they did so Larrañaga passed the bundle holding the bone to the elder McClendon who then gave it to his son and motioned him away. Again, James ran. McClendon and Larrañaga slowly turned and followed.

The trio almost made it back to where their gear had been stored, almost back to Lalo and Bisa when a voice from behind them stated with authority, "Gentlemen, General Kearny requests your immediate presence. We are setting up his tent now" he paused, pointing. "Over there. And he wants you to bring whatever that is you have there."

"Thank you, Corporal Sampson," McClendon said and held up his bloody hands. "Give us a few minutes to clean up and we'll be right over.

"Yes, sir." Sampson said, saluting.

Colonel McClendon and Larrañaga walked across

the seemingly darkening field—or maybe that was just in their minds—the former carrying the hollowed-out log and the latter the stone effigy. They didn't speak, both dreading the confrontation that was surely awaiting them. Entering the General's large tent that had two sides rolled up for ventilation, they were surprised by the rather large crowd. All were silent, all eyes locked on them.

"Colonel McClendon, Doctor Larrañaga," General Kearny broke the silence. "Can you tell me what you did back there and what in the hell are those?" McClendon had to catch himself from laughing at Kearny's choice of words.

"Sir, may I?" McClendon gestured at the field table that stood on one side of the tent. Kearny nodded. McClendon and Larrañaga walked over to the table, set the items down, and stood shoulder to shoulder. Together they took a deep breath. Colonel McClendon spoke.

"Gentlemen," McClendon started, addressing the entire crowd. "I have been tasked by General Kearny to be on the lookout for artifacts of significant cultural and historical significance. Doctor Larrañaga here has also been given this task and has been at it for over a decade on behalf of Queen Isabella II. During his travels, he has come across a few items of…significance. His deep connections with the local indigenous tribes gave him valuable information about the possibility that something very significant was hidden—or left—here in Pecos Pueblo. That was why he was here when we arrived. And that is how I was reunited with my son."

McClendon paused, looked at Larrañaga. "Together

we searched every kiva—ceremonial room—up there on the hilltop. And we found the two items sitting before you. This," he said, picking up the stone effigy, and connecting eyes with Donovan, "is what we believe to be the most significant of the two. For countless generations, the Anasazi kept this in their largest kiva and believed its presence protected them from all evil. Pecos Pueblo is the oldest pueblo in the area so ..." McClendon's voice trailed off. Larrañaga picked up.

"It is believed that the spiritual men could invoke the powers in this stone to accomplish any great task. And as a result they were able to build five story structures which I am sure many of you have never seen the likes of."

"Right," McClendon picked back up. "Now, this item is altogether different." Gently McClendon began to unwrap the bone. *The closer this is to the truth the more believable it will be.* He thought. Once complete, he carefully held it aloft. It was not glowing, and for that McClendon was grateful. "This is what we believe to be a femur from a being unlike we have ever seen. It is too large to be human, which average sixteen to eighteen inches in length. You can see this is much larger. The Anasazi traditions tell us that bones like this sometimes hold the power to heal. We believe we saw that yesterday when Señor Larrañaga severely twisted his ankle and struggled to walk but after he held the bone, he no longer experienced any pain."

Scanning the audience, Larrañaga saw shock and disbelief written on the officers' faces. *Perfect,* the Spaniard thought. He added, "We really aren't sure of anything at this point. These items are clearly excellent finds that would please either of our governments. General, perhaps you could take one and I could take the other?" There, it was out. Make or break time. A rumbling in and amongst the officers gave him all the evidence he needed to know this was not going to end the way he had hoped—with the bone in hand.

General Kearny thought for a moment and then pulled the man named Smythe, the gray-haired recorder who was the only one in the room not in uniform, aside. Neither McClendon nor Larrañaga could make out what they were saying.

After a few minutes Kearny turned his attention back to the men at the table. "Doctor Larrañaga, we thank you for your insight and expertise. I also want to personally thank you for rescuing and returning Colonel McClendon's son. But at this time, your services are no longer needed here. Please gather your things and depart at first light." A wave of the hand dismissed the stunned Spaniard who bowed slightly at the waist and stepped out into the night.

McClendon started to speak but Kearny's raised hand stopped him before he could get a word out. "Colonel McClendon, you have been charged with finding items such as these and find them you have. Well done, sir. I am ordering you to personally ensure they travel with us safely to Santa Fe. Once we've taken the capital and east-bound wagon trains can resume, you will then escort these items back to St. Louis where they will be retrieved by someone from the President's office."

"Yes, sir." McClendon said in a voice barely above a whisper.

"Dismissed."

As the officers made their way out of the tent and McClendon delicately re-wrapped the bone, Smythe approached. "Fantastic finds, Colonel." The old man then did something quite unexpected—held one of his hands up to his face. Two of his fingers were grotesquely curled over. *Too much pencil pushing,* McClendon first thought. Then he remembered his father had something similar: Dupuytren contractures in the tendons of his palms and fingers. Smythe placed his distorted hand on the now-wrapped bone. When he held it up again, Smythe's hand and fingers looked completely normal. The old man smiled at McClendon, a self-satisfied, knowing smile, then patted the bone. "You take good care of this. Guard it like your life depends on it."

Later that evening, Private Frank Edwards wrote of what he saw, of what saved him, in his journal. "The bone was of gigantic size…a thigh bone that could never have belonged to a man less than ten feet."[2]

---

2. Hampton Sides, Blood and Thunder The Epic Story of Kit Carson and the Conquest of the American West, (New York, Anchor Books, 2006), 115.

6. August 12, 1846 — Glorietta Pass

By the time the morning light caressed the upper reaches of the mountains that stood watch over the ancient pueblo, Donovan and his escorts, as well as McClendon and his Dragoon detachment (now *guards*, McClendon felt), and Kearny and a small entourage had traveled more than half the distance up the trail between Pecos Pueblo and Glorietta Pass. The light illuminated a narrow, boulder strewn and tree-lined gap between the mesa to the south and the ridgeline to the north, the last summit before Santa Fe.

When the Army of the West had entered New Mexico, they'd heard that whatever remained of the Mexican army in New Mexico was positioned here in the pass, ready to defend the capitol. But when the governor reportedly fled, the few remaining Mexican soldiers drifted away like the dust behind his southbound horse.

McClendon marveled at the magnificence of the force that lifted the mesa to his left (south, he thought, always trying to keep his directional bearings), up from the valley floor, its sheer cliffs and perfectly flat top completely foreign to anything he'd ever seen. To his north, a densely vegetated downslope and the faint sounds of Glorietta Creek rose from below. The former professor's mind raced. He'd been forced to leave James behind, and with him Larrañaga, Lalo, and Bisa. The soldiers there, the Mormon Battalion, had been left with three explicit orders. First, to safely guide the Army of the West up to the pass the following morning. Second, to bring James with them. Third, to ensure the departure of the Spaniards and Bisa only after the Army of the West took Santa Fe; General Kearny did not want them to aid the Mexicans in any way. *At least*, McClendon thought, *I had a chance to say goodbye. I hope our paths cross again.* A hawk's cry joined the steady clip clop of hoofbeats.

The procession of soldiers to McClendon's front ground to a halt and Colonel Donovan, who had been riding in the center of the formation with General Kearny and McClendon, spurred his horse forward. A minute later he returned, and McClendon listened intently. "A couple of large trees fell across the trail. We can likely get around 'em but the wagon trains won't be able to. We'll take a break here while the men clear the way." And with that, he turned and galloped back towards the front. The soldiers spread out, forming a loose perimeter around the General and his entourage and remained vigilant perched atop their mounts.

Hearing the gurgling of the nearby creek, McClendon's horse turned towards the sound of the water. McClendon had tethered the hollowed-out log with the bone inside to the back of his saddle and felt the nearly incapacitating spiritual weight of his cargo with every step his horse took. He was well aware of the questioning, even fearful stares of the men. Allowing his horse to guide itself to the side of the trail, McClendon reined in his mount before it went too far. Before him was what appeared to be some kind of small animal path leading down to the creek. He turned to the soldiers on either side of him and said, "I'm going to get some water." The Dragoons on either side of him looked at each other, then nodded.

The path down to the creek wasn't long—maybe a hundred paces. But the further McClendon descended, the more out of place he felt. Everything seemed different—especially James. The journey west from Charleston started out as an adventure with a singular focus: to provide he and his son with a new beginning away from the fledgling farm and the high, closed society he had grown to detest. Away from the pain of losing Annie. There had to be a better place, he remembered feeling. And that feeling compelled him to action after he met Kit Carson. McClendon's horse plodded down towards the creek while his mind drifted to that day.

* * * * *

"Kit Carson is one of the most renowned frontiersmen of our time. Hunter, trapper, explorer, Indian-fighter—he even makes his own buckskin clothing. You name it, if it's to be done out west, I do believe he's done it," laughed the dean of Georgetown University's newly established history department as he and Professor McClendon walked up the steps to a grand, marble-faced building on campus. "He's here to present the President and Congress his findings from a recent trip to the Pacific."

The dean had invited Professor McClendon up from Charleston in an attempt to lure him to the nation's capitol, to Georgetown University. This event, this gathering of important visitors to and residents from the capitol was meant to impress and introduce Professor McClendon to what he and his family could be a part of. "I hear Mr. Carson is married to a New Mexican woman and they have a home in Taos—the 'land of the red people.'"

Lowering his voice as they spotted the short frontiersman, the dean continued, "And unlike many of my boisterous colleagues here, Mr. Carson rations his words like one does water in the desert. Come, let me introduce you to him."

McClendon's conversation with Carson had been brief but impactful. The frontiersman passionately described the unimaginably tall mountains, the endless supply of game, and the intriguing people—New Mexicans, Spanish, French, British, and, of course, the natives.

McClendon asked about those—the natives—to which Carson replied, "Indians are like wolves. Run and they follow. Follow and they run." This produced laughter from all within earshot. Carson reached up, put his hand on McClendon's shoulder and, stepping close, concluded the conversation by saying, "Professor, out there, you are truly free."

* * * * *

The water in the creek is free to go wherever it wants, Mc-Clendon thought as he watched his horse dip its head and drink, *pulled only by that which nothing can escape — gravity.* McClendon slid off the beast and, using both hands, scooped up some water and splashed it over his face, its coolness offering a welcome respite from the dust of the trail and the August heat. His horse suddenly raised and shook its head and stomped a foot. McClendon stood, looked all around, and finding nothing and no one, patted the horse's moist neck. "Easy, boy. Easy," he said.

"Yá'át'ééh," McClendon heard from behind a Pinyon. He knew that voice. He knew the Navajo phrase for 'all is good.' *Bisa.*

"*What...? How...?*"

Stepping out from behind a tree and into the creek, his deer-hide moccasins impervious to the water, Bisa said, "We must be quick. Hand me the log with the bone and put this in its place." McClendon didn't think, he just did. With trembling fingers, McClendon quickly undid the leather straps holding the hollowed out log and handed it to Bisa. Bisa handed him the identical but empty log.

While McClendon finished rigging the new log, Bisa whispered, "In three days meet us at the Black Rock Canyon by the Rio Grande. This is a sacred place, near Albuquerque, where the ancient ones have left their symbols on the black rocks." And then he was gone.

* * * * *

Back on the trail, the former professor felt deeply conflicted as they all waited for the trees to be cleared. *What have I just done? Where is James?* He wondered anxiously. He imagined the eyes of the soldiers looking right through what he hoped was his unchanged, calm demeanor—and the empty log. Just when he thought he'd somehow given himself away, the shout to move out came from up front and the mounted soldiers resumed their trek towards Glorietta Pass. The echoing footfalls of the horses now sounded less like clip clops and more like a death march to Colonel McClendon.

* * * * *

The shade of a rock overhang just over the summit of Glorietta Pass provided General Kearny with a perfect vantage point. Colonel Donovan had led the command element to it after checking in with the Dragoons he'd left here the day prior. "All clear," he'd relayed to the General.

Holding his looking glasses to his eyes, Kearny scanned first the New Mexican capital and surrounding landscape. He took his time; "the devil is in the details" he muttered to himself. The rest of the leadership entourage, including McClendon, stood back in silence. When Kearny lowered his glasses, Donovan strode confidently to the front of the group and, like a professor teaching a class, spoke.

"Sir, the main north-south road there is the Camino Real—the Royal Road—runnin' from Mexico City to Santa Fe. The Governor's Palace is the two-story adobe and wood structure on the north end of the plaza. There," Donovan pointed, and Kearny followed along. "Prior to yesterday, the presidio on the western, downhill side of the plaza contained horses and wagons and approximately twenty-five troops of the Governor's guard. As you likely noticed, that stable now stands empty, which confirms our reports that Governor Armijo has indeed left the palace. Early this morning, we moved a thirty-man platoon of Dragoons up to within three miles of the plaza with the order of sending a runner back if any miliary personnel show themselves. No runners have returned so it would appear Santa Fe has been left completely unguarded."

"Thank you, Colonel," said Kearny, who once again raised the looking glass to his eye. A few minutes passed. Kearny lowered the instrument, found a rock, and sat down. "Colonel, how many armed citizens have you seen in and around Santa Fe?"

"We've seen a dozen or so, sir," Donovan responded quickly, knowing where the General was going with this. "And while we cannot rule out that those under arms will put up a fight, we can say that we have not seen them manning any of the towers or defensive positions nor running any security patrols. All the movement down there has been civilian in nature. It's a crossroad town with the biggest marketplace I've seen this side of the Mississippi. People are always coming and going."

Kearny was silent for a few minutes, radiating an intensity not seen down on the trail. His gaze never left the town wedged between the river and the mountains.

The town whose name evoked strong passions in political and military minds from Madrid to Mexico City, from Albuquerque to Washington. And the town—and territory—which soon would become a part of the United States of America.

"Just to make sure I understand what you are saying, Colonel Donovon, is it your assessment that there would be no opposition from the Mexican army to our taking of Santa Fe?"

"Sir, I'd say we'd have a near-certain chance taking that town with only the thirty man platoon we have out there right now. With all 300—it's as sure of a thing as there can be in this business."

"Colonel Donovan, overconfidence has been the downfall of many an army. It will not be the downfall of this one." Donovan, to his credit, nodded his head in what could only be interpreted as both acknowledgement and agreement with his commander. "Let's keep our eyes on the objective until the sun no longer allows." Kearny ordered. "We'll reconvene the leadership group down by the horses after that."

McClendon, like the others, could not take his eyes off of Santa Fe. He too saw the crossroads, the constant movement of people, horses, and wagons bringing goods to and from the plaza in front of the Governor's Palace. He witnessed the crowds entering and then exiting the imposing cathedral with a belltower that must be five stories high on the east side of the plaza. Finally, he looked to the south and west, towards Albuquerque, silently searching the horizon for a Black Rock Canyon.

* * * * *

That evening, sheltering from the incessant wind and potentially prying eyes, General Kearny and his entourage reconvened around a small fire between a handful of wagon-sized boulders. The meal of beans, bison, and bread sat heavy in their stomachs. Lively talk of past exploits, run ins with wild Indians and great beasts, encounters with French and British trappers, and the seemingly endless headaches caused by naïve and inexperienced American settlers filled the air. A runner from the platoon down in the valley returned and brought the group back to the present. He offered news that a handful of soldiers had left Santa Fe on horseback, heading south and west, towards Albuquerque.

"Gentlemen, I do believe the time is nearly upon us," General Kearny said, the light from the flames reflecting off his cheeks and forehead. "Colonel Donovan, send a runner down to the wagon trains. Tell them to break camp and begin their march up and over this pass at first light." Donovan nodded to the Dragoon who ran off into the dark and the sound of a galloping horse soon followed. Kearny continued, "Gentlemen, we too will move out at first light. We'll ride hard and fast and take the Plaza by surprise. Colonel Donovan, you'll lead with all of your Dragoons with the exception of the platoon you have down there now. They will provide overwatch and will be our reserve." He paused. Almost every officer around him was doing their best to hide the eagerness that coursed through their veins. Even Smythe, pencil and paper in hand, had a new energy about him.

General Kearny continued, "By the time the mid-day bell rings in that great church of theirs, the flag of the United States will be flying over the Governor's Palace."

7. August 13, 1846 — Santa Fe

The sun took longer to reach the southwest side of the Sangre de Cristo Mountains but that did not hamper the lead element of the invading army. The cooler morning air and knowledge that the successful completion of the first part of their mission, the capture of Santa Fe, was close at hand amped up the battle-ready men. Colonel Donovan rode close to the front, his carbine- and saber-toting Dragoons surrounding him in a tight, fast-moving formation through the still-silent small villages on the outskirts of the capital.

Each man's face was painted with a confident determination, each horse seemingly attuned to the importance of the moment at hand. As the wave of Dragoons flowed through the villages, all eyes scanned for threats and, finding none, pushed on. McClendon, riding at the rear of the formation, noticed the presence of all kinds of people cautiously emerging from their homes and shelters: red, white, black, brown. *You saw something like this in 1821*, McClendon thought, recalling the year the Mexican army pushed out all remaining Spanish forces. *And now, twenty-five years later you are seeing it again. God, protect us all*, he prayed.

* * * * *

As with Pecos, Santa Fe served as a hub of a civilization well before the arrival of the Spanish. For thousands of years, people lived in villages along the Santa Fe River, a tributary of the Rio Grande. Santa Fe officially became the Spanish capital of New Mexico in 1608, some sixty years after explorer Francisco Vásquez de Coronado and his conquistadors arrived in the area in search of the "golden cities."

It was 'founded' as the capital by Pedro Peralta, the second Spanish military governor of the territory, who successfully made the case to those that mattered that the location met all the necessary prerequisites: the Santa Fe River and its 180,000 acre watershed provided plenty of water, the mountains to the east served as both an excellent defensive barrier and were heavily forested, providing more than ample building material for construction, game for food, and perhaps even minerals.

And the presence of multiple indigenous villages provided the critical labor and goods that Spanish settlers in and around the capital would need.

Governor Peralta followed the Spanish blueprint for new territorial cities, a schematic based on Roman Mediterranean cities, that had been implemented all over the New World as he laid out his plans for Santa Fe. By 1620, when all construction had been completed, the indigenous people, settlers, soldiers, and clergy arriving or living in the area could not help but be amazed by the sight of the place.

The two-story Governor's Palace lined the entire north side of grand plaza and faced south, towards Mexico City. The Royal Presidio which contained barracks, a guardhouse, a high protective adobe wall with towers, the jail, and stables lined the west side of the plaza and backed up to the river. On the south side stood a towering, fortified archway and gate flanked by adobe walls to 'welcome' travelers who reached the northern terminus of the Camino Real—the Royal Highway.

The east side of the plaza with the breath-taking backdrop of the Sange de Cristo Mountains contained the most significant structure of all: the Cathedral of St. Francis. At over five stories tall, not including the bell tower, this religious and spiritual center of power faced the plaza and the valley beyond. From this high perch, the might of the Spanish and the weightiness of their Catholic faith could be seen and felt for a hundred miles.

Time and events took a heavy toll on the Spanish capital. In the 236 years since the Roman blueprint took form on the high desert plain, the grand cathedral, luxurious palace, fortified presidio, and imposing gate bore witness to indigenous revolts, hangings (settlers who attempted to flee were treated as traitors), and, in 1821, Mexican Independence.

When the Spanish government fell, the structures remained as if in an act of solidarity against the whims of mankind. But the two plus decades that had passed since then had taken a toll. The lavishly furnished and well-stocked Governor's Palace which had served both as a symbol of superiority and a place to go for much needed supplies and reminders of "home" no longer fulfilled those functions. The same held true, for the most part, for the Royal Presidio.

The Cathedral of St. Francis and its clergy, however, continued on its mission unabated. Unlike the disrepair that befell the palace and presidio, the Cathedral, and the higher power that it symbolized, attracted the kind of attention that ensured its focus on bringing people to God (and God to the people) proceeded even amidst national turmoil. Financial support for upkeep and operations came from as far away as the Vatican City State and Holy See and as close as wealthy settlers in and around Santa Fe.

One of those wealthy Mexican frontier settlers, perhaps the most successful and influential in the mid-nineteenth century, was Juan Felipe Ortiz. He rallied support to not only maintain the Cathedral but continually improve it despite—or maybe even because of—the Mexican Revolution. Juan Felipe gave more than treasure to the universal cause. He gave his son as well. Father Manuel Ortiz, oldest son of Juan Felipe, was the first non-full-blooded Spaniard to be ordained by the Durango-based Roman Catholic Bishop who oversaw all Catholic churches and missions on the Mexican frontier. For the Spanish, Mexican, and indigenous people within sight of the magnificent Cathedral and its seventeen-foot-tall carved wooden doors which stood open to anyone, the church represented hope in an immense and often times violent land just like it's namesake, St. Francis of Assisi.

* * * * *

Colonel Donovan, surrounded by a dozen of his most imposing Dragoons, trod unopposed into the plaza that had born witness to Spanish Conquistadors, indigenous warriors, and Mexican revolutionaries. The rest of his Dragoons expertly encircled the plaza, carbines at the ready. The lack of gunfire confirmed what the soldiers already knew—all Mexican military personnel, including their commander, had abandoned their posts. With the midday ringing of the church bell just moments away, the daily marketplace in full swing with vendors from nearby villages in the middle of their *negocios* with travelers and locals alike, it was just another day in Santa Fe. It was a scene, Donovan thought, that had likely been the same for centuries. Only today would be different. Despite the sun being near its apex in the mid-August sky, this was the dawn of a new day for these people, Donovan thought, and smiled. But what Donovan didn't know was that soon he would look back on this moment and see it as the high-water mark of his career.

The church bells sounded their call to service, almost as if scripted, as General Kearny and his entourage entered the plaza. The soldiers' sweat-stained backs stood straighter, higher in the saddle, one hand holding their rifle or saber and the other holding the reins. Cragged mountain peaks and a few emerging mushroom-shaped cumulus clouds beginning their early afternoon stretching up into the turquoise sky provided an epic backdrop. This very scene had been imagined thousands of times in the minds of the Americans, from the most inexperienced private to the President of the United States. Not only was this the first foreign expedition of the relatively young country, but the taking of this old and symbolically powerful city and the territory it commanded nearly doubled America's size and elevated its place in the world order.

Father Ortiz, dressed in the brown habit of the Franciscan order tied at the waist by a rope with three knots representing vows of poverty, chastity, and obedience, stood on the steps of the imposing cathedral like a shepherd calling out to his flock. Which, of course, he was.

Despite all the dust kicked up by the American soldiers or maybe because of it, settlers and Indians alike moved towards him, making their way between and around the Dragoons as if they were hardly even there at all. Colonel Donovan, perhaps out of a desire to ensure the spotlight fell on the conquering army or out of some disdain for the religious establishment, galloped his horse over to and up the steps of the stately Cathedral, blocking the otherwise open doors. In so doing, he thrust his leg out from the stirrup, knocking over the portly padre, who hit his head on the stone steps where drops of his blood gathered like the clouds above.

The shot rang out before most had even noticed the commotion on the cathedral steps. Donovan, hit in the arm by a rifle round remained steadfast in his saddle. A fire burned in his eyes as blood stained his blue coat. His horse, however, was not comfortable with the near miss and growing crowd and bolted down the steps and out into the Plaza. Quickly surrounded by Dragoons with rifles at the ready, the soldiers searched for the source of the shot while others urged their wounded leader to the recently secured Royal Presidio where they helped him dismount and led him inside. Out in the Plaza, the shooter, an older 'Mestizo', a man of mixed Spanish and Mexican descent, was identified, briefly pursued, and swept up by angry Dragoons. They took him to the Presidio as well and threw him, bloody and unconscious, into the jail.

General Kearny, assured by his staff that Donovan was very much alive and being tended to and the assailant had been dealt with, maintained his focus on the symbolically palatial but physically dilapidated Governor's Palace that made up the northern boundary of the Santa Fe Plaza. Tying his horse to the graying pole of pine spanning the entire front of the two story, city-block wide wooden structure, his eyes never left the Mexican flag flying atop the palace, it's vertically aligned stripes of green, white, and red overlaid with the depiction of an eagle sitting on a cactus. Kearny turned to find Corporal Sampson at his side. He pointed at the flag. The unspoken command as clear as the bell that just rang: take that flag down. Nearby, Smythe noted the date, time, and a few other details in his journal.

* * * * *

When the shot that struck Donovan echoed off the adobe walls of the plaza, McClendon's horse nearly bucked him out of the saddle. Having just reached the arched gate, the animal wheeled and sprinted away from the

Plaza. The Dragoons around him who were much better riders, watched and laughed before riding into the Plaza to investigate the commotion.

McClendon, struggling to regain control of his horse, sensed an opportunity. Without thinking, he stopped struggling and let the horse run. He remembered the rough map Donovan had drawn of Santa Fe in the dirt back at Glorietta Pass. His horse followed the path of least resistance—towards the town's namesake river which runs from the Sangre de Cristo Mountains in the northeast to the Rio Grande in the southwest.

Something clicked in his mind. The southwest, just across the Rio Grande, was where Bisa had told him he'd find Black Rock Canyon. The Black Rock Canyon with all the petroglyphs. Faced with a decision that he knew could bring terrible repercussions, the former professor dismounted as soon as his horse permitted, wiped the sweat from his brow, and tried to still his shaking legs.

His horse stepped carefully down the loose gravel at the river's edge and dipped its head in the water for a drink. McClendon followed, removed his hat, looked back towards the Plaza. His eyes settled on the Cathedral, as if knowing, deep down, there must be something at work here bigger than himself. He too lowered his head to the water and drank.

* * * * *

Back at the Plaza, the Dragoons, minus Colonel Donovan and the handful of men tending to him and guarding the prisoner in the Presidio, stood in formation facing the Governor's Palace. The flag of Mexico no longer blew in the westerly breeze. The locals, having scattered like ants when the shot rang out, slowly returned to the Plaza, a mixture of curiosity and acceptance on their faces. General Kearny saw this and remembered that the transition from Spanish to Mexican rule here in Santa Fe had taken place peacefully.

For an instant, Kearny felt that perhaps something bigger than a flag united these people. *Worldly powers have come and gone here, but the people have always remained*, he thought. A blast from the bugler returned his attention to the recently vacated, sun-bleached wooden pole atop the Palace. The notes of "Reveille" filled the plaza as Corporal Sampson pulled on the dry, frayed rope affixed to the pole. For the first time, the Stars and Stripes flew over the oldest city in North America.

* * * * *

"Goddammit, where is McClendon?" Colonel Donovan shouted, wincing in pain as a medic cleaned the wound that had grazed his humerus, but fortunately passed clean through the arm. A fraction of an inch one way or the other would have meant the loss of Donovan's arm, if not worse. But it wasn't McClendon that Donovan sought; it was the bone. The bone that somehow had cured the wounded soldier back at the Pecos Pueblo. The bone that fixed Smythe's crippled hand.

Donovan had last seen McClendon an hour before

as the Army of the West's lead element entered a village just outside of Santa Fe. Ignoring the question or perhaps not wanting to provide an answer the hot-tempered commander wouldn't like, the men around him remained silent. Donovan's anger grew and his face turned beet red. He changed the question to a demand. "Find McClendon and bring him here!" The men looked at each other and a sergeant standing by hustled away.

At that moment, a mile away, McClendon was fighting his own battle. Deep in thought while sitting at the river's edge, his well-educated mind wrestled with what he knew could be a life-changing decision. Perhaps a life-ending one. Despite being surrounded by a vast, open landscape, he felt boxed in between two options.

The first was to remain devoted to his country's mission and the man that had taken him in and given him purpose. This option is what McClendon's father and grandfather would have stoically advised since both had served in the U.S. Army, the former during the Revolutionary War and the latter in the War of 1812. Both had adamantly told McClendon to follow in their footsteps and make a career out of the service. A more noble profession did not exist, in their minds.

Much to their dismay, McClendon had chosen an alternate form of service, that of a teacher. History was his passion. And here he was, in the middle of the making of it, just like his predecessors. As he glanced back over his shoulder, he could make out the American flag rising atop the Governor's Palace. With that sight and the distant call of the bugle resonating in his mind, McClendon also heard his father's disappointed voice when he announced his intention to attend the College of Charleston. He hadn't been much older than James is now.

The second option was to flee. Find James. Reunite with him and Larrañaga, Lalo, and Bisa in Black Rock Canyon. *Easier said than done,* he thought, *especially with the army in hot pursuit.* He turned back and looked to the southwest, between the distant mountains around Albuquerque and what appeared to be a caldera—the base of a volcano, much closer to where he now sat. Between the geological features, the terrain rolled like ripples in an ocean, but these were brown and bare. And James was out there, somewhere.

That the four of them had remained together, "escaping" from the protection of the Army of the West with the mysterious bone had surprised the former professor. It also told him much about how close they had all become. *Like family.* A hint of a proud fathers' smile erupted on McClendon's troubled face as he recalled the stories Larrañaga had shared about how James had been both brave and strong during their crossing of the trail.

With each passing minute, the clouds to the north grew darker and closer. Rain would soon be upon him. Something Larrañaga said to him back at the pueblo about a key difference between the Spanish and indigenous people suddenly jumped into his mind. "They go inside a building to talk to their god," he said, referring to the Spanish. "We go out into the natural world—and our Creator speaks to us."

Jonathan McClendon closed his eyes and took several

deep breaths and focused on the sound of the river. Opening his eyes he saw, just in front of his feet, an eddy—a circular pattern—and McClendon had his answer. James had told him about the circle of life, the importance of connection and relationships. He stood, scratched his horse between the eyes, grabbed ahold of the saddle horn, and took one last glance back in the direction of Santa Fe. He then hoisted himself up and turned the horse southwest, downriver, towards the Black Rock Canyon.

* * * * *

While General Kearny gave a rousing victory speech to the three-hundred soldier strong formation and a hundred or so locals, and Colonel Donovan barked out orders to assemble a search party, and McClendon traded his blue officer's coat for a serape, Larrañaga trained his field glasses on Santa Fe. He watched, for the second time, one country's flag being lowered from atop the Governor's Palace and another country's raised in its place. *Like sand shifting in the desert*, he thought. *Nothing of this world is permanent.*

Larrañaga, Lalo, Bisa, and James had managed to sneak out of Pecos with their horses in the night. Once a safe distance away, they found shelter in a cave at the base of Glorietta Mesa and together devised a plan. So far, it was working.

The plan was both simple and heavily reliant on Bisa. For the first phase, the young Navajo had been tasked with riding cross-country up the valley between Pecos and Glorietta Pass, finding a way to link up with Mc-

Clendon, and exchanging the log with no bone for the log with the bone. This he did, thanks to some quick thinking and a sharp axe. He'd also been tasked with telling the elder McClendon about Black Rock Canyon and then returning, safely and with bone in hand, to the cave.

With this done, phase two began. Bisa, with his native appearance enabling him to blend in with other Indians and crossers on the Santa Fe Trail, rode back up and over Glorietta Pass, around Santa Fe, and out to the west through the pueblos that dotted the landscape between the capital city and Albuquerque like stars in the night sky.

Larrañaga told him to stop in each pueblo and spread the word that they'd found something from the ancient ones and that Doctor Larrañaga, known throughout the area as a good man with the interests of the people in his heart, was coming their way with it. The Puebloan people, Larrañaga knew, would not want the bone to fall into the hands of the Americans. Bisa would ask them to be on the lookout for the Spaniards and, if need be, help them steer clear of the soldiers.

Meanwhile, Larrañaga, Lalo, and James bypassed Glorietta Pass and the soldiers who'd likely be on it. They rode south around Glorietta Mesa on a trail known only to the locals before making their way west towards the Rio Grande and Black Rock Canyon.

Anxious to remain undetected by the Americans who were likely looking for them, the unlikely trio kept to the low ground—the dry riverbeds, or arroyos, that snaked through the arid, piynon-covered terrain. Surrounded by steep walls of loose stone and sand, the arroyos, often up to a hundred feet below the crusty plateau, served as funnels for any rain that fell. Hours passed uneventfully, and progress for the single file line of weary travelers was slow but steady. James rode behind Larrañaga and Lalo brought up the rear.

Larrañaga filled the time by telling James stories of his interactions with the Puebloan people. As he listened, James remembered Larrañaga telling him about the responsibility of the listener, to absorb and be able to repeat with precision and accuracy what the speaker said. Larrañaga's heavily accented English filled James' attentive ears as they walked along the sandy bottom of one arroyo, made their way up a rise to check their direction, and carefully eased down into another, the only trace of their passage being the prints of their horses' hooves.

When the sun was halfway through its descent, Larrañaga halted the horse and studied the path before him. James, now half asleep in his saddle, failed to notice that Larrañaga had stopped. His horse nearly ran into Larrañaga's, evoking a muffled laugh from both of the older men. Larrañaga cleared his dry throat and caught James' startled attention. "Mi amigos. We're coming up on the Santo Domingo Pueblo, one of the oldest active villages. The people here are direct descendants of the Anasazi who lived in Chaco Canyon."

Larrañaga paused, choosing his next words carefully to ensure maximal impact, "Every aspect of the lives of the Chacoans aligned with the environment around them. They built wide roads that ran for hundreds of miles in each cardinal direction as well as thousands of dwellings with "T" shaped doors oriented east towards the rising sun. They celebrated and based their very lives around the 18.6 year lunar cycle. Chaco, James, was the center of the circle of civilization in this land for thousands of years." He paused again, then spurred his horse forward. James and Lalo followed, still listening.

"The first Spanish explorers who came here named the pueblo we'll soon arrive at after Saint Dominic, a Castillian priest who lived four hundred years ago. St. Dominic is the patron saint of astronomers and natural scientists, which seemed a very appropriate name for these people so attuned to the sky." Just then, a cacophony of coordinated drumbeats, whistles, and flutes filled the air. James watched as Larrañaga smiled and began humming along to the strange song.

"I'd forgotten all about their "Feast Day" celebration. It takes place in early August every year. People from pueblos far and wide come here to take part in the event. This is perfect for us." Larrañaga smiled and spurred his horse forward.

* * * * *

The Dragoons had never seen Colonel Donovan this worked up. An aide helped him onto his horse, both beast and rider still visibly shaken from the shooting. With a mood as dark as the cumulous clouds overhead, Donovan galloped around the interior and then exterior of the dusty Plaza hollering for McClendon. His steadfast confidence and disciplined approach to soldiering seemed to have bled out, replaced with anger and perhaps a hint of fear.

Having completed the circuit without success, an out of breath, sling-armed, sweat- and now rain-drenched Donovan burst into the Royal Palace looking for General Kearny. He found the man examining a formal dining room complete with polished tile floors, a dark mahogany table large enough to sit twenty people, and over a dozen paintings of famous Spaniards. All this went unnoticed by the commander of the Dragoons. Before Donovan could begin, Kearny held up a hand, silently advising his subordinate to catch his breath, to regain control. Words matter, especially at a time like this, Kearny had repeatedly told him. Donovan did his best to collect himself.

"Sir, we have a problem. McClendon is nowhere to be found." And he has the …" he paused, hoping his tone didn't make him sound overly anxious about an ancient relic in the midst of what he knew was a triumph of epic proportion for his commander. For his country.

General Kearny took in the sight of his trusted subordinate. What he saw did not please him in the slightest and what he heard did not—would not—take away from the significance of the moment. Awkward silence filled the room as the two men looked at each other, one with fire in his eyes and the other trying to maintain a fatherly patience.

Finally, from the shadows in the corner of the room, Smythe stepped forward, and ordered with a military authority that he did not officially possess, "Take whomever you need then go find him and bring *it* back." Surprised by the source of the outburst, but in tacit agreement with the content, General Kearny nodded and turned his attention back to his inspection of the Royal Palace.

* * * * *

In the now-muddy Plaza, the detachment of Dragoons who had previously been assigned to watch over McClendon sat wet and embarrassed on their mounts as Colonel Donovan burst out of the Palace. Dripping with disdain as well as water, Colonel Donovan barked, "Men, you have failed in your duty to guard a *professor*. I pray, for your sake, that your tracking skills are better than your guarding skills."

The experienced fighters had proven they could track anything—that was their job, to find and destroy. Now they were being told to do just that but instead of going after Indians, they were going after one of their own. Amidst questioning glances, Donovan awkwardly mounted his horse and asked, "Which way was he headed?" The two Dragoons who had last seen McClendon pointed west in unison, neither wanting to speak. "Then get on with it!"

The rain, mud, and rising waters made tracking where McClendon had gone next to impossible. All they could do was use the mindset of their target. *The easiest way is usually the right one,* Donovan thought as he looked downhill to the west. "Go!" he commanded, pointing in the direction he had been looking. The Dragoons pushed their horses to their limits and followed the banks of the now murky, angry river west—their moods a solid match. After a while, the rain stopped as suddenly as it had started, an act followed by many silent expressions of gratitude.

Pausing at every place that afforded a comprehensive view of the terrain to the west and south, a still angry but visibly tiring Colonel Donovan raised his field glasses to his eyes with both arms, wincing at the pain, and scanned the horizon. With a head start of at least two hours, McClendon could be miles in front of them, he knew. But Donovan's riders were unmatched in their ability and had his wrath and their reputation as motivation. Each time they stopped, they saw the same thing: a steady stream of civilian activity flowing away from Santa Fe, just like the river. Fortunately, Donovan thought, the uniformed "officer" would stick out like a sore thumb amongst the brown and green terrain. They pushed on.

* * * * *

Bisa made it to the periphery of Santo Domingo Pueblo and wearily and gratefully dismounted. He stretched, taking in the sight of the festive village before him. He walked his trusted horse towards the busy plaza which, like all the other pueblos he'd been to, was lined with people both buying and selling food, pottery, tools, jewelry, and even colorful, exotic birds that must have come from far away. As he took in these sights, the mouth-watering smell of the food of the pueblo nearly made him buckle at the knees.

A young boy ran up to him and offered to water and feed his horse. Bisa smiled and reached into his pocket for a single silver Spanish coin—a "real"—and tossed it to the boy, handing him the reins. Larrañaga had instructed the young Navajo to seek out the elders upon arrival, so he asked the boy where he might find them. The boy pointed and Bisa nodded in gratitude, hoping he could find something to eat as well.

Larrañaga's instructions were both clear and intimidating for the young Navajo who didn't particularly enjoy the role his given name called him to be. At each pueblo he was to seek out the elders and inform them of the discovery and the travelers who sought to protect it, to keep it away from those who would remove it from the land of the people. Bisa's sense of duty—both to the Spaniard and to his own spiritual traditions—compelled him forward. As the Navajo walked towards the elders, he could not help but notice that he stood nearly a head taller, with higher cheekbones and lighter skin than the Puebloans. The men, Bisa also noticed, looked like they were about to eat. A table with the four basic foods of the Puebloans: bread, corn, beans, and squash stood in the shade just outside a three-story building. Bisa's empty stomach spoke just as loud as his voice as he introduced himself, causing the men to laugh and invite the young Navajo to join them.

"My name is Bisahalani—Bisa—and I am from the Tsegi." At the mention of the great rock canyon to the west the elders exchanged glances, a few whispering to each other. Bisa continued, after devouring a piece of bread, trying to use the exact words Larrañaga had given him. "I have been traveling with Señor-Doctor Larrañaga and his nephew. We found something from the ancient ones. Something the foreigners want for themselves but that belongs with the people…"

Bisa and the elders spent the next hour eating and talking, not just about recent events but also about Bisa's life in the Tsegi—a place that held as much cultural and historical significance for the Anasazi / Ancestral Puebloans as it did for the Navajo. A common bond, a shared past.

As they finished eating and the time for talk concluded, an elder stood and offered Bisa a place to rest. Walking him into the three-story adobe structure behind the table, the elder told Bisa that he and his people would help the travelers. He also told him to take what they had found back to where it all began. To Tsegi.

* * * * *

The intensity of the late afternoon sun and the hardness of the land around him combined to wipe away all evidence of the rain that had fallen, McClendon noticed as he walked his horse towards a distant village. He was not alone. Indians in what he assumed to be traditional, colorful dress were walking or riding bareback on the trail. Settlers and farmers who greeted him in Spanish and English or some combination of the two from atop horses or wagon benches traveled alongside the South Carolinian. Movement was all around him and somehow, it was comforting.

He'd removed his blue jacket and white shirt underneath, trading the former with an Indian just outside of Santa Fe and replacing the latter with a brown pullover he'd kept in his saddle bag. He wished he had a spare, non-uniform set of pants. The former professor nodded and tipped his hat to those around him doing his best to blend in, to hide in plain sight. Every few minutes McClendon turned in his saddle, looking back for signs of the pursuers he knew were coming.

At the outskirts of the village, McClendon dismounted and walked in, smiling in awe and appreciation. Four-story buildings the same color as the ground itself gave the appearance that the structures simply sprung right up out of the ground on their own. Tall wooden ladders connected one floor and roof to the next, creating a maze-like appearance. Bright colors adorned the locals' attire, and the sounds of drums and flutes filled his ears. The delicious smell of cooking meat caused his dry mouth to water. McClendon stood six feet tall but the people here barely came up to his chest. What they lacked in height they seemed to more than make up for with a radiant sense of…community. Energy. Passion for life.

A group of older gentlemen, their faces creased with lines and their heads and torsos wrapped in colorful, intricately woven fabric, pointed at McClendon—specifically at his blue army-issue pants—and beckoned him closer. Bisa stepped out from behind them. McClendon dropped the reins of his horse and ran, like a student being released on the last day of school, to the young Navajo.

McClendon's initial joy at finding Bisa diminished slightly after hearing that James was not with him. Bisa, speaking too slowly for the anxious McClendon, relayed all that had transpired. He both started and finished with his confident belief that Larrañaga, Lalo, and James were coming from the east and would arrive soon. And then all joy faded when the former professor realized that Donovan and his goons were out there in the same direction. McClendon panicked. *I've led them right to us-all of us.* McClendon knew he had to do something.

* * * * *

With the Santo Domingo Pueblo in rifle range, the Dragoons tried to pick up their pace but were hampered by all the other travelers on the trail. In frustration, Donovan pulled out his pistol and fired a shot in the air. The people parted like the Red Sea. While firing the shot successfully cleared the way, Colonel Donovan, full of anger and frustration—and maybe a touch of fear of what he'd become if he did not find the bone—had pulled the trigger without thinking. He'd used his right/wounded arm. The recoil of the .54 caliber pistol broke open the bandage and the wound, the pressure shattering what was left of Donovan's already damaged humerus.

The Dragoons closest to the colonel would never forget the grizzly and unexpected sight: the pistol firing, the nearly detached arm dropping instantly to their commander's side, the pistol hitting the ground, and the colonel's initially surprised eyes registering what happened and then rolling back in his head before he too hit the ground.

* * * * *

Larrañaga stopped his horse abruptly as the sound of gunfire echoed off the sandstone banks of the arroyo. First, he'd heard a single pistol shot—likely from the Johnson Model 1836 .54 caliber. After a few minutes, two more shots rang out. These he was certain were from the famous 1843 Hall breech-loading percussion carbine. Both were standard issue for the U.S. Army's First Dragoons. *How could they have tracked us here already?* Startled, Larrañaga hesitated. Jumping from his horse, the Spaniard commanded the others to do the same.

* * * * *

McClendon hadn't seen the approaching Dragoons until he heard the boom of the pistol. He also didn't see Donovan fall from his horse or else he might have chosen to react differently. But he wasn't really thinking. Knowing that the Dragoons were after him and the "prize" he was supposedly carrying, he ran back to his horse. The only thing he could think to do was to lead the Dragoons away from the pueblo before Bisa and the others were detected.

McClendon had just swung his leg over the horse when he was surrounded by four pissed-off Dragoons, the business end of their carbines pointing straight at his chest.

* * * * *

The rest of the Dragoons, seeing that their objective — finding and detaining McClendon who now sat on his horse with wrists bound, a lead rope stretching from the reins of his horse to the pommel of one of the other horses — had been accomplished, established a security perimeter around their fallen colonel. But their attention was largely inward, toward the man who had led them so far, sustained them through so much. It was clear that the damage to Donovan's arm could not be repaired; it was only attached by a few strands of skin and tendon. The best they could hope for was to get him — still alive — back to the surgeon in Santa Fe.

They wasted no time. Fixing a tourniquet on the commander's arm above the shattered bone and applying a splint to hold the floppy mess together, they carefully lifted Donovan's limp body up and across his saddle, tying a rope from his good, left arm under the horse to his left ankle to prevent him from falling off. The Puebloans watched closely, slowly and ominously closing in on the soldiers from all directions. Two Dragoons firing rounds in the sky gave them the space they needed to begin their return to Santa Fe.

* * * * *

The Dragoons' snatch and grab operation seemed to pull away all energy in the previously vibrant plaza. What had moments before been a kaleidoscope of life was now a somber stillness. Bisa admonished himself for standing by while it all went down. He remembered when, many years ago, he had been led away from his parents and taken into slavery by Utes. Bisa sat down, his back against a wooden pole and felt the too familiar sense of powerlessness overtake him.

When the soldiers were no longer visible from the pueblo, life slowly resumed as it always did.. A familiar sight snapped the young Navajo out of his gloom. He stood and watched as Larrañaga, Lalo, and James walked their horses into the plaza with looks of first surprise and then relief on their dirty, tired faces. As they got closer and saw the look on Bisa's face those looks turned to something else.

Bisa's demeanor filled in the gaps that his carefully chosen words left out. He told them of the sudden appearance of the Dragoons, the gunshot, the taking of James' father, and the hasty departure. In his mind, the young Navajo could still see the resignation on the elder McClendon's face to whatever terrible fate would now be his. He could also still hear the professor's voice calling back to Bisa, "Tell my son I love him." *Did my father say something like that as I was taken away?* Bisa asked himself.

Looking James in the eyes, Bisa conveyed his father's parting message. And deep inside, James could *feel* his father's words. He could also hear something his mother repeatedly told him back home. "Showing your emotions to people is like bleeding next to a shark." James struggled to keep tears from falling from his eyes. *I have to be strong.* He thought.

Larrañaga turned to see the elders staring. Several of them he knew from when he traveled, pueblo to pueblo, administering vaccinations. The Spaniard approached them, said a few words that the others could not hear, and then pointed at the hollowed-out log tied on the back of his horse. He led them over to it, untied the bundle, and opened the log. The elders' initial hesitancy and doubt vanished faster than the retreating Dragoons as they took in the sight of the colossal bone. To a man, the elders stepped back just enough for the Spaniard to register their profound respect for the artifact. Holding it out to them, he slowly described where it had been found, what it had done, and that they were doing all they could to keep it out of the hands of the American soldiers. He told them briefly about what he had learned about the Incan culture's belief in Viracocha. Their eyes never left the log.

"V is still present. In this. In us," one of the elders said and smiled a toothless smile before reaching out and touching the log.

* * * * *

It had been nearly a year since Santo Domingo had seen violence of this nature from soldiers, but the Puebloan people were by no means new to it. They had been fleeing the destructive nature of newcomers since the dawn of what they believed was the fourth world, this world. The harsh reality that warring tribes, soldiers from far-away places with devastating weapons and a desire to possess that which, the Puebloans believed, could not be possessed was as evident on their faces as the deep creases from squinting into the sun. As was their custom and the custom of many others, the Puebloans turned to their higher powers, the ones they believed existed all around them for direction.

Late that night, inside a kiva reserved for only the pueblo's elders, Larrañaga, Lalo, Bisa, and James huddled beside the Puebloans in a spiritual ceremony. James marveled at the dimly lit space, feeling completely safe for the first time since leaving the Charleston. The bone had been taken by the elders, prayed over, cleaned, covered with some sort of paste to aid with preservation, and then re-wrapped in beautiful beaver skin.

One of the elders began to pray and Bisa, who sat next to James, translated. Together they prayed for guidance and protection for the bone. They prayed for the well-being of the land and the things and people that inhabited it. And they prayed for each other. Since it was wrapped, none of them noticed that the bone began to glow.

8. August 14, 1846 — Rio Grande

Like the first people in the Anasazi creation story, Larrañaga, Lalo, Bisa, and James emerged from a hole in the ground to a sparkling night sky. With the sound of their boot heels hitting the hard ground echoing off of interwoven mud-brick homes, they walked four abreast a short distance to where the elders had told them they would find their horses and a place to sleep. In safety. Larrañaga carried the hollowed-out log.

"I do not know about you, but I am tired…all the way down to my bones!" Larrañaga said, hoping to lighten the mood, even if just momentarily. He looked at his small band hoping for a laugh but received none. Deciding to take a more serious approach, he continued, "Dijo un hombre *mucho* más inteligente que yo, 'A gem cannot be polished without friction, nor a man perfected without trials.'"

"Then God sure is busy with his polishing powder!" James snapped before finding a corner and taking a seat in the three-sided structure where their horses and gear had been stowed. With his head between his hands, the young South Carolinian couldn't keep the tears away any longer. All that he'd lost since the turn of the year coursed through his mind. Life back home wasn't perfect, he thought, before …. But he'd take it in a heartbeat if he could have his mother, sister, and father back.

Even after his mother and sister died, he still had his father. They still had their home. The community had wrapped itself around them for a while, as well-meaning people often do, but as time passed that waned, as did the Dean's patience with his father's frequent absences from the classroom. The elder McClendon hadn't been a big drinker before, but without mom there, James imagined, he found escape in the bottle like so many do.

But still James hadn't been alone. After his father returned from the trip to Washington with his stories about Kit Carson, he seemed to have found a new reason to live, a new purpose: to go west, to find a new home, start a new life. So, they sold everything and made their plans. They joined the westward flow of Americans. And then the attack on the trail, the unlikely escape, and the heartfelt reunion. Only to be separated once again. This time, he feared, for good.

Lalo untied James' bedroll from the back of his horse and sat down quietly next to the young man. Placing an arm around James' shoulder he said, "Your father was doing all he could to get back to you. Because he loves you. Because he wants to be a part of your life. And when he saw the soldiers coming he tried to lead them away."

Lalo paused and sighed deeply before continuing. "James, your father risked everything to protect us. To me, my fair-haired amigo, that is the best gift a father can give his child. To show what it means to be a good man in a world full of…bad. Your father tiene un corazón puro—a pure heart."

"But if we had gotten there…" James looked up through swollen, pleading eyes.

"Then we'd all be dead, and the bone would be in their hands," Larrañaga said from a few feet away. "Maybe even on its way to Washington, D.C." James shot a fierce look at the elder Spaniard, clearly not buying that anything could be worse than losing his father.

Larrañaga took a deep, settling breath amidst the sounds and smells of sleeping horses before he continued, "James, we are human beings. We cannot change the past—not even with this bone," the Spaniard knelt and traced a circle in the loose dirt before looking back at James. "But one of the things you can control is your outlook and it begins and ends in your mind. Let me put it this way," he said, pointing at the circle and tracing around it.

"What you think about drives how you feel, which then determines how you act. And the cycle repeats itself, never stopping. If you choose to focus on your anger or your loss or all the "what ifs" running through your mind, then that will sour your feelings like milk left in the sun. Those sour feelings will lead you to make poor decisions, do things not well thought out—like go after him. And where will that lead? I tell you I've seen it countless times in men far older than you. It leads to the next bad thing. The next bad feeling. The next bad act."

Larrañaga now stood, his voice softening. "Or we can

choose to focus on the blessings—the positives, like the example he set for you and for us. Like the fact that we still have each other and many who will help us. We have the bone. And we have the power to do the next right thing. So tell me, young James, as I described those two circles which one do you think your father would want you to choose? Which one do you feel in your heart is the right thing to focus on?

"Focusing on the good makes me feel better. But the hurt…is still there," James begrudgingly replied.

"Yes, and that is good, mi hijo. Hurting is a part of love. It helps us remember. And it drives us to share that love with others. Each one of us has witnessed tragedy, has felt hurt. Each one of us has lost people we've loved."

With that James leaned back on his bedroll and closed his eyes. The others gathered theirs and did the same, deep in their own thoughts and reflections. There were still a few hours left before daylight and the travelers would need all the sleep they could get.

* * * * *

Father Ortiz hadn't always wanted to be a priest. In fact, as the oldest of the four Ortiz siblings, he recalled spending more time thinking about following in his father's footsteps than he ever did about church or God. When his father introduced him to Bishop Zumbria who was visiting from Durango fifteen years prior, the seed to become a man of God had been planted. The next year,

Manuel found himself traveling to Durango to study and pray. To learn to live the life of a priest.

Three years later, Bishop Zumbria, who had become like a second father and took great personal interest in the spiritual development of the young Ortiz, ordained him as the first non-pure blooded Spanish priest in New Mexico. But at times like this, Father Ortiz questioned his chosen path.

Father Ortiz, to be sure, had a heart for the people. For more than a dozen years he'd attended to their physical, mental, and spiritual needs. He was also a smart man, like his father, and quickly learned that while political entities come and go, real and lasting influence was attainable through the less transient religious establishment. By providing the people a means to escape the unforgiving frontier life as well as hope in the afterlife, Father Ortiz knew he was doing good in a land full of bad. He also knew that as the direct link between New Mexico and the Vatican he stood on the precipice of eclipsing his own father as most powerful man on the frontier. Perhaps, he thought, that was his father's intention all along.

But now the priest who had served so many and, in his mind, sacrificed so much for the greater good — for the people — saw his grand plan unraveling. Unable to sleep, he dressed and wandered out to the stone patio beside the entrance to the Cathedral. Here, just a few steps from where the American officer had been shot, was a labyrinth — a set of concentric circles made out of different colored stone tiles set into the ground. Labyrinths like this had been etched into the floors of churches for two thousand years and served as meditative walkways.

Father Ortiz had walked its path countless times, usually doing so amidst the early morning stillness. It always helped him center on the Franciscan virtues of humility and patience. But not this morning. This morning, he was overcome with anger, with fear. He wasn't centered at all.

As he paced the circles, head and shoulders stooped and hood pulled up both for warmth in the cool morning air and to help him focus on the ground at his feet, Father Ortiz reflected on the present state of things. First, he'd given Larrañaga the most likely location of the hueso grande, as he called it, the big bone that both the Bishop and, more importantly, the Pope had desired for so long.

Father Ortiz had Larrañaga and his crew followed and watched, with the intention of taking the valuable artifact from the Spaniards if/when they'd found it and then personally delivering it to Rome. They had found it, his watchers reported. But the 'taking' part of the plan unraveled with the arrival of the Army of the West. Ortiz's men had to fall back lest they have a run in with the feared Dragoons.

Second, and just as disturbingly, the fear that the invading Americans would have little regard for the traditions of the Catholic church and specifically for him and his Cathedral, was coming to fruition. The fact that the American officer rode his horse up the steps amidst the mid-day call to service angered the holy man incredibly. It had been one of Father Ortiz's most trusted men who shot the American and while on one level that provided some satisfaction, the act itself and the loss of a good man increased his already high blood pressure to dangerous levels.

Slowing his pace and focusing on his breathing in an effort to regain his composure, Father Ortiz prayed for the soul of his man and for guidance.

The plan that began to take form in his mind would require the assistance of his father—his human father—as it called for an outlay of cash and supplies. Father Ortiz resolved that the hueso grande, now, was both his redemption from being stuck on the frontier and his salvation for the next life. *I must find it, no matter the cost.* He thought. *Then the Pope will have to grant me my request to lead a larger congregation in a much more desirable location.*

* * * * *

Across the Plaza from Father Ortiz, Jonathan McClendon, through the haze of an oppressive headache, was praying. He had awakened on the dirty floor of the jail in the Presidio in a cell next to the man who had shot Donovan. Overwhelmed by the emotional hole in his heart that had started to heal but now had been torn open, the former professor turned officer turned traitor feared less for his own fate than that of his son.

Please, dear God, guide and protect him. Somehow, in the midst of his prayers, a calmness began to settle in his mind like the morning dew. Everything, he realized, was out of his control.

The Dragoons had traveled straight back, stopping

only once, shortly after leaving Santo Domingo when the lieutenant in charge recommended that they immediately try to use the bone to heal their commander. Although McClendon could not recall much about the rest of the trip back, thanks to the blow to his head, he replayed the fateful scene that led to that blow knowing that he'd have to answer to the man who he'd ultimately betrayed, General Kearny.

They'd been traveling only a short while when the small detachment of Dragoons stopped along the Santa Fe River so the men and horses could get a drink and refill their canteens. During the stop, McClendon heard the lieutenant order two men to retrieve the hollowed-out log from behind McClendon and bring it to the horse where the unconscious Colonel Donovan lay across his saddle. As McClendon watched, the knowledge that this would not end well crept over him like an afternoon storm.

The men did as directed, holding it away from their bodies in apprehension until they set it down at the feet of the lieutenant and, not turning their backs, slowly backed up and stood behind their horses. McClendon saw that all the men had put their mounts between them and the log. The lieutenant got down on his knees and carefully lifted the top half of the log and gingerly set it down to the side. The look of fear he'd had on his face quickly turned to anger as his eyes took in the bare wood of the inside. Eyes that then shifted to McClendon. That was the last thing McClendon remembered before his world went dark.

* * * * *

One reason Kearny had been recommended for the role of commander of the Army of the West by peers and superiors alike was his ability to maintain a calm and collected demeanor and make sound decisions, even in the most trying of circumstances.

Once, with only two platoons—about 60 men—of Dragoons, he'd been ordered to physically remove one thousand Cheyenne Indians from a junction of rivers in Wyoming where American trappers wanted to hold their annual Rendezvous—a meeting, trading, and drinking extravaganza where a season's worth of work, hardship, and solitude was exchanged for money, ample food and drink, and companionship. Kearny hadn't been a fan of the drinking and debauchery that always resulted in at least a handful of deaths, but he knew what the event meant to the trappers.

Captain Kearny took one platoon and headed straight into the Cheyenne camp while the second held back, "Just in case this doesn't work," he'd said. The Cheyenne chief was ready for confrontation and, Kearny imagined, was feeling confident about his odds when the thirty-man platoon rode into the village. They were immediately surrounded by over a hundred shouting warriors armed with rifles and bows and arrows. The Dragoons braced for the inevitable attack, but Kearny had other plans. He'd brought with him a bear-claw necklace that had been a gift from an Osage chief the previous year. When Kearny pulled the necklace from his overcoat and offered it to the Cheyenne chief, all shouting ceased and was replaced with a low murmur.

The Cheyenne chief took it, nodded, and beckoned Captain Kearny to sit down next to a fire with him. By the end of that day the Cheyenne had vacated the area and not a drop of blood had been spilled, all because of Kearny's ability to stay calm and make good decisions—an ability that thirty years later an officer named Custer did not possess.

The events of the last 24 hours combined with the national spotlight this army had trained on it, however, severely tested General Kearny's ability to remain calm. He hadn't been sleeping well knowing that for the first time in his career, people all over were watching, recording, and judging his actions and decisions in real time and those judgements would ultimately determine his place in history. And while he and the Army of the West had successfully taken Santa Fe, *I can no longer say without a shot being fired, can I?*

A few of his command staff had openly criticized his decision to bring Jonathan McClendon into the ranks. Smythe berated him for losing the bone. And speaking of bones, the surgeon had reported that he'd had to amputate Colonel Donovan's right arm at the shoulder and that he might not make it through the night.

On the positive side, Kearny knew in his heart that the capture of Santa Fe—of New Mexico—with just a single shot fired, was a resounding success by any measure. He'd also received word that the rest of the Army of the West had marched straight through from Wagon Mound and was now at Glorietta Pass. They would likely arrive the following day.

He had dispatched a messenger to return to Fort Leavenworth carrying the news of the success and his plans going forward. And he'd been pleasantly surprised by the arrival, just prior to dinner the night before, of his colleague and friend Kit Carson whose home was in the nearby village of Taos. Over dinner Carson confirmed that the "Santa Fe Trail" did not actually end in Santa Fe. The well-traveled road, the legendary frontiersman reported in his humble yet confident manner, continued west all the way to the Pacific Ocean.

Carson himself had made the crossing earlier in the year and offered to travel with the Army of the West to show them the way. All of this was extremely positive news that would make his family proud.

As General Kearny sipped a steaming cup of coffee on the wood plank deck outside the Governor's Palace and looked out across the Plaza, he realized one more matter would require his attention this morning. Colonel McClendon's hasty departure, while wrong—some were even casting him as a traitor—did nothing more than ruffle some feathers. But the embarrassing reveal of the empty hollowed out log not only cost Donovan's arm, Smythe's unflinching support. The civilian recorder made it clear that Kearny's failure to maintain possession of the ancient and seemingly powerful artifact would indeed be relayed to the President. Unless, of course, Kearny could get it back. *How difficult could that be?* He snickered. *Like finding a needle in a thousand haystacks.*

Slugging down the remainder of the hot brew, General Kearny set his cup down and strode purposefully across the Plaza to watch the sun rise over the Sangre de Cristos. He hoped it would help him clear his head and provide the direction he needed. Never had Kearny been issued a mission like this, a unique juxtaposition of military conquest and treasure hunting.

He felt a tremendous weight on his shoulders and something else. Something tugging at his soul telling him that this missing artifact was something…different. Something life changing. At that the sun crested the mountains. Energized by its warmth on his well-traveled face, Kearny resolved that today he'd put together his plans to continue the march and resume the search. Failure was not an option.

* * * * *

As Kearny raised his face to the sun and Father Ortiz paced the labyrinth, Larrañaga, Lalo, Bisa, and James were already on the move, west of the Santo Domingo Pueblo heading towards the distant high desert plain and the fertile, narrow valley of the Rio Grande just before it. The Puebloans had offered an old, covered wagon. James, to everyone's surprise, quickly and expertly assessed the apparatus and fixed a cracked axel plate and several missing wooden spokes before hitching up two onery mules, also provided by the Puebloans. Lalo and James rode in the wagon with their horses tethered to the back while Larrañaga and Bisa rode their own horses, the former to the front and latter to the rear.

Speed was of the essence, so they kept to the well-worn northeast-southwest road paralleling the river. Their goal for the day was to cross the Rio Grande and make it into the relative safety of the Black Rock Canyon just north and west of the town of Albuquerque.

In and around Santa Fe, the towering ponderosa pines so valuable to people and the blue grama grass so valuable to livestock were plentiful, but between Santa Fe and the Rio Grande the boundless landscape was devoid of all things green. The ponderosa's smaller cousin, the pinyon, dotted the otherwise burnt, rocky, undulating land. Every so often James caught sight of Indian shelters tucked underneath overhanging rocks or in the crooks of old riverbeds where faces of the young and old emerged from the shadows, watching but not saying a word.

And occasionally, as they moved down the rutted trail just as fast as the mules would take them, they'd see the footprints of mountain lion, coyote, and deer. Perspective, here, was difficult for James to grasp. *How can I see so much but so little at the same time?* He wondered. His mind struggled to estimate distances with any accuracy. Only when he trained his eye on something specific, like another wagon far ahead on the trail heading in their direction, and watched it grow as it came closer, did he begin to gauge the immensity of the land around him.

Lalo, having handed James the reins, watched him closely. His attention was not out of worry but rather admiration of how well the young man seemed to be doing in the face of all he'd been through since leaving his home. James was resilient, that was for sure. And just a handful of years older than his own son. Slipping into the fatherly role he'd left behind—and missed—Lalo cleared his throat, pointed to a green strip of land in the distance and began to teach. "The Rio Grande runs from the mountains in Colorado—at over 12,700 feet above sea level—all the way to the *Gulfo de Mexico*. This is about the same distance as from St. Louis to Santa Fe and back. It is not very deep and often has so little water in places that you could walk across it and water wouldn't even get into your boots.

Most of the river's water that leaves Colorado doesn't even make it to the Gulf as it is used by all the people between Colorado and there. For drinking. For farming. For living. There have been many years when there just isn't enough, so people are forced to leave. But there are many other tributaries to the Rio Grande that also contribute…like the Pecos, the Conchos, the San Juan, and the Solado, just to name a few. In some places the river's canyon walls are 800 feet tall—like up to the north near Taos. In others they are less than twenty feet tall.

Larrañaga rode up beside the wagon and caught the last couple of sentences. "Talking about the river, sí? Well, right up there is where we'll cross. Should be shallow enough to get the wagon through." James followed Larrañaga's outstretched hand to an 'S' shaped bend in the river valley with what looked like a dry sand bar extending a good bit of the way across. Lalo nodded and took the reins from James who feigned disappointment. Both Spaniards smacked the reins against the back of the beasts and shouted "Vamos!" The mules might have picked up their pace by a half step, but Larrañaga shot ahead. For the first time James could remember, Lalo laughed.

* * * * *

General Kearny did not laugh when, after breakfast, Smythe tried to command him to go after the bone himself—but he wanted to. In fact, had the old man not been so…old…Kearny would have physically tossed him out of the Royal Palace himself. Having captured Santa Fe, General Kearny's next priority was to take the Port of Los Angeles, and he gracefully reminded the civilian of that fact. But since seeing what the bone did to Smythe's severely misshapen hand, it seemed the old man's new religion, his every utterance was centered around the relic. Around what it could do for President Polk, what it could mean for the United States. And unfortunately, Smythe had as direct a line as possible to the ear of the President. The wrong words said here, and Kearny could be forced to hand the command over to someone else—perhaps even Smythe himself. *Now that would be a hoot,* he thought.

General Kearny dispatched the runners to round up the command staff for a meeting in the Palace's dining room. As he awaited their arrival, his mind wandered. Who all had been in this room and what kinds of decisions had they been faced with? At nearly 250 years old, this was by far the oldest building he'd ever spent a night in and was certainly the oldest building of European origins in the United States.

He recalled learning, while a student at Columbia University, about Marco Polo's 13th century overland exploits to China which opened European markets to Asian spices, silk, and gold. Kearny had never been a gambling man, but as he walked around the Governor's Palace, he admired the portraits hanging around the great room and he began to comprehend just how much the Spanish royalty, like the Venetians before them, had gambled—and won.

Kearny adjusted a slightly-askew portrait of Vasco Nunez de Balboa, the man who established the first European settlement in the New World in 1510 and subsequently marched across the thin strip of land to find the Pacific Ocean in 1513. Next to Balboa's was one entitled "Pascua de Flores" depicting Ponce de Leon in what is now Florida. Beside that was the long, bearded face of Hernan Cortez who conquered the Aztecs in 1519, one hundred and one years before the pilgrims touched the rock in Massachusetts Bay.

Kearny paused before the next depiction, this one of a Spainard walking in a desert leading a few horses and three others and he recalled the story of Alvar Nunez Cabeza de Vaca, the explorer whose ship had wrecked off the coast of Florida. The story went that Cabeza de Vaca and three of his crew had endured eight years as captives—slaves—of the native tribes there in Florida. Once they earned their freedom, they walked from what is now the southern United States all the way to Santa Fe to become the first Europeans to lay eyes on the interior of North America.

And finally, Kearny stood before the largest painting in the grand room: one of Francisco Vásquez de Coronado. Unlike the other paintings which displayed their subjects from the front or side, this one depicted the Spanish conquistador and explorer from the ground level, clad in armor, sitting atop a white stallion. In the foreground of the painting and standing next to Coronado's horse was a Catholic priest in his traditional brown cloak, holding and reading from a Bible. Behind the two men were many other mounted, armor-wearing and spear-yielding soldiers.

Coronado's name and legacy, Kearny knew, were well known in these parts. In fact, Kearny fashioned himself as having much in common with the vaunted conquistador. While Coronado had never found the cities of gold, his exploits spanned from the Pacific to the west to the Mississippi River to the east, from Mexico City in the south to British Columbia in the North. Kearny smiled. His career was on the same trajectory.

No painting of Santa Anna, Kearny observed as his commanders filed into the room. *Perhaps you wear too many hats, compadre.* The renowned 'Hero of Tampico' and the man who'd put down the Texans at the Alamo had been an officer in the Spanish army before fighting against Spain for Mexican independence. He'd been an ally to President Jackson before he betrayed President Polk. He'd even been a practicing Catholic before casting aside the Roman Catholic Church. *Principles matter,* he reflected.

General Kearny's audience, once assembled and read into the plan, was not surprised by its simplicity. Another trait Kearny was known for. Less opportunity for confusion, he'd often say. The Mormon Battalion would remain in and around Santa Fe and help bring American law and order to the area. The settlers and natives here, Kearny knew, were critical to "win over" now that all threat of the Mexican military had quite literally run off. And as much as he did not like losing one third of his trusted Dragoons, General Kearny ordered that one company, one hundred of the mounted, saber- and carbine-bearing men, would be tasked with pursuing the escaped Spaniards and more importantly, the bone.

Sketches of Larrañaga had been made and handed to Lieutenant Colonel Peter Thompson, the executive officer and second in command of the Dragoons who stood in for the recuperating Donovan. In one week's time, the main element of the Army of the West would continue their journey towards the Pacific and the Port of Los Angeles. All—including Smythe, Kearny was pleased to notice—nodded in agreement with the plan. The officers stood as their commanding officer concluded, coming to attention as Kearny left the room.

Corporal Sampson had been one of those who rounded up all the various commanders and support leaders earlier that morning and, weary from the ride around the hills surrounding Santa Fe, sat on a surprisingly comfortable wooden chair in the shade near the entrance to the Governor's Palace as the leadership convened. He'd been there long enough to begin to do what most soldiers do in the absence of orders—doze—when a hand gently came to rest on his shoulder. Before even opening his eyes Sampson put his hand on the pistol in his belt.

When he did open his eyes and took in the sight of a priest, Sampson blushed and relaxed his hand. A large man donning a brown cloak said, "Soldier, would you please take me to General Kearny? My name is Father Manuel Ortiz. I have information I think will be of great interest to him."

At that very moment, as if on cue, General Kearny strode out the wooden doors of the palace and into the oppressive mid-day August sun. Waves of heat radiated up from the gritty Plaza. As his eyes adjusted, he nearly ran into Corporal Sampson and the priest he'd seen on the steps of the cathedral the previous day. "Excuse me, sir," Sampson stuttered as he stood and backed up right into the priest who also backed up. "General Kearny, may I present Father Ortiz, from the…church," the young man awkwardly added.

Kearny's first thought was of the painting of Coronado. *This priest looks just like the one standing beside the conquistador's horse*, he thought. Kearny shook the priest's outstretched hand in greeting. "I am heading over to the Presidio to check on the officer who was shot on the steps of your church, Father Ortiz. Care to walk with me?" And then to Sampson, Kearny continued, "Please run ahead and inform the doctor I am on my way." Sampson, grateful to extricate himself from the awkwardness of the moment darted off and the priest, in an attempt to exude some sort of control in the moment, pointed in the direction of the presidio. Kearny nodded and as the pair walked towards it, Father Ortiz began his well-prepared speech.

"General, my father first laid eyes on the Sangre de Cristos fifty years ago. Back then the Royal Spanish Governor offered the people here whatever they needed to wrest a living from this difficult land. He and his soldiers provided protection from raiding Indians. And most importantly, in my humble opinion, he gave the Church all we needed to oversee the saving of the eternal lives of God's children.

Sir, I have lived my whole life here, a life dedicated to discerning God's will, to saving souls, and being His hands amidst this beauty…and this turmoil."

The priest's hands had been wildly gesticulating and either that or the weight of this speech seemed to leave him out of breath, sweat breaking out on his fleshy face. Pausing and placing a moist hand on the General's arm, the priest continued. "I witnessed how the Spanish ended their rule here. They just rode away, leaving us to fend for ourselves. Many died as a result. Governor Armijo and his soldiers followed their example. It breaks my heart to think what all of us will have to suffer through in the coming days and weeks. The Spanish and Mexican governments knew their place and role and I—the Church—knew ours as well. I hope we can continue that tradition."

"Father Ortiz, I mean no disrespect, but I have an army to lead and a mission to accomplish. Santa Fe will be well-cared for; you have my word." General Kearny said, pulling his arm away from the religious man and resuming his walk to the Presidio. Father Ortiz, not ready to give up, followed closely behind.

"*Mi General*, I can be of great value to you. I possess knowledge of and tremendous influence over these people, the settlers and natives alike. *And, sir, I know where the bone is going.*" General Kearny stopped in his tracks.

* * * * *

The dark clouds just a few miles to their north worried Lalo as the wagon started across the Rio Grande. For James, the hot but humid air of the river valley offered a welcome change that made him think longingly of Charleston. The wagon they rode in was largely empty save for the hollowed-out log and a few food bundles and water barrels the Puebloans had graciously provided. Lalo assured James as they approached the river that because of this, they needn't worry about sinking too deep into the sand.

As the wooden wheels dipped into the water, Lalo did his best to steer the mules towards the tracks on the far side where previous travelers had emerged from their crossing. Larrañaga sat on his horse on the high ground above those, alternating his focus between the wagon and the river upstream. Bisa did the same from a similar position on the near side. Suddenly a deep rumble from the north filled their ears. Lalo instinctively looked upstream and in so doing pulled back on the reins, just briefly. Larrañaga hollered, "Apurarse—Hurry!" Bisa also yelled something that James did not understand. Lalo, realizing his fateful mistake, did all he could to get the braying mules moving again.

To James it looked as if the previously placid river was being swallowed up by an angry torrent of murky water of biblical proportions. Great billows of beige foam and large tree trunks surged at its forefront. Lalo, urging the unruly mules onward amidst the rapidly approaching surge yelled to James to get the log out of the back and hold onto it for dear life. James had it in his hands before Lalo finished issuing his command. *I'm going to have to jump out of the back of a wagon again!* James realized. Turning back to the front, his last clear vision was of the mules being swept away by what looked like the trunk of a tree with Lalo still gripping the reins.

Larrañaga had left his perch atop the far side of the river and nearly reached the tumultuous water's edge when he realized it was too late. He'd seen James hop into the back and grab the log. He'd locked eyes with Lalo before the crest of the murky wave struck the side of the wagon. He'd watched James leap from the back before the patched white canvas toppled over, pulling the wagon downstream as a sail filled with wind would pull a ship. Larrañaga turned his frightened horse away from the water's edge, retreating to safety but never took his eyes off the wagon.

Dios, por favor protege a mi sobrino, Larrañaga prayed. He looked downriver and spotted a sand bar around the next bend and wasted no time in getting there. Larrañaga spurred his horse to the point where he hoped he would be able to pull his men to safety. Bisa had done the same on the opposite side of the river. They watched and waited. A sense of dread coursed through Larrañaga's veins like venom from a snakebite.

Over the roar of the river, Larrañaga heard Bisa shout something and saw him plunge into the river. Moments later he saw the Navajo struggling to stand in the surging water while pulling James, still clutching the log, towards the shore. Larrañaga returned his focus to the water. *Por favor…* Larrañaga said over and over as critical moments and then minutes passed with no sign of his nephew.

Larrañaga found Lalo's broken body almost an hour later as the raging river subsided; his head and shoulders wedged between two boulders not far from where the wagon initially upended. The force of the water seemed to have pinned him there. Larrañaga, a man who had witnessed more death and destruction in this land than most, carried Lalo's body to the shore, collapsed, and wept. Bisa and James heard his cries from across the now-calm river. They carefully picked their way across to Larrañaga, the Spaniard's tears dropping into the unforgiving river.

As Larrañaga cradled his nephew's head, James held out the log to the Spaniard with the bone inside and asked, "Can we use this…?" An expression of hope darting across his and Larrañaga's face like the last glimpse of the sun before it dips beneath the horizon.

It was Bisa who responded. "No."

"But…why?" James pleaded.

Bisa tightened the sweat-soaked headband that bound his long black hair around his head before answering.

"Death is not to be feared. It is a part of nature, a part of the circle of life. Lalo is back with the spirits now."

An hour later, as they stood over Lalo's grave, Larrañaga removed his hat and said, "Eduardo Larrañaga Garcia. Mi amado sobrino. You are the salt of the earth." While the tears had stopped, Larrañaga's shoulders remained slumped with grief. He kneeled and placed his trembling hand on the loose dirt. "You dedicated your life to helping others and I can think of no more noble pursuit than that. You made the world a better place. Mi sobrino, I am forever in your debt. What I could never have hoped to accomplish alone, we were able to do together. I will keep my promise to you—I will look after your family." Larrañaga stood, collected himself, and continued.

"Your favorite prayer was that of St. Francis who said, *'Lord, make me an instrument of your peace. Where there is hatred, let me sow love. Where there is injury, pardon; where there is doubt, faith; where there is despair, hope; where there is darkness, light; where there is sadness, joy. Divine Master, grant that I may not so much seek to be consoled as to console; to be understood as to understand; to be loved as to love; for it is in giving that we receive; it is in pardoning that we are pardoned; And it is in dying that we are born to eternal life. Amen.*"

James dropped to a knee and silently thanked Lalo for all he'd done for him. Bisa, in his own way, did the same. The love behind the Spaniard's words, the love that connected all things drifted around them like the drone of the river. Larrañaga hugged the two young men and together they solemnly walked back to their horses.

Anxious to change the mood, Larrañaga said, "Let's take a quick inventory." They did. Three men. Three horses. A small amount of dried meat Larrañaga and Bisa had stashed in their saddlebags. Two full canteens. Two rifles and two pistols. And the bone. Deciding to make camp just up from the river in the shade of an overhanging cliff, they built a fire to help dry out their boots and sat quietly, the only sound the now calm but steady whisper of the river below them.

As the stars began to appear in the evening sky, Larrañaga spoke, "I'd like to tell you a story of one of our ancestors." At this the Spaniard pointed in the direction of where Lalo was buried. "His name was Francisco Eduardo Pizarro. He was the born the illegitimate son of Captain Gonzalo Pizzaro and Francisca Gonzales in Trujilo, Spain in 1478. Francisco was raised by his maternal grandparents, far from the cities of Madrid and Seville where his parents lived, and for much of his youth was a swineherd with no real prospects for what we'd call advancement.

Around that time, King Ferdinand II and Queen Isabella I sought out young men like Francisco, promising them great wealth and important titles in exchange for becoming conquistadors — explorers — for Spain. Francisco jumped at the chance to leave his pigs behind and in 1510 signed up to accompany explorer Alonso de Ojeda on a mission to the eastern side of what is now Mexico. He handled himself admirably, proving he could be trusted to do the right thing in even the most difficult of situations. His performance caught the attention of another er conquistador who was planning an expedition to the western side of the New World. That expedition resulted in our—in Spain's—discovery of the Pacific Ocean.

Francisco Eduardo Pizarro earned the recognition and respect of his peers and the Spanish royalty. From 1519-1523, he served at the Queen's request as the mayor and magistrate of the newly founded village of Panama. It was there that he began to accumulate his fortune as well as a deep knowledge of and interest in the native peoples. So when he came up with the idea of leading an expedition of his own down the west coast of South America he approached Charles I, the new King of Spain, with his proposal. The king not only approved of Pizarro's plan, but bestowed upon him a *coat of arms*, along with the title of Captain General, and the official role of Governor of New Castille, a distance of some 600 miles south of Panama along the Pacific coast. From pig farmer to governor. Quite the achievement!" The rock cliff behind Larrañaga amplified the pride and enthusiasm in the Spaniard's voice.

He continued, "Pizarro took with him a senior military officer, Diego de Almagro, and a high priest, Hernando de Luque. Remember that name? It was his journal that I read from—about Viracocha. Anyway, in 1530, Captain General Pizarro disembarked for the land he named 'Peru' with 168 men and 37 horses aboard three ships. The name Peru likely came from a river of a similar name, 'Viru'. Do you remember how the Incans believed Viracocha always came from the water?"

"When Pizarro and his conquering force arrived off

the coast of Peru, they sent messengers to King Atahualpa, the leader of the Incans, with the request for a meeting. What Pizarro did not know was that the Incan Empire spanned nearly 700,000 square miles and contained over 12,000,000 diverse peoples, 1,500 capitol cities, 15,335 miles of roads, and, perhaps most threateningly, over 300,000 warriors. The Incan Empire was by far the largest and most advanced civilization in the New World."

"King Atahualpa, unthreatened by the small Spanish force, granted the conquistadors safe passage to his lavish residence in the coastal city of Cajamarca. Placing their lives on the line, Pizarro traveled there and made his pitch to the emperor and his court under the watchful eyes of dozens of his personal guards: keep your empire by swearing loyalty to King Charles I of Spain and accepting Catholicism."

"King Atahualpa, perhaps finding humor in the audacious proposal or taking offense from it accepted neither. Pizarro, having known this would be the likely outcome of his audacious proposal, launched a surprise attack with his heavily armed and armored albeit significantly outnumbered conquistadors. The story goes that the Spaniards killed 7,000 Incan warriors without losing a single one of their own."

"But one thing was for certain. During the melee, Pizarro kidnapped King Atahualpa and took him out to one of the three ships. Within a year, between the lack of unified Incan leadership and the advanced Spanish armor, weaponry, and tactics, the capital of the Incan Empire fell to the Spanish."

"As with any expedition or plan, there are bound to be difficulties." Larrañaga's previously prideful tone turned downcast, and he continued. "Pizarro's was no different. For the rest of his life, he and his leadership council worked day and night to govern the disparate Incan tribes over vast distances and terribly difficult terrain. But his personal efforts to permit, even encourage, the Incan life to continue as it had for centuries were largely undone by De Almagro and De Luque's own personal missions: to clear away everything about the Incans, the people included, from face of the earth.

Because of this, Pizarro made tremendous efforts at great personal risk to collect valuable Incan artifacts, filling many boats with precious metals and stones, carved statues, embroidered fabrics, and anything else that might have some financial or historical significance and sending them to the safe estates of trusted colleagues elsewhere in the New World.

Pizarro's growing wealth and collection of artifacts drove a wedge between him and his military and Catholic counterparts. De Almagro and De Luque each expected to receive an equal portion and the priest, acting on orders from the Pope, expected all items of cultural or religious significance to be destroyed."

"This…conflict…led to De Almagro's decision to overthrow Pizarro. On June 26, 1541, twenty soldiers under the military officer's command raided the governor's palace, killed him, and then at the pointy end of a sword forced the governor's leadership council to appoint De Almagro as the new governor."

"So what does this all have to do with us, here—today, you might ask? I am getting to that, so listen closely. Knowing that De Almagro and De Luque had something terrible in mind for him, Pizarro placed the most valuable and sacred Incan artifact, something he'd learned had mysterious—even miraculous—powers, in a large trunk aboard a small but fast boat captained by a man he trusted. Pizarro ordered that man to deliver the trunk far to the north, to a great civilization living atop a high desert plain in a deep red rock canyon that he'd learned of from King Atahulpa."

"The people there, King Atahualpa had said during one of the many long talks the two leaders had on the prison ship, had both ancestors and beliefs in common with the Incans and would forever protect the ancient artifact from those who would either destroy or misuse it. Pizarro ordered the captain to set sail the night before he was killed. While Pizarro knew he couldn't control the fate awaiting the Incan people, he could certainly honor the King's last request. Neither De Almagro nor De Luque tracked it down. Neither did anyone else, as far as we know."

"Shortly after assuming the throne, Queen Isabella II, anxious to keep Spain at the top of the list of the most powerful countries, set her sights on creating the world's largest museum filled with the most valuable artifacts from the New World. Knowing of my ties to Pizarro, she offered to fund an expedition of my own. To find that artifact. And Lalo decided to join me." Larrañaga took a drink from his canteen before continuing.

"Together, using the cover of a doctor and his assistant giving out immunizations, Lalo and I have scoured the land from the Pacific to the Mississippi for the descendants of the captain Pizarro trusted. For the trunk. For the ancient artifact. We have dedicated a large portion of our lives and all of our hearts to this. We have heard many things that led us to believe that the ancient artifact did make it here, safely, as Pizarro had instructed, but we never found it. It took your arrival to accomplish that, James."

"So now that we have it, what are we going to do with it—take it to your Queen?" James asked.

"No, mi amigo."

"Then…?" James asked.

Larrañaga looked at Bisa with an expression on his face that puzzled both James and Bisa. It was like he knew the answer but was not yet ready to speak it. He said, "We need to get it to where Pizarro wanted it to go," Larrañaga said. "But that will not be easy. Now that word is out that it has been found, many will be after it, just like old times."

* * * * *

As Larrañaga finished that sentence, some thirty miles to the south, on the outskirts of the crossroads town of Albuquerque, populated largely by still active pueblos and private ranches owned by Spanish and Mestizo settlers, an exhausted Father Ortiz heard the driver of his horse-drawn carriage holler back that they were nearly there.

Minutes later the two men waiting for him looked at each other in disbelief. The carriage was painted glossy black and had gold-embroidered white curtains drawn across the windows. The priest's mode of transport seemed more suited to the cobblestone streets of Rome, they thought, than this frontier town.

The pair wore fine albeit dust-covered dark, pin-striped coats and pants emblazoned with gold buttons. Each wore black, round-brimmed hats similar to those Father Ortiz had seen other priests wear, and bandanas around their necks. Unlike any priest, each had a dual-holster pistol belt around their waists. They'd been dispatched from Rome to the central Mexican town of Durango earlier this year and then again from Durango north to Albuquerque once the Diocese there received word that the Army of the West had left St. Louis. That word had traveled down the Mississippi on a riverboat, by ship from New Orleans to the port of Matamoros, and by horse from Matamoros across to Durango. There it had been given to Bishop Zumbria.

Father Ortiz exited the gaudy carriage anxious to get this meeting over with; he knew the men only by their fierce reputation. They were professional soldiers, part of the elite and secretive Swiss Guard. Established by Pope Julius II in 1506, the Swiss Guard's principal mandate was to protect the Pope and the Holy See. In the 340 years since its establishment, the Swiss Guard had been deployed countless times both in and around Rome as well as abroad, always at the behest of the Pope to further his interests or the interests of those who contributed large sums of money to the Roman Catholic Church.

The Swiss Guard's ranks were filled by some of the most skilled and oftentimes most ruthless mercenaries from Switzerland and France: fierce fighters who would neither abandon their mission nor give their enemies quarter. The Swiss Guard had only sent men like this to the New World once before and they had returned without completing their mission. These two, eager to demonstrate their prowess, had vowed only to return if successful.

Bishop Zumbria had informed Father Ortiz that if the United States made a play for New Mexico, these two men would be responsible for collecting anything of value. The Americans, the Pope knew, held little allegiance to the Catholic religious institution. The assumption the bishop maintained was that all of God's work that had been done by the priests here over the past few centuries would be undone by the largely Protestant Americans despite their country's adopted motto, "In God we Trust." And he, Father Ortiz, was to help provide these two men with any and all resources and information that could help them complete their mission.

As the heavy-set padre stepped out of his carriage and into the cooling evening air, he assessed the two fair haired and lighter skinned men with angular faces and piercing eyes. *Nothing good will come of these two*, he thought. Little did he know how right he was.

* * * * *

As Father Ortiz introduced himself to the Pope's men, General Kearny concluded his final meeting of the day, this one with Lieutenant Colonel Thompson. He'd ordered Thompson and the detachment of one company of Dragoons to depart at dawn the next day and travel west with the sketches of Larrañaga. They'd ride through each pueblo between Santa Fe and Albuquerque, pick up and follow the Spaniard's trail until they found him. And the bone. Thompson's men would serve an additional purpose: to clear Albuquerque of any potential threats to the Army of the West. All military-aged males with weapons of any sort were to be relieved of those and, if necessary, detained or eliminated, whichever most expeditiously met the needs of the mission. When Thompson asked if that included the native population, Kearny had simply nodded. *The devil is always in the details*, the commanding general thought.

9. August 15, 1846 — Tewa Pueblo

Larrañaga hadn't slept much; the darkness of the night seemed to penetrate and lay siege to his broken heart. Not only had he failed to keep Lalo safe, but his nephew's wife had lost a husband, his son a father. He knew he'd honor the promise to return to them in Chihuahua City, to raise Lalo's son as his own. But then he thought of James. Of Bisa. Of the bone. Looking up at the stars above, the man who'd saved countless lives felt both powerless and insignificant.

As the first rays of the sun silhouetted the Sangre de Cristo Mountains to the east, Larrañaga sat next to Lalo's grave and prayed for guidance. As he did so, he watched the shadowy river before him, his eyes focusing on a branch of a tree about the same length as the hollowed-out log. He watched it drift unencumbered for a few moments and then get hung up on something, the force of the water holding it in place. Then enough pressure would build on one side or the other and the branch was free once again. This repeated several times before the branch caught up on the rocky shoal closest to Larrañaga and there it remained.

There it would remain, he thought, until the next surge of water pushed it along. *I am like that branch,* Larrañaga thought. *I cannot control the current nor the ultimate destination.* As the temperature climbed with the sun, Larrañaga felt himself surrender to that knowledge and do the only thing he knew he could control which was making one right decision at a time. And the first right one was to stand up and get moving. Taking one last look at Lalo's grave, he also caught movement on the shore. The branch was once again drifting downriver.

Larrañaga stretched his stiff legs and back and walked back to the cliffside where he gently nudged the two sleeping young men. As they sat up and rubbed the sleep from their eyes Larrañaga, ever the caretaker, retrieved a cloth-wrapped bundle of dried deer meat from his saddle bag and handed them each a piece. "Eat something and then let's get moving," he said. James and Bisa silently ate. Then they stood, brushed the ever-present dust from their clothes, slipped on their now-dried boots, and began to ready the horses.

By mid-morning, the Spaniard, the Navajo, and the American could see the rim of the Black Rock Canyon a few miles to the southwest. For the most part they followed the western shore of the Rio Grande whose banks were green and dense with river grass. Larrañaga regaled them with stories of some of the things the Spanish had brought to the area—like the tall cottonwoods now lining the riverbank. A ways up, out of the reach of the river, Larrañaga pointed out fields of corn, beans, squash.

"This is the land of the Tewa," Larrañaga announced with enthusiasm. "Good people and very friendly!"

They all spurred their horses forward, Bisa and James passing Larrañaga as they galloped up the hillside into the busy Tewa Pueblo adjacent to mouth of Black Rock Canyon. Smiles and cheers greeted the two surprised young men. James raised his hand to wave before realizing that all the people were focused on Larrañaga. As they entered the pueblo's main plaza, the smells, sights, and sounds of the vibrant village embraced them like a mother would a child returning home from a long absence. Larrañaga beamed with pride as the threesome dismounted their horses and approached a group of elders.

After making the introductions and having a brief conversation with the elders in their native language, Larrañaga turned to James and said, "Lalo, Bisa, and I came here several years ago and gave the entire village the smallpox vaccine. The elders just told me that since then no one has died of the dreadful disease." Neither Bisa nor James missed the gratitude and pride in Larrañaga's voice. *Just what he needed,* James thought. *Everything happens for a reason,* Larrañaga thought. *This reminds me of home,* Bisa thought.

As they sat on the ground under the shade of a colorful canvas supported by several wooden poles and ate a midday meal, one of the elders told the story of the three sisters. Larrañaga translated for the young men.

The three sisters — corn, beans, and squash — provide all people with two things: an important lesson and vital sustenance. Both are critical to life. The lesson the three sisters offer us is a simple one. We are stronger together. The oldest sister, the one that is planted first, is the corn. As the corn grows, the stalks provide the beans with something to wrap themselves around. The bean plants nourish the soil. And the large, spiny squash leaves offer shade from the sun which helps the soil retain moisture. For the people, a meal of corn, beans, and squash provides all the nourishment we need. And if you look just over the crest of the hill behind us, you'll see three mounds that at one time breathed fire and created the Black Rock Canyon. Now they are cool and at peace. We call them the three sisters. They help us remember that we are stronger together.

James, taken both by the story and the soothing manner in which it was told, blurted out his own eloqui, as his father used to say. "And everything else is gravy." James was pretty sure no one understood his reference to his mother's tasty sauce but thinking of his parents made him feel still connected to them.

* * * * *

The Dragoon detachment under the command of Lieutenant Colonel Thompson departed Santa Fe as ordered and rode hard to the west. They stopped in each village and asked if they'd seen Larrañaga. Most of the time their questions were met with silence, but the Dragoons were not easily dissuaded. They began to offer Spanish silver in exchange for information—not to village elders but to those looking most in need of money. At Santo Domingo they struck…silver. A thin old man tending a booth at the outskirts of the pueblo told the Dragoons that a man who looked like the one in the sketch came through and was last seen heading towards the Rio Grande and Black Rock Canyon. But, the man warned, Black Rock Canyon is a sacred place. A place of the ancients. He pointed at the Dragoons and said, "You cannot go there."

Thompson tipped his hat and spurred his horse west.

* * * * *

Father Ortiz had given the two men who had introduced themselves as Jules and Auguste, obviously their noms de guerre — war names — taken from the great uncle-nephew Roman Emperor combination, a copy of the sketch of Larrañaga and a map of the area. As with the emperors, Jules was clearly the senior of the two Swiss Guardsmen. Standing over the map which was spread across a table on the first floor of a dimly lit two story hotel that Father Ortiz knew doubled as a brothel, Jules inquired about each town his gold-ringed pointer finger came across.

Doing his utmost to ignore the noises coming from upstairs, Father Ortiz answered the man's questions, giving him just enough but not too much information. Father Ortiz knew he had to control these men and the only way to do that was through knowledge. After finishing with the map, the man called Jules sat down in a chair and looked at Father Ortiz with the intensity of a starving hunter sizing up its prey. His questions shifted from places to people — starting with Christoval Maria Larrañaga and his nephew — and the weary priest answered to the best of his ability. Ortiz hadn't known of the Spaniard's ties to the conquistador Francisco Pizarro, but these men did.

Now that adds another wrinkle in the story, Father Ortiz thought. Jules then asked about the American General Kearny, both as a man and in terms of the capabilities of his Army of the West. Ortiz saw no reason to hide what he knew on these topics. In fact, he embellished. As the hour got late and the rapid fire of questions waned, Jules asked if Father Ortiz could indeed confirm that the "artifact," was in Larrañaga's possession. Father Ortiz simply nodded his head in the affirmative. "Has it been…used?"

Ortiz had heard whispers of the 'miraculous healing' that took place at Pecos Pueblo but hadn't seen it himself. Not wanting to confirm rumors, he answered truthfully. "Not that I am aware of." *Used. Intriguing choice of words. What can this do?* He wondered.

Finally, after nearly an hour in the "hotel" and the embarrassed looks of the men and women who had come down from upstairs when they saw Father Ortiz, Jules folded up the map and conferred with his partner in French. Ortiz did not know French well but understood enough. They planned to start their search by heading west towards a dormant volcano peak named "Cebolleta" on the map. The Navajo called it Tsoodzil, or Turquoise Mountain. Before taking their leave from the holy man, they gave him very specific instructions. "You will station men here in Albuquerque as lookouts. If they see Larrañaga, they are to detain him. *Just detain him*. And then send for us."

Grateful to be free from the brothel and the Swiss inquisition, Father Ortiz climbed up into his carriage and instructed his driver to take them to one of his father's ranches on the northern edge of Albuquerque, an area known to the locals as "Old Town." He had arranged to meet a dozen men who were fiercely loyal to the Ortiz family there the following afternoon, men skilled in tracking and fighting and extremely loyal if the money was right. Which it would be, thanks to his father.

On the way, a solitary tumbleweed rolled past the carriage's window. Moments later it was followed by a swarm of others and Ortiz smiled knowing that he'd soon enjoy a good meal and get some sleep…but only after he set in motion the plan that would make him the most important man in New Mexico.

10. August 16, 1846 — Black Rock Canyon

At the insistence of the Tewa elders, Larrañaga, Bisa, and James stayed the night in the pueblo. As usual, Larrañaga rose before the sun. He walked the short distance to the mouth of Black Rock Canyon in the darkness and found a boulder to sit against. He had a big decision to make and realized that this was the first time since finding the bone that he had a chance to come up with his own plan, not one forced upon him by others. He recalled the old saying, "by our actions, not our reactions, do we govern our destinies."

He had always had Lalo to bounce his thoughts off of, but sadly that was no longer the case. His nephew's death and his responsibility for Lalo's family and for Bisa and James added a tangible density to the high desert air. So Larrañaga did what he'd been taught to do; he sat in the stillness of the predawn darkness and tried to clear his overwhelmed head and heart. He imagined the river again, of the floating stick but this time, he visualized it drifting unencumbered by snags or shorelines. Larrañaga sat there, casting his own thoughts aside whenever they arose, and opened his searching, aching heart as he waited for the next right thing to come to him.

* * * * *

Black Rock Canyon[3], a place of tremendous cultural and historical significance to the Anasazi and their descendants, is a U-shaped geological structure with its open side pointing east, towards the Rio Grande and the rising sun. The rim of the canyon stands a few hundred feet above the floor, its gradual walls thick with piles of jagged basalt boulders as large as wagons and as small as water pots, their varying sizes and irregular shapes the result of rapidly cooling lava exposed to the air at or near the earth's surface.

The black rocks stretch as far as the eye can see around the three mile-deep and one-mile-wide wide canyon. The expansive canyon floor is just like the ground Larrañaga now sat on: loose brown sand over hard brown rock, mostly flat, and dotted with scrub brush and the tracks of rock or spotted ground squirrels, black-tailed jackrabbits, western diamondback rattlesnakes, and mountain lions. It is also tracked—and guarded—by the Tewa who believe their ancestors' spirits still inhabit the area.

What makes the Black Rock Canyon so special to those who know it is how it connects the people of the

---

3. Black Rock Canyon was designated Petroglyph National Monument in 1990.

present to the people of the past through hundreds of petroglyphs etched on the rocks. Different from hieroglyphs which are symbols used to represent words, petroglyphs represent much more than words; they tell stories. Also unlike hieroglyphs, the meaning of each marking can only truly be interpreted in the context of the other markings around it, their alignment to the sun or stars, and even their placement in the canyon—high or low on the ridge. Some petroglyphs are tribe, clan, kiva, or society depictions identifying who had been there and what their lives had been like. Others represent religious or sacred entities in the act of serving the people.

Still others convey information such as direction of travel, the locations of water, animals, or people, or, in the case of the Spanish, warnings about strange new people or things. For a civilization that did not write books to preserve the past, the petroglyphs serve as a timeless means to pass along information and insights that resided in the hearts and minds of the people who lived there.

* * * * *

As the sounds of the Tewa starting their morning routines filled his ears and the smells of morning fires and cooking food filled his nose, Larrañaga's drifting mind latched on to Bisa. The boy who had so harshly and suddenly been taken away from his family and his culture. The young man who had proven himself time and time again to be a valuable member of Larrañaga's small band. Somehow,

Larrañaga knew, Bisa would play a large part in the plan that began to take form amidst the petroglyphs.

Not far away, James was awake but hadn't yet risen. Bisa continued to sleep fitfully a few feet away. James silently watched the Navajo and noticed the many characteristics they shared: no facial hair, thin, strong frames, and calloused hands. They both had been forcibly separated from their families, their homes. James respected and admired Bisa and, he noted with some surprise, felt at home in his presence.

The two young men and Larrañaga had gone to sleep in a small room in a two-story structure nestled into the cliff that separated the high plateau from the Rio Grande outside the mouth to Black Rock Canyon. The adobe structure contained many such rooms, the different levels and sections connected by wooden ladders and flat rooftops like those they'd seen at the Santa Domingo Pueblo. With the growing intensity of the morning sun, James looked around the one-window room. In the corner stood the only furnishing, a glazed black and yellow bowl decorated with the images of ducks and wavy lines that reminded him of snakes sitting atop a thin but wide, flat rock. The bowl could easily have held a couple of dozen of his mother's buttery biscuits.

As James lifted it to study the bowl's perfectly circular top and bottom and its artistic renderings, the rock beneath it moved slightly. James carefully set the bowl down and quietly slid the rock to the side revealing, to James' surprise, a hole in the ground. He immediately thought of the hole he had crawled through to find the tunnel that led to the bone, and he didn't think twice about see-ing where this one led. After slipping on his boots, James shimmied his way through the dark opening. There was just enough light to make out handprints etched into the walls as he descended into the tunnel below. He also saw where other holes, like the one he had crawled through, connected to the tunnel.

Squirming his way through the tunnel for what seemed like a terrific distance, James finally came to its end. But the tunnel ended not with the opening he'd ex-pected but rather a rock. James' heart raced with panic. He could neither go forward nor could he turn around and go back, there wasn't any room. James did the only things he could think of. He yelled and pushed on the rock.

No bueno, Larrañaga would say, James thought, des-perate to find a way out. Again, he yelled. Moments later the rock began to move, slowly at first and then all at once the tunnel flooded with light making the air seem to glimmer as the stirred-up particles of the sand and dust caught and reflected the rays of the sun. Larrañaga's face appeared, as did his hand.

"We seem to be establishing a bit of a pattern here," Larrañaga said as he once again helped James out of a tunnel. "Buenos dias, mi hijo. What kind of trouble are you getting into this morning?"

James, red with embarrassment, shrugged his shoul-ders and dusted himself off. "I found this hole in the room we slept in and that led me…here." Larrañaga slid his arm around James' shoulders and together they laughed, the Spaniard's calm, kind demeanor quickly putting James at ease. It was then that James realized they were actually inside the Black Rock Canyon.

The suddenness of a soft but strong voice startled the pair. "I thought I might find the two of you here," one of the Tewa elders who welcomed them the previous day said in Spanish, which Larrañaga translated.

Replying in Spanish, Larrañaga said, "It seems our curious young friend has an affinity for exploring new things." The elder smiled at them, then looked at the tunnel.

"New things. Old things. How do we know the difference? Well, where is your Navajo friend? We are planning a special ceremony. Please, join us. You are welcome."

Larrañaga and James looked at each other, nodded, and strode back to the pueblo.

The three travelers met the Tewa elder who'd invited them outside a kiva twice as large as the one where they had found the bone which Larrañaga now carried. One by one the other elders disappeared from view as they descended the wooden ladder through the hatch in the earthen roof. Once the elders were all down inside the circular structure, Larrañaga handed the wrapped bone to James. He too climbed down into the darkness. James handed the bone down and followed, as did Bisa.

As his boots hit the hard dirt floor, and his eyes began to adjust to the semi-darkness, James was struck by the uniqueness of the situation. *I wish Dad could be here,* he thought. He scanned the room, unsure of what to do. On the bench that spanned the room's circumference sat the Tewa elders and just behind the ladder they had just descended was a large, flat-top stone where the bone now sat. Casting a glance at Larrañaga for guidance, James saw a similar, awestruck expression as the one that was likely on his own face. The last thing he wanted to do was make a fool out of himself or offend anyone. The elder who had invited them pointed to space on the bench, waited for them to take a seat, and then addressed the entire group.

"Here, in this sacred place amongst the markings of the people, we gather to give thanks for the return of our friend, Doctor Larrañaga, who made his own mark by giving life to so many. And we welcome his friends. We begin by honoring those who have come before and pray that with their wisdom and strength we can continue to honor them by living our best lives until we too are called back to the spirit world. That is the circle of life. The way of the people," the elder said.

For several minutes the elders sat in silence with their eyes closed. Fragrant pinyon chips smoldered in a bowl beneath the rock that held the bone, the smell and smoky appearance reminding Larrañaga of the incense used in Catholic traditions to purify the altar and signify the lifting up to the heavens of the celebrants' prayers. Humbled to be in the presence of these wise men and grateful to have been included in this traditional ceremony, the Spaniard closed his eyes.

One of the other elders began to make wordless sounds that seemed to Larrañaga to be almost yearning in nature, as if the elder was calling out to someone or something.

What Larrañaga could only think of as a chant grew in volume and intensity as each man added his own voice to that of the group. The Spaniard joined in, nudging James to his left and Bisa to his right to do the same. With some reluctance the two young men complied.

Soon the chant rose to a level where dirt from the earthen roof above them began to drift down on their faces. Feeling this, Larrañaga opened his eyes and when he did so his voice caught in his throat. The bone glowed with a brilliant turquoise light, as if a chunk of the sky now existed in the dark space around them. Slowly it began to rise into the air of its own accord, coming to hover midway between the perch it had been on and the roof. Staring on in amazement, he again nudged the others, but they were already watching. The elders continued with their chant. They did the same.

When Larrañaga had thought he'd seen it all, Lalo appeared standing before him. The life-like apparition reached out and placed its hand on Larrañaga's shoulder. In consolation? Encouragement? Larrañaga couldn't tell but he could smell his nephew's familiar scent. He could see the love in his eyes and felt it in his heart. While his mind raced make sense of what was going on, he felt a welcoming and calming warmth spread throughout his body.

"Lalo?" he whispered amidst the chants. Next to him he saw James reaching out to what appeared to be the young man's mother. An older Indian man had his arm around Bisa's shoulders in a fatherly embrace. The spirits of men, women, children, and even animals seemed to fill every available nook and cranny in the illuminated kiva. Never had anyone in Larrañaga's band felt such love, such a powerful connection to those who had come before. Words escaped them as the ethereal experience unfolded amidst the illuminated and levitated bone. Time seemed to stop—no, Larrañaga thought, not stop. In here, right now, *time does not exist.*

At some point a commotion outside the kiva made all eyes turn towards the hatch, even those of the spirits. The bone continued to hover and glow, but its hue shifted from turquoise to a deep, blood-like red. The senior elder stood and while he never ceased chanting he did walk to and grasp the glowing bone. He then ascended the stairs and all those around him followed, including Larrañaga's band.

Once outside, Larrañaga scanned the area to discern the source of and reason for the commotion. It did not take long. Several women pointing to the northeast drew their attention to a cloud of dust that seemed to be heading in their direction. The elders formed a circle around the one holding the bone and continued their chants which gained a level of intensity as they did so.

"It's the Dragoons," Larrañaga whispered to James.

As the Spaniard said this, the world around them shifted as if turning on an altogether different axis. While every Puebloan dashed for the relative safety of their homes, all sound seemed to evaporate like water. Even the white noise of the nearby river seemed to have been pulled away as if by some great sponge. Larrañaga's mind struggled to wrap itself around this when something started happening to his vision. The entire pueblo, its structures, farmlands, kivas—absolutely everything—began to shimmer like a mirage. It was as if the thick adobe walls that kept the interiors cool in the summer and warm in the winter had taken on a slightly, then mostly, then entirely transparent, vibrating quality. Something special was happening and they watched in amazement.

Through the shimmering, James began to make out the stern faces of the blue-clad, mounted soldiers and while his instincts told him to run, Larrañaga and Bisa held him in place. *Could Dad be here?* He thought, hoping. The elders had not yet broken their circle around the one holding the glowing bone and in fact seemed to be either unaware of or unconcerned about the impending danger the Dragoons carried like the swords on their belts.

The soldiers advanced two-abreast into the space where the village had stood for hundreds if not thousands of years, the footfalls of their horses producing a dull, thud-like sound off the surrounding cliffs. Their commander rode by within inches of the chanting elders, seemingly impervious to their presence, and then raised a hand signaling for them all to stop. Within moments what looked to be over a hundred soldiers formed a circle around their commander, encompassing the small group of elders, as well as Larrañaga's band.

"Well gentlemen, this looks like the famous Black Rock Canyon," the commander said. Although he was sitting atop his horse just a few feet away, the man sounded like he was speaking through some kind of distant tunnel. "Not much to see here." He paused, turned his horse around to take in the depths of the canyon to the west. The trail they had ridden in on to the north and east. The Rio Grande to the east. The Sandia Peaks, watching over it all. "Sergeant, where's the nearest town?" Thompson asked the Dragoon with the map.

"About fifteen miles in that direction, sir," the sergeant said and pointed towards the Sandias. "Albuquerque." All heads looked in that direction. All except the silently chanting elders.

"Then let's get moving," the commander said.

Like a choreographed dance, the circle of Dragoons morphed back into their marching column and galloped away. As their dust cloud diminished in the distance, the chanting of the elders stopped. The previously invisible pueblo reappeared as if nothing had happened.

"What in God's name…?" Larrañaga said under his breath as the Tewa elder carrying the previously illuminated but now "normal" bone placed it back in the animal hides. Each elder silently turned to the ones next to him and locked arms in a manner that resembled a handshake and then melted away into the village amongst the people resuming their daily lives as if nothing out of the ordinary had taken place. Had it—Larrañaga thought? Judging by the looks on the faces of James and Bisa, it most certainly had.

While Larrañaga and James wandered back into the pueblo, Bisa walked up into Black Rock Canyon. What just happened, both the visitation in the kiva and the vanishing of the pueblo triggered long-suppressed memories of his early childhood. As he walked amongst the basalt boulders, he traced his fingers over the carvings left by those who had come before. Unknowingly he stopped before a depiction of a duck. His thoughts turned to his home.

* * * * *

Bisa was born and raised in a place the Spanish call Canyon de Chelly, 'de Chelly' the Spanish interpretation of the Navajo word for 'rock'—Tsegi (pronounced Tsay-yi). Looking north and west above the boulders of Black Rock Canyon, Bisa saw in his minds' eye the great sandstone cliffs and pillars that formed the land his people called home. He saw the abundant carvings and cliff dwellings high on the ridge that those of the past had left for his people. He wondered who might still be there after all these years.

The last time Bisa was amongst his people was eight years prior. It had been a time of great drought which took all water and as a result all wildlife from the Tsegi. Bisa's clan, like many others, decided to leave their home in the hopes of finding a better place, a better life. Carrying all they could manage; they walked south for many days to a place his mother told him would have plenty of water and food. The place, according to his father and the Navajo tradition, was near where the Twin War Gods killed the monster *Yé'iitsoh* (Big God) atop Tsoodzil (Turquoise) Mountain.

As the monster lay dying, his blood flowed down the mountain and congealed all around its base forming vast fields of black, hard rock. When Bisa's clan arrived at their destination, tired and hungry, Bisa remembered not being able to believe his eyes at the breadth of the black fields before him. He remembered his father telling him that the Spanish called the place "El Malpais"—the badlands—because they could not get their horses and wagons across the rough, broken terrain.

His father, of the Hónágháahii clan, led them to a hidden but well-worn path in the lava field which ended at the mouth of a great cave. For more than a year, Bisa and his family lived in what turned out to be a vast array of caves connected by tunnels. Many others lived there as well, people from all over, and not just Navajo. Water was plentiful—the hard ground collected it, and large, subterranean pools provided all the people needed. And with the availability of water came the animals, both in and around the black fields. Bisa and his family quickly adapted to their new home, grateful for all it provided.

One day, after a particularly rainy season, Bisa's clan decided to leave El Malpais and return to Tsegi. As the clan walked along the raised plain just west of the Ch'óshgai or Chuska Mountains towards their home, they came across a trading post that hadn't been there on their way south. Two large wooden buildings, each with its own corral filled what had been a lightly forested field adjacent to a creek flowing out of the mountains. Outside one of the buildings stood a number of men and horses. When Bisa's clan saw the armed men begin to ride in their direction, they scattered. With bullets smacking into the trees and zinging off rocks, Bisa tripped, hit his head, and blacked out. When he came to, his arms were tied in front of him and several natives speaking the Shoshonean language of the Utes hovered over him. He was still where he had fallen and he anxiously looked around, hoping to find his parents, his clan, but to no avail. The men picked the boy up and put him on a horse behind a man whose smell nearly made the young Navajo wretch. As they rode off, Bisa saw a few broken, bloody bodies in the tall, dry grass.

* * * * *

James and Larrañaga spent the day listening to, watching, and admiring the people of the Tewa Pueblo. Everyone, it seemed, had a purpose. Larrañaga told James that prior to the arrival of the Spanish, this place and many like it were thousands of people strong. A great city in a canyon called Chaco a few days ride to the north had been the center of civilization here for hundreds if not thousands of years. It had attracted people from far away, both as a refuge and as a center of trade. By the time the Spanish came to this land, Chaco had long been abandoned. But their descendants, the Puebloan people, remained. Living in what to both Larrañaga and James seemed like the most inhospitable place on earth amidst the most difficult of circumstances, the Puebloans displayed a pervasive resilience and inherent connection to each other and their environment.

"Tenalach," James said under his breath. Larrañaga, sitting next to the young man after they had hauled up several large pots of water from the river to the pueblo, looked at him quizzically. "'Tenalech' is an Irish word used to describe the relationship a person has with the land, the sky, the water; the deep connection that makes someone able to, as my mother used to say, 'hear the earth sing and be one with nature.'" Larrañaga nodded, committing the new word to memory.

Bisa silently walked up behind Larrañaga and James and startled the pair with a war cry. Together, they laughed. "It seems Bisa has found his voice," Larrañaga said as he stood. "Vamanos…" Larrañaga nudged James with his boot. "Los tres amigos," the Spaniard joked as they picked up their empty pots and headed back to the river.

* * * * *

More than a little frustrated with their lack of success, the detachment of the Army of the West's Dragoons trod into the town of Albuquerque as the sun began to set over the high desert plain. They'd followed the Rio Grande south on both sides of the river, hoping to discern some sign of the fugitives but they'd found nothing. Now, amidst the waning light and blowing grit, the first American soldiers in Albuquerque looked more like ghosts of the past than they did a modern-day conquering force.

After making a complete sweep of the crossroad town, Lt. Col. Thompson ordered his detachment to split up with one platoon covering the south side of the town and the Camino Real leading to Mexico, one on the far west side of town on the high ground just across the Rio Grande, and one on the northeast side of town on the Camino Real leading towards Santa Fe. Thompson went with the latter. All three posted lookouts and security while the others tended to the horses, cleaned weapons, ate, and made camp—in that order. They were, after all, professionals.

* * * * *

Lt. Colonel David Thompson of St. Louis, Missouri bore no physical resemblance to the broad shouldered, square-faced, ruddy-complected Colonel Donovan. Neither did he possess the same short temper or pejorative view towards the Indians. Thompson was a man of slight build, and the men joked behind his back that if he turned sideways, he could dodge a bullet. An engineer who specialized in well-digging in before joining the army, Thompson was first and foremost a thinker who also possessed an uncanny ability to see through rock (for water) or into the heart of another man (for character). Useful traits for a man in charge of the lead element of the Army of the West.

11. August 17, 1846 — Albuquerque

Having been up the first half of the night ensuring the men were appropriately situated and animals and gear cared for, Thompson rose slowly with the sun, cast his perceptive glare over the still landscape and, shaking off the cobwebs of sleep with a cup of coffee so thick it looked more like syrup than a beverage, engaged his analytical mind. Where would these Spaniards go out here? Who would they seek help from? Like a lock clicking into place, the "who" question spurred a line of thought that triggered immediate action.

Turning to Lieutenant Joseph "Pete" Peterson who had been following behind the senior officer, he asked, "Pete, how many ranches did we see on the way out here from town?"

"Just one, sir. It was a big one. A hunnerd head of cattle and fields of corn and sech down by the river."

"Send a squad back to get eyes on that ranch. Do not have them engage in any way. On the quiet-like. I just want them to find out who is down there and report back."

"Yes, sir. Right away."

Lt. Colonel Thompson, satisfied that all was as it should be, headed towards the fire—and a second cup of coffee.

* * * * *

As Thompson took the first sip of his second cup of coffee, Larrañaga woke up from the first full night of sleep he'd had in over a week. He knew he'd need it with the plan that was unfolding in his mind. Waking Bisa and James, the three men packed their gear and readied their horses. The Tewa elders saw this and ushered them over to a large table filled with food. The smell of fried bread made their empty stomachs grumble, and they ate as if there was no tomorrow.

Satiated, Larrañaga pulled a handful of silver Spanish coins from his pocket, placed them on the table, and patted his heart and stomach in gratitude to the Tewa. James and Bisa made the same motions, their mouths still full. One of the elders handed Larrañaga three cloth-wrapped packages of foodstuffs and then turned and handed Bisa what at first seemed to be a rolled up, tightly woven blanket. As Bisa placed his hands on the item he realized the bone was inside.

With the elder's hands resting atop Bisa's, the Tewa slowly spoke the chant he'd said the previous day, the one that made the bone glow and…Bisa repeated the chant, trying his best to catch the tone and inflection. The Tewa said it again, faster this time, and Bisa followed suit. And judging by the blue glow coming from inside the blanket, he got it right. The Tewa smiled and let go of the artifact.

Larrañaga had never been to Canyon de Chelly but had heard much about the sacred home of the Navajo—and the Anasazi before them. The journey there would not be easy; the first half, from where they stood out to and past Cebolleta Mountain and El Malpais to the north-south running Chuska Mountain Range was wide-open terrain. They'd be able to see for miles, sure, but if the Dragoons followed them out there, they'd have nowhere to hide.

The good news, Larrañaga thought, was that they had Bisa. While it had been some time since the young man had been there, the Spaniard knew that not only could the young Navajo help guide them through the Chuskas, but his mere presence would also prevent other Navajo from attacking them. Maybe.

As Larrañaga, James, and Bisa carefully picked their way up and over the rim of Black Rock Canyon and across the high desert plain towards their first landmark the three small dormant volcano cones that the Tewa had named 'The Three Sisters,' a hawk's 'kee-aaah' pierced the air. *Two good days of riding and we'll be in the mountains,* Larrañaga thought. *Please watch over us,* he prayed.

* * * * *

The men calling themselves Jules and Auguste were not used to the intensity of the sun at 5,500 feet above sea level, nor the complete absence of anything even remotely resembling shade. While the pair had brought as much water as they and their horses could carry, they had ridden hard to the west the previous morning and consumed much of it. They'd found some shelter from the oppressive sun and hot wind at the base of three hills that looked like miniature volcano cones. From there they could see for miles in any direction, so they decided to ration what little water they had left and wait until the sun set before moving on in search of water, the Spaniards, and the bone.

* * * * *

Another thirsty man lay on the dusty floor of the dimly lit Presidio jail cell some 100 miles away. Jonathan McClendon, the former professor, waited to learn of his fate like a schoolboy outside the principal's office. He had a gash across his temple, a swollen-shut eye, and bloody bare feet—all the result of the discovery that the hollowed-out log no longer held the bone and the forced march back to Santa Fe.

In the cell next to him sat a middle-aged mestizo rancher, the one who had shot Donovan. He seemed to like to talk—had been doing so in Spanish since the sun came up—and McClendon only partially listened, occasionally catching words he knew like peligro (danger) and muerte (death), and one, "verdugo," that he discerned through the man's hand signals to have something to do with hanging. McClendon sat silently in the corner of the cell, his knees to his chest, both his head and disposition downcast, tracking the progression of time by the movement of a beam of light that came and went through the single, small window high up on the wall of the cell.

Sometime after mid-day, he heard a commotion outside the window. McClendon yelled out, pleading for water. Laughter ensued. "Please," he begged. Moments later two Dragoons burst through the wooden door of the presidio. One dropped his trousers and began to urinate through the cell bars.

"Here, have you some o' this!" one said.

"You'll be lucky to get a rope after what you've done," said the other who laughed while standing by the door.

A third, booming but slightly shaky voice that he knew was Donovan's, came from just outside the Presidio's adobe walls. "That'll be enough." And a moment later the tall, broad, and much paler Colonel Donovan walked slowly into the jail. His right arm was gone, replaced by a blood-soaked bandage that stretched across the man's ample shoulders. Dismissing his men, Donovan used his remaining arm to pull a stool up to the edge of the cell. He sat, wearily, his gaze both intense and searching. "You've betrayed your people, McClendon," he started. "Now, maybe you can save your soul by telling me where the bone is."

* * * * *

Back on the outskirts of Albuquerque, angry words from another interrogation filled the dry air. The riders that Lt. Colonel Thompson dispatched had returned with the news that the "padre's chariot" was inside the barn on the ranch they'd been told to watch. When they'd told Thompson the news he'd sent them back with orders to escort the priest and whomever else was with him back to their makeshift camp. Now Thompson had one foot propped up on the step of the carriage and Father Ortiz, with sweat on his brow, shifted nervously in his seat.

"So you want me to believe you came all this way yourself just to pick up some new Bibles?" the officer said.

"Why yes, the Lord's work is never done. Did you know we only have two Bibles in all of Santa Fe? One is my personal Bible and the other belongs to the cathedral. We are in desperate need of more, especially with all of you coming into town. You see…"

Thompson cut him off abruptly. "Who owns that ranch, padre?"

"My father." Ortiz responded indignantly.

"And what does your father have to do with Bibles?" Not waiting for a response, Thompson continued, his keen eyes never leaving Father Ortiz. "One of the ranch hands there told my men you'd been in town yesterday, meeting with someone. Who might that have been?"

Father Ortiz thought carefully and then responded. "Two men from the Diocese in Durango. They had been instructed to deliver the Bibles, which they did." He said and patted a small brown satchel that sat on the seat beside him.

"What are their names? What do they look like?" Thompson demanded.

The officer continued his interrogation of Father Ortiz whose confidence and indignance had blown away with the wind. Thompson made some notes in a small leather journal he'd pulled from his pocket and then took another good look at the perspiring priest and the interior of the carriage. When he'd finished, he stepped back and told the priest's driver to wait a few minutes and then he'd be able to proceed back to Santa Fe.

Lt. Colonel Thompson then strode over to the lieutenant who, accompanied by four other Dragoons, had been observing the interrogation.

"Pete, I want two of your men to take this note," he handed the junior officer one of the pages he'd written on, "and escort the padre back to Santa Fe. No stopping. And have them deliver it to Colonel Donovan or…if he's…indisposed…to General Kearny himself. Then I want two more of your men to ride to the west and pass along the names and descriptions of the men the padre met with. They are to be apprehended and brought to me."

"Yes sir," the lieutenant replied and ran off.

Turning back to the carriage, Thompson waved the driver on and tipped his cap to Father Ortiz.

"Hold on one more minute, sir," Thompson yelled to the carriage driver as it began to pull away. The officer briskly walked up to and threw open the wooden door. "Padre, hand me that satchel of Bibles."

Father Ortiz had reflexively put his hand on the satchel when the door flew open where, with white knuckles, it firmly clutched the well-worn handles. The look on his face was one of shock and…fear, Thompson thought. "I'll do no such thing. You have no right to interfere with the business of the church. For all I know you'll…."

This time it wasn't Thompson's words that interrupted Father Ortiz. It was his action. With surprising speed, the officer climbed into the carriage, tore the satchel from the padre's grasp, and stepped back out. He opened the bag to find silver coins. A great many silver coins. When Thompson looked back up at Father Ortiz he smiled. "The Lord's work, huh?"

At that moment, the two Dragoons who were to escort the padre back to Santa Fe rode up and he handed one of them the satchel. "Give this to the general with my compliments—and those of Father Ortiz." And with a shout and a wave, Lt. Colonel Thompson bid adios to the carriage and its escort.

* * * * *

Larrañaga led the trio of horses across the plain as shimmering waves of late summer heat emanated from every surface. While the Spaniard could clearly make out pointy tops of the Three Sisters, it was difficult to see what, if anything, might be on or around them; the heat waves close to the ground distorted everything. Deep down, Larrañaga knew that if he were looking for someone west of Albuquerque that's where he'd be—on one of those cones. Sweeping his eyes back and forth across the endless horizon, Larrañaga let his mind drift to what had happened back with the Tewa. *Those soldiers couldn't even see the village,* he thought. Larrañaga wondered if Francisco Pizarro had known about the bone's power.

Larrañaga felt the bullet impact his horse before he heard the report of the rifle. And then he saw a puff of smoke midway up one of the cones. The horse's front legs buckled, launching Larrañaga out of the saddle and over the animal's head. A good thing, he would later think, as the horse then collapsed to the side and rolled over. He would have been crushed. But these thoughts weren't going through his head now. He'd tried to roll as he hit the ground, but he'd struck a rock and, at least momentarily, was unable to move.

James' and Bisa's horses reared at the crack of the shot and instinctively they sprinted away from the fallen horse, back in the direction from which they'd come. Barely able to stay in the saddle, James did his best to gain control of his spooked horse and at the same time stay with Bisa who raced towards a small depression—a dry arroyo.

Moments later, Bisa disappeared from view. James headed for the same spot and suddenly he and his horse were airborne; the flat bottom of the arroyo rapidly rising to meet them. The force of the impact was too much and the hard landing propelled James into what fortunately for him was loose sand. Realizing that he'd survived, James' eyes locked in on Bisa who held the bundle that contained the bone and realized that his friend was chanting, his mouth moving silently at first. But moments later James heard it. The chant.

The bone began to emit its reddish glow. James tried

to emulate the chant, hoping—praying—that it would somehow save Larrañaga and protect them from whomever was out there. With the bone glowing in Bisa's arms and the two of them chanting, James collected their horses and together they made their way, slowly, up to the crest of the arroyo. They kept up the chant, their hearts racing, their eyes just about the rim of the arroyo, searching. Hoping.

One man stood over Larrañaga and appeared to be kicking the Spaniard. Larrañaga curled into a ball to protect himself from the violent barrage as another man, this one on horseback, rode up and searched Larrañaga's saddle bags and bedroll. Apparently, he didn't find what he wanted because he climbed back on his horse, hollered something at the other man, and pointed in the direction of Bisa and James. The man who'd been beating Larrañaga began to tie the Spaniard's hands.

Bisa's chanting and look of determination conveyed the confidence James desperately needed to follow the young Navajo's lead. They climbed back on their horses and pointed them towards Larrañaga. First they walked tentatively, as if barefoot across a floor covered in broken glass, unsure of just how invisible they were. With each step, however, their faith in the power and the goodness of the bone increased. *Help us,* James thought, unsure of what they'd do once they got to Larrañaga. *Trust in something bigger than yourself,* a voice (was that Lalo?) somewhere deep in his head said so loudly he looked around to see if there was someone else there.

Taking a deep breath in between the chanting, the

young men looked at each other and simultaneously spurred their horses into a full gallop towards Larrañaga and his assailants. Like at the Tewa Pueblo, the world around them began to shimmer. Based on their lack of reaction, the assailants had not yet seen the two young men riding towards them.

Bisa's horse slammed into the unsuspecting man who'd just finished binding Larrañaga's hands. Never before had James seen a man fly as far as this one. He didn't have an opportunity to watch the conclusion of that flight, however, because his horse was three lengths behind Bisa's and heading straight for the other assailant, the man on the horse. James watched in what felt like slow motion as he saw a look of surprise on the face of the man in front of him that was quickly replaced with anger and a grim determination.

The man reminded James of his grandfather: a soldier. For the briefest of moments, shorter than the appearance of a shooting star, James made eye contact—or at least felt he did—with the mounted man who had drawn his gun and pointed it at Larrañaga. The gun in the man's hand exploded as James' horse passed between the shooter and his Spanish friend.

In the moments that followed, James expected to feel the searing pain of a bullet wound or his horse give out underneath him. But neither happened. As James turned his horse around, he saw that the pistol had literally exploded, the end of what had been a long metal barrel now a twisted mess as was the hand holding it.

"Normal" time started again as Bisa and James trotted

their horses back to where Larrañaga now kneeled. The man with the wounded hand was in full gallop away to the southeast. The other was still and lifeless. The surprise and elation at what they'd done caught in their breath, their chants fell away and with them the glowing of the bone. Larrañaga stood and turned to his two friends who had just appeared, as if out of nowhere. He held up his bound hands in triumph and laughed because he knew not what else to do.

James jumped off his horse and threw his arms around Larrañaga. Realizing the Spaniard's wrists were still bound, he stepped back and cut them with his Bowie knife. Then he hugged the man again. Bisa sat on his horse and watched the figure of the stranger disappear below the crest of the mesa. "Let me collect my things and let's get moving. We need to get to Cebolleta tonight," a grateful Larrañaga said.

* * * * *

The veteran Swiss Guardsman pushed his spooked, sweat-soaked horse just as hard as he could over the open terrain. His hand hurt but pain, he knew, was only temporary. Pain could not ruin a life like his. Failure could. The fear of failure compelled him forward; the desire to complete his mission at any cost kept him focused. He needed water, supplies, and a few men and then he'd be back on the trail of the ancient artifact whose power, he believed, he just fell victim to.

He held the reins tightly with his only good hand,

the other tucked into his shirt vest. Jules slowed his brain down and replayed the scene as he rode. He'd seen some unbelievable things in his life, but he'd seen *nothing* here. One moment his partner had been standing next to Larrañaga, tying the Spaniard's hands, and the next his body was flying through the air, parallel to the ground, before crumpling against a rock like a sack of corn. And Larrañaga! He had him dead to rights and pulled the trigger. *How in God's name did my pistol explode?* He asked already knowing the answer.

He remembered feeling a rushing presence just before the explosion. An outside force. *Against me?* He seethed as the adrenaline wore off and the extent of the damage to and pain in his hand began to register in his mind. *I must get that bone,* he thought as he drove his horse over the last hill before the downslope to the Rio Grande.

* * * * *

The lieutenant in charge of the platoon of Dragoons on the west side of the river had received the message from Lt. Col. Thompson: to be on the lookout for the kind of man they now saw riding down from the crest of the mesa. In short order, the Dragoons had the wounded man surrounded and in custody. The man had a sharp, angular face and the eyes of a warrior, but had lost two fingers from his right hand. The platoon's medic wrapped it tightly while several others conducted a thorough search of his person and saddle bags. They found a lever-action rifle, a pistol, a knife, a bag of gold coins, and a black leather-bound journal.

The prisoner was non-responsive to the lieutenant's questions, so the officer did the only thing he knew to do; he gave the order to take the prisoner to Lieutenant Colonel Thompson.

* * * * *

As the brilliant turquoise sky melted into a reddish-orange glow that reminded him of wildfires on the grassy plains of Kansas, Lt. Colonel Thompson stood from where he'd been sitting on a rock overlooking the Rio Grande. Over the din of the rushing water he heard the unmistakable sound of riders approaching: five riders, four in blue. The commander stood and stretched, his heart picking up its pace at the sight. Perhaps they had their man.

As they approached, the squad leader held up his gloved hand signaling the others to halt and then saluted his commander. Thompson returned the salute, but his eyes had not left those of the man who was riding with his wrists bound to the saddle horn. This slight, fair-complected man had the eyes of a soldier. He was not Larrañaga.

His hopes dashed, but his mind already working the situation, gathering and organizing facts and impressions, he pointed the squad leader in the direction of his command post and instructed him to take the prisoner there, keeping him under guard.

The prisoner had yet to speak after finishing a plate of food and two canteens of water on the ground outside the commander's tent. While he was eating, Thompson flipped through the pages of the journal found on the prisoner. It was written in French. Thompson, who frequently interacted with French traders and trappers in Colorado, knew enough of their language to be able to understand most of the finely penned—both in style and grammar—content.

The journal started by recounting orders from the Pope to travel to Mexico, to seek out the Bishop in Durango, to wait for orders to pursue the "item" once it was located. And to return the item post haste to Rome. The bulk of the rest detailed the journey itself. The concluding pages described the meeting with Father Ortiz, the search for Larrañaga, and most importantly, the reported discovery of the bone.

"Well, sir," Lt. Colonel Thompson said in French to the surprised prisoner, "It looks like we are after the same person, the same…thing. And when the Army of the United States wants something," he paused for dramatic effect. "We get it." Thompson then showed the prisoner the sketch of Larrañaga. "Have you seen this man?" The prisoner's chiseled face betrayed a hint of recognition, but still the man remained silent. "Was he carrying anything…out of the ordinary…?"

After a few awkward moments, the prisoner nodded and gestured towards a canteen one of the Dragoons was drinking from.

"Get this man more water," Thompson said. "But before I give you anything else, you will tell me your name, who you are working for and with, and what your mission is."

With the Dragoon soldiers murmuring in the background, the prisoner weighed his options. Thompson waited patiently then asked, "Well?"

No response. Thompson paced around the prisoner, keeping a tight leash on his own emotions. The sounds of distant coyotes broke the oppressive silence. Turning to the Dragoon who stood behind the prisoner, Thompson ordered, "Sergeant, keep this man under guard through the night. At first light I want this platoon to pull stakes and escort the prisoner back to Santa Fe. In two hours, I will accompany you and your squad back to your platoon in the west and we shall round up this Spaniard."

12. August 18, 1846 — Cebolleta Mountain

Forty miles to the west, Bisa tossed and turned as he tried to get to sleep. Where they had chosen to spend the night was in the foothills of Tsoodzil, the southernmost of the four Navajo sacred mountains that marked the land of the Dine—the Navajo people. The last time he had been this close to where the Changing Woman defeated the monster that threatened to devour his people he had been with his mother's clan.

He could still see his mother's patient smile, remember her voice. Like all Navajo, Bisa believed—he knew in his heart—that no one was ever "gone." The word for "goodbye" does not even exist in the Dine language. But would he ever be able to see her smile or hear her soothing voice again? For the first few years after he'd been taken, Bisa could feel her presence. But with each passing day she seemed further and further away. Was she now with the spirits?

The events of the day also kept him awake. Something in him had changed when he'd repeated the chant, over, and over, and over again. It was as if a door had opened in his soul—a door to a life filled with as many possibilities as there are stars in the sky and the kind of love his mother had talked about, a love that put the needs of others before his own.

Bisa searchingly gazed up at the sacred and weathered peak, now faintly lit by the light of the nearly full moon. As the stillness of the cool night air settled in around him, Bisa, for the first time since that fateful day in the forest near the trading post, felt purpose pouring into him. As his mother used to fill bowls with food or water, Bisa felt his soul filling with the intrinsic strength of the mountain, the passion for life, and love of all those who had come before.

When Bisa's eyes finally closed, they did so with the certainly that he now had his own mission: protect the bone and serve those he loved. Tomorrow he would guide Larrañaga and James to safety.

* * * * *

Lt. Colonel Thompson said a quick prayer of thanks for the cooler night air and the light of the nearly full moon as he and the platoon of Dragoons rode west. As they ascended the river valley onto the high desert plain, the once far-off outline of Cebolleta Mountain got closer and larger with every passing minute. The Dragoons had commandeered a wagon from the ranch where Father Ortiz had been, filling several barrels with much needed water. The information and insight they'd gained from the French-speaking prisoner's journal and demeanor provided him with an actionable lead as to the whereabouts of Larrañaga and the bone. But all of that also raised number of weighty questions in Thompson's mind.

What interest does the Pope have in Larrañaga? Are there other soldiers like the prisoner out here? Who or what is helping Larrañaga? And what is the story with this bone? The questions repeated over and over in his mind. The occasional howling of coyotes and the incessant footfalls of the horses provided the only answers he'd receive.

As the night began to shed its tight hold on the open landscape and the eastern sky behind the Dragoons lightened, word from the lead horsemen came back that they'd located a small spring. Having traveled for hours, Thompson gave the okay to take a break, but was wary of the fact that they were out in the open. And somewhere out there was Larrañaga and his crew who had clearly bested at least one proven warrior.

As the Dragoons watered their horses and stretched their legs, Lt. Colonel Thompson scanned the horizon with his looking glasses. He estimated they were a dozen or so miles from the foothills of the dormant volcano. The high desert plain stretched as far as he could see to the north and south. Far in the distance to the east he could just make out the Sangre de Cristo and Sandia Mountains casting shadows over the towns of Santa Fe and Albuquerque, respectively. And further to the west he could make out another range of mountains.

A hint of a feeling of isolation and concern began to

creep into Thompson's veins. *Just like the plains ... so much open space that it's hard to make out the small things, the important things.* He thought. Thompson did his best to take solace in the knowledge that he was on an important mission and at least had the benefit of being in the company of proven warriors. As he pondered his situation, Thompson recalled a conversation he had with Kit Carson before he departed Santa Fe.

"That land out there, its like nothing you've ever seen," the renowned explorer and trapper had told him. The quizzical look on Thompson's face implored the soft-spoken man to continue. "Stay away from tight spaces where the Indians can sneak up on you—they're mighty good at that. Oh, and if you see one Indian, know there are probably twenty more close by."

Thompson did not lack courage, but as he remembered this last statement, the hair on the back of his neck stood up. With thirty Dragoons he had no concerns about his ability to capture Larrañaga.But a surprise strike on unfamiliar terrain by a similar-sized force would not end well for him or his men. He resolved to avoid tight spaces and not stay in one place for long. "We leave in ten minutes," Thompson barked.

* * * * *

Larrañaga woke with a start, stiff and sore from the fall from his horse. As he shook off the cobwebs of sleep, he turned to the side and saw a still-sleeping James. He turned to the other side and saw Bisa's empty bedroll.

With a burst of energy, he stood and searched the arroyo. "Bisa" he called out, his voice echoing off the rocky walls. James sat up immediately and grabbed his rifle. Larrañaga repeated his call, this time his voice betraying a hint of concern. Maybe more than a hint.

"I am here. Come," Bisa said from somewhere above them. The calmness of his voice relaxed Larrañaga, but the command surprised James. Together Larrañaga and James scrambled up the loose sand on the sides of the arroyo and up and around dozens of boulders to a vantage point where Bisa sat. When they arrived, out of breath and sweating despite the early hour, they sat down on either side of Bisa who was pointing to the east—and a rising dust cloud. Larrañaga pulled his looking glass out of his pocket and scanned the area.

"Looks to be about 30. Plus a wagon. My best guess based on their formation is a platoon of Dragoons. The sun is still behind them so I cannot be certain," the Spaniard said, now fully awake. "Maybe five miles out."

Larrañaga lowered his looking glass and began to think. Then he raised it again and panned from the approaching Dragoons in the east across the mesa to the south and then west. He lowered the glasses again. "I don't think we can move out without being seen."

Bisa spoke next, with content and tone saturated with wisdom. "No, we cannot. The eastern sun would light us up like a fire does the night. Let's let them pass and then we can follow behind them until we hit the Chuska's. If they see us, we lose them in the lava fields." For James' sake he pointed, this time to the southwest. "The Spanish call that area El Malpais—the bad country. They say that because their wagons and horses cannot cross it. But what they do not know is that long ago the Anasazi and more recently the Hopi and Zuni and Navajo found good lives there. Plenty of food and water. People, I believe, still live there."

He paused and looked at Larrañaga. "Maybe my people." Bisa turned back to James, "I lived there many years ago." Looking back at the dust cloud to the east Bisa stood, the others following suit. "We should get ready. Now."

*****

The two lead Dragoons, rejuvenated by the stop at the spring and at full alert as a result of the proximity of their objective—Cebolleta—caught a glint of a reflected light from a ridge along the base of the mountain. The uncertainty of whether they had really seen something or whether their tired eyes or some desert illusion had caused the flash vanished when it happened again, a minute later. "Contact," the pair screamed over their shoulder, pointing out the location.

While they waited for orders, they pulled their sweat-encrusted hats down on their heads out of fear of losing them in the pursuit. An unwritten tradition in the Dragoons was that any man who lost his hat in pursuit had to buy all the others a drink. They did not have to wait long. Thompson pulled up beside the men and after a quick assessment gave the command for the first two squads to push ahead at all possible speed while the third remained as security for the wagon. In a rare burst of emotion he yelled, "Go Dragoons!"

* * * * *

Having issued his own command, one that Larrañaga and James were more than happy to follow, Bisa was the first to reach the bottom of the arroyo where he quickly grabbed the strap of leather he'd placed around the blanket-wrapped bone and slung it over his back. By the time he'd done this, James and Larrañaga stumbled down into the arroyo and started to gather up their gear.

"No time. They have seen us. We have to get to the lava fields," Bisa commanded. James threw a questioning glance at a stunned and winded Larrañaga who shrugged in agreement. Larrañaga grabbed his pistol belt and saddle bag and James, rifle already in hand, slung it and a bladder of water over his shoulder and all three sprinted further down the arroyo to where their horses were tied to a pinyon. Bisa quickly untied all three sets of reins handed the others theirs. James had little bareback riding experience, but given their situation, he knew it was his only option.

Once they were up, Bisa let out a cry and the animals jumped from the arroyo. James did all he could to hold on. Larrañaga followed closely behind, keeping an eye on both young men, knowing that the loose sand and boulder mix of these foothills could topple a horse on a moment's notice.

Minutes later the ground leveled out and became

more hardpan; good news for the horses, bad news for the fleeing riders who no longer had any cover or concealment. It was two miles at least, Larrañaga knew, to the wagon-sized black boulders that marked the front edge of the lava field so detested by his Spanish predecessors. For the first time since mounting up, Larrañaga snuck a glance to the east and inhaled sharply when he saw the Dragoons less than a mile away, the disciplined, professional riders gaining ground with each step. "Rapido! Rapido!" the Spaniard shouted.

Bisa, by far the superior rider, pulled out ahead of his traveling companions, he and his horse moving as one over the hard, grama grass covered ground. Turning his head from side to side, his long black hair stood out directly behind him, his strong legs keeping him firmly in place as he scanned the black boulders for the size and shape of a rock he had committed to memory—one his parents had called 'the turtle' for its rounded back and skinny upward protrusion on one side. Motivated by the necessity of saving his friends, protecting the bone, and perhaps even finding his clan, Bisa silently encouraged his horse to go even faster. It did.

Larrañaga followed closely behind James, keeping worried eyes on the young man and the rapidly approaching Dragoons. James was in the fight of his life with the dark horse that seemed intent on slowing down or even stopping. The Spaniard pulled up alongside James and yelled, "Just hold on! Focus on Bisa!" James, breathless, simply nodded as Larrañaga pulled out his pistol, aimed it up in the air, and pulled the trigger.

No further motivation was needed; James' horse took off in a full gallop towards Bisa. *Como alma que lleva el diablo*—like a bat out of hell—Larrañaga thought. And that was good because the Dragoons were just about in range.

Moments later, the zing of poorly aimed bullets filled the air like buzzing insects in the wetlands. In perhaps a minute or two, Larrañaga figured, the Dragoons would be close enough to pull up and take well-aimed shots whose sting would be far worse than that of insects. At the same moment that realization coursed through Larrañaga's mind, Bisa, far ahead now, stopped next to a large boulder at the edge of the lava field. Larrañaga couldn't believe his eyes when the Navajo jumped off his horse and began shouting something and waving his arms to follow.

Larrañaga again pulled up alongside James, keeping himself between the young man and the Dragoons whose faces the Spaniard could almost make out and seemed to be slowing. "They think they have us," he said as the crack of a well-aimed shot sliced through the air close enough to Larrañaga's face that he felt the heat of the bullet as it passed. "Keep going, I'm going to buy us a bit of time," and with that, Larrañaga slowed his horse and hunched over, feigning that he'd been hit.

* * * * *

The pursuit was just about over, Lt. Colonel Thompson thought as the exhausted horses slowed and the excited

223

men whooped at the sight of the wounded Spaniard waving his hat in what appeared to be surrender. Knowing they had their prey cornered against the ragged black lava-strewn field that stretched as far as their eyes could see, Thompson, out of an abundance of caution, told his Dragoons to hold back while he scanned the boulders with his looking glass. He fixed his attention on the lead rider who had reached the edge of the field and dismounted. *Strange,* he thought. The second rider would reach the first any moment now. The commander lowered his looking glasses while his horse shifted underneath him. Were they leading him into a trap? Some sort of ambush? As Thompson began to raise his glasses once again, he saw the Spaniard resume his sprint towards the two others and gave the command to follow, but cautiously.

* * * * *

James, needing no encouragement to dismount, slid off the beast's back even before he had come to a full stop. Bisa pointed him to a two-foot-wide path between the turtle-shaped rock and another of similar size. "Give me your rifle and follow that path," Bisa's calm voice made it impossible for James to not do as his friend instructed. Bisa shooed the two spent horses away and shouldered the rifle, taking steady aim at the closest Dragoon some two hundred yards away. Larrañaga was coming in fast but wasn't out of the woods yet. It was going to be close.

When one of the Dragoons raised his rifle, Bisa pulled the trigger, dropping the soldier into a heap on the hard ground. This bought Larrañaga the time he needed. With a wild look on his sweaty face, the Spaniard hopped from his horse and followed Bisa's outstretched finger towards the path between the boulders. Bisa let loose one more well-aimed shot and fled down the path as well.

* * * * *

Lt. Colonel Thompson was furious, mostly with himself. Had they been just a bit quicker (or less cautious) on the march or faster on the pursuit, they'd have the Spaniard and be on their way back to Santa Fe.He could still see the ploy Larrañaga had used to buy his men more time, and shook his head in frustration, knowing he'd been bested. This time.

As the Dragoons caught their breath some hundred yards from the boulders marking the edge of the lava field, Thompson slapped his leg in disgust, the three riderless horses almost mocking the men in blue. One of them asked, "Are we going to go in after them, sir?"

"If we go in there we'd have to dismount. We'd be easy targets," Thompson replied with a tinge of misplaced anger that he regretted as soon as the words left his parched mouth. This failure certainly wasn't the fault of his men. No, this was all on him. As their leader, Thompson knew he had to fix this, or he would suffer the consequences—plain and simple.

Scanning the terrain with the hopes of finding a path that would accommodate their horses but finding none, he took off his hat and thought. The only thing that came to mind was to wait them out. Surely this trio could not hide in there for long.

"Grab their horses and let's pull back a bit," he ordered.

* * * * *

While Bisa led James and Larrañaga into the lava field, and Lt. Colonel Thompson and his platoon made for the cliffs to the north in search of a suitable vantage point, a great commotion erupted back in the plaza at Santa Fe. It had been five days since the Army of the West had taken their objective and General Kearny was quickly learning that for a professional soldier, conquering was much easier than governing.

Tuesdays, he had been informed by a rather insistent Father Ortiz, were traditionally "dispute settlement" day. And since the disappearance of Governor Armijo over a week ago, the Spanish, Mexican, and American settlers, the Indians, and travelers of all sorts in and around the Santa Fe area had been forced to put their disputes on hold until…now. Tuesday.

So, after breakfasting this morning, Father Ortiz set up something resembling a stage under the shade of the honey locust trees in the center of the plaza. Appropriate, Kearny thought, noticing the thorn-ridden branches as he took his appointed seat—one of two—behind a small desk atop the stage. A line of disgruntled people had formed under the overhang of the Governor's palace.

Father Ortiz, the self-proclaimed grand marshal of

this civil ceremony, the likes of which Kearny had never witnessed, let alone been a part of, ushered one of his scribes up onto the stage to take the other seat so that each case's participants, complaint, and resolution would be noted for the record. *Whose record?* Kearny thought. *I will not do this again.*

As the sun beat down on the plaza and the scribe noted the payment required to settle a dispute over a man's chickens that had been killed by another man's dog, the bass of hoofbeats caused all heads to turn in the direction of the arch gateway to the Plaza.

A platoon of Dragoons trotted proudly in with what looked to be a prisoner in tow. Kearny's heart leapt—both for his Dragoons' success and for the excuse to be done with the tedious civil proceedings. The commander of the Army of the West stood and adjusted his gold-star-emblazoned blue coat. Father Ortiz, doing his best to keep those in line at peace protested in vain. Kearny strode across to the Plaza to receive the platoon leader's report.

After returning the younger officer's salute he said, "Lieutenant, welcome back. Get your horses into the presidio's corral. See to your men and then meet me in the Royal Palace." The words 'Royal Palace' forced a raised eyebrow from the junior officer. "Is Lt. Colonel Thompson with you?"

"No sir. He's hot on the trail of the Spaniard, west of Albuquerque. Apparently this one," the lieutenant gestured over his shoulder, "had a run in with Larrañaga. We think he had a partner. By the looks of 'em they didn't make out too well. I'll be right over to give you a full debrief, sir."

General Kearny stepped back from the lieutenant and took a closer look at the prisoner. He'd seen soldiers of every creed during his career, but few had the look this one had about him. Like a caged lion, the prisoner looked both regal and capable of the kind of violence that filled nightmares. The General and the prisoner locked eyes and neither flinched nor spoke. *Interesting*, Kearny thought. The previous day he'd received word—and evidence—from his Dragoons that Father Ortiz had been up to something nefarious with a large sum of money.

Does the padre have an interest in the bone? Was this man somehow connected to Ortiz? Kearny hadn't yet said anything to Ortiz about this, figuring it best to keep your friends close and your enemies closer.

An idea took shape in the commander's mind. General Kearny turned and looked across the Plaza to the line of "citizens" and panned the crowd for Father Ortiz who had been there just minutes before. But he was nowhere to be found. "Corporal Sampson," the general said over his shoulder to the soldier he knew never left his side. "Please go find Father Ortiz and offer my apologies for having to cut those proceedings short. Tell him I request his presence in the Palace at his earliest convenience."

"Yes, sir," Sampson responded and quick-stepped off towards the cathedral.

* * * * *

The fecid smell of the century-old, two-stall jail wasn't getting any better for McClendon. Neither was the food the guards brought in twice a day. To the former professor who was more accustomed to defining schedules and activities, not having any control over his life was more painful than having teeth pulled.

Donovan continued to visit at random times of the day and night. McClendon figured it was intentional—designed to keep him off balance. Every time the brute of a man came in, he'd ask about the bone and Larrañaga and every time he stormed away with no more knowledge than he'd come in with. But other than the interactions with Donovan, McClendon's only company was the middle-aged mestizo.

Unlike McClendon, that man had no doubt of his future. The proclamation that he'd be hanged at mid-day on the 19th had come down the previous day. *Not a good way to die,* McClendon thought when he'd heard the news, but was there any way that was "good?" The historian in him knew the Spanish had introduced the practice of hanging criminals here well before America had even been a colony.

It seemed to McClendon, based on what he'd heard the guards discussing, that General Kearny was anxious to get back on the trail and that they'd be doing so on the 21st. *Three "wake ups",* as he used to joke with his wife, Annie. The "wake up" reference was a reflexive thought that propelled McClendon down the proverbial rabbit hole into his memories of her. What he loved most about Annie was how she made him a better person.

For her, there was no gray in life. Things were either good or bad, right or wrong. She had a deep-seeded passion for the good, the right, both in words and deeds. Posed with even the most complex dilemma, Annie could and would distill a solution, one based on what she called "unconditional positive regard." Her love for all and ability to overcome any obstacle bathed her in a light that few radiated, McClendon thought, a light that others wanted to follow—or run from if they acted selfishly.

She was also a truly captivating beauty. Her straight auburn hair was neither thick nor thin—it felt almost divine between his fingers when he had the chance to run them through it and provided a perfect frame for her oval shaped face, her blue-grey eyes. And her lips…how he loved the look and feel of her lips. McClendon closed his eyes and transported his thoughts across both land and time as he embraced her intimate presence.

A sharp clang against the metal bars brought McClendon back to his present predicament. The latch to the cell next to his, the one containing the doomed mestizo, opened and a man McClendon had never seen before walked in. The first thing McClendon noticed was the blackened right hand the man held close to his chest with his left. The second was the large, gold ring on his left ring finger emblazoned with what McClendon knew was a Latin cross, its descending arm longer than the horizontal one.

The ring caught the attention of the mestizo as well, who immediately crawled towards the man and reached out from a kneeling position as one might do for a priest, *or someone with royal blood.* Reflexively the stranger let go of his damaged hand and extended his left hand out to the man who took it between his own. Then he kissed the ring.

The familiar voice of Colonel Donovan snapped McClendon out of the fog he'd been in, watching the out-of-place scene of respect and devotion play out in the adjacent cell. "On your feet, McClendon. General Kearny has requested your presence," he said with disdain as he unlocked the cell. "You smell like you've been rolling around with the pigs. You need to get cleaned up first."

With that, he nodded to the guards. Surprised, confused, and most of all, ready for some kind of resolution, McClendon stood on shaky legs and walked out of his cell.

* * * * *

McClendon, cleaned, dressed in second-hand clothes not dissimilar from what he used to wear when working his fields, and appreciating the fact that he was sitting on a cushioned chair rather than the floor of a repugnant jail cell and drinking water from an actual glass rather than a bucket that served the dual purpose of latrine and trough, marveled at the Royal Palace's formal dining room that had become General Kearny's meeting place.

The paintings of conquistadors, priests, and governors on the walls, the cool and clean tile floor, and the grand, dark wood table made the former professor feel like he was right back at the College of Charleston. After a few minutes, Smythe came in and sat across from McClendon and raised his formerly crippled hand offering a wave more appropriate for a parade than … this. Colonel Donovan followed and sat two cushioned seats away from McClendon.

McClendon was about to say something snarky to the Dragoon commander when the great wooden doors to the dining room banged opened and the silent prisoner with the gold ring was escorted to the chair next to McClendon. The man's right hand was now bandaged, and in a sling. He rested his left hand on the table. Once again, the ring captured McClendon's attention.

"You are a long way from home, sir," McClendon said in low, drawn-out voice. When this did not provoke a response he continued. "Swiss Guard? One of the Pope's soldiers," he stated more than asked.

The surprise on the previously stoic prisoner's face was as unmistakable—and confirming—as the church bell that rang just before the prisoner arrived.

General Kearny strode into the room. "Gentlemen," he said even before both feet were squarely on the hard tile. "It's time for a little 'come to Jesus' moment. Wait—where is the padre?"

"Sir, he's just entered the Palace. He'll be here momentarily," clipped Corporal Sampson from just outside the ornate room.

"Very well," the commanding officer said, striding confidently around the table to its head. Kearny remained standing, eyes alternating from one man to the next. McClendon had admired and respected Kearny from day one, both for his leadership skills as well as his character. He didn't know whether he should apologize or extend a hand or just smile. He settled on an awkward wave of his own and felt his face redden with embarrassment.

Father Ortiz, sweating and, judging by his constant fidgeting, clearly anxious about something, shuffled into the great room. Kearny gestured the padre to the open seat between Donovan and the recently outed Swiss Guardsman. Kearny saw Ortiz nod ever so slightly to the man. *One question answered*, the commanding officer thought. All parties in place, General Kearny took a seat and placed his hands on the table.

"Gentlemen, something is going on here and no one will leave this room until we either figure out what that is or," Kearny stopped, letting that hang there. In the silence that followed, the commander's eyes shifted between Ortiz and the unnamed prisoner. "So, Father Ortiz, let's start with you. Tell me what you were up to in Albuquerque."

* * * * *

Thirty-three minutes later, Smythe noted in his journal, General Kearny held up his hands, open faced, towards the priest. "Enough. Father Ortiz, I didn't ask you here for a history lesson nor do I need an education in how the Catholics run their business. I specifically asked what you were doing with all that coin in the wee hours of the night."

Ortiz, having rambled seemingly without a breath for all that time now sat silently. "You leave me no choice, padre. Until you feel moved to *confess,* you're remanded to your church. You, sir, are dismissed."

Corporal Sampson emerged from the shadows of the corner of the room and guided the stunned priest out the door.

Turning to the silent prisoner, General Kearny continued, "Now. Let us start with introductions. I am General Steven Watts Kearny, Commanding officer of the United States Army of the West. Who, may I ask, are you?"

After a few moments, Colonel Donovan slammed his only fist on the table. "Sir, he's one of the Pope's bastards—soldiers. A Swiss Guardsman." As implications of Donovan's words sank in, Kearny turned to Donovan.

"And how, Colonel Donovan, did you come to know this with such certainty?" Now it was Donovan's turn to hesitate.

"Sir, McClendon figured it out," he stammered, his voice ripe with feigned humility.

"Is this true?" Kearny said, now speaking to McClendon who responded with a silent nod, held up his left hand and wiggled the ring finger. A hint of a smile broke out on the general's face.

Turning back to the prisoner, Kearny continued his interrogation. "What, pray tell, is a soldier for the Pope doing in United States territory?" Again, silence. Kearny's patience had run its course. "You leave me no choice, sir. I am putting you, under guard of course, on the next wagon train east. Our friends in Washington will surely have some…questions…for you."

With a wave of his hand, the two Dragoons who had

escorted the man in lifted him out of his chair and ushered him out of the room, leaving Donovan, McClendon, Smythe, and Kearny seated around the table. After the doors closed behind them, Kearny sat with hands folded in front of his face, eyes closed. Opening them, he continued.

"Colonel Donovan, thank you for your presence. It looks like your wound could use a fresh dressing." The indirect dismissal took Donovan by surprise, but nonetheless he stood, nodded to his commander, and took his leave, but not before casting an evil eye towards McClendon.

Turning to Smythe who, by the expression on his face was enjoying being a part of this circus as he'd later pen, General Kearny said, "Mr. Smythe, I'm going to take a different track with our friend here. I'm hopeful that with just the two of us we'll be able to have a productive conversation." This time the indirectness of the dismissal did not immediately register.

Corporal Sampson stepped forward and placed a hand on the older gentleman's shoulder. "Thank you, corporal," Kearny added. To McClendon's surprise, even the guards exited the room. Kearny walked around and closed the doors behind them. When he returned to his seat, he pulled out a piece of paper, and scanned it in silence. The former professor began to tremble. He too would later write about this moment, describing it as "life-changing."

* * * * *

After yet another harrowing escape from the Dragoons, Larrañaga and James followed Bisa through what felt like a maze of narrow pathways. They walked for over an hour along the ancient trails in eerie silence—even the wind that roared in their ears during the sprint across the desert floor seemed reluctant to enter this space. At high points on the path, they could see towering sandstone cliffs on the far western boundary of the lava field. To the north were the Chuska Mountains. To the east, far in distance, they could just make out the Sandias. And to the south they could see…nothing. It was as if the lava field stretched into eternity. With each step they seemed to be going deeper into the heart of what to James and Larrañaga felt like the most inhospitable terrain they'd ever encountered. *El Malpais is right,* Larrañaga thought.

A sudden screech snapped their attention to the sky. "That's a Buteo Regalis—what some call a Ferruginous Hawk," Larrañaga said, shielding his eyes from the brilliant sun, also noting the dark cumulus clouds to the northwest. "It is said they make that call as a warning, whether for their chicks or for…" He stopped talking when the piercing sound came again.

What the sharp eyes of the hawk saw would have surprised—even shocked—Larrañaga and James. The path they'd been following was a series of concentric circles with a large, dark opening at the center.

* * * * *

Sensing that wherever Bisa was taking them was close,

Larrañaga watched the two young men before him on the path as a father might over his own sons—or as that hawk might have over its chicks, both protecting and admiring. James had come a long way since he'd been discovered under the overturned wagon bed. Gone was the scared boy. In his place was a studious, open-minded, very capable young man who not only had survived several life-changing events but had learned and grown from them.

Larrañaga knew he himself had had a difficult time adjusting to this land, this life, and he *chose* it. For all intents and purposes, James had not. *Yes,* Larrañaga thought, *James will do well out here, will become a man of great character if we can steer clear of any more run-ins with soldiers or treasure hunters.*

Bisa too had changed. He'd only been a small boy when Larrañaga had crossed his path. From what the Spaniard had been able to piece together, a small band of Ute and European renegades had kidnapped Bisa and taken him up to the pine-laden forests of northern New Mexico. Early one spring, Larrañaga and Lalo stumbled on the small band and gave the Utes the smallpox vaccine. In exchange, the Utes offered the dirty, shivering, and undernourished Navajo.

At first, Larrañaga turned down the offer, not wanting to have anything to do with slavery. But Lalo wisely urged him to accept. "We can save him from this life, give him a purpose," Lalo had said. With all possible humility, Larrañaga knew they had saved the boy. The cleaner, warmer, stronger Bisa had decided to stay with the Spaniards when given the chance to go free. And in many ways, Bisa had saved them. He'd taught them the Navajo language and culture, educated them on the different Indian tribes, and even got them out of some tough situations. *I would not be alive if it were not for Bisa*, he knew.

The trail, descending now, turned sharply like a prairie dog's burrow. The twenty-foot tall jagged-edged walls closed in around them. The wind on the plain above them shifted and with it a beautiful noise—a song—enveloped the weary men, reminding Larrañaga of the tales the sailors told of sirens who lured ships into the rocks with beautiful songs. Larrañaga couldn't discern the source, but sure enough a soft, feminine voice emanated somewhere in front of Bisa. In mid-stride, Bisa froze and fell to his knees. Larrañaga and James, fearing the worst, ran to his side.

Bisa knew that face, that song. Both had resided deep in his heart for as long as he could remember and, now he was looking at and hearing them. The combination ignited a long-dormant love deep in the young man's soul.

He ran to the seated elderly woman who surprisingly didn't stop singing but did lock eyes with Bisa as he knelt before her. She cupped his now tear-streaked face in her hands, looked deep into her son's soul. Neither noticed the bluish glow of the bone slung across his back.

"Shima," Bisa managed to say. "Mother."

* * * * *

Larrañaga and James stood frozen in bewilderment at the

sight before them. The tearful reunion, the glowing bone, the mouth of a cavern large enough to swallow a wagon with countless, dimly lit faces looking on. Friendly faces. Tears filled James' eyes. How many times had he dreamed of embracing his own mother one more time? People of all ages slowly emerged from the cavern's depths as molten lava had thousands of years earlier. *Can this be real?* James looked at Larrañaga and thought. Larrañaga answered the unspoken question by putting his arm around James.

Standing together, Larrañaga and James watched as 'Shima' slowly stood from the rock she'd been sitting on and took Bisa into a full embrace. Her long gray hair was pulled back in a tight knot behind her head, her weathered face, high cheekbones, and dark eyes at the same time elegant and strong. She wore a brown blanket-dress laced together on the sides, allowing her sinuous arms freedom of movement. Nearly a foot shorter than her now full-grown child, Bisa's mother stood on her toes to place her head against the top of his shoulder. She fixed her mahogany eyes on the pair standing behind Bisa, silently thanking them both for returning her son.

A rumble from above the rock walls and a perceptible drop in temperature interrupted the moving scene. James watched as Bisa's mother stooped to pick up the half-made basket she'd been working on, placing all the dried grasses she hadn't used in its shallow bottom. She said something to Bisa and then beckoned Larrañaga and James to follow. Together, safe, they descended into what had, just moments before, been an almost impenetrable darkness. Now the glowing bone and radiant hearts lit the way.

* * * * *

Several miles to the northeast of El Malpais Lt. Colonel Thompson and the platoon of disheartened Dragoons sat in the shade of an overhanging sandstone ledge in the foothills of the dormant volcano. They too heard the screeching hawk and watched as the late afternoon thunderclouds advanced across the desolate landscape. *Everything is framed by perspective*, Thompson thought, looking at what he knew was a cloud thousands of feet wide and even more tall, but seemed the size of a tick on a dog compared to the amount of space the eyes could see. He watched the first drops of rain fall on and instantly evaporate from the hot rocks at his feet. *Just like the Spaniard—and the bone.*

Calling one of his sergeants, Thompson decided it was time to bring up his third platoon—the one he'd positioned on the south side of Albuquerque. He issued the order and began to formulate a plan. He had Larrañaga cornered somewhere out in that vast lava field. *I will not let them vanish again*, he said to no one in particular as more drops fell and evaporated.

* * * * *

Back in Santa Fe, Father Ortiz went through the motions of the Mass to a slightly larger crowd than usual, thanks to over a dozen new congregants: soldiers of the U.S. Army. He'd been somewhat surprised that out of what looked to be a thousand soldiers, only fifteen were Catholic. Ortiz knew that his role was to invite people to have a relationship with the triune God. *How much more effective would I be with the bone?* He thought as he held up the 'cup of life' and blessed it.

The meeting with General Kearny had not gone well. After he'd been so rudely dismissed, Ortiz stopped and prayed in front of the statue of Saint Francis adjacent to the steps to the cathedral. As he completed the Lord's Prayer, he'd heard the footfalls of two American soldiers who were to be his 'guardians.' *How dare that pompous Norteamericano restrict the movements of a man who had dedicated his life to God's work?* He thought.

A few minutes later, as Father Ortiz pulled a piece of bread from the loaf and placed it in the mouth of one of the soldiers, an idea began to form in his mind. For the first time that day, Father Ortiz smiled. *Perhaps this new following of Americans was a gift from God after all.*

* * * * *

El Malpais — 'the bad place.' Larrañaga saw in his mind's eye the name he'd written over the approximate forty by sixty-mile rendition of the area on the map he'd copied into his journal. The empty space on the map was an area he'd been warned by others to avoid at any cost. As his sunbaked eyes slowly adjusted to the cavern, his preconceived notions dissipated.

They'd been descending carefully on well-worn paths atop undulating, ropy black rock before Larrañaga realized that they were navigating a series of interconnected lava tubes. Hushed voices echoed off the cavernous walls, excited chatter mixing with apparent warnings advising him to watch out for sharp edges along the sides or potholes in the floor. After ducking underneath a low ceiling, he emerged into a great tunnel illuminated by light and surprisingly, water, from a large opening in the cavern's roof.

Larrañaga's eyes followed the water from the opening in the roof to the floor of the cavern. A deep and wide pool reflected the grey of the sky above. *Water attracts life*, Larrañaga recalled. He passed through another small portal and came to an even wider part of the tunnel—this one capable of fitting several wagons abreast. A hundred curious faces turned towards the new arrivals. Larrañaga remembered Don Bernado de Miera y Pacheco's description of 'finding' the deserted Chaco Canyon village. *Is this where all those people went?* He wondered.

While the Spaniard's mind attempted to grasp both the geological and human significance of the scene before him, Larrañaga and James were directed to a place to make their own. They watched as Bisa's clan wrapped itself around the young man like the tight-woven blankets the Navajo were famous for. At first everyone seemed to be talking *to* Bisa, filling him in on the lives of the people he once knew and loved. The storm overhead passed, and the brilliant turquoise sky emerged through the opening and with it the Navajo went silent.

Bisa cleared his throat and for the first time Larrañaga watched as Bisa's noble spirit came alive in the telling of his story. For the rest of the afternoon, Bisa lived up to his name as he told his mother and all the rest of the journey he'd been on, frequently pointing over at Larrañaga and James. The look on Bisa's mother's face as she smiled and nodded at the Spaniard at each mention of his name said more than any words could.

As James gave into the weariness that settled into his bones, he recalled a time many years ago when he and his father were fishing. Summer had come early to Charleston and even at eight o'clock in the morning the late-May temperature was close to 100 degrees, the humid air thick enough to cut with a knife. They'd been fishing since dawn and James hadn't reeled in a thing. After losing his bait for what seemed like the fiftieth time, the boy threw his pole down in frustration.

"James, do you know the difference between happiness and joy?" Jonathan McClendon asked.

Like any early teen posed with such a question, James rolled his eyes. "No, but I'm sure you'll tell me."

"In my opinion, happiness is dependent upon circumstances. For example, you'd be happy if you caught a fish. You'd be happy to have a cold glass of Mama's sweet tea in your hand right now. Those things are not under your control, so if they do not come to fruition—if our circumstances do not align with our desires, it is easy to be *un*happy.

"Joy, on the other hand, is a state of being. It's a deep, inner knowledge that even amidst circumstances we neither desire nor control, we are still loved. We are still valued." They sat in silence for a few minutes before the elder McClendon continued. "A very wise man named Paul who survived some of the most terrible circumstances a man could face wrote in a letter to the Romans, "For the Kingdom of God is not a matter of eating and drinking, but of righteousness, peace, and joy in the Holy Spirit.""

As James drifted off to sleep, Larrañaga felt like a protective blanket had been pulled over his soul. While finding the bone had been his proclaimed mission, Larrañaga realized that finding, getting to know, and doing life with Bisa and James — the good and the bad — was God's plan for him. He said a silent prayer of gratitude and knew in his heart that somewhere, somehow, Lalo was smiling down on them all.

13. August 19, 1846 — Santa Fe

In two days' time, the commanding general of the Army of the West would be leading the majority of his troops to their next—and final—objective: the Port of Los Angeles. *Not a moment too soon,* Kearny thought. Before finalizing his route of march, however, the commanding officer wanted to have one more conversation with his friend and renowned frontiersman. As he awaited Kit Carson's arrival, Kearny sat in a wooden rocking chair on the decked patio of the Governor's Palace.

Steven Watts Kearny lived and loved the life of a professional soldier. He'd spent two frustrating years at Columbia University before joining the New York Militia and the fight against the British in the War of 1812. He'd fought and led with distinction, earning both commendations from superior officers and the respect and trust of the men he led.

The only blemish on his record, if one could call it that, came from the aftermath of the Battle of Queenstown Heights where he'd been wounded and captured by the British. Kearny was a POW—a prisoner of war—for three agonizing months, held against his will on a ship in horrid conditions. He was eventually paroled and, after fully recovering from the ordeal, was offered the assignment he'd hoped for: that of a company commander on the frontier.

The unbroken horizons, imposing peaks, breathtaking valleys, and cliff-lined coasts called out to his soul. Before he left for his new posting, Kearny met the stepdaughter of William Clark of the Lewis and Clark expedition. She captured his heart and soon they married. Together they shared both the love of the west and the love of children—they had eleven, six of whom died in childhood. He hoped to bring all who could to California once this mission was over.

The thoughts of family brought Kearny back to the conversation he'd had the previous day with Jonathan McClendon. The former professor reminded Kearny of himself in many ways. An intelligent man with a passion for adventure and for his family, McClendon had demonstrated that not only could he adapt to new, challenging situations, he'd proven he could work with all kinds of people. He'd also proven himself capable of action.

As Kearny considered what fate should befall the former professor, he chose not to listen to his subordinate commanders' opinions. Many wanted him strung up like the mestizo. *No,* he thought, *that would not only be wrong but also counterproductive to the mission.*

Perhaps selfishly, the General thought, if he offered McClendon the opportunity to get out of this predicament with his life, the former professor would forever feel indebted to Kearny. *Shoot, he might even see his son again*. All of this had led the general, a master of putting the right people in the right place at the right time, to offering Jonathan McClendon the role of interim Governor of New Mexico. James Silas Calhoun, the politician from Georgia would be formally given the position by President Polk once the War with Mexico came to its inevitable, victorious conclusion for the United States of America, but until then McClendon could manage the administrative functions the role demanded.

A self-satisfied smile broke out on Kearny's face as he recalled how shocked McClendon had been when he first heard the proposal. Kearny concluded his prepared speech with a statement that made the choice not really a choice at all. He'd simply said, as he rounded the table and put his hand on McClendon's trembling shoulder, "Jon, there are two paths ahead of you. One path is very short and does not include even the possibility of reuniting with your son. That path serves neither of us well. The second path is as long as you choose it to be. And it offers you the chance to both reunite with your son and prove to me and the United States of America that, like your father and grandfather before you, you are an American patriot."

McClendon had been staring at his hands. After several moments of silence, the former professor stood and looked General Kearny in the eyes. "'I believe the true measure of a man is what he does with power.' Yes sir, I accept your proposal." Kearny knew the Plato quote. He also knew he'd played his cards well.

Two men who did not approve of Kearny's proposal

were Colonel Donovan and Smythe, but they didn't have to. They simply had to accept it, which they did, albeit under formal protest.

As Kearny rocked in the chair, he could hear the two very different but passionate men yelling at the prisoner, desperate for information about the Spaniard and the bone. Again, the beat of the footfalls of several horses redirected the general's attention to the gate of the Plaza.

"Good to see you again, General Kearny," Kit Carson said as he reigned in his horse. Behind him, on their own horses, were Carson's wife Josefa, their oldest two sons, and an older but distinguished mestizo Kearny hadn't yet met. Carson continued, "And this is Josefa's father, a prominent New Mexico businessman and landowner—Juan Felipe Ortiz." General Kearny's shoulders slumped noticeably at the man's surname.

* * * * *

Corporal Sampson had his hands full. The larger than expected Carson party had forced General Kearny—and therefore Corporal Sampson—to change what was to be an informal meeting across a table covered in maps to a formal mid-afternoon meal that out of necessity would have to include Señor Ortiz's troublesome son.

As a result, Sampson had to advise the cooking staff of the change of plans and to personally invite Father Ortiz. The first took only a moment. The second he did not look forward to.

Sampson pulled open the heavy wooden doors to the massive cathedral as the final hymn concluded, grateful not to have interrupted the service. He stood in the back and watched the diverse mix of congregants—Spanish, Mexican, Indian, and even some Americans— file out of the huge room.

While he waited for his opportunity to approach the priest, Sampson studied the seven intricately designed and expertly crafted stained-glass windows on each side of the room, the sunlight casting its radiant beams through the fourteen depictions of the stations of Jesus' final journey as a man. When the great room had finally emptied, he watched two army soldiers approaching Father Ortiz on the chancel—the stage, as Sampson liked to call it.

He'd been raised a Baptist and had listened to more sermons from fire and brimstone pastors than he cared to remember. The stout priest held out his hand for the soldiers, which they both, in turn, took and kissed. Then he led them into what seemed to be an office off one side of the great room, closing the door behind them. Sampson walked up the aisle, over to the door, and listened. He could just make out Father Ortiz's deep but hushed voice and imagined the man's already inflated chest growing even more so.

"The Pope himself has given us a very important mission my brothers. He rightly feels this…artifact…will pull people away from the La Palabra de Díos, the Word of God—and the message of the Holy Catholic Church. Out here, we have so many…distractions. Gods of rain and corn and then there's that kokopelli who our *Indigena* friends say brings stories, magic, and trinkets to those he visits. And where does any of that get us?!"

Sampson heard a fist strike something wooden and Father Ortiz's voice had become angry. After a few quiet moments, Ortiz continued, "As such, His Holy Eminence has ordered me to do whatever I can to retrieve that artifact, to include providing a handsome reward for any and all who help."

A creaking of the giant church doors behind him caused Sampson to duck down and hide in the shadows of the long wooden pews just a few feet from where he'd been standing. He strained to continue to listen to the padre's conversation with the American soldiers and was only able to catch a few words such as "prisoner," "wagon," and "Canyon," before deciding it was time to work his way along the outside of the pews to a side door he noticed on the way in.

Sampson's heart raced, knowing that he needed to get this information to the general ASAP. In his haste to do just that, he ran into one of the padre's assistants. After offering an apology, Sampson told the young man that he'd been looking for Father Ortiz and wanted to extend General Kearny's request to join him for a meal in the Governor's Palace.

* * * * *

The party from Taos gathered around the formal dining table where maps and canteens had been replaced with fine silver and large trays overflowing with food of the kind Sampson hadn't seen since, well, ever.

General Kearny took his seat at the head of the grand table, the heroic depiction of Coronado behind him on the wall. On one side sat Donovan, Smythe, and Mc-Clendon, whom he introduced to the guests as the interim governor of the New Mexico Territory, effective upon his own departure in two days' time.

On the other side Kit Carson sat closest to Kearny, alongside his wife Josefa and two sons, and the elder Ortiz. Sampson and another soldier stood along the wall.

"Corporal Sampson, were you able to get word to Father…" General Kearny started, only to be interrupted by Father Ortiz pushing his heavy frame through the door, sweat once again trickling from his brow.

"Apologies for my tardiness, señora y señores. Am I too late to offer a blessing for this feast?"

Kearny gestured for him to continue, casting an inquisitive eye towards Corporal Sampson.

After the meal, General Kearny invited the men outside for a cigar and the real meat of the conversation. Lighting his, Kearny said like a fisherman casting his line, "So tell me what I should worry about on this next leg of our journey?" Carson took the bait.

"The biggest worry you have is water and food. The fastest way there is the Old Spanish Trail which heads northwest out of Santa Fe, across the high desert plain of New Mexico and the Colorado Plateau, before descending into the Great Basin and crossing the Mohave

Desert. You'll need to pack a great deal of both for your horses and mules. Ever thought of taking camels?"

"Camels?" The general raised an eyebrow amidst a puff of sweet-smelling smoke.

"Yes, sir. Señor Ortiz here has been using camels to bring up goods from Mexico City for a couple of years now. You can load 'em down with 600 pounds *each* and they'll go ten times as far as mules without water. I've been trying to tell those *politicians* in Washington to get their hands on as many as they can but haven't heard a peep back. Juan Felipe here, he can get things done. He brought up another dozen from Mexico City last month. What's that bring the total to?" Carson asked the elder Ortiz.

"Cuarenta, mi amigo. 40."

Kearny smiled, knowing this next proposal would be key to his success. "Very well then. Señor Ortiz, I'd like to hire your camels and their drivers and Mr. Carson, I'd very much appreciate it if your lovely bride would allow you to accompany the Army of the West on this march to the coast. Your expertise would be invaluable, and you could bring Mr. Ortiz's property back once the mission is complete."

Father Ortiz, for the first time since the blessing, jumped into the conversation. "Gentlemen, I would very much like to join the march as well. I would certainly be of service to the men, am familiar with the terrain and the Indígenas on the proposed route, and I could also see to the safe return of my father's property."

General Kearny's face reflected both surprise and

conflicting emotions. He'd hoped not to have to broach the subject of the priest's shady dealings and recent reprimand and until now that hope had been realized. But if he rejected the offer he'd be forced to say why. Setting aside his personal disdain for the scheming man, General Kearny quickly weighed his options.

Father Ortiz, Kearny realized, had played his hand well. The general stubbed out his cigar, giving himself an extra moment to come up with the response most likely to contribute to the success of the mission.

"Yes, I think that is an excellent idea. But Father Ortiz, you must be able to keep up with us. We will be riding hard and cannot afford any unnecessary delays."

Turning back to the elder Ortiz and Kit Carson, he asked. "Are we agreed then?" General Kearny, anxious to have both his capable friend and the use of the camels in his kit, so to speak, extended his hand first to Señor Ortiz. With handshakes completed all the way around, Kearny turned to his former Dragoon commander.

"Colonel Donovan, I'd like you to take charge of the camel detachment and coordinate with Señores Ortiz on the details. Also, please get me an update on the status of the rest of the Dragoons. We'll need them to link up with us as well. Men," General Kearny concluded, "the Army of the West will depart on the 21st via the Old Spanish Trail. Thank you for coming today and Godspeed."

* * * * *

Alexander William Donovan fumed as the gathering dispersed. He'd lost more than an arm since the taking of Santa Fe. From the vaunted position of commander of the Army of the West's most elite unit to the babysitter of a loaded down camel brigade and a Catholic priest.

He had seen, firsthand, the power of the bone they'd found. Now, more than ever, he wanted it back. He wanted it all back. Yes, he'd agreed to execute the orders of General Kearny, but deep inside he knew he'd do whatever it took to get his hands on that bone.

* * * * *

Tucked safely inside what felt like the center of the earth, Larrañaga and James took the opportunity to catch up on some of the basics, like sleeping and bathing. It had been over a week since Larrañaga had been able to write in his journal, so he did that, bringing his well-traveled book up to date. He also sketched out a map of what he could remember of their journey inside El Malpais—something he figured might be useful to have someday.

James, having collapsed from exhaustion, was now clean, well-rested, and most of all curious. Deciding to explore the cavern, he crept away from the main area and walked quietly back into the shadowy depth. Small shards of white pottery along the edges of the path caught what little light there was and guided him through the narrowing space. Soft voices echoed from all directions, giving James a feeling of being surrounded by spirits. When he felt a hand on his back he jumped, nearly hitting his head on the ceiling.

"I thought I'd find you here," Bisa said. "Let me show

you something." Bisa shouldered past James and together they picked their way deeper into the cavern, the cool air beckoning them onward. After a while they came to what James could best describe—more from sense than sight given the darkness—was a caved in section of the cavern. James' outstretched hands felt the rough edges of huge rocks, heard the faint sound of his breathing bouncing off the closed walls around him.

"This is new. Two days ago this was open," Bisa whispered, his voice coming from all around. "This is the way to get out of the lava fields to the north and west. The way home. My mother says a great trembling in the earth caused this on the morning they were planning to return to our homeland. It was a sign, she said, that it was not time for her to leave. Had this not happened, they would have already left."

Stunned, James silently nodded. "Everything is connected."

* * * * *

Late in the afternoon, Larrañaga and James followed Bisa, his mother, and several others out to the mouth of the canyon. Bisa, as usual, walked with the bone slung over his back. As they approached the blazing sunlight, they shielded their eyes in silence for a few minutes. Once adjusted, the group climbed up a path on a rock that had toe-holds chiseled into it, onto the lava-field plateau. Warily, both Larrañaga and James scanned the horizon for any sign of the Dragoons.

They didn't see any and relaxed.

What seemed to hold the attention of Bisa's mother and the others, however, was the wide opening in the ground just a stone's throw away. A perfect circle with sharp, overhanging rims in the black, ropy lava that could swallow something the size of the church in Santa Fe. Bisa's mother indicated they should sit, so sit they did. In a voice that resonated both humility and wisdom she began to tell a story. Bisa translated.

According to our tradition, all life came from the feminine and all-powerful darkness. By life I mean all things—trees, birds, insects, animals, and of course, man and woman. At first this life was simply a connected awareness. Today's animals, plants, and people were like the mist: very much present and connected, but shapeless. The Great Spirits changed that—for us and for all things. They gave everything their physical forms and bestowed upon us a way of living through appreciation for all things.

Our ancestors made their way out of the darkness and into the light. Up from below. But that did not change our connectedness. Nothing except our own selfish thinking can do that. When we live in connection with all things, past and present, we are strong and can emerge out of any darkness. But when we become selfish, wanting more than we need, causing harm to others, forgetting the past and looking only towards the future, we step away from the connectedness and become lost and alone.

My clan came here to escape the sickness — the small pox — that the foreigners brought to our home. Many died. But is time for us to return, to rebuild, together.

So here we each sit together, having emerged from our own darkness. I ask you. Do you feel connected?

As she spoke her last word, the sun dipped behind the cliffs to the west and the sky took on an orange hue. The storyteller looked around the circle of people and began to chant, quietly at first, reminding James of Bisa's chant a couple of days back, of the elders at the pueblo. Different words and tone, James thought. He cast a quick glance at the bone strapped across Bisa's back just in case but didn't discern anything unusual.

With the suddenness of a lightning strike a screeching black cloud erupted from the hole in the ground. A near-solid mass composed of tens of thousands of bats beat their wings against the evening air as they emerged from their roosts below the sharp edge of the great opening. The small creatures flew as one in a tight circle mere feet over the heads of the seated people. The wind swirled; the air filled with chirping.

And just as suddenly as they emerged, all but one departed — off to the northwest. The largest one remained for a few moments longer, as if to ensure it had the attention of the gathering of people. And then it fluttered off, but this one headed east. A blanket of silence and stillness fell upon the gathering.

Bisa's mother picked up where she left off.

We have much in common with bats. The wings of each bat are unique, like the circles of hair on each horse, like the nose of each dog, like the tips of our fingers. Those all are unique; they set us apart. And sometimes we are meant to be apart. Like that lone bat, like Bisa has been. But we are better and stronger when we are together. When we are living with purpose.

Everything has a purpose — the plants and trees, animals and insects, and the people. This purpose is not something we decide, it is what we feel and do when we choose connection. The bats we just saw have and continue to fulfill their purpose of dropping seeds from fruit they've eaten so those seeds can grow and provide for the people. They eat the insects that bother us. And one more thing they do … they give us direction.

I invite you to sit here, with a grateful and open heart, and listen. Quiet your minds and hear all that has come before. Feel the life all around you. Bathe in the connection. Do this and you will know your purpose.

With that she promptly stood and stepped down the face of the rock they'd climbed, vanishing into the cavern. Her clansmen followed soon after, leaving Larrañaga, Bisa, and James beneath the first of the night's glittering stars. The orange sky in the west turned red and then purple as if preparing to embrace the rapidly approaching night sky. The three who had traveled so far and experienced so much together sat quietly.

Bisa was the first to stand and climb down the rock face. James followed a short while later.

Larrañaga hadn't expected any of this: James, the loss of Lalo, reuniting Bisa with his mother, being on the run with the bone. He'd started this phase of his life on a grand adventure, hoping like many Spaniards to find fame and fortune in the New World, hoping to find what his ancestor Pizarro had hidden from the military and religious establishments of his time.

He hadn't found fame or fortune, but that wasn't his purpose. He had found the mysterious, ancient bone and that, he thought, had been his purpose. But again Larrañaga realized that more importantly, God had led him to a place and people that sorely needed his presence. A peace settled over him unlike anything he'd ever experienced.

Larrañaga stood and stretched his tired and sore legs and back and realized those weren't the only tired and sore things. Without thinking he took a few steps in the direction the solitary bat had flown and again sat down. He'd heard the Navajo creation story many times, the progression of the Dine through the Four Worlds, but this was the first time he'd truly connected the similarities between his Catholic-Spanish beliefs and those of the Navajo. What Bisa's mother had said resonated in his soul more loudly than any church service he could recall.

What is my purpose now? Larrañaga brought himself back to the original question. His heart told him that he still felt personally responsible for Bisa and James, and as such should remain with them, protecting, teaching, and guiding the young men. But now that Bisa had found his mother and clan…Larrañaga's heart then focused on James.

The South Carolinian had a father out there, somewhere. A father who should know of his son's whereabouts and who should have the opportunity to see that son become a man. *But is he still alive?* He questioned. And then his heart turned to Lalo's son and wife, who he'd promised to return to.

Over the course of his journeys, Larrañaga had learned many valuable lessons, but one in particular now came to mind. One that had helped him navigate challenging and complex situations that could have overwhelmed him if he gave them that opportunity. *Do the next right thing,* he thought. *God has a plan and as long as I remain open to His will, I cannot go wrong.*

Amidst the silence and openness of the lava fields, the Spaniard quieted his mind to see where the 'river' would take him. The river, Larrañaga realized, was the *His*—God's—journey that meant so much to so many throughout history (*His story*). The Incans named that entity Viracocha and with it achieved great things that benefited all their people.

Francisco Pizarro had recognized this, had been willing to give everything to protect what remained of *Him*. Pizarro had done all he could to keep *Him* from certain destruction or even worse, keep *Him* from those who wanted to live as *He* did. And now the mysterious artifact that was as symbolic as it was tangible was in his well-traveled hands. At that moment, Larrañaga knew the next right thing was to see the bone get safely to where Pizarro had wanted it to go. His purpose crystallized, Larrañaga stood and descended into the cavern.

14. August 20, 1846 — Cebolleta

"Dawn on August 20, 1846…" Lt. Colonel Thompson scribbled at the top of a new page in his journal as the sun cast its first rays on the top of the volcano behind him. "The third Dragoon platoon has rejoined the second here at the base of what I am naming Mount Taylor after "Old Rough and Ready" General Zachary Taylor. Our force numbers 61 Dragoons, 2 Ute trackers, and 66 horses. One day water supply, three days' food rations, thirty rounds per man."

He paused, scanned the jagged plain of black rock and continued. "We are unable to pursue our primary target into the lava fields on our horses. As such, having watched and waited for the Spaniard's emergence for as long as our supplies permit, we will move north to our secondary mission—that of providing scouting support along the Old Spanish Trail for the advancing Army of the West."

Before riding away, Lt. Colonel Thompson turned one last time to the lava fields and said, "Our paths will cross again Spaniard. And next time…"

* * * * *

Just a few miles away, Larrañaga nudged James awake. The soul- and purpose-searching had sapped their energy more than expected. The Spaniard had caught more than a few hours of much-needed sleep, and his heart was once again focused on his purpose. As James rubbed the sleep from his own eyes, he looked into Larrañaga's.

"I remember when our paths first crossed, mijo, back in the Cimarron Desert, and you were just a boy who'd lost nearly everything—from the passing of your mother and sister to the leaving of your home, to the wreckage of your wagon train, and separation from your father. Do you remember telling me the reason you'd started on your journey?"

As Larrañaga spoke, James sat up, his head downcast. Larrañaga put his hand on James' shoulder and continued, "You told me that you and your father were looking to start a new life, one filled with adventure and, if I recall correctly, some kind of service. Sí? A more noble purpose does not exist. But noble purposes do not come without extreme hardships—look at what Jesus had to go through!

Someone once told me that a man who knows and remains focused on his "why" can bear with almost any 'how.' Mi hijo, we have been through much together. And we're not through it all yet. But you have proven that not only are you capable of looking after yourself, tienes un puro *corazón*."

James stood eye to eye with his protector, mentor, and

friend. Two very different, unique men who had found that more important than the differences were the commonalities — what they shared. James did not know where this heartfelt speech was leading but felt an overwhelming sense of gratitude. "I would not be alive if it weren't for you and Bisa and … Lalo. I owe you everything."

Larrañaga smiled compassionately, humbly, and continued, "James, I will travel with you to Canyon de Chelly to see that the bone gets to where my ancestor Pizarro wanted it to go. And then I will leave you. I must get back to Lalo's family, as I promised to do."

* * * * *

Hours later, Larrañaga, Bisa, and James stood with straight backs and renewed spirit deep within the cavern where the massive boulders blocked the subterranean passageway. Together they held the bone out to their front and together they started to chant. Soon the bone grew light in their arms and began to glow its blue hue. Their voices resonated throughout the cavern, bolstered by those of the rest of the clan behind them.

Miraculously, the rocks before them began to vibrate as the structures in Tewa Pueblo had, and with that vibration they too became transparent. The cavern grew brighter as light from the far side came through what had been a solid wall of darkness. Larrañaga, Bisa, and James took one hesitant step forward, and then another, and soon they and all the others walked through the vibrating, nearly invisible rocks into the open cavern beyond.

"Vamanos!" Larrañaga said with a contagious confidence as the threesome emerged from the cavern at the far northwestern edge of the lava field. The Chuska Mountains stood before them and somewhere deep within them, Canyon de Chelly. Bisa's mother and the rest of the clan filed past them, energized as they began their journey home.

"Soon, shi'kis—my friends—we will be back with all my people," Bisa said and, in a move that surprised both Larrañaga and James, handed the young man from South Carolina the re-wrapped bone. "And the bone will be safe."

15. August 21, 1846 — Santa Fe

General Kearny was up well before dawn with a child-like energy that he could feel in his toes. Perhaps it was the excitement of the adventure ahead that caused it. Or the leaving behind of the mundane administrative activities of a stationary army. Either way, as he dressed he silently acknowledged that while the Royal Palace had served as a fine place to hang his hat, he was glad to be leaving it behind. The palace — not the hat. He strode with a purpose out into the darkness to his waiting horse, calling Sampson as he did so.

"Bring me the sergeant in charge of the eastbound wagon. I want to bid our foreign friend adieu. And please awaken the professor. I want to get this ceremony over with and be ready to move out at first light."

While Sampson hastened away towards the Presidio, General Kearny mounted his horse and prodded it out the southern gate and up the hill to the east of the town. From there he could hear more than see the sounds of an army preparing to move. The sound invigorated him. Commanding an army, he knew, was his calling.

* * * * *

Dawn in Santa Fe, a moment most inhabitants regarded as a grand opening act of each day, found itself nearly upstaged by the lengthening arm of the United States and its conquering army. Men and horses loaded down with gear shifted nervously outside the arched gate. Inside the gate, the Plaza buzzed with activity. The wagon with the prisoner and several bundles of mail inside, and a handful of small trunks filled with artifacts strapped to its roof, began its eastward journey from outside the Presidio. Once clear of the Plaza, the platoon-sized command element of the Army of the West formed up in front of the Palace.

Interim Governor McClendon, begrudgingly recorded by Symthe, had already been sworn in on the steps of the church. And most importantly, at least to General Kearny, the Army of the West was lined up in their order of march and ready to go. Only the troops from the Mormon Battalion remained in place, ordered to ensure that Santa Fe did not fall back into Mexican hands.

From atop his horse outside the Royal Palace, General Kearny looked out at his army and issued his final order in Santa Fe: "Move out!"

* * * * *

After cresting the ridge at Glorietta Pass, the driver of the east bound, prisoner-bearing wagon slowly brought his four-horse team to a halt and engaged the brake handle. As devout Catholics, both he and the sergeant on the bench next to him silently traced the sign of the cross from their foreheads to their chest and shoulder to shoulder before jumping down and opening the wagon door.

One unlocked the shackles binding the prisoner's good/left wrist to the wagon while the other untied the horses. Moments later, with the wagon pushed over the edge of the trail, Jules launched himself up onto one of the horses and, with his two new partners in tow, turned around and headed back towards Santa Fe.

* * * * *

The professor/officer/governor, albeit interim, once again felt overwhelmed at the course his life had taken. Never could he have imagined *this*. As Governor McClendon sat down in the same chair as General Kearny had used in the formal dining room—the one beneath the depiction of Coronado—an image appeared on the horizon of his mind: *James*. From somewhere deep inside, McClendon heard a voice repeat something he'd read; *the two most powerful warriors are patience and time.*

The sound of boots on the wooden floor outside the dining room snapped McClendon out of his stoic contemplation. A company commander and a young sergeant from the Mormon Battalion strode purposefully through the open doors of the dining room. This was the normal routine, General Kearny had told the interim governor. Every evening at sundown he'd receive a report on the events of the day. But the manner in which the two men burst into the room betrayed the likelihood that something outside of the "routine" had happened.

Standing to greet the soldiers, the freshly shaven Governor who wore a new brown herringbone suit and white shirt—all gifts from Juan Felipe Ortiz—said, "Good evening, gentlemen, what do you have for me?" he asked, using his best professor's voice.

"Governor," the blond-haired captain with a sun burned face said, "A west bound caravan just pulled into town and reported seeing the wreckage of a wagon near Glorietta Pass. I had some of my men check it out and it is, without a doubt, the wagon that pulled out of here this morning with the prisoner. There was no sign of the prisoner or his escorts." As McClendon opened his mouth to speak, the officer continued. "I've told a platoon to head out that way at first light to scout around for any sign of them."

"Understood, Captain. Sounds like a solid plan. Anything else?" McClendon asked, trying to disguise the worry that started to creep into his mind like the evening's shadows across the Plaza.

Now it was the sergeant, who upon closer inspection could have passed for the captain's younger brother, who spoke. "Yes sir. We've just received word from Lt. Colonel Thompson of the Dragoons." The stiff collar around McClendon's neck now feeling a size too small. "He advised that he and his unit are on their way north along the east side of the Chuska Mountains to reunite with the Army of the West."

McClendon tugged at the constrictive collar and

leaned forward, waiting—hoping—for news of Larrañaga, of his son, but none followed.

"Thank you, Captain. Sergeant. Good work. I appreciate you and your men. Please keep me posted on any further news on either of those fronts."

* * * * *

At that very moment, thirty miles to the northwest along the Old Spanish Trail, General Kearny finished documenting the progress of the Army of the West in his journal. They'd successfully linked up with Colonel Donovan and the detachment of supply-bearing camels and made their way across the Rio Grande. With the faint outlines of the San Juan mountains to their north and the sunbaked, high desert plain to their west, Kearny stood from his field table and chair, stretched, and said a silent prayer of thanks for being back on the trail.

Corporal Sampson approached. "Good evening, sir. Might I have a moment of your time?" After a few minutes of hushed conversation about Father Ortiz's secret meeting with the soldiers in the church, Kearny removed his hat and looked up as the first of the night's stars made their appearance. *And the drama continues*, Kearny whispered to himself. *But at least he's not my problem anymore.*

16. August 22, 1846 — Albuquerque

The Pope's soldier rode west as quickly as the horse, terrain, and Mormon Battalion patrols they had to avoid permitted. When they finally arrived at the crossroads town of Albuquerque, tired and with worn out horses, they made their way to the church near where the meeting with Father Ortiz had taken place. The man known as Jules went inside while the other two who'd been told to find fresh horses made their way into the saloon across the street.

Two hours later, Jules walked out of the church, frustrated that the men Father Ortiz had enlisted to help him were nowhere to be seen. Neither of the two could compare to Auguste but he couldn't do this alone, and pride kept him from sending for more help from the Diocese in Durango.

The American soldiers initially demonstrated a willingness to support the Pope's wishes and had greedily accepted the offer for more money than they'd make in a year with the Army of the West in exchange for a month of their time. But now they were nowhere to be found. *All these men are the same, their actions and values align with whatever or whomever gives them the most pleasure today, rather than God's eternal promises,* he thought as he crossed the street towards a bar. *At least that makes them easy to understand. And manipulate.*

As Jules approached the bar's swinging doors, the sound of a fiddle filled his ears. In all his years and travels in service of the Pope, music had been Jules' one true escape from the violence and oftentimes boredom that comes with being a soldier of God. He'd tried several times to learn how to play the violin as its notes both soothed and excited his soul. As he listened to the fiddle—a cheaper version of the violin and thus more accessible to the masses—he detected an interesting blend of British, African, and Indigenous progressions, all synthesized into one melody. *Beautiful,* he thought.

Finding the two men and a half-empty bottle of some dark liquid in the back corner of the bar, Jules pulled up a chair and outlined his plan. When he finished, he placed two small bags full of silver coins on the table, one in front of each man and concluded, "Together we will do what no Supreme Pontiff has been able to accomplish for three centuries. This is your first payment. You'll receive the rest once we take possession of the bone." The men nodded in agreement, refilled their empty glasses, and called to the barkeep for another glass.

"No thank you. I will bid you adieu for the evening. Meet me outside the church tomorrow at dawn. Do not be late—and do not forget the horses," Jules commanded.

* * * * *

The Old Spanish Trail—Viejo Sendero Español—was first documented in the late 16th century and served as a means to connect Spanish settlements in Santa Fe with those along the southern California coast. It followed the 37th parallel (north) out of Northern New Mexico and across the Colorado Plateau before turning southwest into the Great Basin and the Mojave Desert beyond before emerging into the coastal lowland area within sight of the Pacific.

The approximately 700-mile-long trail tested even the most experienced early travelers with sharp mountain ridges, plummeting canyons, and bone-dry deserts. It wasn't until the early 19th century that the Old Spanish Trail became a regularly traveled route of commerce. John C. Fremont and Kit Carson were amongst the first Americans to cross from Santa Fe to Los Angeles, using the Old Spanish Trail, in 1844.

* * * * *

"The second time is always better than the first," Kit Carson joked to those within earshot as the lead element of the Army of the West emerged from a wide, dry riverbed onto a barren mesa. Through the dusty haze to the north, several 14,000-foot peaks poked into the turquoise sky. "Except in the case of marriage. My second lasted barely a year. Her native name was 'Making Out Road.' Well, she hit the road pretty darn quick."

Chuckling, General Kearny turned back to assess the progress of the slow-moving but all-important camel detachment that had just descended into the riverbed. "Let's hold up here for the night," he said to his entourage. "Those camels move slower than molasses. Corporal Sampson, please head back and inform Colonel Donovan that he can hold his detachment on the near side of the riverbed for the night."

Kearny felt a twinge of sadness for Colonel Donovan, but knew if he could fully recover, he'd have his cherished Dragoons back.

The jury is out on the 'camel experiment,' Kearny wrote later that evening, *and it likely will be until the conclusion of the mission. The amount the beasts can carry is astounding, but their speed, especially for a former Dragoon like me, leaves a great deal to be desired. Interesting, though, that the dozens of camel drivers, as well as the beasts themselves — Camelus dromedarius Linnaeus — were "imported" through Mexico and Spain, having started their journey in the Middle East. Their language and customs remind me a great deal of the natives here. And they appear to be right at home here.*

17. Early September 1846 — Tsegi/ Canyon de Chelly

Are you the same hawk? **James' inner voice asked. It** drifted high overhead on invisible yet ever-present updrafts, casting its shadow on the sheer cliffs of the place the Spanish named Canyon de Chelly. Larrañaga and James brought up the tail of the procession and tried in vain to pacify the anxious, even disdainful looks they garnered from the Navajo who were tending crops, sheep, and goats along the canyon floor. *That hawk may be a regular here, but people like me clearly aren't. At least not yet,* the South Carolinian thought and nervously smiled at a couple of children who stood as still as statues, watching.

They'd entered the mouth of the canyon an hour earlier where the red walls were only thirty feet tall and the river wash that had cut the canyon like a knife through butter finished its journey west off the high desert plain and angled north where it fed into the San Juan and Colorado Rivers and end its journey in the Gulf of California. As the weary travelers continued to wind their way deeper into the canyon, the rock walls that might have been easy climbs at the entrance now stretched straight up a thousand vertical feet. The height and proximity of the north and south rims flipped the tables on the 'normal' reality of the high desert plain; instead of the vast, open sky all that was visible above was a sliver, a proverbial river of cloudless turquoise. Instead of being surrounded, front and back and side to side by blue tones, every shade of brown from bisque to bistre enveloped them. James was quick to notice that any significantly sized crack or crevice on the walls contained some type of mud-brick structure. Some were as low as the canyon floor while others were mere feet below the rim.

"Tsegi," Bisa said as he rejoined his friends at the back of the clan. "Pronounced TSay-ih." He repeated the word phonetically and continued, raising both arms in an animated gesture that took both Larrañaga and James by surprise. "The literal translation is 'inside the rock.' These are my people," Bisa said in what James sensed was a mixture of pride and sadness. "The Dine have lived here for many generations. You can see — life is bueno Larrañaga! Here along the wash, you see our fields have the same crops as the Tewa: the 'three sisters' of corn, beans, and squash. We also grow cotton — for weaving baskets and clothing. You see those trees over there?" Bisa pointed. "Peaches! Down here we hunt rabbits and deer and above the rim the antelope are plentiful."

They rounded a corner deep within the winding canyon and a herd of fine-looking horses came into view, all grazing on wild sagebrush near the base of a rock formation. "Wild horses. Fast and smart. I will catch you one!" Bisa proclaimed. "And that is 'Sleeping Duck Rock.' There are tunnels behind there," his jovial laugh echoing off the canyon walls.

Something had changed in Bisa over the course of their thankfully uneventful journey from the lava-fields, Larrañaga and James realized as they listened to and watched their companion. *The contrast is incredible,* Larrañaga thought, *like this place.* Bisa had been silent most of the way here, especially when they'd walked across the field by the trading post where he'd been taken from his clan. But as Bisa enthusiastically pointed out plants, rock formations, carvings, and cliff dwellings, Larrañaga realized he had done so not as slave or servant, but as a Navajo who was *home.* As if to put an exclamation point on this, Bisa nudged Larrañaga and pointed to a petroglyph twenty feet up on the wall. A series of concentric circles emanating from a central point.

"El cículo de la vida," the Spaniard whispered.

Bisa nodded, a knowing smile on his face. Turning, he pointed in the direction they were heading, towards a towering cliff tucked behind yet another bend in the canyon. *This is like a maze,* James thought. *No wonder they've lived here for so long. No one can find them!*

James tried not to trip while gawking at the crumbling structures tucked high up into a ledge on the cliff's face. Minutes later, he saw a second set of dwellings a few hundred feet up from the canyon floor. Both were devoid of people, standing like silent guardians over Bisa's clan. That silence was shattered as a final set of dwellings, these on the floor of the canyon, came into view and a cacophony of joyful screams resonated all around the canyon floor. People poured out from the dwellings and the fields around them like the bats from the cavern back in the lava field. Larrañaga and James stopped and watched as Bisa and those who'd left Tsegi reunited with the rest of their people. A twinge of sadness, of longing for his own home coursed through James' heart like the river in the canyon.

Seeing the change in James' demeanor, Larrañaga stepped close to the young man and said, "An important lesson here, mi hijo. I too miss where I grew up. But in my opinion, *home* is wherever you are surrounded by people you love, people you can depend on who tell you both the good and the bad, who help you become all that you are meant to be—even if that means great sacrifice.

"You've seen some excellent examples of that, from your father who put on a uniform to find you, to Lalo who told you to save the bone and yourself just in the nick of time, and to Bisa who rode like the wind to lead us into lava field."

Larrañaga motioned towards a flat rock, walked towards it, sat down, and beckoned James to do the same. "I believe our paths crossed for a reason, James. Before I left my home in Spain, I believed that the most important mission was to find this…bone…and bring it to my Queen," he said and patted the bundle tied across James' back. "Only after I began interacting with the Indians and Mestizos, only after bearing witness to all of their pain and suffering did I begin to understand that my real mission was much bigger than that, just as it had been for my ancestor Francisco Pizarro. Ciertamente—I'm grateful we found the bone, but for me, and I know Lalo felt the same, reflecting God's light and love on others, bringing hope to people in a world full of...terrible difficulties...that is the only true mission.

I've tried to do this as a doctor and as a...father and friend...for both you and Bisa. And now, it is my opinion that God wants you to find way to do the same, find people you can share your pura corazón with. James, I believe you are *el hombre mas capaz* to not only protect the bone but use it and what is inside you to help others believe in...something bigger...than themselves."

The words and message resonated deep in James' heart. The happy sounds of reunion diminished, replaced with the confirming whispers of the ancients channeled through the wind and water coursing through the canyon. James had heard that same message before, many times, from his mother: Reflect His light and love. "I can do that."

Bisa ran excitedly towards them. "Come! There are people I want you to meet!"

* * * * *

Back in Santa Fe, Governor McClendon emerged from the cathedral feeling refreshed and restored. *Refreshed* because while he had not been raised as a Catholic and as such did not know how to react to some of their traditions, he hadn't been to a service since leaving Charleston and the service the young Spanish priest who'd come in from Durango had overseen had enough in common with his own that he felt connected.

Restored because God had always been his and Annie's compass. In this land, he knew the compass was often the difference between living and dying. He'd witnessed the disastrous results of others' actions when they'd acted solely in their own interests. The priest's concluding message today struck a particular chord with Governor McClendon. He'd said, quoting Saint Augustine, "It is no advantage to be near the light if the eyes are closed."

Well, McClendon thought, *the events of the past couple of months have proven both His existence and the need to keep my eyes and heart open.*

The interim governor had made the decision to spend as much time as possible with the people; listening to, learning from, and, where possible, helping make their lives just a little easier. Jonathan McClendon, as a husband, father, and professor, had experienced tremendous satisfaction in being in relationships with others—and that had been difficult while as an "officer" in the army where rank and pedigree seemed more important than what was in someone's heart or mind.

As a result of his connection-based approach, Governor McClendon was welcomed into the homes of Spanish and Mestizo settlers and invited to participate in Puebloan celebrations and ceremonies in the large villages of Taos and Santo Domingo as well as numerous smaller ones around Santa Fe. He'd also managed to plant a very important seed: he was looking for James and his travel companions. The people he wanted to help also seemed to want to help him. *Funny how that works,* he ofen thought.

Shielding his eyes from the bright, mid-day sun, the Governor strode across the Plaza to the marketplace just outside the Royal Palace where a few dozen local vendors set up "shop" on blankets and makeshift tables. They offered colorful blankets and baskets, jewelry, tools, and his personal favorites, fresh vegetables and the pan-fried bread that had helped him put on a few pounds since coming across the country.

Time permitting, McClendon liked to visit with each vendor and did his best to spread his purchases out amongst them, but when he saw the familiar face of an old man from Jemez Pueblo who always had delicious food, McClendon unconsciously rubbed his belly and approached him. "For some reason, Church always makes me hungry. What do you have today?"

"For you señor, I have something special." Reaching back into a covered basket the old Puebloan picked up a bundle of something wrapped in a colorful cloth. He set the bundle on the table and began to unwrap it. As he did, McClendon's eyes fixated on the depiction on the cloth—it was of a scene, a place. "These are what we call *tuna,*" the old man said. Noting the look of confusion on McClendon's face, he continued, "It is made from Prickly Pear Cactus. We remove the thorns from pads, cut them into strips, and boil them in water. They are very sweet. Please, try one."

McClendon slid one into his mouth, his taste buds

exploding in delight as he devoured the sweet treat. He picked up another and took his time with this one.

"We also use this to make jelly. Would you like some?"

"Yes…por favor!" McClendon struggled to communicate after regaining control of his overwhelmed tongue. *I haven't tasted anything like this since…Annie cooked for me,* he thought, a tear—either from his memory or his overwhelmed taste buds—tricked down his cheek.

He reached into his vest-pocket, pulled out a silver coin, and set it down on the colorful cloth, his eyes lingering. "What is that place?" McClendon pointed at the depiction and inquired.

"Ah, that is the home of the Dine. Tsegi. It is a place muy especial. Sacred."

Governor McClendon set two more coins down on the table, his mind grasping at, trying to connect, what the old man was saying with a sensation that was rising in his heart. "Where is this place, Tsegi?"

"In the direction of the setting sun. A week's ride, mas o menos. But it is hidden. Very hard to find, señor." The old man beckoned McClendon to move closer and placed his hand on the governor's shoulder. "It is not far from the Hopi village of Oraibi—but you cannot go there. 'New people' are not welcome," the old man warned and then did something that surprised McClendon—he handed the McClendon the cloth.

"Muchas gracias. Por todo—for everything—señor."

* * * * *

Colonel Donovan desperately wanted to regain the command of his beloved Dragoons. The broad-shouldered, ruddy-faced officer who'd lost an arm over a month prior, no thanks to Jonathan McClendon, now rode at the tail end of the Army of the West, his face almost painfully caked in the dust kicked up by thousands of boots and hooves to his front.

Instead of leading elite troops at the cutting edge of the army's sword, his orders were to keep an eye on a fat padre and the pack of slow-moving and ill-tempered camels. *They're not the only ones in a foul mood,* Donovan thought as his horse walked into some rare shade; the bluff they'd been following for miles on the north side of the monsoon swollen San Juan River now directly overhead.

For the past week, the Army of the West had followed what Kit Carson explained was the first leg of the Old Spanish Trail. They'd spent almost a week on the northern edge of the high desert plateau in New Mexico before crossing the San Juan River into Colorado, the 14,000-foot snow-capped peaks the only witnesses to their progression. It was there that Lt. Colonel Thompson and his Dragoons who'd been pursuing the Spaniard, and the bone, rejoined the Army of the West and reported negative results.

This had infuriated Donovan. *I wouldn't have let them get away,* he seethed. A few miles to the southwest of their crossing point they'd seen a rock formation that resembled a ship's sails jutting high up from the desert floor. "Shiprock," someone had called it.

It was near there, one night, that Donovan had seen Father Ortiz sneak away from camp. He'd followed the wily padre down to the riverbank where three shadowy figures waited for him. The rushing water masked their voices, but Donovan thought he detected something familiar in the accent of the man who spoke with Father Ortiz.

From there the army continued west into the Utah Territory. Occasionally word would come down the line that natives had been spotted on a ridgeline or plateau far in the distance, but they'd quickly vanish into the seemingly endless landscape. *Lots of good hiding places here,* Donovan noted more than once.

With a mind fueled by resentment and, although he'd never admit it, fear, he decided to do his best to befriend the pious man and prod him for information. *Keep your friends close and your enemies closer,* he reckoned.

"Colonel, look—there it is," Ortiz said from atop his horse alongside Donovan's. They'd been talking about waterways, how the San Juan River served as a major tributary to the Colorado River and also marked, according to native lore, the border between Navajo and Ute territory. Knowing that water meant life and the absence of one meaning the absence of the other, Donovan asked about other sources of water in the area. That was when Father Ortiz told him about and pointed to what the Navajo called "Chinle" wash. "Chinle—means 'flowing out.'"

Sitting as high as he could in his saddle, Colonel Donovan scoped out the area to the southwest that Ortiz pointed towards. The setting sun was a glowing ball of red hanging low on the horizon, which made discerning anything more than a strip of what could only be water reflecting the sun's glare impossible. *Lots of good hiding places...*

Later that evening, after making camp, cleaning weapons, looking after the horses and camels, washing, and eating, Donovan finished adding the Chinle wash to the rough map he'd sketched in his journal—not an easy task for a man with one arm. He stood and stretched, deciding to follow the unmistakable sound of Father Ortiz snoring to where the sleeping man reclined against his saddle. Nudging him with the pointy toe of his boot, Donovan knelt down beside the padre and showed him the map he'd drawn. "You said this Chinle wash means 'flowing out.' What does it flow out of?"

Reluctantly, Father Ortiz sat up. "I've never seen its source, but somewhere...here," Father Ortiz said, pointing at an area almost due south of their present location. "My Navajo friends tell me that somewhere in there is the fabled Tsegi—or as the Spanish call it, Canyon de Chelly. The Chinle, I believe, flows out of that place. No non-Navajo has ever been there, or, rather, has ever come back alive from there. I cannot think of a better place..." Father Ortiz stopped talking abruptly.

"A better place to hide," Donovan completed the sentence.

Ortiz realized he'd crossed a line and did not say anything for a few moments, his mind searching for how best to continue. "Especially if he who wanted to hide had native friends," Father Ortiz said quietly, realizing that perhaps this disgruntled officer might be *useful* in his desire to retrieve the bone. The two men of vastly different worldviews and backgrounds spoke in hushed voices until the first glow of light emerged in the east.

* * * * *

"Nakai," James repeated slowly, questioningly, doing his best to get the pronunciation right. A Navajo elder named Narbona had listened intently to Bisa's animated telling of his journeys and had pointed at the South Carolinian and said "nakai."

"It means one who wanders around," Bisa said.

"Well, I reckon you are right, sir. Course, it seems like we've all been doing some nakai," James laughed as the light of the fire cast their long shadows on the petroglyph covered sandstone walls behind them. The juxtaposition of old and new did not go unnoticed—or unfelt. The night was almost chilly in the depths of the canyon.

Chief Narbona laughed at this as well, clearly understanding what James had said. He sat slightly apart from Bisa's extended family, whether out of deference to Bisa's clan or something else, James wasn't sure. Perched on a higher ledge than anyone else, they'd all gathered to hear Bisa's story. Narbona had steely grey hair tucked into a headband, a Romanesque nose, and a colorful blanket wrapped around his shoulders. He'd joined the festivities earlier in the day, bringing with him several sheep as gifts to Bisa's mother.

Later that evening, James would learn from Larrañaga that Chief Narbona was no stranger to wandering. In 1822, Larrañaga explained to James, Narbona and fifty warriors traveled to the Santo Domingo Pueblo under a flag of truce to discuss territorial boundaries with the New Mexican governor. But it had been a ruse, a fact Narbona realized too late. Twenty-four warriors under his command who had laid down their weapons were butchered by the Mexicans. Chief Narbona had barely made it out alive.

In the twenty-four years since that bloody day, Chief Narbona largely focused his time and attention on caring for the physical health and spiritual well-being of his clan.

But Narbona, born in 1766 to the Tachíí'níí clan (Red-Running-Into-The-Water People), was neither a recluse nor a pushover, Larrañaga further explained. He'd ushered in great prosperity for his people by taking valuable livestock from Spanish and Mexican settlers. He'd also gathered many historically and spiritually significant artifacts and hidden them deep in the canyon in a place, according to Bisa, called the Cave of the Ancients. The Mexican Army did occasionally venture into Navajo territory and when they did, it did not end well—for the Mexicans. In 1835, just to the east of Tsegi at a place now called Narbona Pass, the Navajo chief and 200 warriors ambushed—and decimated—an entire Mexican expedition not too dissimilar in size to the Army of the West.

As the night wore on and Bisa's clan retired to what they called their hooghan nímazí, which means 'round home,' Narbona stood to leave. But before he did so he beckoned to James and Bisa who quickly got to their feet and approached the chief. Seeing this, Larrañaga quietly stepped away knowing that he'd need a good night's sleep before heading out in the morning.

"Let us meet tomorrow, at the canyon floor below the Cave of the Ancients," Chief Narbona said to the young men in a low voice that seemed to emanate from deep inside.

* * * * *

As the stars faded and the canyon walls caught the first rays of morning light, Larrañaga sat with his toes in the river, having just finished a much-needed bath and a painful but necessary shave. Smooth-faced and clean-smelling, he slid on a new pair of moccasins and white shirt the Navajo had given him before pulling another gift—a flat brimmed hat—over his salt and pepper hair. As Larrañaga looked at his reflection in the slow-moving water, he smiled at image looking back at him, especially as he realized that his hair was now more salt than pepper. *No te preocupes, Señor Larrañaga*, he said to himself and smiled. *Pareces un hombre nuevo.*

After the previous evening's stories had come to their necessary conclusions and the young men had retired to their hogan, Larrañaga had approached Narbona wanting to catch up with his old friend. They'd known each other for years—Narbona had led him and Lalo to every Navajo village to vaccinate the Dine. During those early days, they'd learned a great deal about each other as individuals and their respective peoples, values, and be-liefs—and they'd found that they had more in common than they'd thought.

Each considered himself a humble shepherd, but each also stood strong in the face of wrongdoing. In their own ways, they wanted to make the world a better place. Now older and perhaps a bit wiser, Larrañaga and Narbona spoke quietly and sincerely about their experiences since last seeing each other, both the good and the not so good. When there was nothing left to say, Larrañaga stood and somberly informed Narbona that the previous year the Mexicans had put a 'dead or alive' bounty on the Chief's head. Narbona reacted with stoic resignation and said, "Until the hunted learns how to write, every story will glorify the hunter."

After quietly readying his horse in the soft, pre-dawn glow of light in the small strip of sky visible above the canyon rim, Larrañaga tucked two folded pieces of paper that he'd ripped from his journal, one with Bisa's name and the other with James', into the side of the hogan they slept in and, in a well-practiced move, mounted the horse Chief Narbona had provided. With a tip of the hat and bottom eyelids swollen with tears, Cristóval Maria Lar-rañaga turned his horse and followed the water out of the canyon.

* * * * *

They'd known Larrañaga planned to leave, but as Bisa and James walked deeper into the canyon in the morning light towards where Chief Narbona had instructed them, they did so in silence. As if in defiance, neither young man had opened his letter. Like Larrañaga, James had been gifted a pair of new moccasins, a fresh shirt and trousers, and a flat-brimmed hat. But he decided not to wear the hat, opting rather for a strip of his old shirt that he'd cut and now used as a headband, mimicking that which Bisa wore. *When in Rome…* he smiled. The bone, still wrapped in its casing, hung across James' back like an arrow quiver.

"Do you think we'll ever see him again?" James asked, and before Bisa could respond, the South Carolinian pre-empted him with, "Yes. The circle of life."

"El círculo de la vida."

* * * * *

Chief Narbona sat, as deep in contemplation as he was in the canyon, 300 feet vertical beneath the Cave of the Ancients. In this place that the Navajo and Anasazi before them called home, the wind never ceased its whispering and those with open ears could always discern something from its timeless wisdom. The water, however, came and went, depending on the season and amount of rainfall. So too will the Dine, Narbona thought, just like the Anasazi.

Before walking up into the canyon towards the Cave of the Ancients this morning, three of his best hunters returned from a venture up above the rim. The hunt had been successful, but the bounty was overshadowed with the news that the 'New Men's' army set up camp north of

Tsegi, where the Chinle met the San Juan. *Perhaps they will pass uneventfully,* Narbona thought, knowing, however, that even if they did pass quietly *this* time, it would not be long before the cries of his people would echo from the canyon walls as surely as the Anazazi's had.

As a both a tribal leader and spiritual man, this deep-seated awareness pained him even more so than the vision he'd had of his own death—at the hands of a white man. *But none of that will happen today.* Today he'd do his best to ensure the values and traditions of the people would not be lost. An old saying ran through his mind, *In our every deliberation, we must consider the impact of our decisions on the next seven generations.*

Raising a wrinkled and slightly forced smile, Chief Narbona held out his hands to the two young men as they approached. They wore different shades of skin but seemed to be of one heart. Lightly they touched hands in the traditional Navajo greeting. James glanced at Bisa, silently thanking him with his eyes for teaching him this.

"Where we are about to go is as much about what's here," Narbona said as he pointed to the hearts of the young men, "as it is about what's around us." Looking deep into first Bisa's and then James' eyes, giving them time to absorb the words his own father had said to him, Narbona then turned and walked away from the side of the canyon with the cave's opening high above. James and Bisa looked at each other and then followed him across the water. "Roll that boulder aside," Narbona said and pointed to a rock as big as a wagon wheel propped up against the cliff wall facing the opening far above. James and Bisa, working together, did as directed. Their efforts exposed a narrow, dark tunnel.

"The Anasazi were a small people," the Navajo chief who stood over six feet tall said over his shoulder as he somehow managed to fold his shoulders in and, despite his age and size, gracefully entered the tunnel as if he'd done it a hundred times. James and Bisa followed, albeit in a less practiced manner. James unslung the bone and carefully pushed it ahead of him into the darkness, careful not to jam it into Bisa's feet to his front or on the unforgiving tunnel walls around him. The cool, moist air in the tunnel would have been a pleasant respite from the rocks that radiated dry heat outside had it not been for the passage's narrowness and steep incline.

After several switchbacks, James detected light ahead. Soon the tunnel opened up enough to stand. They were somewhere within the rock walls of the canyon, a secret passageway, and James recalled where he'd found the bone. The tunnel he'd traversed in the Tewa Pueblo. Finally able to stand, the trio emerged into the sun's blazing light and stood silently while their eyes adjusted.

"You lead now. That way," Narbona said to Bisa and pointed up the face of the cliff. James looked on incredulously.

"Here, use these," Bisa demonstrated as James reslung the bone, and followed his friend up the rock face using barely noticeable hand and foot holds carved into the stone.

With their shirts soaked with sweat, their fingers, hands, and knees scraped, they climbed up into an opening in the cliff face more than a hundred paces long, the rock 'ceiling' some twenty feet high, and the village tiny far below on the canyon floor. The Cave of the Ancients. Narbona placed a well-timed hand on James' shoulders as the young man's legs wobbled with vertigo. "Look over there," he said and pointed towards the far corner of the opening and away from the ledge.

James' legs steadied as his gaze settled on a two-story rock and dried mud structure that rose from the floor of the cave to its ceiling. Walking towards an open portal, James saw that much of the floor inside was covered in small rocks and shards of black, red, and gray pottery. Carefully and quietly, Narbona slid past James and pointed at a dark corner where two small bundles were laid side by side wrapped in what looked to be yucca leaves. On either side of the bundles, stretching the length of the room on two sides were large baskets, bowls, and pottery of all shapes, sizes, and colors. Many were filled with cloth-wrapped items.

"This is what remains of the ancient ones. Those," he said, pointing at the small, wrapped bundles, "are adult bodies curled up like infants. It is forbidden to touch them, but their spirits and wisdom, like the baskets and pottery, are very much with us. Come, let's sit over there," Narbona said in a voice that reminded James of his father. He led them to and sat down on a small rock wall behind which were a number of grit-covered wooden crates. He closed his eyes and took several slow, deep breaths. James and Bisa followed his lead, grateful for the opportunity after the steep climb.

After several minutes of silence, Narbona opened his eyes and spoke in little more than a whisper. "For more than 10,000 years, the Anasazi lived between these ledges, in these cracks, amongst this rock debris. Their lives were not easy. When they came here, animals such as the wooly mammoth, ground sloth, giant beavers, and saber-tooth cats roamed freely and posed great danger to the people, as did times of drought, sickness, and evil men—just as we find today." Narbona stopped talking as if he needed to listen to something or maybe he was just choosing his words carefully. Perhaps both.

"They listened to and learned from the Great Spirit, from those who came before.. It was the Great Spirit that showed the people how to make weapons so they could hunt and provide for their people. And when those beasts perished and the people went hungry, the Great Spirit is what showed them how to farm.

It is this that brought Larrañaga here with medicine when it looked like the Dine would follow the mammoth and saber-toothed tiger to extinction because of the smallpox. It is this that brought you two together." Again, Narbona paused. "And it is this that helped you to find what you did. Before I ask you to show it to me, I'd like to tell you one more thing.

Your friend Larrañaga and I, during our time together, found that we share many beliefs. Like him, and like you two, I have spent much of my life as a *nakai*—one who wanders. In my wandering, I have seen and experienced much, not only of the Navajo but of all those who wander these lands. The most significant discovery I have made, and I believe this to be true of Larrañaga as well, is not of a particular thing or place. It is the knowledge that all people are connected. To the Great Spirit. To each other and this world. And to the past. But they must *choose* that connection. If they do, life continues as it always has. You two have chosen connection. To each other. To your people. To learning and surviving … together. You, Bisa and James, give me hope."

"But I caution you. When people choose something *other* than connection, they see differences, not commonalities. They use words and names to separate, to diminish. All people are capable of seeing the world through hateful eyes. Fear and pride stand in the way of connections.

So whatever we choose to call this …," he said, pointing at the wrapped bone, "let us always remember that it is a part of what connects us. All of us."

* * * * *

Some five hundred vertical feet above and not more than a few hundred paces northeast, wedged between an Organ Pipe cactus and a cluster of sage brush at the northeastern rim of Canyon de Chelly, the Swiss Guardsman studied the Navajo village down on the canyon floor. For two weeks he and the American soldiers had wandered through the Chuska Mountains looking, unsuccessfully, for this hidden refuge. Jules had begun to doubt the place even existed. He'd decided to turn north towards the Old Spanish Trail and the Army of the West to find Father Ortiz. Maybe he'd know something, Jules had thought.

Unlike Canyon de Chelly, the Army of the West was not difficult to find but approaching it was another matter. He'd waited for the right opportunity to approach the priest and on the second night his patience had been rewarded.

Jules had quietly thanked the Holy Father as well as Father Ortiz for the two Ute scouts Ortiz had slyly broken off from the camel train and temporarily assigned to Jules. Ortiz had said they could find anything, and he hadn't been wrong. The Utes led Jules' band south, right to the rim where the Swiss Guardsman now watched from above. Having fulfilled their duties, the Utes turned and headed back north.

Now it is time to watch and learn, the man who had fought for the Vatican on four continents thought.

* * * * *

"It's more like a maze than a canyon," an old trapper who'd recently returned from Wyoming and the annual Rendezvous told Governor McClendon beneath the shade of a tree in the Plaza of Santa Fe. "Yessiree, it was near on two years ago, right about this time. I was on my way back and the outfit I was workin' for an' ridin' with wanted to check out the place where the San Juan meets the Colorado. Some Indians had told us that where the rivers meet a great whirlpool appears; huge, powerful circles of water."

"Well, sir, we found it, and it was like nothin' I'd ever seen. We weren't there but for a couple o' minutes before a hunnerd of those damn Utes ambushed us. I took off and jes' kept on ridin' until my horse gave out, which it did at the mouth of a canyon. To be sure, there wasn't much there. Red Rocks. Trickle of a creek runnin' out. Maybe a couple a hunnerd feet wide. But it was getting' dark and I hadn't a drop of water or a morsel of food, so I wandered in. Don't know how long I walked before I realized I was loster than a buggy on a mountaintop. Twists and turns aplenty. And that was when I came across them Injians. Navajo I reckon. Thought I was dun fer. Well, they gave me some food and showed me out and got me pointed in the right direction to the Old Spanish Trail. Figgerd I'd used up all my luck, so I high tailed it outta there."

As Governor McClendon captured the meat of the conversation he'd had with the old trapper earlier in the day in his journal, the idea of writing a book about all the characters he'd met crossed his well-educated and inquisitive mind. Amidst the flickering of the candlelight, McClendon set his pen down, rubbed his face, and glanced over at the large—and largely blank—map that he'd found in a desk in one of the many rooms of the Governor's Palace. Outside of a handful of mountain ranges and rivers, Albuquerque, and of course, Santa Fe, the map was as devoid of content as the landscape was of civilization. *Where are you, James?* He traced his finger along the San Juan River to where it met the Colorado and then glanced at his notes. *South. Maybe a day's ride. Water.* A sudden, heavy rapping at the door interrupted the silence.

The door opened and a young soldier leaned in. "Pardon the interruption, sir, but an old man from Santo Domingo is requesting to see you. Should I tell him to come back tomorrow?"

"No private. Please send him in."

Two hours later, Governor McClendon lay in his bed, sleep eluding him despite the late hour. The elder from Santo Domingo Pueblo had conveyed that he'd received word that both James and the bone were safe with the Navajo. The two men had then spent an hour filling in the map, adding both useful landmarks and places to avoid in as much detail as time and language barriers permitted.

When they'd finished, McClendon, with glassy eyes and a joyful heart, startled the elder with an affectionate bear hug. Once the Puebloan recovered from the foreign gesture, he added something else. The following morning a wagon train of Hopi traders who'd been in Santo Domingo Pueblo would be leaving there for their home in Oraibi—just a day's ride from Canyon de Chelly.

I'm coming, son, McClendon thought and willed himself to sleep.

* * * * *

One of the American soldiers ran up to the concealed spot on the canyon rim where Jules had spent most of the daylight hours for the past two days. "Sir, five riders are heading this way from the north. Moving fast."

Jules' reached for the lever-action rifle next to him, then slowly pulled himself away from the rim. Once he'd cleared the line of sight from the floor of the canyon, he stood, and followed the man back to the nest of boulders where they'd made camp.

"Two blue coats. One Father Ortiz. And those Utes. I knew their assistance was too good to be true." Jules said as he peered through his looking glass at the dust cloud in the distance. As a rule, he didn't trust any man who didn't have the personal discipline to accept God as his Lord and Savior. *And there are some of those that do that I don't trust either,* he thought. *This is not part of the plan,* he seethed.

"Go out and meet them. See what they want. Do not let them come here—we don't want them giving away our position. Now!" Jules barked.

The American soldier mounted up and rode away. But again, the plan did not go the way Jules wanted. Less than an hour later, the men, now walking their horses, strode determinedly into the makeshift camp amongst the boulders.

It took a lot to make Jules angry, but a lot had just happened. In a low, penetrating voice he said, "Father Ortiz, I don't know what you are doing but this is not what we agreed. You and your party need to turn around and…"

Father Ortiz held up his hand to the man who was clearly used to issuing orders—and having them followed. "Stop right there," Ortiz interrupted. "We all are after the same thing, the BONE," he yelled, his voice bouncing off the rocks and cascading down into the canyon. Realizing his mistake and knowing that, with all the very capable warriors around, he needed to maintain control of the situation, Father Ortiz took a moment to remove his hat and run his hand over his glistening forehead and through his black hair. "Now let's figure out how we can work together."

Colonel Donovan quickly assessed the situation amongst the boulders. He'd expected to find the man who called himself Jules—Father Ortiz had told him much. But outside of that brief interaction in the Governor's Palace, Donovan hadn't had an opportunity to digest the steely-eyed foreigner's capabilities. What he now saw impressed him. What he didn't expect was to find two American soldiers accompanying the Vatican's soldier. He hadn't recognized them at first, but his aide, a young, dark-haired lieutenant who stood a full head shorter than his commanding officer whispered this in his ear while Jules had been talking with Ortiz.

Having always been quick on his feet, Donovan smirked as an idea took form in his mind, and as usual his mouth soon followed. "Now look here, padre and *Jules,* all of this here is now the territory of the United States of America. Four of this group are official representatives of that government and as such I will be issuing the orders here. You *gentlemen* are welcome to assist in this endeavor and will be compensated for that. Your other options are…less pleasant."

This turn of events did not surprise Father Ortiz. In fact, he'd counted on it. Father Ortiz had been able to use Colonel Donovan's personal desire to regain his position of prominence to his advantage. With two more soldiers to bolster that desire, their chances of recovering the ancient artifact increased significantly. And what Donovan didn't know was that the Utes had been loyal to the Ortiz family for years. Jules, however, was a dangerous man — a soldier no one but the Pope could control. The Swiss Guardsman could be of some use in getting to the bone, but eventually his interests would conflict with Father Ortiz's.

A thunderclap over the mesa to the west interrupted the tension and testosterone-filled standoff. Father Ortiz was the first to speak after the rumble subsided. "Gentlemen, let us take it down a few notches. I propose we achieve together what we could not separately. In three nights, we'll have a new moon. We can use that to our advantage. The Ute scouts will lead us around to the mouth of the canyon and, under the cover of nearly complete darkness, deep into the canyon. I believe I know where they are keeping the bone. And with your arms…" Father Ortiz paused, realizing his poor choice of words, and then continued. "With your rifles and skills and the element of surprise, we should have no problem getting it and getting out with what we all want."

Jules' body language reeked rage amongst other things, both towards himself for underestimating the ambitious priest and for being forced to work alongside troglodytes like the Americans and the Utes. But any advantage lacking in the present situation he more than made up for with experience. Confident he could figure out a way to regain the upper hand he said, "Tell me where they are hiding it."

"The Ancient will be with the ancients," Father Ortiz

responded, knowing he'd successfully defused the situation — at least for now. "That is all I will say on that at the moment. Now, what does a faithful servant of God have to do to get something to eat?"

* * * * *

Hundreds of feet below the rim, Narbona marveled at the bone's size and condition but refused to touch it. He even held his own leg up against it to compare lengths. Convinced it was something truly special, Narbona asked James to set it on the floor of the cave so that it nearly touched the back wall and pointed out at the opening and the canyon below. Confused but mindful of the elder, James did as he directed then stood back and watched as the Navajo leader sat down next to the bone, his back against the wall and his legs crossed in front of him, and beckoned James and Bisa to do the same on the other side of the artifact.

"Let us sit in grateful silence with the ancients. Perhaps they have something to tell us."

After a few moments of eerie silence, several voices filled the opening in the cliff. Voices from far below, speaking hurriedly, saying words James did not understand. Bisa stood reflexively and rushed to the edge of the opening. "Something is wrong," he said. Without another word he stepped to where they'd climbed up from below and began descending. James looked from his friend to Narbona, who had not moved, and back to his friend before he dipped from sight.

"Tell me, James, what does this bone mean to you?" Chief Narbona asked unperturbed.

James started to speak and then caught himself—something his father told him to do many times. "Think before you speak," he'd say. "It is not the quantity or speed of your words that matters. It is the quality."

James began again. "Larrañaga spent his whole life pursuing…"

"No, I did not ask what the bone meant to Larrañaga. I know what it means to him and his ancestors. I also know what it means to Bisa: finding it brought him back here to the people he loves. I asked what the bone means to you."

James' thoughts shot through his mind like fireworks on the 4th of July, but each one had to do with others' views. Narbona waited patiently, silently watching the young man as he processed his thoughts. Finally, James responded, speaking slowly. "To me, it is a physical reminder of all that is good."

If James had been nervous about the quality of his response, the slight upticks in the corners of Narbona's eyes and mouth put those fears to rest. "And what would you do with such a reminder?"

"I would want people to see it, experience it, as I have." James stopped for a moment and then continued. "I would want them to feel its presence in their hearts and realize that there is, indeed, 'something bigger'—regardless of what they choose to call it. My father once told me, 'you become what you give your energy to.' I want to give my energy to something…good."

Chief Narbona nodded his head slightly, the smile crossing the entirety of his weathered face. After a few minutes, he stood and extended an arm towards James. James accepted the assistance and stood. But it was more than that. Once again, as two very different people stood nearly eye to eye, something connected them. Something passed between them. Both felt it deep in their hearts. "Let us go see what is going on down below," Narbona said. Together they climbed back down, leaving the bone with the ancients.

* * * * *

When James and Narbona walked back into the ring of hogans on the floor of the canyon, Bisa was taking off his plain white shirt and putting on something much more…purposeful. The new shirt was made of tanned hide of some sort with patches of red stroud—what looked like heavy, dyed wool—with blue and green pigmented symbols that reminded James of the petroglyphs. Attached to it were long strings of beads and seeds. Narbona leaned in close to James and said, "That is a Navajo man's war shirt. Something must be wrong."

Moments later, Bisa and two other young Navajo men, all carrying rifles, sprinted effortlessly across the canyon floor and disappeared behind 'Sleeping Duck Rock.' Narbona, who had left James' side and went to speak quietly with another elder, returned. "There are white men up on the rim," he said with a voice more sad than angry. "Bisa is going to see how many and what they are up to."

James was torn. A part of him felt like he should be with his friend—they'd been through so much together. But he also felt like maybe he'd slow Bisa down. He didn't want that, not when the safety of the village might be at stake. Narbona must have recognized the conflict on James' face because he quickly followed with, "I am getting old, James. And soon this clan will need a new chief. Now that Bisa is back, with all of his experience with the 'new people,' I think perhaps he could be the one."

Gesturing towards the rim, Narbona continued, "Like any young man, he is anxious to prove his abilities. It is good that you remain here. Let us go and see which horse chooses you as its next rider," he said with a smile, taking James' arm. He silently led the young man from South Carolina towards a herd of wild horses grazing on a grassy field.

Narbona and James spent the remainder of the day together, telling stories and laughing as the younger man did his best to learn how to ride bareback like Bisa on a particularly ornery, leopard (white body with dark spots) colored horse that did not want to leave his side. But neither did he immediately obey the young man's commands.

Bisa returned well after dark. The news he brought wasn't as bad as Narbona had expected; he'd feared that the Army of the West had turned south but only seven men with rifles camped just over the top of the rim. As Bisa sketched a quick map with a stick in the dirt next to the fire, he described what he'd seen and learned. The most interesting part Bisa saved for last. The one-armed

Colonel Donovan and the man who'd tried to kill Larrañaga by the Three Sisters were amongst the seven.

When he finished, Chief Narbona spoke. "It is good that you learned all of this. And it is even better that you did not confront them." Turning to James, Narbona said, "Does it not say in your Bible that we should, 'clothe ourselves in patience?'" James could only nod, surprised that the Navajo chief knew this.

"We should keep watch especially as we begin to lose the moon," Bisa said and pointed up at the waning crescent shape directly above them. Narbona nodded. Bisa stood and directed several others to various points in the canyon. The rest of the village quietly went about its business, an uneasy feeling drifting with smoke that filled the narrow valley.

* * * * *

The Hopi village of Oraibi was both older and more populous than Santa Fe. According to those who live there, the Hopi Indians first occupied what some called 'Old Oraybi' half a millennium before Spanish explorer Pedro de Tovar set foot on the mesa-top village in 1540. Jonathan McClendon slung his saddle bags over his shoulder after completing the journey from Santa Fe. He'd ridden in the back of a covered wagon all the way out of precaution. McClendon took in the scene, amazed at the staggering number of rock and mud constructed homes and buildings. Must *be at least a thousand people living here,* He correctly surmised.

Leaving Santa Fe had not been an easy decision. McClendon had made many friends and was grateful for all the opportunities to meet and hear about the journeys of so many people from so many different places. He'd also been entrusted by a man he respected and admired, to fulfill the duties of interim Governor of New Mexico Territory. For all intents and purposes, by deciding to leave he abandoned those duties just as surely as he'd abandoned his duties as an officer of the Army of the West.

To mitigate the impact of his departure and hopefully cover his backside with Kearny, he appointed the more-than-willing commander of the Mormon Battalion to act in his stead. *Have I made the right decision?* he asked himself as he scanned the horizon to the east—the direction of Canyon de Chelly.

The Hopi traders who'd traveled with McClendon from Santa Fe to Oraibi hadn't spoken much English and as he stretched his legs, he noticed another significant difference between this place and Santa Fe: *not much Spanish influence here now.* The only structure that looked like it might have been a mission lay in hundred-year-old ruins.

McClendon retrieved a small bag filled with silver coins and the map he'd made with the help of the elder from Santo Domingo from his saddlebag. The language barrier made communication with these benevolent, soft-spoken people (McClendon would later be told that the name 'Hopi' actually means "friendly, peaceful, and civilized people) challenging at best. McClendon glanced around at the men he'd traveled with, trying to figure out who he should ask for help. And how. The man who'd led the wagon train was the only one who'd spoken any English and that is who McClendon strode over to, map and coins in hand. He pointed to the spot on the map labeled, 'Canyon de Chelly' and pleaded, "Can you take me there? Or close to it?"

"Please, take this," McClendon said, handing the man several silver coins.

The Hopi man's expression turned from surprise to suspicion in an instant, but McClendon continued. "That is where my son is. I need to find him," he pleaded, offering the man the entire bag of coins.

"White people cannot go. Without…" the Hopi man said reaching for English words.

Unsure as to whether he was being played by the man he'd just traveled hundreds of miles with, McClendon enthusiastically offered, "Invitation? Yes, I have an invitation. My son…we…" Now it was McClendon's turn to struggle to find the right words to describe how his son came to be in the homeland of the Navajo. The Hopi man studied McClendon's face and seemed to consider before breaking into a smile and pushing the bag of coins away.

"I will take you there," the man finally said. He pointed to a flat-top ridge a short distance west of where the Chinle turned north towards the San Juan River. "We go there in morning."

* * * * *

As it had each morning for hundreds of millions of years, the sun rose over the gritty, burnt desert plain. The relatively few insects, reptiles, animals small and large, and people who now inhabited the area that 500 million years earlier had been covered by an expansive ocean used the more 'comfortable' pre-dawn hours to forage for their livelihood. Before long the oppressive late-summer sun made all movement life-threatening. In this place, for all but a few, the sun's heat and extreme desolation made self-preservation the only objective that mattered.

* * * * *

For the Navajo, the coming of a new moon was a cause of celebration; a time to pause and unite their clans and honor their tribe. With this new moon, however, as foreigners prowled the rim above, a darkness seemed to penetrate what should have been the light hearts of the Navajo. Neither the beating of painted drums nor the sounds of the vibrant, thousand-person strong village filled the Tsegi air. A foreboding air wafted around the Navajo hogans, pinned in by the thousand-foot-tall canyon walls.

The men atop the rim had left the previous day, Bisa's lookouts reported. The 'new men' headed north from the east-west running canyon at first, then swung towards the setting sun, before heading down the gradual slope towards the mouth of the canyon. Unable to follow due to the chasm that separated the north from the south rims, the Navajo 'watchers' as James nicknamed them, returned to the village. Chief Narbona quietly advised Bisa to send them up the north wall and out to the mouth of the canyon to keep eyes on the enemy, but the newly emerging leader of the clan had other plans.

"They are coming for the bone. We must be ready for them," Bisa said to the gathering of Navajo. Narbona nodded in agreement. "They are only seven. I know these men. They are soldiers, skilled with horses and rifles. They fight for themselves, for their own pride. But we are warriors, and this is *our home*. We will fight for our brothers and sisters, our clan, and all those who came before us. Let us remember this and draw our strength and courage from …"

Bisa looked now towards James and then out to the rest of the clan before continuing. "Something much bigger than ourselves." All eyes closed, including Narbona's, and the hushed prayers spoke volumes to those who were listening.

18. September 20, 1846

What the Navajo had no way of knowing was that two days prior, while they waited for the new moon, Donovan had penned a convincing note to General Kearny. In it, Donovan advised that soon he'd have the opportunity to knock out two very important birds, *well, many more than two if all goes well*, Donovan had thought, with one stone. He'd conveyed that with the help of Father Ortiz, he'd tracked down the ancient artifact as well as the feared and troublesome Navajo raiders following Chief Narbona. And now both were within the grasp of the United States' Army of the West.

All he needed to accomplish this was the swift deployment of the Dragoons to the south of their present position and, of course, a resumption of command. *He has always had a soft spot for me,* Donovan had thought as he dispatched his lieutenant with the note. And just in case General Kearny balked, he sent a copy to the recorder named Smythe.

General Kearny, after quite a bit of prodding from Smythe, had begrudgingly dispatched one hundred of the U.S. Army of the West's Dragoons to aid and assist in the mission Colonel Donovan proposed. Smythe had been adamant about the importance of getting the bone and returning it to President Polk.

While General Kearny understood and appreciated that desire, he also knew taking care of Chief Narbona would earn him even more coverage in the press, as well as the history books. But in no way would he let this detract from his mission to capture the Port of Los Angeles. That was why he'd decided to keep the rest of the Dragoons under the command of Lt. Colonel Thompson with his army.

The hundred person strong Dragoon detachment, excited for the reprieve from the tiresome and uneventful march and the opportunity to once again serve with Colonel Donovan, spent the day traveling south. They were led by the lieutenant who'd delivered the messages. The rest of Kearny's army continued their slow progression west.

As the sun dipped below the high mesa to the west, the detachment linked up with Colonel Donovan five miles north of the canyon the Navajo called home. Amidst raucous cheers and the bravado of a conquering force, Donovan resumed command of the men he'd recruited and trained and led all the way from St. Louis. Gathering his officers, he outlined the plan.

* * * * *

As the last light in the sky vanished like rainfall on the hot rocks, Bisa placed two of his most dependable warriors on opposite sides of Sleeping Duck Rock. It was a wise move in Chief Narbona's opinion. The location was a critical juncture of paths deep inside the canyon with ample avenues of retreat if and when those were needed. These warriors would serve as the advance guard, tasked with relaying the message that the 'new men' were approaching by mimicking an owl's screech—a sound the bird made when something threatens their nest.

One screech would mean the north side of the river and two would mean the south. With that warning and knowledge, Bisa and Narbona could deploy their warriors accordingly so as to ensure maximum protection for the village and keep the Navajo from getting caught in any crossfire. It was a good plan, both Navajo leaders agreed. Rifles and bullets, bows and arrows, knives, and equally lethal yet ancient atlatls and axes made from meteorite—anything that could be used as a weapon—were checked and cached in hidden locations as darkness enveloped them.

* * * * *

As the Navajo made ready for the coming fight, a mile down river, Jonathan McClendon bent and drank deeply from the clear, cool water at the entrance of Canyon de Chelly. He was exhausted yet hopeful, despite the fact that he'd not seen another living soul since the Hopi man dropped him off on the mesa to the west. He had, however, nearly tripped over the half-exposed skeleton of a dinosaur that lived only in history books. *Or nightmares,* he'd thought.

Desperate to maintain his more often than not positive outlook, he focused on the water and the dark shapes of what must be trees around it.. *This place must be truly beautiful in the morning light,* he thought. Ankles and feet aching and wary of the deep shadows along the canyon walls, McClendon stood and chose to walk along the sandy bank of the gently flowing river in search of the Navajo village — and his son.

* * * * *

Seven darkness enshrouded men froze at the sucking sound of footsteps in the mud along the bank of the river. The source was hard to pinpoint given the lack of light and the fact that any emitted sound bounced off the rock walls several times before reaching its destination. They'd climbed down to the northern bank of the river a few hundred yards inside the mouth of the canyon in the likely event that the Navajo had posted lookouts and had been using the shadows of the cliff walls to slowly make their way into the canyon.

The two Ute scouts led the small procession and were tasked with leading and getting them, undetected, into the village. Father Ortiz and Jules followed right behind them; the religious man was more than slightly uncomfortable that the Swiss Guardsman was behind him. Then came the two American soldiers whose heavy breathing conveyed their readiness for a fight.

Donovan's trusted lieutenant, after leading the detachment of Dragoons to the rendezvous point, had ridden ahead and rejoined the small group so as to ensure they stuck with the plan and now brought up the rear.

After several tense moments, Father Ortiz gestured to the Utes to continue. *It is only a matter of time before we are discovered. We need to be as close to the village as possible when that happens*, he whispered.

* * * * *

An hour earlier, James had found and climbed up onto a ledge some ten feet above the canyon floor. He'd used mud to darken his face. He did the same with his white shirt and arms. By Navajo standards, it wasn't quite a war shirt, but it brought him some much-needed confidence. *Whatever happens, I will forever be a part of this*, he thought.

A dozen or so petroglyphs were etched into the wall just above the ledge. It was another rendition of the circle of life that now caught his attention. As he traced his finger around the carving, he thought back to how he and his father had fled South Carolina after all that had happened there. He recalled the terrible attack on his wagon train, the losing of his father that led Larrañaga to him, and to Autograph Rock where he'd first seen the carved circle.

He then remembered the compassionate tone in Bisa's voice as the young Navajo described how the Dragoons had taken and beaten his father in Santo Domingo before hauling him off to what would likely be a hanging. Tears fell from his eyes. He closed them and saw the last glimpse he'd taken of Lalo before jumping out of the wagon and saving himself from the roaring Rio Grande.

All those times, he thought, he'd *reacted* to the circumstances that came his way, much as an animal might have. He'd lost so much that, at times, feelings like gratitude and faith in something bigger seemed as foreign here as a four-poster bed. But now, as he sat and prepared for what likely would become another tragic memory, James thanked God for all that had brought him here, to this place and to these people. *They are family,* he thought, *and I will not run from this fight, from them. And the bone … wait, the bone!*

James launched himself off the ledge and the moment his moccasins sank into the loose sand beneath, the utter stillness of the now dark canyon broke. A single, shrill, owl-like screech. *North side — the side where the hogans are and the side that, 300 feet up, is the Cave of the Ancients.* The thoughts instantly coursed through James' mind. *GO!*

Unsure of whether he yelled that or something inside yelled it at him, James' legs reacted accordingly. He sprinted towards the boulder that hid the entrance to the pathway up to the Cave of the Ancients.

* * * * *

The Utes knew their sole advantage, the element of surprise, was blown when the screech echoed off the canyon walls. They looked back to Father Ortiz for guidance, hoping that perhaps their benefactor would decide to pull back and reconsider. They knew that the Dine did not hold the Utes in particularly high regard, given their participation in the Navajo slave trade. They also knew that hundreds if not thousands of Navajo inhabited this canyon—and that they'd not surrender willingly.

The Ute's hope was dashed as Ortiz commanded, "Vamos con Díos. Keep going! *I* can barely see you, so they cannot see *us*!"

As if confirming his proclamation, a spattering of ill-aimed rifle shots pinged off the rocks above them and thud into the wet ground at their feet. The Utes broke into a run, their athletic prowess soon putting a distance between them and the portly priest and those behind him. But what Father Ortiz did not have on the fitness front, he more than made up for with the knowledge he'd gained from a Navajo man he'd converted back near Wagon Mound. Knowledge that would make finding the bone not only possible, but probable. *The Navajo don't know that I know about the Cave of the Ancients*, Ortiz assured himself. *All I have to do is get there....*

* * * * *

Jonathan McClendon, far from his comfort zone of a classroom or the Plaza in Santa Fe, dropped to the ground when the first shots rang out. With water coursing all around him and flashes from gun barrels briefly illuminating the narrow valley like shooting stars in the night sky, he knew only one thing for sure. *No bueno.* Having no idea what to do other than keep down and find his son, he crawled a few feet forward, taking shelter at the base of a small boulder. He tucked himself as close to it as he could.

* * * *

The sound of gunfire, magnified by the thousand-foot-tall rock walls, rolled out of the canyon and towards the Dragoon detachment like the roar of a flash flood. They'd been waiting for the prearranged signal to advance: a blow of a whistle that would come once the small advance party found the village.

Colonel Donovan, anxious to fulfill what he knew in every fiber of his being to be his destiny of greatness, his name printed alongside the likes of great cavalry commanders like "Light-Horse" Harry Lee and Richard Mentor Johnson, and desperate to prove to General Kearny that he deserved to have his full command back, ordered the mounted soldiers to advance, despite the fact that the signal had not yet been given.

Any lingering doubt he might have had at making his hasty decision dissipated just a few moments later when the high-pitched sound of the whistle drifted out of the canyon. The hoofbeats and blood-chilling war cries of his Dragoons reverberated off the rock with a nearly impenetrable density. But despite the utter darkness accompanying the new moon, penetrate they did. Half the unit headed up the north side of the river and the other half took to the south, exactly as planned. Within minutes they were deep inside.

A Dragoon riding abreast of Donovan fell from his

horse, groaning in agony as the they approached what looked like a pile of boulders in the middle of the slow-moving river. Colonel Donovan's blood boiled, not so much as a result of losing a man, but at the thought that these subhumans were trying to keep him from achieving what he knew would be a victory shared across tables and campfires for years to come.

Realizing, once again, that he could not ride and return fire at the same time on account of having only one arm, he slowed his horse and leaned over the saddle, keeping the horse between him and the source of the gunfire. He swung his leg over and strode confidently towards the pile of boulders directly to his front, with the zing of bullets whipping through the air. *No way a few Indians can take all of us in this darkness before we take them,* he thought and drew one of the two pistols from his belt.

* * * * *

James' grandfather, an immigrant from Scotland and veteran of the 'Second War of Independence," had tried to describe what being in battle was like. "It's chaotic," he'd said, "where anything and everything can happen, often for seemingly no reason at all." He'd often used words like "chance," and "fate." "Few," he'd said, "kept cool heads on their shoulders, clear eyes focused on the mission, and hearts driven to doing whatever it took to protect each other. Even if that meant stepping out in front—which it usually did. Those were the ones I tried to emulate."

When he hopped down from the ledge, James' heart

was focused on his grandfather's words. Even in the darkness. Even amidst what he recognized as the war cries of the Dragoons and the sounds of the dead and dying. It was as if something, somewhere, was guiding him and all he had to do was follow.

Follow he did. Through the tunnel and up the rock wall he climbed, his every move conducted with precision and speed. As he pulled himself up and into the Cave of the Ancients, he rushed to the back wall and sat next to the unwrapped ancient and mysterious bone that hadn't been moved since he'd last been here.

Taking several deep breaths to calm his pounding heart, James focused his mind on all that he was grateful for: His parents, Larrañaga, Lalo, Bisa, Chief Narbona, and, most importantly, God. "Your will be done," he whispered, and then he began to chant. Quietly at first, the wordless sounds emerging from deep inside the young man barely made it to the opening of the cave, even with the echo effect.

But with each repetition, James' confidence grew. With confidence came volume. From behind closed eyelids James felt, rather than saw, the bone begin to glow. He didn't stop; rather, he stood and spread his arms wide and belted out the chant from the mouth of the cave, hundreds of feet above the melee below.

Who knew how long it had been since the sounds of life and divine love projected out from this cave, but when James realized that the gunfire below had nearly ceased, he opened his eyes. The sight before him took away what little breath he still had in his lungs.

* * * * *

While the water kept flowing out of the canyon, the bluecoats flowed steadily in. Colonel Donovan's face broke into an ear-to-ear smile which no one was able to see—except for Jonathan McClendon.

"Look what we have here," the one-armed Dragoon commander said. In a fluid and startling fast movement, Donovan holstered his weapon and reached down and seized McClendon by the throat and lifted him to his feet. Wisely placing the governor between him and all the action to his front, Donovan seethed, "Let's you and me go for a walk." Donovan's calloused hand held McClendon's throat a moment longer, rage and spittle erupting around the Colonel's words.

When he finally let go, he spun McClendon around and pushed him forward. "Move!" he barked and once again Donovan drew his pistol, pulled back the hammer, and thrust the short barrel into McClendon's back.

Speechless and with legs that felt like they were full of lead, McClendon obeyed. What Donovan didn't know was that McClendon had a pistol tucked between his belt and his belly, well-concealed by the brown jacket he'd been given back in Santa Fe. Remembering this did not give the governor any confidence; McClendon had never shot a man and wasn't sure he could bring himself to do so.

Donovan prodded McClendon forward. Shadows of men engaged in brutal, hand-to-hand combat danced around them as they approached what both men realized must be the Navajo village; the sounds of women and children screaming adding a new depth to the darkness.

"We're going to burn this place down along with everyone and everything in it. Everything, that is, except the *bone*," Donovan seethed. McClendon heard Donovan inhale sharply, suddenly, and then no longer felt the business end of the pistol against his back.

Is he still there? Is this my chance? The thought sped through McClendon's mind. Then something from above interrupted his panicked thoughts. A penetratingly *hopeful* sound. McClendon couldn't help but look up.

* * * * *

Chief Narbona had discarded his rifle and stood back-to-back with Bisa, both holding now blood-covered axes as they awaited the next wave of Dragoons. Both had minor wounds, but the knowledge that they were fighting for the survival of their people released a seemingly endless quantity of adrenaline that kept them going, ready to take on the next Blue Coat.

While they fought, they directed. They did their best to orchestrate the most effective defense against the flood of invaders. As Narbona corralled several children towards the relative safety of a rock wall, a sound from far above reached his ears. Then his heart. *Someone is up there. Chanting!*

The thin yet sharp point of a rapier erupted from the front of Narbona's shoulder as he gazed up at the Cave of the Ancients. As pain erupted so too did a light from the cave. A light that glowed as if the sun itself was rising from deep within. The blade withdrew and the stern face and narrowed eyes of a white man stepped around to his front. The Navajo leader sank to his knees. For the angry, hopeful, wounded, and perhaps most of all, sad, Narbona, just breathing required a conscious effort.

The steely-eyed man began to ask something in an unfamiliar language and then restarted in Spanish. "Donde esta el hueso grande?" Where is the big bone?

A tear began its journey down Narbona's painted face. Dropping his ax, he raised his good arm out to his side, mimicking the figure he now saw outlined by the light far above. He prayed for the preservation of his people, of their way of life, accepting that he would likely not survive the night. It had been in his dreams, being killed by a white man. With a focused mind and yearning soul, he added his voice to the chant that had caught everyone's attention.

* * * * *

Behind James, the glowing bone had, like in the pueblo near Black Rock Canyon, risen from where it had been laying. Only this time it tipped up on end. As the chanting continued—not only from James but from people down below—other bones began to appear from the baskets in the cave as if a magnet was pulling them from their humble containers.

James, now trembling in his moccasins, watched and chanted as a full skeleton took shape. It appeared to be kneeling there in the cave. *A good thing*, James thought, given its tremendous size. Once the skeleton was fully formed, muscles and then skin grew over it. White skin. A beard. A white, flowing robe. Jesus? Viracocha? God.

Within moments, the head of the giant, glowing man raised up and looked at James. Eyes of indescribable depth that conveyed first sorrow, then love. Emanating a radiant blue light, the giant reached out his hand and took ahold of James' shoulder. What could only be described as a fatherly moment passed between the two before the apparition stepped to the edge of the cliff face and stood with his arms out to his sides. Taking up most of the opening of the cliff face, the brilliant entity surveyed the now illuminated canyon floor below.

A hail of bullets rained into the cave, passing through the giant's body and impacting the rock walls behind. Instantly the giant's blue glow turned blood red. The giant pointed first towards the sky and then the earth below. James dove behind the small adobe wall he'd sat on in the nick of time. He would struggle, later, to put down in words what happened next.

* * * * *

When light from the Cave of the Ancients caught his attention, Father Ortiz had been hiding in the darkness across the water from the village, away from where most of the fighting was taking place. That was where his Navajo friend had told him to look for a secret passageway that would lead to the location of the bone. He'd been hoping—praying—to find what he sought, but the darkness had been all-encompassing.

But now, with the growing light from above, Ortiz saw a small opening in the rock just a few paces away. After scanning the canyon floor for threats, he dashed towards it, hoping he could fit his rather large frame into the tight space.

Every foot of progress came with tremendous physical exertion. Even when he'd worked on his father's ranch as a young boy, he'd never done anything like this. Soon his clothes were torn, drenched in both sweat and blood. He realized he was pouring, literally, everything he had into accomplishing his objective. *Like the flagellation of Christ,* Ortiz thought.

After what seemed like an eternity, Ortiz emerged from the tunnel. The man's pained eyes took in the scene of someone or something of immense size standing in the opening of the cliff face. The final hundred-foot climb, he also saw, would require him to shimmy up a near vertical cliff face. Father Ortiz took a deep breath and, knowing he was close to claiming the ancient artifact as his own, he began to climb.

* * * * *

The emergence of what could only be the Great Spirit above the canyon floor gave Bisa an opportunity. He'd been fighting not just for his own life but for the lives, past, present, and future, of his people. He'd been wounded; deflected a soldier's thrust of a knife with the outside of his forearm which had left him with a deep gash. He wrapped his sweat-soaked headband around the wound to staunch the bleeding and as he did so, a calmness began to wash over him.

But now, with all eyes trying to make sense of the sight above, Bisa yelled to his tribe, telling them in the Dine language to retreat to the caves behind Sleeping Duck Rock. Like a rabbit in a garden, Bisa moved swiftly but purposefully from one hogan to another, from one hiding spot to another, corralling his people towards safety. He found the seriously wounded Narbona, the man's trademark bear claw necklace dripping with blood as if the claws themselves had ripped open his shoulder. The children the great chief had been protecting were still cowering in the shadows of the rock wall.

Bisa scooped Narbona up into his arms and, with the children in tow, made their way towards Sleeping Duck Rock where the rest of his people sheltered deep in hidden caves. Casting one last look over his shoulder, Bisa stood transfixed by the giant red figure who had been pointing at the sky and was now pointing at the canyon floor. Behind the figure, Bisa could just make out, was his friend James. Quickly he ducked inside.

* * * * *

The opportunity that Bisa seized when the Great Spirit emerged from the depths of the Cave of the Ancients was also afforded to Jonathan McClendon. Like everyone else on the canyon floor, McClendon's first reaction to the glowing far above was one of paralyzing confusion. Amazement mixed with fear like some noxious cocktail. And like Bisa, McClendon made the most of the opportunity. With a decisive and almost graceful movement, he turned and knocked the pistol from Donovan's hand while at the same time pulling his own.

But in the moment that followed, he lost his footing in the wet sand along the bank of the river. He tripped and fell. His world went dark.

* * * * *

The great glowing entity that had placed its hand on James' shoulder looked just like the depiction he'd seen of Moses at the Red Sea. While that painting conveyed power and meaning, it dwarfed in comparison to the power and meaning that now stood before him. Blinding bolts of light now streamed from the entity's red fingertips. James slowly climbed out from behind the short wall and moved around to the side, towards where he'd climbed up from below.

What he saw surprised him. Tears flowed down the giant's face as he directed the beams of light at the attackers. James cringed as he saw Blue Coats turn into dust that hovered for a moment before falling to the canyon floor.

This went on for what seemed like an eternity; bursts of light sending those without love in their hearts into what James would later describe as the 'forever darkness.'

Just as suddenly as it had started, it stopped.

329

The glowing Great Spirit pointed a finger at a solitary man below. With a firm, penetrating voice that resonated from every angle of the canyon, he said, "Warrior from afar. In your heart I see that you fight for something bigger, for something you believe is for the good of the people. But you have allowed yourself to be misguided. You have chosen to place something between me and you."

He lowered his finger as the man holding the rapier fell to his knees. "Leave this place and never return. Tell those you follow, as well as those who follow you, that you have seen *my* light. And never again let *any man* or thing get between us."

Silently Jules nodded, his brain unable to grasp the enormity of the grace he'd been afforded. He stood and found a nearby horse. Casting one last glance over his shoulder at the entity far above, he prodded his horse into the darkness.

* * * * *

Father Ortiz watched this scene play out from beneath the Cave of the Ancients, almost within arm's reach of where James now knelt. *El Espírito Santo. Could it really be?* he thought, sensing a seismic shift in every fiber of his being.

An incapacitating awareness of how egocentric he had become flowed through him, a feeling that was quickly followed by an overwhelming desire to replace that with something more … *soul centric,* more connection based. He'd felt that in his early days of priesthood. He'd promised himself, back then, that he would emulate Saint Francis in his belief that "God lives in your nearest neighbor, in every man." As he listened to the glowing entity, he realized he'd broken that promise.

His hold on the cliff face tenuous at best; Father Ortiz shifted his weight from one foot to another and in so doing pried loose a small rock. It tumbled down, sounding like thunder in the newfound stillness of the canyon.

Startled at the sound and movement, James' first reaction was to fight. With anger in his eyes, he jumped to his feet and raised his foot to stomp on the priest's hands. Or maybe his head.

"James, *stop*," the glowing entity commanded as the red glow faded to purple and then to blue. James immediately felt ashamed and lowered his foot. Once again, he knelt. Only this time he did so towards Father Ortiz. The young man extended a helpful hand towards the trembling priest.

"It is not always easy to *love* one another. Or to *love* me," the glowing entity that James would later call the 'Big Man' in his journal said. He too knelt right beside James, also extending a helpful hand. His voice now lowered to barely more than a whisper, the 'Big Man' said, "Love is a big word. My teachings always begin with the simple. Find what you have in common with each other and follow that with expressions of…*kindness*. Let us be kind to Manuel Ortiz."

Together the 'Big Man' and James plucked Father Ortiz from his precarious position and set him down on the floor of the cave. "Now let us sit together. We have much to discuss."

The unlikely trio sat in the same places that Narbona, James, and Bisa had a couple days earlier. Sometimes they spoke; questions asked and answered verbally. Sometimes they sat in silence; questions asked and answered deep inside their beings without spoken words. This went on until the narrow strip of dark sky hundreds of feet above the already elevated Cave of the Ancients broke with the coming of dawn.

After a long period of silence, the 'Big Man' spoke, "I am going now but know in your hearts that I am never gone. In every place, in everything and person, in the past, present, and future, *I am.* Your journeys will not be easy but rest your souls in the knowledge that your destination is assured. Because you have chosen to believe … in something bigger."

"My children, whenever you feel lost or unsure, sit with me, as we have tonight." Then he spread his arms as wide as he could which, given his height, was quite a distance. The 'Big Man' simultaneously embraced both James and Father Ortiz, the feeling of love and belonging penetrating deep inside their souls.

The 'Big Man's' solid form slowly grew translucent, his face, skin, and muscles fading as did all the bones but one. The femur.

* * * * *

James helped Father Ortiz navigate the path back down

to the canyon floor. In more ways than one, they had the light to guide them. When they emerged from the narrow tunnel, James collapsed, but not from exhaustion. Sitting by the river just a stone's throw away stood his father.

19. September 24, 1846

As tradition dictated, the Navajo mourned those that had been killed in the attack for four days. Bisa organized and led the burial ceremonies and, with a weak but recovering Chief Narbona by his side, did his best to console and reassure his tribe. His people were, above all else, scared. Scared of losing their homes. Scared of losing their way of life. While they'd survived this latest attack, they all knew that more would be coming. It was just a matter of time. Narbona's eyes wordlessly confirmed this knowledge.

After the mourning period ended, Chief Narbona called a meeting of all the Navajo at a spot even deeper inside Canyon de Chelly than the nearly destroyed village. Long-abandoned cliff dwellings peppered the canyon walls and a towering monolith the Navajo called Tsé Ná ashjéé' ii, or Spider Rock, stood watch over the fertile canyon floor.

Once they'd all gathered, Chief Narbona told them he had two things he wanted to express. The first was about Hózhó, which, for the sake of the McClendon's and Father Ortiz, he defined in English as the Navajo way of life; a sense of spirituality comprised of beauty, order, and most of all, relationship. A sense of striving for balance in all things—including humility and gratitude. Especially gratitude, he told everyone.

And then the Navajo chief had each member of the tribe speak of something he or she was grateful for. The dry canyon walls seemed to drip with echoes of grateful voices once everyone had spoken.

After a few moments of near silence, Chief Narbona called Bisa up to the rock ledge he sat on. As Bisa climbed up the wall, still nursing the wound on his forearm, James thought that it looked like Bisa had aged ten years since that dark night.

Putting his good arm around Bisa's shoulders, Chief Narbona's voice circled Spider Rock and the entire assembly as he expressed gratitude for Bisa's timely return. Narbona then expressed gratitude for Bisa's mother, for all she did early on in Bisa's life to build a good sense of character in the young Navajo.

And then he announced that the Navajo elders had met and agreed that in the months to come, Bisa would step into the role of chief of the Tsegi Navajo. As Narbona said this, he took the bear-claw necklace he wore off and laid it around Bisa's neck. Hundreds of drumbeats cascaded across the canyon floor. Later Bisa would tell James that clapping is not a Navajo custom, hence the drums.

"One last thing I would like to say before I rest," Chief Narbona said. "I ask for your forgiveness in advance, as this is quite unusual." The lively crowd grew silent, only the distant echoing of a red-tailed hawk's calls to its life-long partner filled the air. "James, please come here."

20. September 25, 1846

By the time the sun was high enough in the sky to be visible from the canyon floor, the relocation of the Navajo village was nearly complete. *Amazing*, James thought, as he dropped an armful of logs by a half-constructed hogan and watched men and women, young and old, work together, not an idle hand in sight, nor an audible complaint. Many families had lost loved ones; warriors or parents or children who would have been instrumental in the rebuilding process.

But those families were tended to first by the all the rest. It was as if the effort itself, James observed, was the most important part of the healing, the starting over process. *Our journey never ends*, the 'Big Man' had said as he drew the circle of life in the dirt floor of the cave that fateful night.

* * * * *

That evening, Bisa found an exhausted McClendon father-son combination sitting quietly at the base of Spider Rock. Something had been on his mind for quite a while now and it was finally time to address it.

"James, can we take a walk?"

James looked to his father whose eyes were heavy with exhaustion and stood. He had an inkling he knew where this was headed—a conversation long overdue. "I haven't read it yet, have you?" The young man from South Carolina said.

"No. It is time. Let's get them and meet up there, on that ledge," Bisa said, referring first to the letters and second to a quiet spot some fifty feet above the canyon floor.

From atop the ledge, Bisa and James could not help but be awestruck at the sight and sounds of the new village. It was as if it had always been there, people living, working, and loving—together. "Beauty and…" James said.

"Hózhó," Bisa agreed.

"I wonder where he is now," James asked, not expecting an answer.

"Let us sit with his words now. Should we read them out loud?" Bisa asked, knowing that is what he'd prefer. James nodded and gestured for Bisa to start. He read,

Bisahalani—Bisa, el hijo que nunca tuve. It warms my heart that you are once again amongst your people. I smile knowing all of the experiences we've shared across this great land, the good and the bad, have given you the insight and wisdom that you might otherwise have not received, the insight and wisdom that will be valuable to your people. You are one of the few in my life who gave as much as you received; your impact on me has been life changing. I am grateful for you, Bisa.

In the days to come, your tribe will need you. In the days to come, life will not become harder, but it will change. It always has. And you are the one, I know, who can lead your people into the future so that the next generation and the generation after that not only survive, but thrive.

I believe our paths were meant to cross. Something bigger than us knew we should walk this earth together. I am grateful for every step. I hope our paths cross once again, mi hijo.

James' eyes were both wet and wide as the sound of Larrañaga's accented voice replaced Bisa's for the last bit of the letter. All he could do was nod his head. Bisa's normally stoic face broke. Chin on his chest he sobbed, silently, for a spell. James put his arm around his friend.

"Yá'át'ééh abíní. Your turn," Bisa finally said.

James took a deep breath and began to read,

Diego, mi hijo norteamericano. I read something from Ralph Waldo Emerson that made me think of you: "He who is not every day conquering some fear has not learned the secret of life."

You've grown in many ways since we found you beneath that wagon box. You were a scared, lost boy. Now you are a man with a unique and very important outlook in this land. Your open and humble heart is as precious as the bone. While you may have set out for a place to start a new life, instead you have found that it is the journey itself that matters, as we all have a common beginning and a guaranteed destination. That is a lesson I have only recently learned myself, and I attribute that wisdom to you.

As you know, I am heading to fulfill my promise of caring for Lalo's family. That is the next phase of my journey. It is my hope, God willing, that with the news of Lalo relayed and their safety ensured, I can continue on my real purpose, to find and return ancient artifacts to where Pizarro first shielded them from theft or destruction. So, it is with that in mind that I pass along three last things:

1) Your father is alive and well. From what I hear he is the governor of New Mexico—and is doing a better job than any of his Spanish or Mexican predecessors. It seems he too has found his purpose.

2) You have the knowledge, wisdom, and resourcefulness to safeguard the ancient bone. You also know the good it symbolizes, the miracles it can work. Bisa, Narbona, and I have spoken, and we agree that you, Diego, are the most well-suited to do this.

3) Consider finding your way to the Yuma (meaning smoke—they use smoke to bring rain) People at the northern edge of the Sea of Cortez or what some are now calling the Gulf of California. God willing, I will be there in January. I will set sail at the end of that month while the waters are still calm.

Whatever you do, wherever you go, know that it is I who have been blessed by your presence. I will keep you in my prayers and know you will do the same. God bless and keep you safe.

21. November 1, 1846

"You'd better get moving, amigo. Soon snow will cover the ground in the higher elevations," the man with the bear-claw necklace said to the man he now considered a brother. Three saddled horses and as many camels shifted from side to side in the background, hoping to find the perfect balance for all that they carried. *Just like we are,* James thought..

James took two steps forward and embraced Chief Bisahalani for what he hoped would not be the last time. Governor McClendon and Father Ortiz did the same.

* * * * *

At the ceremony where Chief Narbona expressed his gratitude for Bisa's return, he'd also recognized the Hózhó — the Navajo way of being — that James had displayed both before and during the events of the 'Dark Night.'

Chief Narbona had gone on to speak of the changing of the times, the arrival of the 'new men,' and the fact that long ago, the Navajo had likely been called the 'new men' by the Anasazi. Narbona then designated James as the new protector of the ancient bone and the way of life it not only calls for but demands.

After several moments of stunned silence, the drums once again sounded off. Jonathan McClendon clapped.

* * * * *

The bone was now wrapped and bundled, as it had when they'd first found it, in deerskin inside a hollowed-out log that was now tied to the back of James' horse's saddle.

The camels had been found wandering aimlessly by the San Juan River several weeks prior, still burdened down with satchels, barrels, and baskets containing miscellaneous supplies of the Army of the West. Father Ortiz had laughed when several Navajo led a dozen of the odd-looking beasts who spit in the faces of their minders into the canyon.

James recalled the priest saying something like, "Their owners must have forgotten all about them," his belly shook with insight no one else was privy to. He'd then said, "These camels can be quite useful. Let me tell you about them …"

* * * * *

Father Ortiz had, since his own 'Dark Night,' spent much of his time in quiet contemplation. Inspired by the symbols of concentric circles etched by civilizations long since gone, the priest carved his own rendition of the "circle of life" in the hard-packed dirt in a secluded nook near the village. He'd spent hours walking the makeshift labyrinth as he had outside the cathedral in Santa Fe. Between the events of that fateful night and his time sitting quietly with 'something bigger' he felt reborn; his sole purpose to reflect the light and love of God to all he encountered. In small, humble settings. Out in the world.

He'd realized many of the Spanish priests had spoken these words, but few had actually lived that purpose in a way that the 'Big Man,' intended. He certainly hadn't. For Father Ortiz, reflecting the light and love of God meant keeping his own pride and ego quiet—not an easy task for any man.

It was with this in mind that Father Ortiz offered to travel with James on the next leg of his journey—to Yuma.

* * * * *

Jonathan McClendon, having reunited with his son in such dramatic fashion, again, seized the opportunity afforded by the tranquil setting by listening to the young man he'd once held in his arms. He was astonished at how James had helped save Larrañaga, escaped into El Malpais with the Dragoons in hot pursuit, and journeyed with the Navajo through the Chuskas.

But what impacted McClendon the most was hearing, through James' own words, how his faith in something bigger than himself had not only taken root but blossomed into a desire to serve in his own, unique way.. *What more could a father hope for?* McClendon thought.

The morning after the 'Dark Night,' Governor McClendon penned a message to the commander of the Mormon Battalion back in Santa Fe. He gave a brief update on his whereabouts and the order to ensure that Tsegi was now to be considered, by the government of the United States, as sacred land. McClendon did not describe the events of the 'Dark Night,' nor the fates of Colonel Donovan and his detachment of Dragoons—and he never would.

He'd then given the message to a Navajo rider who took it to the Hopi Pueblo and the traders who frequently traveled to the capitol city. Two weeks later, three Hopi traders rode into Tsegi and delivered the first of several replies. The message read:

Glad to hear you and your son are well, Governor McClendon. All is fine here in Santa Fe. News from General Kearny is that the Army of the West accomplished its mission: the seizure of the Port of Los Angeles. General Kearny has even put in the paperwork requesting appointment as the governor of California. Perhaps you'll soon be peers. On another front, we have continued to receive requests for an update on the whereabouts of the bone from Smythe. Should I pass along any reply?

Hope to see you soon. I fear the locals here appreciate your approach to governing more than they do mine.

With the business in Santa Fe effectively addressed for the time being, the two McClendon men had taken long walks, exploring nearly every twist and curve of Canyon de Chelly, just as they explored each other's hearts and minds. It was the father's turn to convey some of his experiences and insights and, to his pleasant surprise, James listened attentively.

In a somber voice, Jonathan told his son about the Comanche raid on the wagon train. How, after several days of unsuccessfully trying to follow the Indians on foot, believing that they had kidnapped James, he had stumbled upon an eastbound wagon train. Jonathan's tone brightened as he told of how General Kearny had taken him in, given him a purpose that previous generations of McClendon would have been proud of. He'd finally worn the uniform that his father and his father's father had worn.

But mostly he spent the majority of his time recounting story after story of interesting encounters he'd had with the diverse groups of people in and around Santa Fe. "I've counted over a dozen different tribes of Indians, six different Christian denominations—and the Mormons of course, and gold seekers and settlers from Europe and even Africa!" he exclaimed.

Gratitude filled James' heart. As he listened, he realized that his father had indeed found something that excited him as much as being a professor had. And based on what Larrañaga had written, James knew his father was serving the people with a heart of kindness.

In a voice filled with respect and admiration James

had said, "You are the best kind of leader Dad, not a king but a servant. You've lost or given up nearly everything, and yet you still want to help people—people you do not even know."

The sounds of their feet sinking into the wet sand along the wash on the canyon floor filled their ears and reminded them both of the long walks they used to take on the beach back…home. It was time, they both knew, to deal with the elephant in the room.

"Where do we go from here?" Father asked son.

James thought for a few moments, praying that he'd find words to effectively convey what he knew, in his heart, was his calling. He heard Larrañaga's voice deep inside, reminding him of advice he'd given back in the Santo Domingo Pueblo. He'd said, "When times become difficult, focus on doing the next right thing."

In a voice that resonated a wisdom far beyond his years, James began, "When you first brought up the idea of crossing the Santa Fe Trail, you said that the reason we were doing so was to find a new life. Father, we've done that and then some!" he proclaimed.

After a moment he continued, a bit more subdued. "I'd always thought that meant a place—and us being together. After listening to you, hearing your words and the feelings behind them, I think you've found your new life," James said as if he were the elder of the two.

Jonathan McClendon was too stunned to argue. A river of gratitude flowed through his soul, but so did a sadness with the knowledge that James could not, as protector of the bone, return to Santa Fe. *Thank you, God, for all that you've done to help my boy become a man,* he thought as he put his arms around James.

The two embraced quietly for a minute before that familiar red-tailed hawk called out. Together they gazed skyward at not one but two hawks flying high above, each on its own path but somehow working together. "I appreciate you more than you know, James. I reckon I'll head back to the Hopi pueblo and catch a ride back to Santa Fe." Then Jonathan asked his son, "What about you—what will you do?"

"Since when do you use the word 'reckon'? You turning cowboy on me?!" Again, the men laughed. *Laughter,* James remember his father telling him when his mother passed, *makes difficult times easier.*

In a somber voice, James continued, "This place has not seen the last of the U.S. Army. Chief Narbona said he had a vision that the mounted soldiers will not leave this place alone even though you ordered them to. Narbona believes they will come here to force the Navajo to give up their home. Their ways.

And if they do not agree, they will kill them, just like the Spanish did the Incans and the Aztecs. And the bone…it cannot fall into the hands of those who would try to use it for selfish reasons, just like it cannot become yet another artifact inside a museum that some politician or Queen can yield to elevate their country's cause.

And the outcome would be just as bad if the Pope got his hands on it and destroyed it like he and his priests have done throughout so much of the ancient world. The 'Big Man' kept those who believe in him and his teachings safe in the face of sure death as he has done, well, since the beginning.

I feel that the next right thing for me is to do my part to keep the bone safe and to give hope to those who might really need it—just like you. So," James paused and took a deep breath before continuing. "Larrañaga told me of a place where the Colorado River meets the Sea of Coronado. The 'foam of the Sea'…"

The pair from South Carolina embraced as fathers and sons have since time immemorial.

"The foam of the Sea?" The elder McClendon pulled back and asked.

"Another name for God. Viracocha—the name means, 'Foam of the Sea.' The Incans believed that every time God came to visit them, He both came and left by the sea," James replied.

"I am proud of you son. You'd better write."

Again, they embraced and this time tears fell freely from smiling faces; whether out of sadness or happiness or some muddied combination neither knew, but what they did know, with absolute certainty, was that despite the extreme trials and hardships of life, Jonathan and James McClendon had accomplished their objective from earlier in the year: to find a new life. They also knew that, like the petroglyph of concentric circles etched into the walls above them, their paths would continue to wrap around each other's.

* * * * *

"Hágoónee'," Chief Bisahalani called after the trio as they turned their mounts and headed out of the canyon. "See you later. There is no 'goodbye' in the language of the Dine. We will always be together in spirit!"

22. Late November, 1846

The dust-enshrouded trail James McClendon and Father Ortiz followed south and west from Canyon de Chelly had been used by native peoples for countless generations. It connected the civilizations in and around the high desert plain with those on the coast.

Bisa had given them a map depicting the route and guiding landmarks to follow to the village of the 'Yuma People.' The first part of the trail ran due south from Canyon de Chelly, bordered on either side by elevated grey and brown mesas protruding from the otherwise flat, open, and barren terrain.

In the low areas, blue grama grass attracted all types of passersby—people and animals—to the likely presence of water and the nutrition to be found in its long, thin blades and curved seedheads. The daytime temperatures were much cooler now, the elk skin jackets the two men had been gifted provided much-needed barriers against the incessant wind. At night, the temperature dipped below freezing, which made the buffalo-hide blanket a very useful addition to each man's kit.

Neither man spoke much, both processing recent

events and praying for continued divine protection. Every now and again, James turned in his saddle and patted the bundle containing the hollowed-out log.

One morning as James sipped a steaming cup of coffee while sitting on a rock at the base of a pair of jagged peaks joined by lower but still elevated ground in the middle that reminded him of Larrañaga's saddle, he opened his map, studied it, and scanned the glowing horizon. It had become his start-of-the-day routine. He wondered who else had slept in this spot and where they might have been heading.

The landscape had, for days, been completely devoid of life. Their supplies, and particularly their water stores, were nearly gone. A place marked "Horsehead Crossing" was their next landmark, somewhere out across the flat expanse to their south maybe half a day's ride.

Bisa had placed a small circle around the location, a symbol he used to denote 'life.' James smiled for his friend and, with quiet confidence, knew that they'd make it and get what they needed.

Meanwhile, Father Ortiz concluded his morning routine of walking in circles in meditation and prayer. He saw James's smile and demeanor and appreciated the young man's silent confidence. James stood as the padre approached the small fire and handed him a cup of steaming coffee, as had also become routine.

* * * * *

Horsehead Crossing was little more than a trail intersection. The only features that distinguished it from the rest of the open landscape were two small, greying wooden structures that looked as if they'd disintegrate in a modest wind. As James and Father Ortiz tied their beasts to a hitching post, five riders and one dust-covered carriage approached in a hurry from the east. James and Father Ortiz watched the convoy slow just before it reached the intersection. At least, they did until the massive cloud of dust following it forced them to lower their heads and shut their eyes. As the cloud started to clear, James spun and saw an identical convoy approaching from the southwest. "They aren't soldiers, so that's a blessing," Father Ortiz said quietly.

"We gotcha this time, Bob," One driver said to the other as both climbed down from respective benches at the intersection. Only 'Bob' came out more like 'Bub,' the man's thick Irish brogue one more unique feature amongst this landscape.

Bob tossed the driver who spoke a silver coin and shrugged his shoulders in defeat.

The men who looked more like ranchers or prospectors than some representation of an official entity, laughed and joked with one another as several hopped off their horses, pulled down the faded, dusty bandanas they'd had over their noses and mouths, and began to transfer wooden trunks and canvas bags from one carriage into the other. The others watered and fed and checked the shoes of the horses. *Just like the Navajo,* James thought, *everyone has a purpose.*

Out of nowhere what sounded like a young woman's

voice rang out. "This one's gotta go." The source of the voice popped up from behind one of Bob's carriage horses. She promptly walked into one of the wooden buildings and James' eyes followed every movement she made.

"Close your mouth, son," Father Ortiz whispered and nudged James' shoulder.

Moments later she reappeared. "No luck, Pops. They're plum out." With this matter-of-fact statement, the young woman sporting chaps and boots, and a dusty tan jacket took off her hat and shook out her long auburn hair. James was speechless but at least he kept his mouth closed.

¿Puedes invocar al Espíritu Santo pero no sabes qué hacer con una mujer joven y bonita? Father Ortiz said, under his breath.

The padre's gentle nudging finally broke the spell and James turned towards Bob who was checking out the lame horse. He was about James' father's age, and, like the young woman, the other riders appeared much younger. James summoned some courage and approached Bob.

"Sir, might I be of some assistance?" He said awkwardly—and knew it. Bob chuckled and looked over James' shoulder towards Father Ortiz who had led their animals to the watering trough.

"Well son, unless you be inclined to sell us one of dem horses I don't think so. And keep dem camels away. They spit!" Ironically, he concluded his statement by propelling a brown wad of tobacco juice out of a mouth well-hidden by a beard. The rest of his crew laughed, and James could feel his face turning a deeper shade of red than the sun had already given him.

Father Ortiz looked from the side of the carriage to James and then back to Bob. He stepped forward and started to introduce himself, but before he could finish, the wagon driver held out an open fist. "Stop right there, padre. You'd be Catholic aye? We don't have much use for your kind. My kin are Protestant. All we need is a horse—preferably two. We've deliveries to make and don't earn a half dime if we don't do them on time."

"I have an idea," Ortiz whispered to James. *"Follow my lead."*

* * * * *

With a few hours of daylight left, the convoys sped off in the directions they'd come from with their respective carriage and crews. Both were a part of what would soon become the Pony Express mail delivery service. The one that had come from and was going back to the southwest had Bob at the helm. James sat next to Bob and admired the new boots Father Ortiz had procured for him as he propped his feet up on the shin-high rail in front of the driver's bench. Father Ortiz was already snoring inside the carriage, having thanked God for the blessing of a luxury he hadn't seen in months.

Father Ortiz had traded their horses to Bob for a ride across the entirety of what would become Arizona Territory. Bob, knowing he'd been offered a tremendous deal by a man that despite being a proponent of a different Christian denomination he had no desire to cheat, agreed to provide whatever food and drink the two would need during the trip.

And thanks to the cantankerous proprietor of the Horsehead Crossing Trading Post who had taken quite an interest in the camels, Father Ortiz now also donned a new pair boots and trousers. He remarked to James that his priest's garb had "grown quite *holey*."

James couldn't believe it — if all went well, they'd be in Yuma in just over a week. *Would Larrañaga be there?* He could only hope. And in the meantime, he tried unsuccessfully not to stare at the young woman riding out in front of the carriage. The hollowed-out log rested safely beneath the bench.

* * * * *

As the sun dipped below a mountain range on the western horizon, the convoy stopped for the night at a place so dramatically different from anywhere James had been that he didn't know what to make of it. The landscape around Horsehead Crossing had been as flat and lifeless as an iron skillet. Now, in the largest ponderosa pine forest on the planet, James felt almost claustrophobic underneath the towering green trees. *Almost like the low country, except no dense underbrush.* James thought. The sound of a gurgling creek filled his ears. And a unique smell…like an old firepit…crept in on a gentle, crisp wind.

"We'll be having somethin' ta eat soon," Bob, whose full name was Robert Quinn, said as he and his crew began to make camp. "How about ya get some wood for us?"

James nodded and checked his saddle bag for the axe Bisa had given him. It was still there and he grabbed it. He looked towards Father Ortiz and together they walked towards an area where several trees had fallen. Their footsteps were quiet, the pine needles beneath their new boots a welcome respite from the hard rock of the desert plain.

When they arrived at the spot of the fallen trees it was as if a stage curtain had just risen before them. Thousands of feet below them, the tops of dense pine forest gave the undulating terrain the appearance of a haphazardly laid green rug. Except this rug stretched as far as the eyes could see. Smooth, light-colored limestone rock lined the ridge they stood on. The blue sky with cotton-ball clouds made the scene look like something out of a fairy tale.

"This is the Mogollon Rim," a friendly, feminine voice said from behind, which caused both men to jump slightly. "It's the southernmost point of the Colorado Plateau and this…" she spread her arms wide along the rim, "runs about 200 miles east to west. Hard to beat this view, that's for sure. If we had more daylight, I'd take you down and show you the old cliff houses that the Indians used to live in."

She turned away, but not before James cleared his throat which caused her to shift her blue eyes to his. *Mesmerizing,* James thought before catching himself. "What's your name, ma'am?"

"I'm Maire—and that's spelled M-a-i-r-e," she said proudly. James raised an eyebrow. "What, you don't like it?" She asked in a huff.

"I like it very much, I mean, I like Maire very much, I mean…uggh." She giggled, taking pleasurein James' embarrassment. "Names have meaning…" he said under his breath, remembering the statement Larrañaga had made.

"It means 'Star of the Sea'." She said and canted her head a bit in appreciation.

James McClendon and Father Ortiz looked wide-eyed at each other.

* * * * *

The evening was blissfully relaxing for all but James. When the food was eaten and a jar of some terrible smelling liquor had been passed around several times, Robert 'Bub' Quinn asked his daughter to sing. If any part of James hadn't already fallen for the young, auburn-haired woman, by the time the fire died down and all pulled their heavy blankets over their heads, James' knew he would jump from the nearby rim if she so desired.

* * * * *

Four dark figures watched and listened to the jovial crew. They'd been traveling west from Albuquerque when they'd passed a number of riders and an eastbound carriage who told them about a unique duo they'd seen at Horsehead Crossing. When they'd arrived at the vacant intersection, Jules saw the camels and confirmed with the proprietor that a young man and priest had been thru earlier in the day. With fresh supplies and watered horses, the four determined men mounted their horses and bolted to the southwest. They'd arrived after dark, lured in by the smell of smoke and … singing.

"Once they're well asleep, we'll sneak in and see what we can find," the steely-eyed leader with a rapier on his belt commanded. The other three cast wary glances at each other and nodded.

* * * * *

James couldn't sleep. He told himself it was the numbingly cold wind that kept him awake, but he knew better. He'd never met anyone like Maire. Her singing reminded him of his mother, as did her outgoing demeanor and strong personality.

Frustrated and cold, James stood, picked up the hollowed-out log, and threw the buffalo hide over his shoulders. So as not to disturb the others, he walked quietly to the rim and sat on a huge slab of limestone that protruded over the darkness below. Right next to the fossil-filled rock, icy creek water slushed over the rim. James looked up at the night sky and focused his mind on the sound of the water. *Drifting with the river*, he thought. *Where will you take me?*

* * * * *

Jules had seen someone leave the nearly extinguished glow of the fire, someone carrying what looked like something large and long. He'd directed his hired hands to go and take care of the small crew and the priest; he alone would be more than enough to take out the boy and get the bone.

With the sound of the creek covering his approach, Jules' skillfully crept towards the solitary figure while the others made their way towards the stationary carriage and the fireside just beyond. They'd agreed to use knives for the first kills, hoping to maintain the advantage of surprise as long as possible. The Pope himself had blessed the two-edged long blade Jules held in his good hand.

* * * * *

"How's she cuttin'?" A deep Irish voice said before three rapid blasts from the window of the carriage broke the silence around the campsite. The dark-clad figures holding knives fell to the forest floor before the echoes of the pistol fire faded.

* * * * *

Jules, distracted but not altogether surprised by the sound of pistol fire, and thinking that his men had likely dispatched the rest of the crew, sheathed his rapier and pulled his pistol as he approached the figure trying to get to his feet on the slab of rock in front of him. "We meet again," Jules said, emerging from the darkness between where James had been sitting and the campsite. Jules stepped onto the rock. "Now hand me that bone," he seethed, studying the young man who'd bested the Pope's soldier twice now—a fact that did not sit well at all. "You aren't so tough without…help…are you?"

The young, seemingly unarmed young man looked strangely calm standing at the rim's edge before the experienced, confident warrior. Suddenly, Jules became slightly less confident as a new sound emerged from the direction of the camp. Keeping his pistol trained towards James, Jules turned his head just in time to see a large figure crash into him. The veteran felt heavy arms wrap around his body. The pistol fired but not before James dove off to the side.

"You were given another chance!" Father Ortiz yelled as he tried to get his feet back under him, to slow his forward momentum, all the while keeping a firm grip on the intruder.

James caught the look in Father Ortiz's eyes as the pious man's new, slick-bottom boots failed to gain enough purchase on the slick rock to stop his momentum. Anger, then fear, then resignation reflected back at James in the flash of a second before the two men plunged over the rim and into the darkness below. James dropped to his knees, shuffled to the edge, and cringed at the thud that followed moments later. *You saved me,* James knew. *Why do I lose everyone who gets close to me?*

Through tear-filled eyes James looked up at the stars. They were still there, shining as they always have. The water continued to fall. And somewhere to the east, the sun was preparing to fill the land with light.

23. Early December 1846

Robert Quinn's tired crew unloaded the last of the wooden crates and canvas bags onto a rickety platform hanging precariously over the frothing Colorado River as the evening sun, combined with the smoke-filled valley, gave their final destination an ethereal feel. Yuma.

James tipped back his hat and took in the scene around him. Looking north, up the river that emerged from the Rocky Mountains some 1,500 miles away, he saw an old church and two Spanish-looking buildings facing the eastern bank of the river. Facing Jaeger Ferry crossing where he now stood. Further upriver, on the gently sloping hillside beyond the 'town,' stood hundreds of Indian hamlets: log structures overlaid with mud and brush. Looking south in the direction of the Sea of Cortez, James saw the river disappear around a boulder-strewn bend. In the lowlands where the water didn't butt up against the rocky shores, dense river grass standing taller than a man grew from the nutrient-rich soil. Directly across the fast-moving, muddy river was the western landing of the ferry and another pair of Spanish-looking buildings.

"My Da helped Mr. Jaeger build that ferry," Maire said, pointing as the wooden barge began to make its way back from the far side. "He says this place will be a boom-town now that the Americans have taken California."

With their cargo unloaded and payment exchanged, Mr. Quinn as James now referred to Maire's father, announced that dinner was on him—but only after they'd all cleaned up.

"He means at my Mum's place. Over there," Maire turned and pointed towards the two-story building adjacent to the old church. "It might not look like much, but the second floor has six rooms and the first, well, offers the best Irish food in Yuma."

"How many Irish restaurants are there in Yuma?" James' joke earned him a solid punch in the shoulder.

"Just the Quinn—get it? The Quinn Inn. The Quinn." He did. Then she leaned in close, and James' heart leaped. "For that you get Haggis," she whispered, her lips lightly brushing James' reddening ears before she turned and walked away.

* * * * *

After the incident at Mogollon Rim and the loss of Father Ortiz, Mr. Quinn had gone to great lengths to ensure young McClendon (a "right proper name," he'd commented) felt a part of his crew. He kept James busy with the long list of tasks required to keep the delivery service moving. "Not only do we not get paid if we break down, but we will almost certainly be killed, whether by Indians or *cladhaire's*—bandits," Mr. Quinn had said more than once.

James had learned how to repair the carriage wheels, change out horses, fix busted breast plates, and steer the patchwork carriage that now had four round trips under her wheels, each one covering nearly eight hundred miles. After one day of driving, James had proven so adept that the older man proclaimed, "Appears this lad is after me job!"

While James' skills and steadfast ability to pick up what he didn't already know quickly earned him a place in Mr. Quinn's heart, the rest of the crew proved a bit more reluctant to embrace him as one of their own. It wasn't until James recounted his journey, from Charleston to Santa Fe, from Santo Domingo Pueblo (a destination for many crates coming into Yuma by steamboat) to the mythical Canyon de Chelly that the tide turned in James' favor.

They'd all heard of the deep canyon and the Indians and spirits that were rumored to reside there but had never met anyone who'd actually set foot inside its steep walls. James took on a bit of a mythical quality of his own—and that was before he told them of the ancient artifact that he and his Spanish and Navajo friends had found in Pecos Pueblo. Before they laid their hands on the gigantic femur.

A whisper from somewhere deep inside did, however, keep James from telling them about the 'Dark Night' or the bone's mysterious, chanting-enticed powers. Whether he wanted it or not, by the time they'd finished unloading the cargo at Jaeger's Crossing, James was officially a member of the Quinn's crew.

* * * * *

Reports of snow in the higher elevations caused Mr. Quinn to postpone the mid-December running of his delivery service. When he'd gathered the crew and made this announcement, he'd not been happy. Mrs. Quinn and Maire, however, let out small whisps of joy, but for very different reasons.

Fiona Quinn, the raven-haired, respected, and no-nonsense innkeeper who always wore a long, billowy dress and clean apron, regardless of the time of day or weather, had walked up to her husband and kissed him on the cheek before turning towards the crew after the announcement was made. "As you know, we be seein' many more folks coming through here these past weeks and more are sure to follow. I need ya—we need ya," she turned and gestured to her husband who couldn't do anything but nod in agreement, "to help spruce up the place and care for our customers' kits and horses. Now get to it!"

* * * * *

While on the trail, James informed Mr. Quinn of Larrañaga's planned January arrival in Yuma. So as the end of the year ticked closer, James politely excused himself from Mrs. Quinn's chores each afternoon and wandered the small town and area around it and watched the ferry make its way back and forth across the river, always keeping an eye out for the man to whom he owed his life.

With each passing day, James' face garnered more and more recognition from those who came and went, as well as those who lived in Yuma. During his walks, James made an effort to be like his father; to kindly greet everyone he passed, including the Indians who had called this place home well before any Spanish or Americans arrived.

For the most part, he'd both heard and witnessed, the Indians around Yuma were ambivalent towards the 'new men.' He'd offer them the hand signal for 'yá'át'ééh', 'all is good.' Whether the Indians knew what the gesture meant or not, they'd often respond in kind.

Early one afternoon, as James wandered further away from the Quinn and deeper into the Indian village, he passed several young boys and girls who stopped playing when they saw him and ran off. *Nothing to be afraid of here,* James thought.

The sound of the river pulled him towards its shores where he found a rock, sat down and stared into the tumultuous flow. Feeling more alone than ever, he yearned for his Spanish friend.

Once again, James put Larrañaga's river metaphor into practice. He 'released' the question that he'd been holding onto so tightly — *What do I do now?* — and drifted on the proverbial river of its journey. Suddenly he heard the 'Big Man's' voice saying, "Put your faith in me above all else." For at least a moment, he felt at peace.

Approaching footsteps broke the peace. Turning, he

saw an old Indian, the short, stocky man's long black hair parted in the middle and held back by a solid black bandana. His face was a deep mahogany and heavily lined. The man walked up to James and gestured as if asking permission to join him on the rock. James nodded and did the first thing that came to mind; he gave the hand signal for 'all is good,' but as the man did not respond similarly, a trace of unease coursed through James' body.

For an uncomfortable period of time, the old Indian did not speak. And neither did James. To the young man it felt like an uncontainable pressure was building and would soon be released—by one or the other of them, for better or worse.

Finally, the old man spoke. In halting English that tested James' patience he said, "I have seen you around. I also see you know something of our ways." With this he gave the hand gesture. "But let me tell you something. We Quechan were here when the men in iron came. We welcomed them as we have welcomed people from far away since the beginning. But they wanted to change us. Their holy men pushed their ways, their beliefs. They made promises of a better life. But life did not get better. We stopped listening."

James let the words sink in, taking a few moments to register that the man was now speaking more fluently.

"But I still hear things. Troublesome things."

The old man reached inside his shirt and pulled out a long, brilliantly blue and red feather and handed it to James. James had seen parakeets in Charleston. And in

Santo Domingo he'd seen the Macaws that the elders there had told him came from distant, tropical lands. They'd also said the long tailfeathers of the Macaw symbolized strength and wisdom. *Is he giving me this as a gift?* James looked on questioningly as he took the feather and spun it slowly between his fingers.

"I hear that you have something too, something of our people," the Indian said quickly and with expectation. As the seconds ticked by, the Indian's friendly façade faded. Replaced by something...darker.

James stood and handed the feather back as the old man's eyes flared. *How does he know?* James asked himself as the hair on the back of his neck jumped like corn in a frying pan. The old man stood and looked up into James' eyes. "We will see each other again," he said as James brushed past him.

* * * * *

"Mum, it's almost Christmas," Maire said to her mother as they prepared the mid-day meal.

"Aye, Maire. Our first one here. Before your Da and I left Ireland, Christmas was the biggest celebration of the year. Here though..." she paused, searching for words as she chopped potatoes.

Maire cut her searching short. "Here there are *so* many different kinds of people. Different...beliefs," the young lady said. Mrs. Quinn reached inside her apron and pulled out a silver necklace with a charm on the end that Maire had seen countless times before. "A Celtic

Knot—a circle with three joined and intersecting leaves," Marie said smartly.

"Aye, lass. All are *connected*, on Earth as it is in Heaven," Mrs. Quinn retorted.

"The book of Mathew, I know. But do you think there is only one right one—*right* belief, that is?"

"I think that's something you have to decide for yourself. But I do know for sure that there is both good and evil in the world. And evil is well-adept at disguising itself as good." Fiona set down her knife and approached her daughter, placing her hands on either side of the younger woman's face. "And as Aristotle wrote, 'It is our *choice* of good or evil that determines our character, not our *opinion* about good or evil.'"

Stepping back to her favorite spot in the kitchen, Fiona Quinn smiled and said, "And God has blessed your Da and me with a *good* daughter." As she picked up her knife she continued, "And don' you let anyone, or anything stand between you and the Almighty Father. He loves us and we must love as he does. We are *always* connected—like the knot!"

Finishing her chopping, she abruptly changed the subject. "Speaking of love, tell me more about James. And don' ya be holding back, or I'll be sure to know!"

* * * * *

Christmas morning started in the same manner as every December morning preceding it, chilly. The ferry shuttled travelers east and west who jostled to keep warm alongside their horses and carriages. The westbound travelers angled mostly for Los Angeles and San Francisco. The eastbound ones towards Hermosillo and Chihuahua City.

Fiona Quinn served her crew and guests of the inn steaming bowls of porridge accompanied by thick slices of bacon and short glasses of milk. But before eating, she asked all to join hands and say something they were grateful for. James, holding Maire's hand, looked on in amazement. *Look for what we have in common*, he thought, remembering what Bisa's mother and Narbona had done in a similar vein.

When all who wanted to offer up their thanks had spoken, she prayed. "Lord, we thank you on this glorious day, that you have blessed us to live in Your great creation. We pray that we can let You move in our hearts to love each other as we do You, to look beyond our differences and divisions and be Your peacemakers, honorably working together for all that is good, and that Your truth, civility, and kindness will prevail. Amen."

After eating and cleaning up, Mrs. Quinn announced that her Christmas gift to the crew was that all regular chores could wait until the following day. She didn't know that tomorrow would be very different.

* * * * *

James and Maire decided to make the most of their day off and, knowing Mr. Jaeger had a soft spot for the Quinn family, Maire suggested they take the ferry across the river and explore the hills on the far side. Seeing the radiance in her eyes, James couldn't say no. He headed up to his room to grab his jacket and the bag he'd rigged with two straps, one for each shoulder, which he could tie the hollowed-out log on top of. Inside his bag he placed a blanket and, after some consideration, the pistol he'd taken from a Dragoon back in Canyon de Chelly.

Amidst the grumbling of the other ferry passengers, Mr. Jaeger ushered the excited young couple to the front of the line and in short order the wooden barge carrying the young couple began its slow but steady path west across the Colorado River.

* * * * *

Cristóval Maria Larrañaga rode east in a hired carriage in quiet contemplation. His long, mostly silver hair tied back in a ponytail and new maroon suit that matched the maroon boots Lalo's wife had gifted him, all of which issued forth an air of royalty. *Royalty.* He pondered on the word and all it brought with it. He didn't feel like royalty, however.

When Lalo's wife saw him ride up to her family's ranch, she'd fallen to her knees in despair. Lalo's son had run out from the barn in an attempt to console her but to no avail. She'd cried herself to sleep that night. And the next.

When the despair began to turn towards acceptance, they sat together on the wrap-around porch while Larrañaga told of all the good Lalo had done, from helping save countless people from smallpox to rescuing a boy about Lalo's son's age, to being the best friend and partner Larrañaga could have hoped for. After all that could be said had been, Larrañaga had helped Lalo's wife and son arrange transport back to Spain and saw them safely to the Mexican port of Veracruz where they boarded an east bound boat. That was a month ago. They should be safely across the Atlantic by now, he thought, surrounded by family. *Family.*

James was a part of his family now and family was and had always been a key ingredient in his mission. He'd traveled as quickly as he could across Mexico to the western port of Acapulco where he knew that with the discovery of gold in California, boats now regularly shuttled prospectors who'd arrived in Mexico from around the world up the Pacific coast. However, upon arriving at Acapulco, the port that Hérnan Cortés claimed for Spain in 1531, he learned that the Americans and British had set up a blockade. They did this to ensure no army units could travel north, via ship, to stand in the way of the United States Army in the rapidly expanding War with Mexico.

That was when Larrañaga decided to hire his own boat and crew under the guise of an official Spanish emissary for Queen Isabella II. His recently re-christened boat now sat in the natural harbor of San Diego awaiting Larrañaga's return.

Now where are you mijo? Larrañaga's thoughts returned to the present. "How much further, señor?" Larrañaga queried the driver as he looked out the window at Sahara-like sand dunes.

"Una hora mas hasta el Río Colorado jefe."

* * * * *

Christmas sentiments of peace and joy, for those who celebrated it, were as prevalent in the air as the dense smoke from hundreds of morning fires trapped in the river valley. That was before the first shots rang out. The ferry was halfway across the broad, shallow river, but those waiting on either side could only make out its faint, almost ghostlike form. Although gunfire was not altogether unheard of in Yuma, it had always been somewhere out in the distance, away from 'civilization.'

For those who could tell the difference, the weapons that fired were muzzle-loaded flintlocks that took a minute or two to reload. For those close enough to see, the three Indian shooters standing outside the Quinn cast their spent rifles aside like the previous day's trash and dashed into the two-story dwelling brandishing axes and knives—much better suited to close quarter combat.

Those within earshot shuffled nervously in the hazy gloom. Some unholstered their own weapons. James, Maire, and the rest of the passengers packed like sardines on the west-bound barge craned their necks and tried to discern the source of the commotion.

A wave of Indians raced towards the eastern ferry landing from the dense grass marshlands, firing many more shots from lever-action rifles. Most of the would-be passengers waiting there fell as bullets pierced the queue. Those that did not fell victim moments later, dispatched by pistols or axes as the wave crested over the landing. One man along the rail of the barge raised and sighted his rifle at the attackers but had it knocked away by another passenger. "Don't shoot—you might hit one of ours!" the man proclaimed.

"Oh God, my parents…!" Maire pleaded.

Two things then happened at the same time, things that many would later write about, but for different reasons. The first was that the Indians on the eastern landing cut the ropes that secured the barge to that bank. Now tethered to only the western bank, the barge and all its passengers began to drift down the river towards the bolder-strewn narrows and the Sea of Cortez. The second was that, between whisps of smoke, James saw the old Indian who'd sat down next to him on the rock stride into the Quinn.

"James, what are we going to do? Maire demanded as panic blossomed from all corners of the barge.

James knelt amongst the hysterical passengers and, as quickly as he could, untied the hollowed-out log and withdrew the bone. He elbowed his way back to a standing position and held the bone up over his head and began to chant. It began to glow its protective, calming blue hue and slowly the bone, James, and the barge and everyone on it began to rise as one out of the water; the thick smoke reflecting the blinding light making it seem that the barge had opened a portal into another dimension.

Hovering with water dripping off the bottom, the barge slowly made its way over the river's western bank and onto a dry field. As the people on both sides of the river fought to make sense of what was happening, all shooting ceased.

When the bottom of the barge touched solid ground, James stopped chanting, and the barge and bone returned to their original disposition amidst the enveloping smoke. Just as quickly as he'd pulled it from its casing, he returned it. Before closing up his pack, James withdrew his pistol and tucked it into his waistband, hoping he wouldn't have to use it, but knowing he would if he needed to protect Maire, himself, and the bone.

James, clutching Maire's hand, raced off of the barge with all the others. Together they ran to the river's edge, hoping that he wasn't too late to help Maire's parents. As he did so, a westerly wind picked up and began to clear the river valley of smoke. What he could do, from across the river, he wasn't sure. Hand in hand they watched. Hoping. Praying. Time slowed as they waited for the smoke to clear. Once it had, the old Indian and one of his warriors walked out of the Quinn, covered in blood and holding a long wooden pole with one end burning. Maire dropped to her knees and wept as the Indian threw the branch through the open door. The Quinn burst into flames.

* * * * *

The lush green of the river valley provided a stark contrast to the lifeless, shifting sandy brown dunes that had comprised the view out the carriage window for hours. The carriage slowed but for what Larrañaga could not discern over the noise of the metal-banded wheels rolling over the hard pan road. Finally, when the carriage came to a full stop, Larrañaga heard gunfire. *Not close, but not too far,* he surmised. Pulling his pistol belt out of his black leather bag, he unholstered a pearl-handled .45 befitting of a royal emissary and reached through the window to the carriage's door handle and flung it open. "Espera aquí!" Larrañaga commanded before taking off towards the landing.

* * * * *

James dropped to his knees and wrapped his arms around Maire as he watched the bloodied Indian man across the river scan first the near and then the far banks for any sign of his target. *Looking for me. For the bone.* James knew with a heavy heart. They locked eyes and the Indian menacingly pointed his knife directly at the young man.

"*Mijo,*" a deeply accented voice said from behind James.

* * * * *

Larrañaga, James, and Maire remained in Yuma long enough to confirm that Robert and Fiona Quinn had indeed been killed in the Indian raid. A guest of the inn who'd survived and made his way by boat across the river had told the gathered crowd that the Indians had been looking for something. When they did not find whatever it was, they started killing anyone who remained. The Quinns, of course, had nowhere to run. James wrapped his arm around Maire's shoulder as the man spoke, ready to catch her if she fainted. But faint she did not.

We will always be connected, Maire said silently, tearfully, to her parents.

Rumors drifted in from the west. As news of the Yuma violence and miraculous 'recovery' of the ferry's barge spread, new arrivals brought word that the American General Kearny had dispatched some of his beloved Dragoons to restore peace and restart the ferry. *And,* James knew, *for the bone.*

Neither James nor Larrañaga wanted anything to do with the Dragoons, not after all they'd been through. Combined with the unspoken threat from the old Indian, the next right thing was to get moving.

"I think it is time for us to leave," Larrañaga said, casting an uneasy glance towards Maire.

"It might be asking a lot, Maire, but would you come with us?" James asked. Larrañaga nodded and walked a few paces away. *She's going to want to stay,* James thought, *and that would break my heart.*

Without hesitation she responded, "You're stuck with me, James." Looking one last time across the river at the smoldering remains of the Quinn, she continued. "We're connected mister. So wherever you two are going, I'm going. Any problem with that?"

24. January 1, 1847

Like Charleston, San Diego possessed a distinct beauty and charm formed by years of the intermingling of peoples and cultures. Unlike Charleston, the first half of December 1846 brought fierce fighting between the Americans and Mexicans to the streets and hills surrounding the town's wide harbor. Even the normally tranquil waters of the Pacific churned with violence as war ships, large and small, jockeyed for dominance. Larrañaga, James, and Maire stood a safe distance away on the hilltop adjacent to the Spanish Mission San Diego de Alcala.

"No sería divertido si todo fuera fácil," Larrañaga said. "It would not be fun if everything was easy." Maire punched the Spaniard in the shoulder. James laughed. "Mijos, we will wait until dusk and then make our way there," Larrañaga said and pointed towards a boat wedged between the three-masted U.S.S Cyane and several smaller boats at the near edge of the harbor. "Until then, let me give you a tour of this place. It is one of my favorites—mostly because it stands in honor of two of my most beloved things: God and…'Diego.'" The Spaniard winked.

Epilogue

LARRAÑAGA, JAMES, AND MAIRE

Under a diplomatic flag, the *Foam of the Sea* and her passengers and crew glided slowly south on gentle winds and a calm sea as the sun approached the horizon. "Doldrums, they call this," Larrañaga said as he sat down next to James on a step that separated the captain's nest from the bow of the boat. Maire had gone below decks to sleep and had taken James' pack with the hollowed-out log still strapped to the top.

"Doldrums," James repeated quietly.

"But do not let the sound of that word get you down. Todo esta bien. You are in for a treat. In a moment we will see the 'green flash.' Legend has it that once you've seen the flash—a burst of green light as the sun dips under the water—you will never go wrong in matters of the heart," Larrañaga said.

They stood and walked to the starboard side, both listening to and feeling the soft creaking of the boat. Moments later, James' eyes grew wide as the bright green ray penetrated his entire being. Larrañaga jumped as James let out an uncharacteristic cheer of pure joy.

Larrañaga let James bask in the glow for a minute before saying, "Mijo, I have a suggestion. As we make our way south, I suggest you write about your journey and especially about what you saw and heard on that 'Dark Night.' Do this while it is still fresh in your head."

Larrañaga turned and retrieved a package from his bag. As he walked back, he said with a fatherly smile, "One day, you will have a son or daughter to pass that along to and it is my experience that our cabezas are not like the steel traps of the Navajo." Both men laughed as the Spaniard handed the young man from South Carolina a leather-bound journal. Its cover artistically embossed with the symbol of concentric circles emanating from a central point.

James took it and inhaled a deep breath of the cool, salty air. Lifetimes of tension, it seemed, began to dissipate with the rocking of the boat. He closed his eyes and saw the image of the green flash burned into his retina. Keeping his eyes closed, James focused on the sensation of being adrift on the water. He saw his father's kind face, even heard his voice saying, "I am proud of the man you've become." He felt Lalo and Bisa's presence in his heart and with them, his mother's.

Larrañaga watched as James let his memories swirl around him like a current. Quiet tears formed and fell from the corner of both sets of trail-weary eyes. Larrañaga put his arm around James and whispered, "Remember mijo, an arrow can only be shot by pulling it back. When circumstances arise that seem intent on pulling you back, it means you are going to be launched towards something…bigger. Hay muchas mas flechas en nuestro carcaj."

THE ARMY OF THE WEST

The Army of the West completed its mission: to capture and control the Mexican territories of New Mexico and Las Californias. General Kearny served as military governor of California until May of 1847. He then traveled back to Washington D.C. and received a hero's welcome. As the Mexican American war continued, he served as governor of the captured cities of Veracruz and then Mexico City where his distinction in service earned him a promotion to the rank of major general. Steven Watts Kearny died in 1848 after contracting yellow fever in Mexico.

THE NAVAJO IN CANYON DE CHELLY

Narbona's vision of being killed at the hands of the white man came to fruition in an 1849 confrontation with the United States Army. Despite this, the Navajo continued to live in relative peace and security in and around Canyon de Chelly until the 1860s. As tensions rose across the U.S. prior to and during the Civil War, Kit Carson joined the Army as a Colonel and led a force of mounted infantrymen into the red-rock canyon with a singular mission: round up all remaining Navajo. It took Carson and his heavily armed soldiers two determined campaigns in the winter and spring of 1864 before they could claim success. After that, only the whispers of the ancients remained as the Navajo were forced into 'The Long Walk' some 250 miles across the desert to Fort Sumter in New Mexico.

JONATHAN MCCLENDON

By the time Jonathan McClendon arrived back in Santa Fe, he was met by Charles Bent, the successful fur-trading pioneer who had been officially appointed Governor of New Mexico by President Polk. McClendon volunteered to stay on in whatever capacity the new governor might require, but Bent refused, likely based on the word of the elder Ortiz who had developed a sincere dislike for anything to do with Kearny and the U.S. Army as a result of the loss of all his camels.

But McClendon knew he had a purpose and as far as setbacks went, this was just a small one compared to all he'd been through. He continued to make his rounds, meeting, listening to, and helping people however he could by leveraging his contacts in the army. McClendon earned the nickname, 'alcalde'—mayor. While some might argue, it was McClendon's relationships that prevented the new U.S. territory from falling into utter chaos when Mexican settlers and Puebloan Indians revolted against Bent and the Americans, killing the new governor in his hometown. Thanks to McClendon's relationships and quick thinking, order was restored without any more bloodshed and life continued as it had for centuries in Santa Fe.

THE BONE

Reference to the ancient artifact found in the abandoned Pecos Pueblo appeared in only one published work. A relative of Private Frank Edwards, the solider who'd been shot with an arrow on his way to Pecos Pueblo and received 'treatment' from a doctor there, published the soldier's journal in the early twentieth century, well after Edwards' death. All other records of the giant femur and events surrounding its discovery have, somehow, been lost to official history, relegated to the content of campfire stories or secret ceremonies. Until…

Endless Horizon is the first in a three-book series cre-ated by JT McKinley with the intent to provide readers with an entertaining and eye/mind-opening glimpse of often-overlooked vistas, intriguing characters, and an empowering worldview surrounding the discovery of something…bigger.

After earning his bachelor's degree from Johns Hopkins University in 1993, JT served as an infantry officer in the U.S. Army, deploying twice overseas. After his military service, he worked as an international business consultant before trading in his briefcase for a higher purpose: to support and be present for his wife and children. To further his education and broaden his spiritual horizons, he earned a master's degree in chaplaincy from Liberty University. Today, when he's not working up new stories and researching compelling historical figures, JT manages the 'Homestead' ranch and is active in his community (Go Hillgrove and be sure to check out The Riekes Center at www.riekes.org). You can also view JT's personal website here: www.jtmckinley.com.